ENTWINED

Entwined

In Mystery & Murder. . . x 2

Thomas E. Cochrane

River Beach Press
The Sea Ranch, CA

RIVER BEACH PRESS
Entwined — In Mystery & Murder…x 2

Book development, editor, cover/interior design:
S.A. Jernigan, Renaissance Consultations (www.MarketingAndPR.com)

If you would like to do any of the above or purchase individual or bulk copies, please contact:

Cochrane Enterprises, LLC, PO Box 358, The Sea Ranch, CA 95497
www. RiverBeachPress.com

Published in the United States by River Beach Press
Printed in the United States

ISBN: 978-0-9985106-2-0
Library of Congress Control Number: 2019919691
Subjects: 1.) Mystery & Detective / General
           2.) Mystery & Detective / Women Sleuths

Dedication

Gee and Karen dedicate this, our first novel, to Tom Cochrane, whom we awoke and pestered nearly every night with a new chapter, a new adventure, or yet another twist to these tales which will unfold inside these pages. Whether this saga leads to a sequel depends on you, gentle reader, as well as whether these two are successful in their continuing efforts to awaken Mr. C with their prattling stories amidst his slumber.

Table of Contents

Major characters:

G.W. Lowell (Gee): Boston Socialite, heroine of the novel, writer of this story
Karen Hunt: private detective, Gee's twin or alter-ego
Percy Lowell: Gee's older brother, he inherits the Taft Plantation which is the setting for several adventures
Ma Mah (Mildred) Lowell: Gee & Percy's mother, Boston socialite
James: chauffeur, and confidante of Ma Mah
Bill Scott: pilot of the Lowell family jet

Gee's Vassar friends:

Jackie Horton: redheaded Chicago socialite and cohort
Rosalie: from Argentina, owns an import/export business based in NYC
Laura Lee: "Southern belle," executive assistant & confidante of Senator Throckmorton
Hollie: runs a rescue ranch for wild animals near Salinas, CA
Debbie: successful stockbroker, recently a blonde again
Kathleen (Katy): a successful accountant and money manager for global businesses with dubious ties
Cassie: a depressed blonde who claims no knowledge of her husband Glenn's dealings with the drug cartels

Other important characters:

Charlie: a detective Jackie hires, he may come to play a larger role
Senator Throckmorton: sits on the Homeland Security Committee, he's also a conduit to the FBI, CIA, and has other significant connections

PREFACE

by G.W. Lowell

This is my story, but others keep butting in with their comments. My asides to the story are denoted in parenthesis.

Tom Cochrane—who claims he is the author behind the author—puts his asides in italicized parenthesis. Occasionally, he even butts his way into my story. This prompts me to scold him in insisting he get out and leave me alone—after all, I'm the protagonist here, mister!

PREFACE

by Thomas E. Cochrane

Why do I think I can write a novel? After all, I am a scientist and read mostly scientific articles and nonfiction books. I have had no prior background in writing, other than authoring various scientific reports. My first book was published in 2017, *Shaping the Sonoma-Mendocino Coast, Exploring the Coastal Geology of Northern California*, and my second book was published a year later, *Tornados, Rattlesnakes & Oil – A Wildcatter's Memories of Hunting for "Black Gold"* (2018), which recounts my days in the Midwest oil patch of yesteryear. Possibly, some of my oil tales sound like fiction though—a few of my friends have accused me of exaggerations.

This story you're about to delve into moves at a rapid pace taking our entwined heroines, Karen and Gee, through many adventures and into numerous countries and cultures. (Note: Ah could 'av done a better job wit de lingo and accents in deese stories.) My characters and those they interact with have accents ranging from Boston (their home), New York, the deep south, Chinese and Japanese, Mexican and other Latino regions. Capturing these distinctive ways of speaking is not as easily dealt with in writing as on the stage or in movies.

The tales herein are permeated with 'spoofs' a plenty, nick-names vs. formal names, idioms, funny sayings, asides of the author and also from some of the main characters. Do these digressions snatch you, the reader, away from the story—or give it colour? You decide.

The multi-beginnings of this novel are different from most but speak to a foreshadowing of future events. The poem *Fear of Waking* is purposely placed opposite the beginning of our journey to underscore the unsettling feeling we experience when awaking in a strange place, or following a traumatic event.

Happy reading...!

Acknowledgements

I would like to acknowledge and thank my love, Susan, and especially S.A. "Sam" Jernigan, my publishing/marketing consultant (Renaissance Consultations), and confidante. They have each put up with and tried to channel the strange ramblings of my mind in a collective effort to bring this novel into a completed form for you, the reader.

No doubt we are affected by the events happening around us daily—and many of these are changing our view of the world these days. Several of the chapters in this story reflect some of these current events and also provide direction to our heroines herein...

Fear of Waking

I wake from my sleep with a start!
What is that strange noise?
Is that a shadow
outside my window?
Maybe it's a wild animal,
Or a burglar?
Maybe it's just a tree branch
hitting the side of my house?
So, what is there to fear?
But no, I have this great
sense of dread.
What was I just dreaming?
It's now slipping away.
What was that dream?
It seems so vague now.
Was there a lurking hulk pursuing me?
Why me?
Was I stranded on a mountain?
Or was I falling?
In that instant of awakening,
There seems to be a void
which I am always tumbling into.
When I awake, should I not
just sense a New Day,
a feeling of a New Beginning?
I will rise to meet it!
Seems better...

CHAPTER 1   Every novel must have a Beginning

(This one appears to have five beginnings. Think foreshadowing.)

As I lie here on the edge of sleep contemplating my life as a wealthy Boston socialite, and my secret life as a private (female) detective, I think I must put some of these rich experiences down in writing. Yes, I will pen this as a novel, changing the names of the innocent as well as the guilty, of course. What is a novel anyway? The dictionary defines it as "a fictitious narrative complexly portraying characters in a sequential organization of actions and scenes." Yet it also should be different from any story told before, right? So, how does one write in that mode? Everyone's life is unique and different. The characters in my life are certainly complex and real to me. How to put this in a sequential organization I wonder, when all of our lives are typically so disorganized and events occur so randomly? How to...................zzzz (it seems your author has unwittingly dozed off).

T'was a dark and stormy night *(don't all good novels begin that way?)*. I wake with a start. *(What is a start?)* There is a shadow of a hulk outside my window. *(Isn't there always a hulk?)* Why am I here, and why am I alone? Last night was the great literary debate gala at the Convention Center. Hmmm...I think perhaps I imbibed a tad too much. Why didn't I just slip out with Bill? It was a boring event populated by socialites who fancy themselves as writers. *(Doesn't everyone want to be a writer? Why do I want to be one?)* The house creaks in the storm and I look again to see if the dark figure is still lurking outside my window. Maybe it was just the branches blowing! I begin to think............zzzz

I wake with a start. I must have drifted off. Again. What happened while I was snoozing? The first thing I notice is that the air is hot and muggy, and there is no wind. The smell of the bayou penetrates the bedroom. There's a full moon and now I do see the hulk slithering across the tidily-mown lawn fronting one section of the marsh which is adjacent to the east side of the plantation. I must have my old handyman, Pegleg Joe, fix the fences so we're sure to keep that gator out of the yard. *(Plantations in Louisiana always seem to be decrepit, old, termite-ridden monstrosities near bayous and populated by neighboring alligators!)*

I just arrived late last evening, tired following the 40-mile drive from the airport to Taft Plantation, the home of Alton Taft, who was a relative on my mother's side of the family. The Taft family moved down here right after the Civil War as they were not in good social standing at that point, having not been on the right side of the war. My bother, Percy Lowell, has inherited the plantation and is due here sometime today. He is.........zzzz

I awake with a start. Where am I? The sun is warm, and I must have dozed off. I am dressed in camouflage clothing and I have a gun at my side. They are out to get me as I'm the chief target of their hunt. Why did I agree to this arrangement? The leaves rustle just behind the bush next to me. One of them must be near, or is it just a squirrel? Must stay awake.....but......zzzz

Yet again, I'm jarred from my slumber. Can't I just one time awake gently, just open my eyes in a languid state of relaxation? But no, this time it's real. I peer out and see two men attired in black uniforms, and they're banging away on my front door, I guess they appear to be police. The Boston D.A. must have sent them. I cannot be arrested as my fingerprints will tell all to the world. This is no dream though and I quickly realize I must get away now! Up, up and away............zoom.

Once more, I'm jolted into consciousness. *(Seems like I typically leap out of bed at a full tilt into my busy life. Remember your kids and how difficult it was to get them up in the morning? I guess some people wake up more slowly than others!)* I look around. Where am I? It's cold and foggy. There's a new moon but it gives enough light to illuminate the moody landscape outside my window. What woke me up, and why am I here? I hear the mournful cry of a wolf out on the moor, I guess he was the culprit. *(There is always a mournful cry on the moor. What proper novel would be without one?)*

We arrived here in Scotland yesterday afternoon in my mother's private jet. We, namely Ma Mah, brother Percy, and yours truly came here to attend a prestigious event at St. Andrews Golf Links. The social life of the Lowell family keeps us jetting around the world, always. But I also have my secret life as a private detective—which the family knows nothing about.

The name I use for my detective business is listed online as Kevin Hunt, but my nom de plume for that work is actually Karen Hunt. People seeing my ads/website, however, see a Google Images photo I snagged of some anonymous male. It seems that when one thinks of a detective, one thinks of Phillip Marlow or Sam Spade, but certainly not a woman. When I'm in my full detective mode, I dress like a man sometimes, and even sport a little Sherlock Holmes type cap on occasion. I don't have a cigarette hanging off my lower lip like Bogart though, so how can I be a successful detective? In actuality, I must keep my identity hidden as I often appear in photographs as G.W. Lowell at various high society events.

Think for a moment about names and how they shape our lives. How many people hate their given name and go by a nickname? My mother's name is Gertrude Mildred Lowell. She loathes the name Gertrude and it only appears on her birth certificate. No one in our social circle actually even knows her first name. So why did she name me Gertrude Winifred Lowell? Was this maternal cruelty? No, it seems the name Gertrude and the name Winifred go back to early ancestors of ours in the Lowell family, dating back to when we first arrived in the U.S. from Scotland. I hate my name and have tried very hard to suppress it. After all, does this hot body look like a Gertrude or a Winifred? And I couldn't stand to be a Gert or Gertie, or a Winnie (a good moniker for a horse). So, I simply go by G.W. Lowell. In my mind G.W. stands for Great Woman! Do I live up to that?

Ok, I'm fully awake now, with no more flashbacks to previous cases in different parts of the world unscrambling my brain. I remember now, today is the event at St. Andrews, so I must focus and gather a few succinct words to say at the fundraiser—this one's to benefit crack babies of unwed mothers. I can't help but wonder if any of these babies will survive and grow to be normal, healthy children?

The event is chaired by a socialite dandy, Tallulu Crackenback. How did she get such a name? *(Are we not acquainted with anyone who has a common name they actually like?)* Today, our Tallulu is wearing a wide-brimmed hat and a long dress splashed with a gigantic floral pattern. I bet my older brother, Percy, twenty bucks that hat of hers will blow off in the first ten minutes. She is such a bore, but the event itself is for a good cause. I lose the bet to Percy as it actually takes seventeen minutes to blow off—it was a marvelous sight though, sailing over the first two rows of donors and hitting the Reverend Jesse Goldheim smack in the eye. He had not been paying attention to the incoming flying object and tumbled forward out of his seat between the rows after letting out a girlish-sounding scream upon impact. I'll bet he ends up with a shiner as it looked like he whacked his face but good on one of the chairs as he ducked!

My mother, the prestigious Mildred Lowell of "THE Lowells of Massachusetts," a true Daughter of the American Revolution (on the Lowell side as they were first to arrive on our shore, but also on the Ross and Taft sides of the family), saved the day with a joke and called two attendants to help the good Reverend to the First Aid tent. Ma Mah, as I call her, gave a moving speech about the poor babies and how her good-hearted group has snatched them away from their poor crack-head mothers. *(I wonder if she had to give them some opiates to get them to sign the release of their children? Certainly they are better off now at the Reverend Jesse's hospital/ farm retreat where they'll be well cared for.)*

After the event, we return back to Boston on Ma Mah's small jet which sports a golden stripe on each side, and a red heart on its tail. How fitting a mode of travel for my mother and her friends! My Ma Mah is tall, perfectly attired for any occasion, and carries herself with an always-regal bearing. Her hair is dark like mine, but with a touch of grey. She is instantly the center of attention at any social event, and also tends to take charge in any situation. I am a little shorter, with fine features, a great figure (pilates faithfully!), and I also have a habit of treating myself to the latest fashions. Our pilot is a tall and handsome young man, Bill Scott, who gives me a wink and an affectionate pinch on the arm as I enter the plane. Occasionally I use the plane for one of my detective cases. Within my immediate circle, only Bill knows of my other life. (We had a brief and wildly sexual affair, but we are two really different individuals, so we ended it with a kiss and a few regrets.)

Back in Boston. Our chauffeur, James, is waiting for us to land. He picks up the luggage and opens the doors for us to enter the black stretch limousine. Our favorite drinks—a perfect martini for Ma Mah, and a shot of Glenlivit with two drops of water for me, along with a Coors Lite for Percy (how crass!)—have been mixed and are awaiting us in gleaming glassware.

Ma Mah asks James, "So, is anything new happening back home?"

James replies, "Mrs. Grayson called. She's having an impromptu meeting tomorrow at one o' clock at her house to discuss the replanting of maple trees on the Boston Commons. She so-o wants you to come, Mrs. Lowell."

We wind our way through traffic out onto the Lexington-Concord Road to our abode, a sizable mansion dating back to the Revolution. Originally it was a modest brick structure consisting of two stories with high ceilings, identified as a four-by-four. As our side of the Lowell clan grew in wealth, a large porch was added on the front with tall, stately white pillars. A section was subsequently added to the back containing a generously-sized kitchen, as well as servants' quarters in the basement.

With the arrival of yet more money came the addition of an enclosed swimming pool and clubhouse. Later still, a theater with seating for 30 was added, along with an apartment on the side nearest the pool. On the far back of the property sits the six-car garage for our fleet of vehicles, and also an apartment for our chauffeur, James.

When I came home on holidays from Vassar, I was installed in the apartment next to the pool, and it remains my current residence. Each morning I take laps in the pool and then have a long run, if the weather is agreeable that is. There's a back gate off the garage which I can slip in and out of without anyone in the house noticing. James knows of my comings and goings, but never shares this information or is purposely vague about my whereabouts when asked. He must think my detective garb is strange but has never commented. At least not to me.

As a poor little rich girl, I have an allowance of $8,000 per month as well as a family credit card: a black AmEx. I also keep a private bank account at Boston Mutual and another credit card under my detective name of Karen Hunt. I have a box at a post office in Concord. Karen also has her own cell phone. (Admittedly, sometimes I get the two phones mixed up.) Karen's car is a modest Toyota Corolla, an innocuous tan color, but with a secret built-in pistol compartment accessible only by her fingerprints. It is parked in an attachment adjacent to the garage and purportedly belongs to the chauffeur.

However, in my life as G.W., I have two cars: a deep red convertible Lamborghini for fast, splashy outings, and a black Tesla S for driving to environmental meetings and related events. To high society do's, if not driven in our limo by our chauffeur, I may drive one of the family cars; of these the blue Mercedes is my favorite.

Ah, the vacuous socialite side of my life—it's actually a long, boring parade of gatherings, mostly in support of various causes. I guess I'm following in the footsteps of my mother…although I avowed I would never go down that path when still in my rebellious teenage phase.

In contrast to all the high-end festivities, I love sports. In high school I played basketball, but at five feet two was not tall enough for college basketball. I swim nearly every day when home, and have won a medal or two in the short races. I also play tennis and handball.

In high school, I became competitive, probably because of the probing from Karen. She asked, "What do you want to *do* with your life? Do you just want to be the pampered little rich girl? What are you going to <u>do</u> with that?" Thus, I graduated from high school in the top ten of my class. However, at that early stage, I still had no great passion or field of endeavor I wanted to pursue.

Why Vassar? I guess a couple of my friends were going there. I was sort of drifting at that point, but hoping something would lead me to advanced studies in a particular field. Vassar was a fun time and also taught me more fully how to belong to a group. In fact, I suppose I was seen as a leader. As I had no great passion, I just took a smattering of courses hoping to find a field that would resonate. In the meantime, my major was Poli-Sci, but I didn't think that would necessarily lead anywhere vocationally. I also took an art course, a music course, a geology course, and a biology course—but nothing much developed from those in terms of sparking any genuine interest for me.

After graduation, I could have gone on to graduate school, but this didn't seem advisable with no field I actually wished to pursue. At that point, Ma Mah talked me into helping her as Pa Pah had recently died and the Lowell Foundation had many projects in process. I did so, although more out of affection and duty than genuine interest at the time—and now, fifteen years later, it's hard to fathom I'm still locked into the do-gooder circuit alongside Ma Mah.

But then Karen asked me to do some minor detective work and surveillance in a divorce case. She thought this was a great field and that I (Gee) should become a detective too. However, I didn't want to reveal these detecting activities to Ma Mah so I decided to let Karen be the detective instead. And, from there, this double life of "ours" soon developed. Even though it became difficult to keep Karen secret in creating her own demanding life.

At the urging of my parents, I had to take dance and ballet. Hell, it wasn't urging, more like demanding on their part! In rebellion, I took up archery and skeet shooting. I became a good shot in both sports, which comes in handy as a detective, as you might imagine. Of course, I (as Karen) visit the local shooting range on a regular basis to keep up my weaponry sharpness. (However, as G.W. Lowell, I am opposed to the use of military weapons by the general citizenry, and the local media have branded me "anti-gun" as a result.)

A favorite hobby of mine is photography which I also studied in college, and I have a small darkroom in my apartment, converted from the second bathroom. I have a long-range camera for spying, and some specialized audio equipment for listening. It was hard to slip these expensive items onto my family credit card though. My cover story was that I was studying the mating of local deer and needed the camera and sound equipment to capture their conjoining. (I actually took a couple of pictures of deer just to provide viable evidence.)

The biggest problem in maintaining my secret life as a detective is hiding it from the family and the numerous friends who seem to always be present at our house. Karen's appearance must be different from the socialite G.W. in case she is photographed at a crime scene. Since we share the same 114-pound body, this is somewhat of a problem. The clothes are not an issue—Karen wears sweatshirts, loose pullovers, tight or loose jeans, sneakers or flats. G.W. always wears very high heels, or deck shoes, or specialty shoes for a particular sporting event. Karen wears a sports bra to diminish her pert figure. She tends to slouch and appears sloppy more often than not. The problem is the fingernails. G.W. would like to have fancy, brightly-colored nails, but this would simply not do for Karen. The compromise is a clear or lightly-colored French manicure. The excuse for G.W. is that longer nails do not hold up in handball or on tennis courts. Karen always pulls her hair back in a ponytail or up into a bun. G.W. always has her hair down framing her petite face. Their styles in earrings are always different. Karen actually keeps hers in her car so as to not be caught wearing G.W.'s earrings. We have no tattoos, but sometimes Karen wears wash-off tattoos when engaged in some seedy undercover work.

It's Easter Week and the family, including some cousins, are at the house. We are lounging by the pool, having a few drinks, and lying to each other about our wonderful lives. Suddenly, there's a buzzing in my jeans, Karen's phone's receiving a call. Shoot. I excuse myself and head for the bathroom. On the other end of the line is a distraught woman who needs my help as her 16-year-old daughter is missing. She fears foul play or kidnapping.

I ask, "Does she have a boyfriend?"

The woman replies, "No, she's too young to date, and is always home." I have my suspicions but agree to come and help look for her. Now what to tell my family about needing to nip away?

Actually, I have this fake friend I use for just such excuses and the call just received provides some inspiration for my ruse. "Her family's fighting. Her new live-in boyfriend is threatening to get out the baseball bat if they don't shut-up. "Josie" needs me to come and calm things down as she doesn't want to call the police." I tell them Josie lives two hours away and that I will stay the night and be back tomorrow—throwing in for good measure that I'll call if I'm delayed.

The frantic mom lives in Pittston, Massachusetts, which is indeed two hours away. I grab my detective clothes and slip out to the garage to my Karen car. The girl has probably just run off with her boyfriend, but I'll take the case. It shouldn't be hard to find out if she indeed has a boyfriend. I jot down what I've learned so far from the mom. I label the file, The M.G. Case #106. (Missing Girl) (Some authors when they run out of names for their novels resort to using letters—M is for Murder, D is for Divorce or is it Death(?), L is for Love, Q is for Queer, etc. I always use two letters to label my cases in a system only I capiche!)

It's now late Saturday afternoon and, thankfully, the traffic's light so I arrive at the woman's house in record time. Her name is Annette Jones, a distraught, divorced mother with one child—Sissy, as her friends call her.

I try to calm the mom and quiz her for details about her daughter.

"So, how old is Sissy, Annette?" It turns out her birthday is coming up in three weeks when she will turn 16. I obtain a description and recent photo of her. "Does she have a boyfriend?" I ask again. Her mother reiterates she doesn't think so. The mother works as a secretary at a local auto parts store, so she's not home until nearly six p.m. each evening.

"Who's her best friend?"

"That's a girl named Joy Tyson, she lives just four blocks away." Ms. Jones tells me she's already called Joy's mother, who then quizzed Joy as to Sissy's whereabouts. She claimed she had not seen her since school on Friday. Thereafter, Sissy did not show for Friday's Mass as she had promised her mother.

I decide to go see Joy in person. Possibly she'll tell me something she wouldn't tell her mother. I pull up in front of her house and call Joy on her cell phone, using the number Ms. Jones had provided.

"Joy, this is Karen Hunt. I am a cousin of Sissy's and her mother is worried about her. I am parked in front of your house. Can you slip out and talk with me please? Y'know, I was pretty wild in high school and once got caught with a hangover after some crazy partying with a basketball player. Maybe you can give me a clue as to where Sissy is? It's easy for unexpected stuff to happen, believe me, I know. And nobody will harm her or blame you for anything. We just want to find Sissy, ok? So please come out front and talk to me..."

Joy slips out the side door and joins me in my car. I've taken off my investigative cap and let my hair down from my detective bun. I look more like a soft-spoken girl vs. the tough dyke I sometimes play in this role. I quickly dab on just a little light pink lipstick which completes the effect.

She is clearly concerned, but also probably afraid of not telling what she knows to an adult. I assure her I will keep her out of trouble.

"Joy, please give me a clue as to where to look for Sissy. Does she have a boyfriend? Why not? Doesn't every girl your age have a special guy? Was there a party last night and were you there?"

Quickly claiming there was no party, she tells me Joy and her boy-friend (I knew it!) had a couple of beers and a hamburger at his house around noon.

"What's this guy's name? Where does he live?"

"Bill Knoff, and he lives on Lancaster Street."

"And how old is Bill?" Joy says Bill's "older," about 18, she thinks.

"Joy, this could be a serious problem, especially since Sissy is not even 16 yet. If her mom calls the cops and they arrest Bill, he could do some serious time as a sex offender! We have got to find the two of them and get Sissy home before this situation gets out of hand."

She then tells me somewhat apprehensively they might be up at Loon Lake in Bill's uncle's cabin. *(Is there not always a cabin and a Loon Lake in these stories? In my personal childhood, we had a small lake named Lake Petunia, which was the site of many a party, I can tell you. Gentle reader, where was your high school get-away?)*

"Do you have an address for this cabin?"

"No, but I was there once."

"Could you help me find it?"

"Um, I think so."

"Can you get out of the house without telling your mother where we're going?"

Joy tells her mother she's heading over to Gloria's house to meet some friends and will be back early evening. I call Ms. Jones and tell her Sissy was last seen with another girlfriend, Janet, who had called Joy and said they had a flat tire late last night and that her father was bringing them a new one. Apparently, they had slept in the car all night. I then tell Annette, "I'm going out there to pick Sissy up. I hope we'll be back in just a few hours."

Well, I think to myself, that should keep her from calling the police or the FBI anyway. I sure hope this lead works out as that was a passel of lies. An hour later, we arrive at the lake with Joy doing a good job so far of remembering the route. At a juncture, she then says she thinks maybe it's the road on the left that goes around the west side of the lake. We cruise slowly along in this direction and Joy squints and leans forward in her seat, trying to find the right cabin. We're about to give up when she spots Bill's car neatly tucked behind some tall shrubbery to the side of the cabin. Wow, good spotting.

Now to confront them.

I pull up behind their car and park, blocking any possible escape. I tell Joy to go to the front door as they'll recognize her. I tell her I'll keep an eye on the back door in case they try to beat it out of here. (I make the decision to leave my gun in its secret place as I think this mild situation can be handled without any tough stuff.) Joy knocks gently on the door and calls out to Sissy and Bill. Can she come in? They open the door and let her inside. She tells them about cousin Karen outside. Sissy of course knows she doesn't have a cousin named Karen.

Before any questions can be posed, I enter through the unlocked front door and explain I'm really a private eye hired by Sissy's mother. I ask what they're doing—the surprised couple quickly announces they're going to elope. I ask Bill if he knows Sissy is not yet 16 and that I could, as an officer of the court, arrest him for having sex with a minor and I warn him this charge is a serious criminal offense. Since Ms. Jones doesn't even know Bill, I tell them with firmness in my voice there's obviously no way she will give permission for you two to marry.

"Sissy, how many years of high school do you have left to complete?"

"Two," she replies softly, saying she's only a sophomore.

"Are you pregnant?"

"No, I've been on the pill for three months."

"I'll bet your mother doesn't know." Sissy then begins crying, I look over and see Bill is actually shaking.

"My suggestion to you two is to cool this romance, and for you to finish school and graduate, Sissy. I'll take you back home and we'll stick with the flat tire story I gave your mom. If you two are really in love, then you can keep it on a back-burner for two years. True love will wait. If it's instead just a passing thing, then it will soon be over. Sissy, do you want to go home, or do I report you as a runaway to the police?"

"Bill says, "Ok, ok, I think we can cool it. Please take her home." Sissy has tears streaming down her face but turns away from him and agrees to accompany me.

After getting back to town, I drop Joy off, then bring Sissy back to her house, presenting the mother with a bill for services in the amount of $500— and head back to my other life. I arrive home at the Lowell Mansion slightly after midnight, slip inside my back door, don my bathing suit, and join a couple of my cousins in the pool.

What a night! I wonder if Sissy will get over her first love? I'll bet Bill will avoid her now, as I could see he was really scared in learning her being underage creates a legal threat for him. This broken romance will be hard on Sissy, but at her age, I'm sure she'll likely have another love before the school year's out. *(Gentle reader, can you even remember the name of your first love? If you remember your first love, don't make the mistake of looking them up. It will burst the bubble of their perfection you retain in your mind!)*

The Easter weekend consists of Sunday 11:00 a.m. High Mass. Bishop Mahaffey stops by the house in the late afternoon for a cocktail or two. He's currently pushing Ma Mah to lead a special fundraiser to help get Christians out of certain countries in Northern Africa. The cousins pack up to leave. I think maybe I'll spend an hour at the shooting range. Perhaps the next gig won't be as easy, and I need to stay on my toes.

CHAPTER 2   Murder in San Diego

I awake with a start! I look around to see where I am. Thank goodness…there's no moor or smell from the bayou, or even a storm brewing. Today, I'm in my socialite life and home in my regular bed. What awakened me? Oh, it's my brother, Percy, banging on my door. Glancing at the clock on my nightstand, I can't believe I slept so late. But then what does a spoiled socialite need to do before noon anyway?

Turns out Percy has something to tell me. He just saw mention in his Harvard Newsletter there's to be a forensic geology lecture on Thursday featuring several noted geologists from around the country. Percy knows about my previous courses and interest in criminal justice, but he does not know about my other life. Thank goodness! When he asks if I'd like to join him, I reply, "Oh, I used to be interested in such stuff. It might be fun to take it in. I'll call one of my girlfriends." Admittedly, the Karen Hunt in me is vitally interested in attending the lecture.

Thursday arrives. *(Don't they always say that in novels? People and trains arrive, but the days just happen.)* I arrive at the lecture hall, dressed in a pullover sweater with tan slacks; I have to appear as Karen Hunt, but I still want to look attractive. I wear no makeup and pull my hair back in a ponytail. (G.W. never wears "her" hair in a ponytail, too sporty.)

The lecture and questions were terrific. I loved the story about the incendiary bombs that were made by the Japanese children during WWII. American geologists identified the location where they were launched from the beach sand used in the sand bags to control the altitude of the balloons. Thousands of them were released and started several fires in the western United States. The media was suppressed from publishing articles on the balloons though as we did not want the Japanese to know their balloons had actually made it to our shores. The Japanese quit sending them as they thought they were ineffective as they had received no news of the resulting fires.

After the lecture, I exchanged cards with most of the geologists, thinking I might need to consult one sometime in the future. Mr. Tom Cochrane pulled me aside for a private talk. He chastised me on my appearance! "Listen, I can recognize you as G.W.—not Karen. Your shoes and purse are way above your pay grade as a private detective." *(I find that as an author I like to make an appearance in my novels—kind of like Hitchcock does in his cameo appearances in his films. I also wanted to check up on my heroine. She seemed to be developing a mind of her own. Other authors tell me that once they introduce a hero or heroine, they then help themselves in developing their own plots. Does this really happen?)*

Karen leaves the conference hall and returns home. She thinks to herself, "What right does he have to weigh in? This is *my* story, or rather Gee's story, not his. However, he was right about the shoes and purse. I will be more careful next time. It's so difficult for me sometimes to stay in this other role."

Two weeks later, I'm just returning (as G.W.) from an early morning run. My pocket begins to vibrate: it's Karen's phone, maybe another case. When I answer, it's a distraught woman, Lisa Casad, from Denton, Texas.

"Can you fly to San Diego immediately? My father and brother have been arrested on suspicion they killed my father's wife. I know they didn't do it. Can you please leave immediately? They don't know what to do and have no bail money to get out of jail."

I tell her I'm free and assure her I'll get there as soon as possible. "I will call you back in a couple of hours for all the background info on the situation and your family."

I ask Ma Mah if she's using the jet. "No, it's available. But where are you going?" I reply that I have a very sick friend in San Diego, possibly on her death bed and I want to see her before she succumbs. I could have used a simple story that I just wanted to watch the sunset in San Diego, but Ma Mah might have wanted to come with me.

I phone our pilot, Bill Scott, and tell him Karen needs to go to San Diego immediately if possible. Is the plane serviced? He says it's always ready, especially for me. I think perhaps he still carries a bit of a torch for me! (Hmmm…should I ask him if he has a current girlfriend?) My mind jumps back in time—how did Bill become our pilot?

Oh, right…I recall now…it seems that while visiting his sister in

Boston, he had answered an ad for a pilot for the Lowell Foundation. Now he has been with us for nearly two years. He often attends the events at which Ma Mah and Gee (I) speak. Afterwards on the flight home we often ask his opinion on our talks and sometimes he makes suggestions of points we might include in our future presentations.

Bill joined the Air Force after he left college after two years. His major was anthropology. During his tour of duty, he flew in the Iraq/Kuwait war, discovering in the process he was a great pilot as well as an accurate shot in discharging the lethal rockets from his plane. His missions helped demolish many enemy tanks which the Iraqis soon just abandoned, running whenever they saw the American planes heading toward their position. Bill actually felt badly about shooting running soldiers and soon began to purposely miss them. He was later admonished for being a poor shot when he failed to hit soldiers hiding in groups of women and children. Bill chose not to re-up for a second tour and left the military.

As he had come to love flying, he decided to put his new skills to use in the workplace, initially finding a job with a small air freight company. One summer thereafter he flew as a crop duster—but he was fired when he refused to spray in a field next to one being harvested by pickers.

My Karen suitcase is always packed, except for my gun. When needed, I quickly retrieve that from my car and slip it into a Mahjong case which is specially painted with metallic paints which contort the X-ray scanners in airports. Of course, this precaution is not necessary in our private plane, but it's definitely handy camouflage for commercial flights. Within an hour we are rolling down the tarmac, on our way to southern California. Wheels up.

Once the plane has climbed and hit its cruising altitude, I call Lisa back for all the details on her family and the murder. She says she's only had a brief call from her brother, Mark, telling her he was in jail and needed help. Manuel, her father, who she refers to as "Snake," was also in jail, but Lisa informs me he's being held separately from Mark so they cannot compare stories.

She then explained she has two other brothers and also a sister, and told me her mother died years ago in a car accident while taking her and Mark to visit their divorced father who then lived in Wichita, Kansas. Her mother, Verna, and her father were raised in Kansas, but lived in Oklahoma at the time of the divorce. Snake had a girlfriend named Beverly, and after more than twelve years of living together, they are now married. Beverly works as a church secretary. Snake pretended to be religious and they were highly respected (or maybe accepted) in their church group. Their female minister finally talked them into marriage. Less than two years ago, Manuel and Beverly moved to San Diego and he got a job as the maintenance contractor for a large condominium complex. He talked Mark into coming out and joining him, telling him there was lots of repair work and he wanted an extra hand. The "Snake' wasn't a hard worker but rather a good talker. Conversely, Mark was a very good worker.

Beverly and Manuel became active in a local church upon their relocation. They rented a condominium for a year and had just bought a house when the murder occurred. Mark and Manuel had a pickup truck and a car, and were moving furniture and household goods from the condo to the new house. Beverly was cleaning the condo after they moved the furniture out. It took an hour per roundtrip between the two locations. When Mark and Manuel arrived back at the condo, they were immediately arrested as Beverly was found at the end of a trail of blood leading from the kitchen to the front lawn. The neighbors called the police.

Landing at the San Diego airport late afternoon, I quickly rented a car from Avis, sent Bill back to Boston, and proceeded to the police station. I actually found a friendly sergeant who clued me in on the basics of the case. He also informed me Mark and Manuel were still being questioned with no chance of release before morning.

I found a motel close to the crime scene and prowled around the complex in the late evening. The condo complex was on the side of a hill, with one row of condos situated above the next row. Of course, yellow crime scene tape was draped around the entrance to the condo. I looked carefully at the sidewalk and front yard. I could still see a ribbon of large dark red droplets down the sidewalk, ending abruptly at the spot on the lawn where Beverly fell and died. Who could have killed her—a church secretary—and why?

The next day, I'm up early and decide to make another swing by the crime scene. Once back at the scene, I look over the adjacent condos and see about finding some residents to chat up, but I can only locate one couple at home as most have already left for work. I will come back at five p.m. and maybe I can talk with some more of them then. Somebody has to know something.

Next, I'm off to the police station where I arrange to meet with the police chief. "Can I see my clients? Are they under arrest?" I'm informed I will be permitted to see one of them. I choose Mark as Lisa says he's a straight shooter. An officer escorts me down to his cell and lets me in after I'm duly searched. I tell Mark that Lisa has sent me and that I'm a private eye. The poor guy's trembling as we shake hands, and his complexion is tinged green with fear. The police have been hard on him for many hours, and he says he has no clue about the murder. Beverly was well-liked by the neighbors and an active church goer. Mark had been staying with them.

"Did Manuel and Beverly fight, or have loud arguments?"

"No, they loved each other and were excited about finally buying a house after all these years." I ask Mark how I can run down their new minister and check on possible church employees as suspects.

Afterwards, I head back to the police chief, demanding he release Mark and Manuel or formally arrest them, and inform him we will proceed to raise bail if so. No, they are not arrested, he tells me, but are 'persons of interest,' "Do you have any evidence that one of them or both of them killed her? Were their stories similar?" The Chief admits their stories were identical and they were seen an hour away at their new house at the apparent time of the murder. "Then please release them," I say forcibly.

And he actually did with the caveat, "Don't leave town!" *(Don't all police chiefs in all novels say that? If real criminals were so instructed, it informs them they're suspects, but the police don't have enough evidence to arrest them. No doubt they will instantly disappear.)*

At this point, everything becomes complex. We don't know who the murderer is. Beverly's mother and her previous female minister from Kansas show up. They meet with the new (also female) minister from the San Diego church. No one knows what to do, so I take over. I get the body released from the morgue after the autopsy, and arrange for a mortuary to cremate the remains. The police were reluctant to release the body, but the autopsy had been complete. The clothes were to be kept in the evidence file, after a search for DNA evidence was concluded, just in case. A mold was also made of the knife wounds for possible future identification of the murder weapon.

A funeral is planned at the local church; however, the ministers get into an argument as to which of them is to conduct the service. Two days of haggling later, I tell them it will be a jointly-officiated service and each will play an equal role. After grumbling, they accept my decree. Beverly's mother can't bring herself to look at urns for the ashes and continually weeps at every meeting. So, I take over the urn-buying duties and purchase a nicely-shaped one of Grecian design. The Kansas minister comes up with a lovely poem written out in a calligraphy font to place in front of the urn. Lisa flies in from Texas and purchases some of the flowers for the funeral.

The police won't release the crime scene, so delivery of the rest of the furniture and household goods are on hold. The mattresses were taken to the new house, but not the bed frames or bedding. Mark and Manuel sleep on the mattresses on the floor. There are still no suspects for the murder, I'm not sure what the police are doing. I interview the church employees and also talk with several of the condo neighbors. No one appears suspicious.

More than a week has passed when the funeral finally happens. It's a beautiful and tearful affair and the two ministers do well sharing officiating duties together, and I think it's over at last. Manuel wants the ashes scattered at the new house, Beverly's mother wants them scattered on the family plot in Kansas. I go out and buy another urn and split the ashes in half. I give the mother one urn and Manuel the other. (Hey, if the detective work peters out, I guess I could become a funeral director!)

The police finally release the crime scene and Manuel, Mark, Lisa, and I finish moving their remaining things to the new house. It still takes four trips to complete. Looking around, I notice a shade is being drawn and lifted on the next row of condominiums above the crime condo. A shadow is behind the shade. *(Could it be the mysterious hulk I sometimes dream about?)* I note the window with the shade looks directly into the crime scene condo's kitchen. I wonder who lives up there?

After everyone has left, I come back in the evening for further investigation. I meet some neighbors near the condo with the window shade in question. Turns out a gruff, single man lives there. Apparently, he doesn't work and spends much of his time at home. Someone saw him at his garbage can just after the murder. I inform the police chief of my suspicions and the window shade incident. They decide to follow-up with him as he had not answered his door on their first round of interviews. He still won't open his door to their knocks this time, even though his vehicle is in the numbered parking space that matches his unit number. A check of his criminal record reveals he has been arrested several times for fighting and even once for stalking, but thus far he has only spent a few nights in jail sobering up. While he has done no extended jail time, it's determined there's enough valid suspicion to secure a warrant to search his place, and the officers have to kick the door in after he refuses to open it. He quickly surrenders and admits his guilt in the murder. He confesses he'd been watching and literally stalking Beverly for the entire year they lived there.

I close the file, and label it, the B.M. (Beverly Murder) Case #114.

It's the simple yet guilty-looking things a perpetrator does—like closing a window shade any time someone looks in his direction—that catches him out. The solving of this crime seemed anti-climactic, admittedly almost too easy. (In high-wattage novels and movies, there's always a spectacular shootout with the perpetrator getting killed at the end. However, in real life, the perpetrator often just gives up and confesses to his crime.) The police should have previously zeroed in on the condos above which had direct views into the crime scene residence.

The family pays my motel bill and other expenses, including the two urns, my return to Boston on a commercial flight, and I settle for $100 per day for each of the ten days spent in San Diego. Wow! At this rate, I'll get rich from my detective work in about 100 years!

CHAPTER 3   Investigating whiskey (or whisky!) in Scotland

Another boring luncheon fundraiser. Sometimes I think I should have an actual job like my, um, "friend," Karen. It would tie me down though. I would hate to think that, like Karen, I would have to make enough money to follow my interests. But, who knows, maybe I'll meet someone new at this luncheon. Managing to arrive just before the serving of the food is to begin, I discover my usual friends' table is full, so I take an empty seat at a table near the exit instead. Maybe I can duck out early.

A nice-looking gentleman is seated next to me, Norman Murray, Chairman of the Macallan Distillery. I introduce myself and then realize I had met him once before at a similar function, and I tell him (again?) I'm an ardent fan of Macallan's 12-year-old Scotch (they call it whiskey), and love its sherry barrel taste. We chat about the do-gooder topic of the luncheon. Norman appears nervous. (I hope I'm not boring him.)

I summon up a bit of gumption and ask, "Norman, is something bothering you? You seem on edge. Are whiskey sales down?"

"Yes, I admit I'm preoccupied just now…and it does have to do with business. What I need is a private detective."

My ears perk up. "Certainly, the prestigious Macallan firm can hire whatever top-notch detective agency you may want?"

He replies, "No, I need a good one-person firm to look into a highly confidential matter. The fewer people involved the better. In fact, I need you to not mention this to anyone please. I shouldn't have said any-thing—even raising my concern might present a problem."

"Rest assured, I won't relay this conversation to anyone, Norman. I do however have an acquaintance who works solo as a confidential investigator and has been involved in some very difficult cases. Do you want me to have her call you?"

"Do you think she can leave for Scotland on short notice—like tomorrow?"

I tell him I will contact Karen on his behalf straightaway. "Give me your cell number and what time you'd like to talk." Norm gives me the number and sets the request for three o'clock sharp, telling me he'll be in his car at the golf club for a four o'clock golf date. "Remember, you will not mention this to anyone!" *(All good detective stories warn the heroine to not tell anyone, right?)*

I slip out early from the luncheon and return home to my quarters. I quickly enter through the back door so no one will disturb me. My head briefly swims as I think about this gig involving a trip to Scotland and the Macallan Distillery, with thoughts immediately turning to their Scotch whiskey, especially Macallan 12. At precisely three o'clock, I call Mr. Murray's number from Karen's cell. I disguise my voice to a deeper pitch than G.W.s in an effort to keep our identities separate.

"This is Karen Hunt. How can I be of service to you?"

"I need this to remain very confidential, Karen, as I fear our whiskey is being sabotaged. The water qualities are slightly off normal parameters. This is now the second year this is happening. We're not keeping last year's runs and probably this year's for long-term aging, but we are putting all the product into blended whiskey for the American market. I'm sorry, but you Americans don't have the subtle taste buds of the Scots!"

He continued, "If we are being compromised by foreigners, or rival whiskey houses, the negative publicity could ruin us. I can see the headlines now: Macallan dumps whiskey and poisons the American market!"

"Wow, that would be problematic indeed for your firm! So, you need me to investigate and get to the bottom of this? I don't really know the whiskey industry, who your rivals are, or how to glean what's in the water. Don't you have staff who test and monitor it regularly?"

Norman replies, "Of course we have state of the art testing, and have monitored this problem for coming up on two years now. We will supply you with all the test data. Maybe, as an outsider, you will see something we've missed."

"Have you checked the surrounding distilleries for any changes they too may have encountered?"

"No, we can't do that, as it would then alert them to our problem. Maybe you can visit them on their whiskey tours and tastings and sneak samples of their water? They will not suspect an American tourist is investigating them. Could you do that?"

"Yes, I could, but I will need to work closely with someone in your organization who understands the testing program. I don't know if I can find the underlying issue, but I am good at asking questions. There certainly has to be a solution to your problem."

"Your contact and the only person you will report to, other than myself, is our Managing Director, Scott McCroskie. You may talk to any of the staff, but what you're investigating is confidential, even to them. Maybe you can be a writer doing a piece on how whiskey is made. Take photographs and play up the article idea. Maybe someone on our staff is doing something to the water—but I doubt it as they have all been with us forever. Give me your bank account number and routing number and I will instantly transfer a $15,000 retainer in your account. If you need more, you may call me on this cell at any time."

I call the airport and get a late flight from Boston to Glasgow, arriving early the next morning. This time I will fly first class, as the money has already arrived in my account. Tomorrow may be busy, and I'm going to need to sleep on the flight. I grab my Karen Hunt passport and driver's license, and pack jackets, sweaters, and wool slacks for the cool Scottish climate. I also toss into my suitcase a blond wig for a possible disguise, and a couple of fancy cameras. I grab $500 in pound sterling and $500 worth of euros from my floor safe. But I decide to leave my gun—if I need one in Scotland, I'll bet Macallan can provide one for me. I don't think a weapon will be necessary, but someone messing with a mega-company like Macallan probably would not think twice about doing away with poor me!

Arriving at the Glasgow airport, I rent a flashy yellow BMW convertible. I toss my baggage in the trunk and roar across northern Scotland to Speyside and the Grampian Highlands. By late afternoon, I'm approaching the Macallan Distillery complex. I get out my compact, apply some very bright red lipstick, and don my blond wig...I'm now ready to meet Scott. I breeze into the impressive building and inform the receptionist the Managing Director is expecting me, saying, "Where's his office, please?" I'm then ushered there and introduce myself. He turns to his secretary, tells her he is not to be disturbed, and then says she can go ahead and go home early. She leaves, and he then locks his office door after her.

"I was expecting a more serious-looking individual who would attract less attention," he says to me, at which point I take off my wig and morph into a less flamboyant look.

"I presume Mr. Murray gave you my cover story, I'm simply acting the part. Mr. Murray has briefed me as to the problem. How are you currently dealing with it?"

"To tell you the truth, I'm not so sure about this whole approach. You don't know anything about us, or the whiskey business, so what can *you* do? We have a highly qualified team here and we can surely find the solution —although the time needed to do so is a problem."

"You're exactly right and I believe you could find the solution. However my approach in helping that process along is to ask you a thousand questions, some of them over and over again. Because there is likely some little nuance you have overlooked. Probably it's too obvious for a second look. My stupid questions pelting you from every direction will, at some point, deliver the solution for you. I'll play the dumb blonde with your staff, and on tour at all the neighboring distilleries. People don't really pay attention to a "tourist" like me so you'll be surprised by what I will hear! Are you okay with this approach?"

Scott nods, says it might work, and agrees to aid me in the search. "The waters in the area may be the key. How are you going to collect them?"

"I need a case or more of small test tubes or bottles with numbered labels on them. I will jot a GPS location for each sample and, later, we can plot the data on maps of the area. On the tours, I can be very discreet in filling the sample. However, to sample the streams in the countryside, I'll need a different and less-noticeable vehicle. Do you have an old truck or low-key car I could use to cruise around the local roads without bringing attention to myself? After we collect the water samples, where do we analyze them or who do we get to do it? We could ship them to a lab in London, or France, or even to the States. They'll only have a number on them, and we will be the only ones with the GPS location cross-reference."

Scott likes the plan. He says he has an old, mud-caked pickup truck and also mentions he can supply me with some coveralls. He might even use me for some minor deliveries in the area, but I need to learn "the language."

"I'm actually a master at dialects," I tell him, then providing him a demonstration of some Boston and New England dialects, a bit of Southern drawl, and finishing with a New York twang. "I will have the brogue down in a couple days," I assure him.

"We have guestrooms in the restored (2006) Easter Elchies House, which was originally constructed in 1700. We will put you in the back, which used to be servants' quarters. You park the yellow BMW in the front and the truck in the back which will allow you to come and go, either in sight or out of sight."

I liked this arrangement and Scott — although he seemed dubious about hiring me at first, he's going to be my greatest asset in solving this problem. I put my wig back on. "Ok, now that we have a plan, take me to dinner please, darling!"

I wake early (thankfully without a start) and decide each morning here I'll begin with a jog. The first day, I'll make my way around the 390 acres owned by the Macallan Distillery, and then each day I will head in a different direction in surveying the neighbors. I have a small side pack with my cell phone (camera and GPS apps on-board, of course) and several small, numbered vials for collecting samples. In my side pocket,

I also have a small recording device I'll use to keep notes or record conversations—with or without others knowing.

I jog out from the manor house to the south and then head east along the River Spey which runs along the entire edge of the property. I carefully examine the riverbank for trash or anything that might have been dumped there. Stopping at three places along the river to take water samples, I pretend to be out of breath and lean over, clutching my knees to complete the effect. I splash some water on my face as though I'm overheated. I carefully manage to scoop a water sample during the process. One time I have to tie my sneaker as I perch at the edge of the stream. I do observe people in the distance, and even if they are watching with binoculars, I doubt they see me scoop the water sample.

Back at the manor house, I shower and dress for the day. I have two cups of coffee and an apple for breakfast, which is my usual fare. Jumping in the zippy BMW, I drive the short distance to the main distillery buildings. I could have walked but wanted to make the splashy entrance for the benefit of the staff, and whoever else might potentially be watching. It's now almost nine o'clock, and Scott is in his office wondering when I'll appear. I report details of my morning jog and ask a few questions about the property I have just been perusing on foot, telling him I have already collected seven water samples—three from the River Spey and four from wet spots along the farm road. I told him how careful I was to conceal my sampling activities.

"Scott, today I would like you or one of your most knowledgeable staff to give me a complete tour of the facilities. I will ask a zillion questions, and will also take some pictures, and you will also take a couple shots of me examining something. We must play up the article angle for anyone watching. I want to take samples of everyplace water is used in the facility. We must figure out how I can do that without it being obvious."

Scott says they have already tested all the water used in the different areas. "I know, but this is a different time and we will want to compare current tests with your previous tests. As I'd suggested, we may want to take them to an out-of-area lab for the testing itself."

He is a well-heeled speaker and, as our tour gets underway, it's obvious he loves the whiskey business. He informs me the Scots spell it "whisky" not "whiskey." (I'm making this adjustment forthwith!) The statistics roll right out of his head as we make our way through various parts of the massive facility where they produce a huge volume of whisky. Do you know one acre of barley will produce 1800 bottles? They have 390 acres and buy select barley of two different strains from many other farmers. Wow! This process must require a lot of water, not only in the product itself, but also in the daily cleaning of the facility. As I look around, I note their operation is immaculate throughout.

"Where do you get all of this water?"

Scott replies, "We get the water for the whisky itself from deep springs here on the property. We use cleanup water from the River Spey, which comes from a pipeline half a mile along the farm road." I did notice a difference in the taste of the water at the distillery, I tell him. At the house and the river, it smelled like there was a little pollution upstream. Tomorrow, I will visit the Glenlivet Distillery—but it's downstream, just to the south, so it's probably not the source of the pollution, whatever that may turn out to be.

That evening, I hole up alone in my room, collecting my notes and considering next steps. The questions bounce around inside my head. I wish I had a course in hydrology in my background. At Vassar, G.W. had the basic course in geology but nothing more. It was not one of her areas of interest.

I call aloud, "G.W, Gee as I called you as a child, please help me brainstorm this problem." We drop back into our childhood fantasy mode and begin talking with each other. (Our parents always left me alone as they jet-setted around the world. The symbiotic relationship of "Karen" and Gee developed out of my need for love and companionship.)

"Gee, how I wish you had taken more geology. I'm going to need that sort of expertise to solve this case."

"Karen or Kevin or whoever you are today, why don't you hire one of those geologists you heard at that recent symposium?"

"Hey, good idea, I might just do that!"

G.W. replies, "Gee whizz! (I sometimes think to myself G.W, stands for Gee Whizz.) This is my novel, but since this is your case, you take the path you think best."

Karen replies, "Do I have to bail you out as usual and help you write this book?"

(Tom, my author behind the author, jumps into the conversation. "Quit squabbling you two. Do I have to come up with a solution? This is your novel and your fantasies! I will withdraw from the conversation and you think about solutions for the problem please.")

The next morning, I'm off to take the 11:00 a.m. tour at Glenlivet. Nearly 20 people are already assembled, so it actually is somewhat difficult to get my questions answered. I guess I will have to come back for another tour. The guide is showing us the huge stills, which are gigantic in comparison to the squatty small stills used by Macallan. (Scott says they are the smallest in the business and one of the secrets of Macallan Whisky.)

I ask the guide, "I thought the secret to The Glenlivet was the waters from Josie's Well. That's what John McPhee told us in his story."

To which he replied, "Yes, we believe the waters from Josie's Well are very special indeed, and all of our whisky uses that water." I then ask to see the well. The guide points it out across the road from the distillery, a small non-distinct looking well-house surrounded by a fence and locked gate.

I press him a bit further, "Is the water here in the drinking fountains the same water as from the well?"

He replies, "No, most of the water we use comes from the River Avon, which is a tributary of the River Spey. We have a half mile pipeline to the river and state of the art filtration and treatment system."

I ask, "Can I have a taste of the Josie's well water as it comes from the well?" They are very proud of their whisky and pour me and others in the group a shot of their precious well water. I hang slightly behind on the tour and capture a sample of the water in one of our bottles. I also get a sample from the drinking fountain. It was a very productive tour.

Afterward, I head over to the tasting room and gift shop. There I buy a couple of bottles of The Glenlivet, including a barrel sample, which has a higher percentage of alcohol. All whisky is cut with water before bottling to reduce the alcohol percentage. Maybe that's the problem with Scott's whisky. I will have to ask him about samples from the barrel versus the final product. When does the problem show up—in the cask or in the bottle?

I look over the other items for sale in the gift shop. I pick up a variety of their literature on whisky making. These will no doubt spur more questions for Scott. I am just about to leave, when my eye lands on a small book, Whisky on the Rocks, Origins of the '*Water of Life,*' by Stephen & Julie Cribb. Stephen is a geologist and the book relates the distilleries and the different whiskies to the underlying rocks which is probably one of the secrets of the whisky. *(I guess author Tom has found me this geologist so I can pick his brain!)* I buy the book and my reading for the next couple of nights has been chosen for me.

As the week progresses, I visit more adjacent whisky distilleries: Aberlour, Glenfiddich, Glen Grant, and Glen Spey. I am learning more about the process: after the initial germination stage, the barley is heated (malted), sometimes over peat fires to give the barley the smokiness that some whiskies retain. After this stage, water is added, and then boiled. (This could be the stage to examine for sub-par water.) It is then cooled, yeast is added, and the liquid is then fermented in steel tanks. The "pot ale" is 9 % alcohol at this stage. Then it is distilled inside the characteristic copper stills, sometimes more than once to purify the product. It's now about 60% alcohol. Then it must go into oak barrels for a minimum of three years to be called Scotch Whisky. A portion is aged for many more years, and of course the price goes up depending upon the length of aging. At bottling time, the liquid is cut with water to 40% - 45% alcohol content. (This could surely be the stage at which that strange water could affect the product, as I had already been considering.)

Most of the distilleries have shallow wells in river gravels or alluvial slope wash off the higher hills, especially in the Grampian Highlands. A few have springs as their water source. A spring occurs where the groundwater table intersects the surface of the ground. The rock types in the area are varied here, and old Precambrian schists, quartzites, phyllites and granite forms the core of the area. Most of the local distilleries I examine are in this core area, but the gravels along the streams contain all these other kinds of rocks. From a geologic perspective (reaching back to those college days), the area has been intensely folded and faulted. No doubt the springs are related to the faults in some manner.

That evening, Scott has me over to his house for dinner with his family. Afterwards, we retire to the library for a bit of whisky, although "no thanks, I do not like cigar smoke nor smoke them." *(In novels, don't they always retire to the library for a shot of whisky and a cigar to accompany a secret talk?)* Scott is eager to hear of my progress at this stage of my investigation.

"Well, I keep collecting water samples wherever I go. I notice a difference between your processing of water from the Spey River versus what Glenlivet is doing. They have a very complete treatment plant for the incoming water whereas you just filter it. Tell me what you encounter in the filtering." He replies that the problem they encounter is an excess of sediment coming into the pipe, so they have to change or clean the filters almost daily. The water currently tests as it always has, with no pathogens or whatever. "

What do you do with the sediment? Do you collect and test it?"

He replies it just appears to be normal, fine-grained sand and that they just dump it out of the filter.

"Maybe we should have it analyzed?"

My visits to the distilleries has impressed upon me the amount of water used at every stage of the Scotch making operation. Every liter of whisky produces nine liters of pot ale. "Scott, what do you do with all the waste products from the whole process?"

He replies, "Historically we have used the spent grain for animal feed. Now it's pressed into pellets and sold both as animal feed and fish food for some of the Scottish fish farms. Some of the grain waste was used as fertilizer, but we have way too much of that to just put it on the fields."

I reply, "Do you think that excess fertilizer might be contaminating the water?"

"No. We quit using it for fertilizer." I return to the question of the pot ale and lees from the distillation process.

Scott replies, "We store and treat the pot ale to remove copper and particulates, to evaporate off-gases, and then we pipe it into the river."

I then ask, "Do you think you are contaminating yourself or others by dumping it back into the stream?"

Scott thinks for a moment and then answers, "The Whisky industry is dealing with the problem of waste. We all want to go green and produce less pollution. Current projects are being undertaken at certain distilleries. One is converting the waste to green bio-gas using anaerobic digesters. To date, certain outfits have reduced their fossil fuel demand by 25%. Some people think bio-fuels from our industry may be the energy of the future as our North Sea Oil runs out."

"Gee wiz, that sounds impressive!" (whoops, I realize I'm sounding like Gee!)

My time in Scotland continues as I proceed to visit more distilleries. At Glenfiddich, I get caught by a guard sampling the water. I try to explain that I just needed a little water to take a pill in an hour, so I wanted to take some water with me, but I don't think he bought the story. After another tour of the Macallan facility, I ask one of the hired hands if they always use the same soaps and chemicals in their cleaning process. He said they have never changed the brands they use in the 18 years he's worked there.

The analyses of my water samples are finally returned from the lab in London. We compare all the readings from preceding years. Yes, not quite two years ago we can see certain changes in the pH and in trace metals. This year seems to be trending back toward the normal readings. Then the analysis of the sand sediment from the pipeline filters arrives by mail. The sand contains a lot of copper, which should not be in the stream. Apparently, the copper must have come out of someone's copper stills, maybe even ours!

I ask Scott, "Where do you think it originated? Was the sediment in the pipeline always a problem?"

"The sediment increased and did become a problem about three years ago, right after a really intense year of rainfall. Lots of sediment was washed down the rivers."

A light flashes in my brain. "Everything settles out in streams in slow-flowing stretches and erodes in the meander bends of the cut bank area. (once again, I'm recalling information from Gee's course in Geology—hey, maybe I don't need a hydrologist!) What if you raise the intake of the pipeline, so it won't pick up sediment? We can't do anything about the copper in the sediment itself, but you don't have to suck it into the pipeline."

Scott shakes his head and says with enthusiasm, "I think you've found it, Karen! It's a simple fix and it looks like we don't have to worry about corporate terrorists or bad neighbors after all! Not attempting false modesty, I nevertheless respond, "No, you have found the problem, I only facilitated in the discovery. I'll wrap this up and send you two copies of my report after I return to Boston. And my billing, of course. This has been a great learning experience for me—not to mention my having thoroughly enjoyed a lot of very fine Scotch whisky!"

We part with a hug as I can see the obvious relief on his face. And, in short order, I'm off to return to Glasgow, and the U.S. Well, I didn't need my gun, and now it all seems like a rather tame solution. Of course, to Macallan this discovery will save them millions of dollars, plus thankfully we Americans will not have to drink bad Scotch whiskey—even though we were not aware of the problem—nor how to spell this sublime spirit properly.

On the return flight, I muse over my success in this adventure. "Well, this detective gig was certainly different for me than past ones. I got to play two different roles too—I was Karen the detective working behind the scenes in collecting the water samples and analyzing the data. The other role was playing the outgoing and flamboyant dumb blonde—a la a Gee role.

"Remember, Gee, when we were kids how we used to love to play dress up? You were always pretending to be a princess or playing some kind of leading role. As Karen, I played the unseen maid, or butler, or even the chauffeur. You were aggressive and overbearing and always "in the limelight!" And I was always the brains in the background. I solved the murder—maybe with a little bit of your help—but it was *you* who always took the credit. Looking back, was that really fair? Must there always be tension between us?"

CHAPTER 4   Reunion time

I t's my (G.W.'s) 15-year reunion from Vassar, and a retreat is planned for 20 of my favorite friends at Bear Lodge in the Catskills. It's an old lodge built out of logs in a traditional cabin style, and overlooks a small lake. There are plenty of canoes and a couple of power boats for water skiing. It should be a good five days. I'm so looking forward to finding out what has happened to my chums in the past decade and a half. With my busy life, it's definitely been difficult to keep up with more than a couple of them. Since we were once so close it should be a grand weekend of reconnecting and reminiscing.

Just as I'm thinking about this, Karen, who always seems to butt into my life, says, "I'm glad I'm not going to be with you. From your description of your college days, I thought they sounded like a pretty dull and vacuous bunch!"

"No indeed, they were a lovely bunch. You just put them down because you decided early on you didn't like a couple of them!"

Karen replies, "In novels, don't bad things always happen on these kinds of weekends? Watch out for the hulk in the woods! Keep your wits about you. Someone in the group may be jealous of your position in society. Luckily, it's not near Halloween, so you don't have to worry about goblins and headless horsemen. But wait, isn't this area close to Irving's "Sleepy Hollow?" What a perfect place for murder, or mayhem (whatever that is). Do you want to borrow my hand gun, Gee?"

"You must be kidding, Karen! You've been spending too much time as Kevin the detective. Remember the fun we had playing in the woods as children? Try to relax while I'm on this great reunion week!"

(The stage has been set for an event to happen. Will it be a drowning, or an assault? Maybe a cat burglar will sneak in and relieve them of all their jewelry. Maybe some terrorists will hold them all hostage for huge ransoms. Maybe nothing much will occur. Don't bet on it! I hope this isn't one of those murder/mysteries that waits till the last page to disclose the murderer!)

It's a short trip from Boston to the Catskills, so I decide to drive the

Lamborghini and show off a little—I wonder what the others will arrive in! I drive up the gravel road just as three of the other girls are unloading their suitcases near the parking lot. They're happy to see me, and we immediately jump back into our college era mode of girl talk.

Mary's a successful editor of a fashion magazine and has run my picture numerous times in stunning new looks created by my designer, Pierre. I modestly try to avoid publicity so I'm certain Pierre's the source of these photos.

Josie is a news reporter for CNN on their international beat.

Cassie is a beautiful blonde but, right away, she seems depressed and, even as several of us try to engage her, she's very vague about what she's currently doing. Instead she says, "Let's talk about your travels and social life. My life is kind of boring." Cassie was always the party girl, but also had her studious side, and I recalled she majored in business.

We check in and agree to meet at the bar in 45 minutes. The rooms consist of individual duplex log cabins scattered throughout the mixed oak and maple forest. Blue spruce trees have been planted between the cabins affording each unit almost complete privacy. The entrances to each of the individual units are on opposite ends of a long porch along one side. Six Adirondack chairs are lined up side by side on the porch. Additional privacy of the two units in the cabin is accomplished with a large planter in the middle which serves to divide it into two porches.

Rafaela is in the other unit of my duplex, Cabin Two. I meet her on the front porch where she's having a cigarette and looking a bit wistful. "Haven't you given those up yet? You surely know they're bad for you, right?"

She nods nonchalantly and says, "I know, but I use them to reduce stress. I'm an executive assistant for a tough boss, and he keeps me jumping. Since this is supposed to be a relaxing vacation, I'll try to give them up during our time together."

I mention to her the girls are meeting up in half an hour. It's a warm afternoon and we each change into shorts, summery tops, don sandals and head for the bar.

The bar itself opens onto a spacious deck area next to a pool. At one end is a large maple tree with several tables clustered around it. We wave to our pals who are already seated at one of them.

Joy yells out for us to join them. She's already on her third drink and is growing very loud. "Oh, I needed this lovely getaway. I'm trapped inside a terrible divorce and need the diversion. Bartender, mix me another perfect martini please."

Melanie exclaims, "Oh get over it, Joy! I went through a divorce last year and am now fancy free, and ready to play. In fact…that bartender's kind of cute. I wonder if he's attached? Hell, I don't care if he is!"

About this time, Jackie swoops into the bar sporting a fancy outfit and wants a Bloody Mary to match her natural red hair. We heard her pull up to the lodge in a green convertible XK8. She lives in Chicago and, like me, she's a full-time socialite. "Darlings, I have missed you so-o much! I hope you're not too far ahead of me with your drinks, I'll try and catch up, ok?"

The bartender delivers her Bloody Mary. (I guess he has decided to take care of us rather than let the waitress do it.) He asks me what I want to order.

"I'll have a Macallan 12, neat." (After Karen's gig in Scotland, I have switched to single malt whisky. That girl may change my whole life!)

Jackie says, "Darling, you should have the Macallan 18."

I reply, "I'll tell you what, let's taste both of them and I bet you'll switch to the Macallan 12 as it has a lovely sherry taste." We order both and the side-by-side tasting commences.

Rosalie, originally from Argentina, then breezes into the bar, "Wow, it looks like a drinking party has begun, ladies. But you all should really sample some high-end tequila! Let me see what they have here." Rosalie owns and operates an import-export business in New York City representing goods from South America and the world.

Laura Lee is the next to arrive, having just flown in from Washington. She's a true southern belle, with the manners and drawl to match. She's currently Senator Throckmorton's office manager, but also serves as his press secretary as well as his campaign director every six years. "Ah normally don't drive much as I am always in the limo with the senator, but I picked up a rental at the airport. Ah need a drink—and definitely not a mint julep! What are y'all drinkin'?"

Jackie tells her, "You should join us in our Scotch whisky tasting. We are now about to order a peaty one. Laura Lee, have you always been a blonde? As I recall, we all were blondes at one time or another during our Vassar days. G.W., weren't you always a blonde? I almost didn't recognize you with dark hair."

I toss my head a little and tell her, "Since I live the frivolous social life, I try to look more serious, especially when I am fundraising for a special cause. I even read my speeches wearing a pair of black framed readers! It was fun being a blonde once in a while though back in the day. Maybe I should do it again?"

Soon Debbie and Hollie arrive in their swimsuits. They are in Cabin Four and just recently checked in.

Debbie's a sunny, slightly overweight, and successful stockbroker. She exclaims, "I just heard the end of your comment, and I actually just went blonde a short time ago, I was inspired by remembering our college days. How do you like it? I thought as a recent divorcee I would have more fun as a blonde. My ex-husband likes me as a blonde too. Yes, we have an amicable divorce; we still work together and are friends. We just seemed to develop in different directions with different goals over time, you know? But I'm happy to report I have an exciting new boyfriend who lives in the Virgin Islands. I wonder…should I stay a blonde?"

Hollie has a ranch near King City in California's Salinas Valley where she runs a nonprofit organization that rescues animals. She has several former circus animals and two children who help her run the ranch. Her husband is recently deceased. "We thought we would take a quick dip to cool off. We didn't know we would start off drinking the hard stuff. I guess I should have remembered our college days! We'll be back for a drink in a bit." She and Debbie turn and head off toward the pool.

Jackie exclaims, "Wow! Can you think of any two professions that are further apart? Were they good friends when they were at Vassar? I don't remember that they were."

Next Kathleen joins us. We knew her at Vassar as Katy but now she prefers to be called Kathleen. "They put me in Cabin Eight. Who's also in that unit?" Melanie replies, "I think it's Cassie. Did you see her when you checked in?"

"No, I just had my things taken to the cabin and came straight here to find you all. I'll check on her after we have a drink or two."

Someone then asks Kathleen what she's currently doing and what's been going on in her life. "Me? I'm married to an accountant who owns his own accounting and investment firm, it's doing very well. I have two children who're in their teens. It's SO great to be here with all of my old friends. Frankly, life with Bill has been a little rocky for the last two years, I think we've been growing apart. I actually can't help but wonder if he might be having an affair." Melanie exclaims, "Maybe *you* need an affair, girl! But stay away from the bartender. I already have my sights on him."

Kathleen responds softly, "Oh I couldn't do that. I'm a good Catholic girl, married till death do us part, for better or worse!" The ladies all look 'round at each other and then suddenly burst into laughter.

"Get over it, Katy!" Joy exclaims, "I think I'm in the same boat, missy. Divorce is probably my answer. There must be a better life! I definitely need another drink."

The next day is the opening luncheon ceremony. We have a retired professor from Vassar from whom we had all taken a course, and she gives an inspiring talk. By this point in our lives, we were supposed to all be nearing the peak of our careers (provided we have one). Our professor charges us with changing our focus toward engaging in something geared to the betterment of the nation, or world. Hollie then makes a pitch for a fundraiser to help her save the abandoned animals she cares for. It's then Jackie's turn who makes an appeal for several of her worthy charities. I'm then pushed to talk about some of my own charity fund-raising activities.

After which I offer, "So, yes, there are a lot of good causes out there to support. Pick one of your own and get involved. However, this week is supposed to be a week of renewing old friendships and fun. Let's focus on that for now. If someone needs my help on a project, call me back in Boston and we'll switch gears then, ok? Now, what's for dessert, ladies?"

Three of the women came up just for this luncheon and had other commitments for the week so they left soon afterwards—as a result, we heard very little about their lives or really had much of a chance to chat. Two others had to cancel. Lou and Ann are scheduled to arrive in two days.

By late afternoon, several of us decide to go sailing on the lake, a few others wanted to swim, a couple others head off to the tennis courts. Cassie was dragged out of her cabin and onto one of the sailboats. I was chosen as captain of the boat and we raced down the lake like when we were 19. Once we were underway on our little excursion, just as we came about, Cassie was somehow hit by the boom and fell overboard. Jackie immediately jumped into the water and swam to her. I came about and we dropped the mainsail. With some effort, Jackie was holding the semi-conscious Cassie afloat and we pulled them both back onboard.

Cassie was crying, "You should have just let me drown!" (Was she being inattentive, was it a suicide attempt…or did someone push her?) We each made an attempt to calm her down and quickly returned to the lodge. Jackie and I took Cassie to her room where Jackie poured each of us a stiff drink. We quizzed Cassie on what happened—as well as what the heck is going on in her life.

Her tears resumed as she plunked down on the side of the bed, her head slumped forward, her elbows resting on her knees, "My life's *a mess*. My promoter husband, Glenn, has been indicted for fraud and money laundering for who knows who? I also think he's having another affair.

But he claims he loves me. I don't know why I've stayed with him for this long!"

I switch places so I can sit next to her on the bed, and put my arm around her shoulder asking, "Does Glenn have any money hidden away or anything you could get outside of the lawsuit? Who's he laundering money for? Do you know his friends and business associates?"

Cassie sobs, "I don't know anything about his business friends, or if he even has any money. Glenn always took care of that part of life. I just signed the tax forms without ever reading them." (This looks like a case for Karen to run down. Someone in the group would recognize her as me, so I can't bring her in. Gee will have to take the lead.)

Cassie lives in a suburb of Kansas City. I suggest to Jackie she find a private detective in Chicago to help Cassie. In the meantime, she clearly needs a warm shower and a nap so she can decompress—we suggest as much and leave her upon the agreement she will meet us for dinner at eight o'clock this evening.

When we're alone, Jackie says to me, "How could Cassie have been so dumb and unaware of what was going on with that husband of hers? Didn't she major in business? Do you think she's trying to pretend she doesn't know anything…to protect herself from these criminal charges?"

"I had almost forgotten that. So where did she meet Glenn anyway? Weren't they both working in a medium-sized firm of some sort? Jackie, talk to her alone and try to run down some of her past details."

The next morning, we have planned a mile-long run down along the lake, then a short swim to a small rocky island offshore where we'll have refreshments, a bit of a rest, and more girl talk and catching up. Then we'll all race back to the lodge where the winner will receive a trophy. Debbie and Kathleen did not run or swim, but canoed over to the island with the drinks and food.

At one point, Hollie corners Jackie and me on our own, pushing us to help her with fundraisers for her animal rescues. "They require so much work, and the vet bills for our injured animals are breaking the bank."

I tell her, "My brother, Percy, has done a lot of work in Africa with animals injured by poachers. He has a friend, Rhanda, who's a veterinarian in Togo, and he's wanting to come to America. Maybe you could make a deal with him to donate his expertise for your help in getting him a green card and working toward citizenship? How about if I have Percy call you?"

Having heard enough of the conversation to join in, Jackie says, "I wish I had some great passion in life like you. Maybe I can give you some practical help too, Hollie, as I once had some volunteer nursing experience."

Joy arrives and Hollie entreats us with an invitation, "Come out for a visit and I'll introduce any or all of you to my sweet critters."

A short while later, the canoe is loaded with the remains of our luncheon, and we get ready for the race back to the lodge. Debbie yells, "Get ready, get set. . .GO!" Everyone hits the lake and Kathleen jabs her paddle into the water. The canoe glides over Cassie, who dives and comes up on the other side, without getting hurt. We all swim and scramble with gusto back to the lodge. Of course, I come in first since I run and swim every day. Oh, I forgot to disclose that little piece of information to the gals.

A round of drinks ensues amidst more shared laughs, then it's on to dinner. Later that evening we have a campfire by the lake, sing songs, and cook s'mores. About 10:00, the group begins to break up and we each head for our cabins, or a last drink at the bar. The main trail goes from the lake to the lodge, but side trails break off toward the individual cabins. Rafaela and I are on the path to ours and we see some lights already on in several of the other cabins. We then heard a noise, kind of like a loud pop.

We immediately hear Debbie screaming, "Cassie! Cassie! Somebody's shot Cassie! Come help her!" Several of us turn around and run across the hillside, heading toward Cabin 8. When we arrive, we find Cassie lying face down outside on the trail. Someone turns her over and a pool of blood flows from her chest. She's quite dead, shot in the back—and right through the heart.

Jackie runs to the lodge office where, just by coincidence *(doesn't it always happen that way especially in novels?),* the local deputy sheriff was chatting up the cute night clerk. Upon hearing the news, he pulls out his gun and hurries down to the crime scene. "My God! We don't have murders around here. Who did it? And who is this girl?"

Since only our group are staying at the lodge plus another couple who'd just checked in, the murderer must be one of us. How can that be?

The Sheriff is called, and he arrives a half hour later. The deputy asked us all to gather at the bar area. A couple of the girls are already getting ready for bed. A couple others are taking showers, Kathleen being one of them. Everyone gets dressed quickly when they hear what's happened and assemble as requested. Joy said she needed a drink—as did a few of the rest of us. The sheriff announces he is placing the whole resort under crime scene status. He tells us to go to bed, and said he'd return to interview each of us separately starting at eight in the morning, saying firmly no one is to check out. He also said he is going to have a search conducted of the entire area for the murder weapon, and also wants each of us to allow him to search our rooms. Several of us objected to that. He replied that if we would not do so voluntarily, he would get a warrant. Reluctantly we agree to let him search our rooms… in the morning.

It wasn't surprising that none of us could sleep. Rafaela and I were on the porch, she with a cigarette, and me with a whisky. We kept saying over and over to each other we just couldn't believe one of us is a murderer. As we visited together quietly, policemen were searching the grounds with flashlights looking for the gun. If it isn't on the grounds someplace, then there was a good chance it must be in someone's room. Not a comforting thought. None of us appears to be the desperate type that would shoot it out with the cops. So, if you had the gun, where would you hide it? And WHY would anyone want to kill Cassie? We mull these questions for a couple of hours and finally decide to retreat to our beds.

Rafaela doesn't seem to have the type of mind to really analyze the situation. I call on Karen to help me. In my internal dialogue, Karen says that I (Gee) must take charge in that it seems well above the sheriff's expertise given this backwater location. I am sure many of our former classmates will call their lawyers and demand that he/she be present for the interview.

She then says inside my head, "The killer had little time to ditch the gun and clean up before we were all herded into the bar. There should have been gunshot residue left on her hands and clothes. By morning, all this evidence will have disappeared. Let's see if we can reconstruct who was late to the roundup, who had just taken a shower, and who was in different clothing? The police will check all the trash bins for the gun and probably be looking for clothing too. I doubt if they'll find anything now though. In the next day or two, before we all are allowed to leave, you, Gee should recheck the garbage cans to see if anyone has disposed of any garments." I agree to become a detective under Karen's guidance.

Eight o'clock comes around and the Sheriff is there right on time to begin the interviews. Other policemen are still searching the grounds for the gun, but to no avail. Four of us agree to do the interview without our lawyers. I go first, followed by Rafaela, Debbie, and then Hollie. (I guess the three of us feel confident we don't have anything to hide.) However, the rest of the girls will not be interviewed until their lawyers are present. It takes all day for these individuals to arrive and Jackie's lawyer does not show yo until the morning after.

The Sheriff wants to search our rooms, which we had agreed to the preceding night. I reply, "I'm hosting this party and I will be present along with the occupant of each room during these searches." The Sheriff isn't happy with this, but with the pressure of a couple of the ladies' lawyers, agrees to my demand. The search takes all afternoon and does not turn up anything of note.

When concluded, I ask the sheriff, "Did you search the bar and lodge area? We were all herded into the bar right after the murder, and the killer could have stashed the gun somewhere in there." Of course, he had not done that search. Several of the girls were in the bar and four had gone back to their rooms. The Sheriff then demanded we all open up our backpacks and purses for an additional search in case the killer had retrieved the gun with plans to dispose of it in a better spot.

At this point, I mention, "Four of the girls have gone back to their rooms. They might have stashed the weapon in anyone's room if it was unlocked, or anyplace else on the premises for that matter."

The Sheriff is red-faced and pissed at me for pointing out his mistakes. He says, "We will do this again tomorrow. I am going to once again search all the rooms. You will be detained in the dining room until my investigation is fully accomplished!"

We retreat to the bar, with our lawyers, and have a long discussion on our rights, thoughts on why this could have happened, and who might have done it. No one confessed to having any problems with Cassie or having any knowledge of her having a problem with any of us. She was such a jovial person in college. Her current state of depression seemed to stem from the woes she shared—but what do we know?

The next day, our group is restricted to the dining room while the new search is underway. We play cards or games on our phones or tablets. I supervise the search and, again, nothing is found that might incriminate anyone. As we make the rounds, Karen had instructed me to 'look outside the box' for a place the killer might have stashed the gun. I keep trying to think like Karen does and come up with a couple of ideas. After this official bit is over, I will check them out.

By late afternoon, the lawyers demand that someone be arrested or that we all be released to go on home. The sheriff gives up and decides to release us at that point. Everyone but me packs up and heads out and we all agree to keep in touch as we say our hurried goodbyes. I arrange to stay the night and leave the next morning. After a drink at the bar, I start talking with the bartender who tells me he had a great time with Joy, but he had lost her phone number. I give him her number, hoping to get a little information out of him in return. First, I try and casually quiz him on what he considered the dynamics of our group—who got along the best, who had any arguments with anyone. Who stood out in his mind based on their actions? Did their behavior(s) reoccur on subsequent interactions? But he reported that, from what he observed, we were mostly just swapping funny stories from our Vassar days; sometimes a comment was made about someone's clothes or hair, but nothing vicious. He said he liked our bunch.

Back at my room, I discuss the situation with Karen. She wants to know where I think the gun is? "That dumb sheriff never searched our cars. The killer could have easily hidden their weapon there. Also, outside Cabin 7, next door to Cassie, there's a potted plant on the porch—I noticed a little dirt next to it and a couple of cigarette butts in the dirt like the pot had been disturbed. I thought the Latina staff kept the place cleaned up. I was told they only work mornings, but wasn't one of them helping us as we returned from the lake in the afternoon? I saw her filling a trash bucket with our leavings at the pier."

Karen replies, "Hmmm, let's go check the planter out." We grab a spoon from the coffee station in our room and head down to the plant. Yes, the soil appears disturbed alright. I dig around in the pot with my spoon and quickly hit metal. It's the gun! I carefully extract it using the spoon handle and place it in a plastic zip lock bag I'd used for packing some jewelry. Karen says, "Take it back to Boston and I'll have my police friends run fingerprints and look up the serial number, hopefully they can track down the gun's owner. Since we don't know the motive for Cassie's murder, we need to do a thorough background check on her too and see where it leads."

I head back to Boston with a thousand thoughts in my brain and I fear this case will take some time to solve. It may also involve more than one of my friends' help before it's over. To solve it, I will have to delve in and get more involved in several of their lives.

(Isn't it interesting how my brain jumps back and forth between Gee and Karen and becomes "we" in our analysis! I have tried so hard to keep Gee and Karen separate, with their own special identities. This trait has allowed me (us) to look at problems or situations from two different perspectives. However, now they seem to be merging into a broader more collective entity.)

CHAPTER 5   Taft Plantation challenges

My morning run is a good time to think and contemplate. I'm glad I do not have children or that I am a young grandmother raising youngsters belonging to a son or daughter who's not capable of doing it themselves. I also hope Kevin/Karen do not get any child molestation cases or wife beaters to deal with. I guess a case like that could always be turned down or referred to someone else. But suddenly I'm dealing with an actual murder—and Cassie lost her life on my (Gee's) watch, and I'm now stepping into a realm that had been exclusively Karen's. To maintain the secrecy of Karen's existence with my friends, I will have to continue the case as Gee. However, I can call on Karen to search out data and leads that will not place her in direct contact with my Vassar friends.

I have called on Karen numerous times to help me through the years. I remember when I was 13 and taking piano lessons at the house and everyone else was away from the mansion. My piano teacher, Mr. S, walked up behind me as I was practicing a piece. He placed his hands on my shoulders and slowly slid them down over my chest.

"My, you are beginning to develop into a woman! Such nice firm little breasts!"

I screamed, "Cut it out, Mr. S!" But he didn't stop. I yelled louder, "Karen, Percy, I know you're outside the door. Call James, call Pa Pah, call the police. Do it NOW!"

Mr. S. then jerked his hands back. "Ok, I think today's lesson is over, I'm going now." He left, and we never saw him again. Not surprisingly, I decided to give up piano lessons that day. Although I can't remember what I told Ma Mah at the time. She never brought it up, and neither did I!

Brother Percy calls and interrupts my morning thoughts. "Gee, I need your help and advice. You know I inherited the Taft Plantation outside of Bixby, Mississippi. I'm down here looking the place over and trying to figure out what to do with it. Can you fly down here and spend a few days?"

"I don't have anything planned for the next two weeks. I'll see if Bill can fly me down there in the morning. What can I bring?"

"Well, there's literally nothing here. The place is overrun with weeds and insects. So please bring some insect repellent. We'll stay in a motel a few miles from the house."

My thoughts flit back to my dream, and the smell of the bayou. I wonder if there really is a Pegleg Joe and a hulking alligator? What did Alton and Leona Taft do down there? They had no children and, thus, Percy was a young male relative they tapped as a beneficiary. Didn't he go down there a couple of times when he was younger? I pack a bag with shorts, jeans, and a designer outfit just in case. I pickup some mosquito spray and a case of bottled water. No telling what the water system is like on the plantation. Bill says the plane is being serviced, but we can leave first thing in the morning. I ask if he can stay with us or if he has flights planned for Ma Mah. He says he's open and is up for a change of scenery.

Even though Bill has been our pilot for the past five years, I have spent little time with him outside of the airplane itself. Well, we did have sex a couple of times! Did I initiate it, or did Bill? Anyway, it was good, whoever made the first move. However, I know little of the real Bill Scott. Superficially speaking though, he's tall, slim, and very good-looking, with fine chiseled features, always clean shaven, and well-groomed. And he smells good too.

Bill consistently seems interested in the family's activities. He asks questions about a current event, fundraiser, or outing we may be attending. He often listens to the presentations we give, I think he focuses his attention on mine more than Ma Mah's. But what are his own personal goals, hobbies (does he have any?), and where does he go when he's off duty? Since he knows about Karen, which one of us does he like the best? I had to reveal Karen and her detective business to him as I was having him fly me while I was attired in her clothes when working on a case. At those times, he often asks about the specifics involved and I review my findings with him during the flight back home. After solving one case recently, I was nevertheless exceedingly depressed and upset. He comforted me and, one thing led to another, and we ended up spending the night together, which led to our first sexual encounter. Looking ahead now to spending two weeks' at the Taft Plantation I guess I'll have time to explore some of these lingering questions. I must see if our relationship might become more serious as he's going to stick around while Percy and I figure out what's what down there.

I call Laura Lee and ask her about the Bixby area. She says, "Senator Throckmorton has his plantation nearly adjacent to the Taft Plantation. In fact, we're planning to be there this weekend. He usually goes to his home in Louisiana, called the Mayflower House, but he needs to manage his plantation in Mississippi also. Come over at two in the afternoon on Saturday for tea—or whatever you're drinkin'—and we'll give you some background plus provide you with some contacts in the area.

Bill and I fly into the local airport early Thursday afternoon. The airstrip is short and poorly maintained, so we come to a bumpy stop. Bill says, "We must do something about this if we're going to have regular flights into this place." Percy is there to greet us in a rental car, and we proceed to the Taft Plantation. The manor house sits back over 1000' from the county road. It's flanked with beautiful trees draped with moss on both sides of the driveway, and it makes for a grand entrance. However, the road itself needs a lot of work. The house and adjacent outbuildings need paint and much more in terms of restoration.

Percy has been there for four days and has contacted house cleaners, contractors, and plumbers—but they're slow in showing up. A couple talk a good line about what they can do, but he's suspicious they're better talkers than workers. I tell Percy about our meeting with Senator Throckmorton, hoping he might be able to provide us with leads to locals with good reputations.

We tour the property and make notes on our iPads. The mansion has 32 bedrooms and four bathrooms, located in two wings off the main part of the house. The plumbing consists of primarily lead pipes and old appliances. The water pressure upstairs produces barely a trickle. If you turn on too many lights, they go dim or blow a fuse. There's a huge old kitchen, three separate bars, three large living (or "sitting") rooms, and a sizable terrace situated between the two wings.

The carriage house contains three old limousines, and three horse-drawn carriages. "Oh, think what we could do with these!" Percy says, his eyes gleaming as he runs his hand atop one the vintage carriage seats, "I'd like to turn this place into a retreat or small conference facility. Do you think it can be done?"

Bill asks, "How big is the plantation and are there other buildings?"

Percy replies, "There are over 10,000 acres. Tobacco's grown on several large fields and there are ten or more drying barns to cure the tobacco. There's also a large sorting/shipping warehouse. I understand 15 people work in the tobacco production, and that many of the other area farmers ship the fruits of their labors from our main warehouse. A manager operates the business from his office in Bixby. But I haven't reviewed his contracts or the books themselves yet."

"Yikes! This looks like a real mess plus a ton of assets to deal with. I hate tobacco though, and wonder if there might be another crop to replace that business but which locals could still be hired to run?"

Percy says, "Hey, don't knock it until we have a better plan. We don't want to alienate these people here…who also don't like northerners, no-how!"

Bill nods in agreement, adding, "I'll put on my old clothes, hang out in the local bars for a bit, and get a run down on the neighborhood."

Saturday rolls around and we three head off to meet Senator Throckmorton and Laura Lee, my college friend, at the appointed time. The butler who greets us at the massive front door then escorts us inside, rematerializing with a pitcher of Mint Martinis, and we settle in for a good visit once seated in a spacious and tastefully appointed library. Percy starts the conversation by telling the senator we'd like to restore the plantation and continue the tobacco business, which we know zip about.

Bill asks, "And, by the way, how do we get the airport runway fixed for our plane?"

Before the senator can respond, I also inquire, "And how do we find competent contractors and other workers to aid us in this sizable restoration project?"

"Well, ah know everyone around these parts and several of them are shade tree relatives. Ah will have a contractor, electrician, plumber, and landscaper show up tomorrow morning. People 'round here work slow though. For one thing, it's too hot much of the year. Ah will push them to help you. The going rate 'round here is ten dollars per hour, so don't let them cheat you."

We thank the senator, ask him if we can see him again if we need special help. He replies, "Call on me any time I'm down here. If I am not here, call Laura Lee in Washington and ah'll get back to you."

It's Monday morning about 9:30 a.m. when the first contractor arrives in a beat-up old pickup truck belching smoke. He introduces himself as Barney and tells us he's a cousin of the senator.

"I've worked off n' on at this place for many years. For the last year or two though nothing much was broken, so I wasn't called."

Percy asks, "What's your experience as a contractor, Barney?"

"Ah have been doing this kind of work for more than 20 years now, so pretty much I can handle any problem, sir."

Percy then inquires, "Do you have a contractor's license and insurance? Do you read architectural plans?"

Barney tilts his head to one side and answers, "Well, my license has expired, and I don't have insurance. But I can read plans."

I then join the conversation, "Do you think this place can be restored in less than a year's time, Barney?"

"Ah don't see that as a problem. I can get five good workers and we can do the job."

"When can you start the work?"

"Well…maybe next week. My tractor's in the shop and ah don't have a dump truck, but my friend, Jackson, has one we can rent."

Percy slaps a hand on Barney's shoulder and says, "Come by at eight on Friday morning with two workers and the dump truck. We'll load it up and I'll have a contract for you to do the rest of the work."

About 10:15 a.m., the electrician shows up with a similarly beat-up work truck. "Ah had a flat on the way here or ah would have been here earlier." We take him to the main electrical box.

Percy asks, "Can you replace this service with a modern panel, say for as much as 400-amp service?"

Ronnie the electrician pauses for a moment and then replies, "Well, that is a lot of panel for this ole' place. The main transformer on the main service line will probably have to be replaced. We will have to special order it…and that'll take some time."

Percy replies, "I've already talked with the power company and the transformer is fine, but the incoming electric line is too small. I'd like to replace it underground. Can you do that?"

Ronnie nods, "Yes, ah can, but we still have to get the wire, dig the trench, and order the electric panel. Maybe in two weeks ah can get it handled fer ya."

Percy tells him, "I can have UPS deliver the panel and wire on next Monday. Can you dig the trench on Monday and install the panel on Tuesday?"

"Well, ah don't know. That is kinda fast. It might take two or three days to dig that trench."

Percy's getting a bit exasperated and says, "The local tool rental store in Bixby has a trencher that can, according to them, cut the trench in three or four hours. I'll have it delivered Monday morning before nine-can you do it, or do I have to look for someone else, Ronnie? This remodel job will require the complete rewiring of the entire mansion and replacement of all the electrical fixtures. Are you interested in the entire job or not?"

Ronnie then noticeably straightens up and replies, "Yessir, I would like the entire job, Mr. Percy. Ah think that we can get the trench and line in on Monday for you if we can have that machine."

The plumber, good old Bob, shows up at 11:30 a.m. Percy quizzes him about the existing plumbing and septic system.

"Why are there lead pipes in the house? Why is there no water pressure upstairs? Where's the septic system?"

Good old Bob answers, "Well, I've been replacing the lead pipes for years, but I guess that ah didn't get them all outta here. I put in a booster pump for the upstairs water pressure, but I guess it must have burned out. You want me to look at it? The septic system is old and probably needs to be replaced, ah guess."

Percy then tells him, "We are going to replace the whole system, put in several new bathrooms, and replace the septic system. Can you handle the work for these new systems? We'll have all the old pipes and appliances taken out and you will be working just on the new installations. I will call you in two weeks to sign contracts and start the work." To which good old Bob nods, smiles, and extends a hand for him to shake.

Once this parade of tradesmen left, we collapse. "I thought Senator Throckmorton was going to send us some good workers! If these are the best 'round here, we all are in trouble."

Percy's arranged for two architects from Mobile to come in and examine the place. They show up in a panel truck just after noon. With state-of-the-art equipment, they measure and photograph everything. They assess the termite damage and major structural elements to be replaced. The new plan will give every bedroom an en suite bathroom. Several bedrooms will be split, forming two bathrooms out of the original room. New water wells will be drilled. The swimming pool will be reconstructed and raised above the flood level which had filled it with mud in the past. The septic system will be redesigned as a water reclamation system and used to water the grounds.

After hearing the breadth of planned improvements, Bill says, "Terrific plan, but how can these clowns get the work done? Their equipment's broken down. They don't like to work, and I'm worried they'll screw off while they are working."

I reply with my own comments, "I'm worried you're right, Bill. I don't see how we can get a diligent level of labor out of them. They don't even seem to have the basic equipment to do what needs doing."

Percy then says, "Listen, here's my plan. We purchase fully-equipped electrical, plumbing, and contractor trailers that contain all the tools and parts that maybe required. We buy three new pickup trucks, a dump truck, and a backhoe. The trailers, dump truck, and backhoe will stay on the property and be locked up at night. The contractor, electrician, and plumbers get 24-hour usage of the pickups. We install a time clock and require they punch in and out. Pay is $20 per hour for each of them plus $1000 per month for the contractor, electrician, and plumber. They come to work at seven in the morning, take a 15-minute break at 10:00 and quit at 12:15 for a five-hour day. We install hidden videocams to keep an eye on them while they work. Their cell phones are off limits except for during break time. No smoking or drinking alcohol during working hours. If they're late, they're docked an hour's pay. If they have a good excuse, we may let them work past 12:15 to make up the lost time. The promise to the three primary workers is that once the project is over, they'll get the trailers and equipment as a bonus. In return, they'll serve on-call for rapid service for breakdowns or repairs. We will inventory the equipment trailers on a weekly or more frequent basis, and any missing equipment will be replaced by the primary three contractors."

"That is a serious plan. Do you think they'll agree to it?"

Percy says, "Shoot, why wouldn't they? Five hours a day for twice the going rate and all that equipment when the project is completed? Of course, the project may not be over until the tobacco barns are revamped."

Tuesday and Wednesday are busy days with lots of phone calls to the major surrounding cites to line up trailers, trucks, and materials to be assembled and then delivered to Taft Plantation by the following Monday.

We also purchase a three-bedroom trailer which we'll park on the property to use as our home base for the next year until the mansion can be restored. We line up a driller for two new water wells on the property, and purchase four large water storage tanks. All this will be installed behind the carriage house, out of view from the mansion.

On Thursday, the three of us visit the tobacco operation and meet the players. We call the manager who, it seems, rarely comes onsite, and set up a meeting for next Wednesday to meet in his office, review the books, and receive copies of the past five years' tax returns.

Friday rolls around. Eight a.m. comes and goes, and no workers appear. Nine a.m. and the old dump truck driven by the black man named Jackson appears in a cloud of blue smoke. The contractor's pickup arrives with Barney, Joe, and Blackie crowded in.

Barney exclaims, "We're here and ready to get started. What are we going to do?"

Percy replies, "First, we're going to clean out all the junk inside of the house. The antiques I want to restore, you will carry those to the carriage house, and the rest goes in the truck." Barney's cell phone rings and he gets into a long conversation. Joe is clearly hung over and appears a bit green around the gills. Blackie excuses himself and pees on a tree in the side yard. So, there's four of them and three of us. We pile into the house.

Percy, Bill and I pull out things more rapidly than the four of them can move them. Barney's phone keeps ringing and he works little. Joe is so hung over he cannot keep the instructions straight—this goes to the dump truck…this goes to the carriage house. Jackson's by far the best worker of the four. I suggest to Bill that he seek him out at the local bar on his side of town and have a couple of drinks. Possibly he can supply us with some other real workers like himself.

After an intermittently productive morning on their part, Barney looks at his watch and announces, "Ok, it's 12:30, time for lunch. We'll be back in an hour or so."

I shake my head and tell him, "Nope, we'll eat right here. I've had sandwiches, iced tea, and potato salad prepared for our lunch."

Barney complains and says he has another job to check on. I reply, "You agreed to work for us today. You can take care of your other business this evening. Call them and give them the word. In fact, I would like you to use your cell phone less and get on with the work at hand."

At 1:15, Percy exclaims, "Alright, boys, time to get back to work. We don't even have half a load in the dump truck yet." We work them till 4:30 and the truck is finally filled.

Percy tells them, "This is going to be a big job, fellas, and when you're done, this will once again be a fine plantation. However, it'll never get done in a year with the level of work you did today. For today's work, you performed one hour before lunch and three hours after lunch. At $10 per hour, you each get $40.00."

Barney complains they worked longer than that, plus says he was the contractor and deserved $20 per hour. Percy gives each of them a 1.5 page contract spelling out the plan he'd previously outlined verbally. Percy gives Jackson an additional $10 for the use of his truck and $20 for dump fees.

"I don't want you dumping this stuff anywhere but in a regular authorized landfill, y'hear? If I find out you just dumped this stuff someplace else, I'll see that the sheriff picks you up and makes you pick it up. Is that clear?"

"Yessir, boss!"

"I want you all to look over and discuss the contract. You will be making $20 per hour for five hours work per day, which is more than you make for an eight-hour day. You will work while you are here with no distractions. We will start in the morning when it is cool and quit during the heat of the day. If you can live with this contract, show up here on Monday morning at 7:00 a.m., with the signed contract. New trucks and construction trailers with new tools will be delivered on Monday. Barney will be responsible to see that all the tools are in the trailers each night. They will be cleaned and serviced for usage the next day. Barney is responsible for broken and missing equipment. He will replace it during his afternoons when he is off work. He will receive $1000 per month for that responsibility as well as the time he'll spend after normal working hours with us, or our architect, or whoever we contract for specific purposes. He'll work with you, teach you what he knows, and what you need to know to complete each task at hand."

They all nod, take the documents handed to them, and leave in the two vehicles, departing in a cloud of blue smoke. I wonder what the discussions will be like in the bar these four are now headed to!

It's Saturday night and Bill heads off for Happy Hour at the "Good Times Bar." It's the deep south and segregation is still a way of life hereabouts so he's heading over to the dark side of town. As hoped, Bill finds Jackson there and buys him a drink. "So, what'd you think of the contract? Is it a sound plan? Will you work for the Lowell's under those terms?"

Jackson nods and says, "I can live with it, but ah don't know if Barney can. I have worked off and on with him for a long time. He ain't a very good worker and is poorly organized. Say, you work for them Lowells, what kind of people are they?"

"Well, I'm just their pilot and normally just fly them where they need to go. Usually I have a schedule, but sometimes it can be on the spur of the moment. If I need time off, I have a pilot friend who stands in for me. They are very generous, with a nice bonus at the end of the year."

Jackson takes a swig of beer and replies, "Mr. Percy and G.W. seemed to really pitch in with the work. I thought they was rich folk and not used to working with their hands, so I was a bit surprised to see that."

"I never met the Taft side of the family. Did you know them? What were they like?"

"Mr. Alton was a fine fellow, and I worked for him on several odd jobs. I think that manager, called Colonel Stanton, used the tobacco farm for his personal means and cheated them outta lot of money though.

You should maybe check on that."

Bill nods, making a mental note to pass the info along to Percy. "So, will we see you on Monday, Jackson? I think you can cut a separate deal from Barney, if you wish, or if he doesn't show up."

Jackson says, "We're s'posed to talk with Barney tomorrow and make up our deal. I need to work under Barney to keep the racial peace, but if he turns the deal down, I will want to work for the Lowell's directly, that'd be just fine with me."

It's Monday morning at ten minutes to seven. The three of us are betting on whether the fellas will show and at what time. Bill bets Jackson will show up in the next five minutes. I bet Barney will not show. Percy says he will show at one minute after seven. Just then we hear Jackson's truck a-comin' up the lane.

"Good morning, bosses!" The clock ticks on and soon it's at the stroke of seven. We hear Barney's truck turning onto the entrance road. I guess Percy's right.

Barney greets them saying, "Ok, I guess we can live with this contract, if it's not quite so tight. I don't like being responsible for the tools. Someone may steal some of the tools, and ah don't want to have to pay for them. You know how these people 'round here are!"

Percy's posture stiffens a bit in response, "Listen, you will be the one to check in the tools from the crew and see that they're cleaned and serviced. You will lock up the trailer and have the key. I will have the other key. You don't think that I will steal my own tools, do you?"

"Well, I guess not…but I still don't like the idea. Tools do break and get out of repair."

"If parts wear out, we will replace them. When this project is over, we have promised that we will sign over the construction trailer to you. It seems that if you want to receive good tools, then you will make sure they are properly stored, serviced, and maintained. Does that not make sense to you?"

They then agree to the contract and deliver their signed copies to Percy. I show them the new check-in employment clock. They all fill out their punch card and officially check in for work. I point out the first task of the day. "Inside that box is a new generator. Unpack it, put in oil and gasoline, and see if it works."

"Why do we need a generator? We have power here already."

About this time two guys from the power company pull up and park. One of them wearing a harness gets out of the truck and heads over to the pole which he then climbs up, unhooking the main incoming power line. Next, a big truck towing a trencher arrives from the rental place in Bixby and unloads it at the street. Ronnie, the electrician, is right behind them with an assistant of his. Percy directs Barney to have Joe help them lay out lines for the trenches to the main box, with feeder trenches to the carriage house and pool house.

At nine o'clock, an electric supply trailer, pulled by a new pickup, arrives at the house. "Barney, pick a spot for the trailers that cannot be seen from the road and yet can be watched from the house. Get the weeds cut around that area. There's a new weed eater in the trunk of our rental car."

At 10:00, a construction trailer, pulled by another new pickup, arrives on site. "Barney, here's your new truck and tools. Ronnie, get Barney to remove the old electric meter and fuse boxes, line out the new service panel, and let's cut it into the wall so it does not protrude from the house. After you do that, look at the carriage house and the pool house and recess the new panels there also."

The generator's running and we now have power to run the saws. The trenching is half way down the driveway and will be at the house in less than an hour. By noon, the trench to the house is dug, conduit has been laid in the trench, and it's ready to have service wires strung to the house.

Barney says, "I know we're supposed to check out at 12:15, but we got started late. We'll go ahead and work till 1:00 and get these other two areas ready for service panels. We need some lumber for headers and to frame out the electric boxes. I'll get it delivered this afternoon and we can install the boxes before noon tomorrow."

Ronnie says, "That'll be good. I'll have the power company inspect the boxes and reconnect us to the power grid."

Percy then tells them, "I got permits from the county for the new service, so I'll call the building inspector to come approve it. The power company will install a new meter and we'll be back in business. Ronnie, give us six temporary plugs inside the panel for construction equipment. We also need a temporary hookup for a house trailer, which should arrive late today, or in the morning."

At one o'clock we shut down for the day. Barney is assigned his new truck. Barney gives his old truck to Joe, who has no transportation. Ronnie is given a similar contract and assigned his new truck. Ronnie is now convinced this is a good deal, signs the contract immediately, and agrees to show up at seven the next morning.

At five o'clock, Barney comes back with some lumber strapped to a new rack he had purchased for the truck. He unloads it and says, "Ah will see y'all in the morning. We will need this stuff first thing." The trailer is soon hauled in and situated next to the house, not far from the electric service. It's then leveled, and we're handed the keys. It's time for us to head to the motel. We have dinner together at a nearby restaurant and crack open a bottle of wine.

Bill says, "Hey, I'm nervous about the new equipment at the Plantation. Word of today's ventures will circulate far and wide—we might have robbers show up there tonight! I've got a pistol in the airplane, let's drive over there and I'll go grab it, and then you can drop me off at the house."

"Do you really want to do this or should one of us stay there with you?"

"No, I'll be alright. A shot or two in the air should chase anyone away."

Percy takes him over to the plane and Bill quickly retrieves his .38, a box of shells, and a powerful flashlight. He settles into the house on an old couch and Percy heads out the front door.

'T'was a dark and stormy night, with far off heat lightning.' *(Something must be about to happen! Isn't this always the case on dark and stormy nights?)*

Bill hears the crunch of gravel outside as a dark car slowly creeps up the driveway with no headlights on. Three men in shadow emerge from the vehicle. One of them points the flashlight and scans the hole in the side of the house, and then the flashlight beam moves over toward the new trailer.

"That wasn't there when I was here earlier," he hears one of them say. They head toward the construction trailers and the new generator sitting nearby. "Crap, they chained it to a tree, and we didn't bring any bolt cutters!" One of the hulks is bending over the generator, and crouches down, appearing to test its weight.

Bill quietly opens the front door. Stepping quickly onto the front porch he aims and fires a shot into the tree just above his head, yelling in as deep a voice as he can, "Get outta here or y'all are dead meat!" The three are visibly startled and immediately turn and run back toward their car, with Bill firing another shot aimed to fly over their heads. Once inside the driver guns the engine, jams the car into reverse and floors it, attempting to turn around, but he instead backs into a tree, the rear bumper crunching noisily into its hefty trunk. They then speed away as Bill watches, stepping back inside to call us with the report. Percy and I get dressed and head out to the plantation. When we arrive a short while later, we give Bill a drink of Scotch and discuss the event.

Bill tells us, "One of them said, 'It wasn't here when I was here earlier'. He was referring to the trailer. It couldn't be Barney as he was with us looking at the lumber right after the trailer arrived. We put the chain on the generator after they had all left, so it could be any of them, other than Barney, since we just eliminated him."

"Did the other two say anything?"

"Bill answers, "No, but one of them screamed after I shot. If I heard that scream again, I think I could identify it. Maybe, we need to hire a night watchman for when we're not going to be in the trailer."

On Tuesday morning, both the contracting crew and the electrical crew arrive a few minutes before seven and check in using the new time clock. Ronnie's clearly happy with his new truck. The work on the electric panels is completed on the house, carriage house, and pool house. The county building inspector arrives and signs off on the installation, and a short while later the power company arrives and configures the electrical hookup.

I have lunch and beer delivered. We setup tables and chairs near the pool house and designate this our future break room and lunch room. The crews are done for the day, but choose to stay for lunch, and we celebrate the beginning of the restoration over our suds and sandwiches. Everyone's happy. We had decided last night not to make any reference to the previous night's trespassing incident. The rest of the week will involve interior cleanup and the removal of plaster and lath covering the walls of the mansion. Ronnie and the electrical crew will begin to rewire the carriage house with new lighting, electrical outlets, and will run 220-volt power to the shop area.

On Wednesday, we three will be in Bixby to meet with Colonel Stanton, the manager of the Taft Tobacco business. Percy had arranged the meeting to review the books of the business some weeks earlier. He'd also hired an accounting firm from Mobile to be at the meeting and pick up all the business records for the past five years. At eleven o'clock, we all descend upon Colonel Stanton's office. He graciously greets us, but we can see right away he's nervous.

I reply to his greeting, "Why, Colonel Stanton, we all have heard so much about you, so it's good to meet you, sir. We know nothing about the tobacco business and look forward to you explaining it to us. You know, up north where we live, tobacco usage is declining. How is that trend affecting the Taft business these days?"

"Why, young lady, is it Miss Lowell? I can tell you all a lot about this business. It is true that tobacco usage is down, so our profits are down. The factory buildings are old, and we have had to do a lot of repairs in recent years."

Percy asks, "But is the business in the red, or in the black?"

"Well, I think it's about even, but maybe a little in the red."

Percy then asks, "That's why I've brought these gentlemen along to pour over the books and analyze the business. We don't want to close your enterprise and put all of these good people out of work, but if the business cannot be made profitable, then we will have to do just that. Colonel, I have a couple of questions. How much of the total production is grown on Taft land? And how much of it do we purchase from other farmers? And how is the price determined?"

"Well, those are good questions, Mr. Percy. The tobacco price is determined in the industry and it's different for different qualities of tobacco leaves. It's actually a complex determination. And, to answer your other question, we grow about half of the factory output on Taft land."

I then ask him, "So who's in charge of our farming production? What does it cost us to produce the tobacco versus what we pay for other farmer's tobacco?"

"Well...my son, John T. Stanton, oversees and runs the production from the Taft lands. We produce the finest tobacco, but maybe it costs us a little more to do it."

Percy nods for a moment and then says in reply, "Well, if we can't produce it cheaper than we can buy it for, then maybe we should shut down our fields and purchase the equivalent amount from other farmers."

At this point, the Colonel becomes visibly nervous. "Well, Mr. Percy, let us not think about that. We don't want to shut down our business. Maybe we can figure ways to cut costs." (I can think of a few right off the top of my head–like cutting out the Colonel and his son. That should save a bundle.)

Percy replies to him, "We're not there yet. Let the accountants look at all the books and tax returns first. Once the business has been thoroughly examined, we'll have high cost areas we can then zero in on. Maybe we'll need some new automation, or some new employees, or maybe we'll see about re-assigning employees to different parts of the business. There's lots to review and consider. Are there other crops which might be more lucrative, I wonder? In the meantime, we'd like you and your son to review the operation for your input. In a month we hope to have the analysis done. You will be provided with a copy once we have it. Then we'll all sit down and make a plan for the future. I hope that you'll be part of this plan."

I then add, "Colonel, could you have John T. meet with us this Saturday at ten o'clock and give us a tour of the fields? It'd be helpful to see those and hear from him about the Taft production from those fields."

"Well, yes, Ah could, little lady. He will be glad to give y'all a tour, I'll get it setup with him."

We pick up our notes, the accountants leave laden with many boxes of materials, and we depart in different directions. I laughed to the others, "Did you see how jittery the Colonel got? What'll you bet on how many suggestions he'll come up with? No doubt this business has many perqs—company cars, lots of trips, personal expenses shown as business expenses. It'll be interesting to see what the accountants unravel. What we also need is someone in the community to spy on them."

"How about your senator friend, or his secretary?"

"Nope, the senator's related to the colonel, so that's no help. He did warn us about the colonel's loose ways with expenses though, remember?"

We head back to the plantation where the demolition/cleanup is progressing nicely. The crew is now settling into a good routine and we believe Percy's plan is actually working. By Friday noon, the trailer's completely operational with water, power, and septic systems in place. We then move our personal items from the motel to the trailer. Payday is at hand and we pay the crew in cash. We give them the choice for future paychecks of cash, check, or direct deposit. For all cash payments or reimbursements, we require they sign receipts. This will provide us with a paper trail and avoid any disagreements in the future.

Saturday morning arrives and, with it, our ten o'clock tour of the

Plantation with John T. Stanton gets underway. He actually arrives on time and we set off in the plantation's van.

"So, John, thanks for meeting with us, and what's the story about the plantation and its farming operations?"

He squints into the bright sunshine and answers, "Of the 10,000 acres, we have 2,000 acres in tobacco, and 1,000 acres as pasture for horses and cows. We used to have an active horse-raising business, but currently we only have five old horses in retirement. The cows are a small herd of 100 beef cows which we sell locally in Bixby."

I ask him, "What's the rest of the property consist of? Can more of it be farmed? How much is bayou or wetlands?"

John T. answers, "Well, nearly 3,000 acres are fallow with basically worn-out soil from the previous tobacco growing. Only a small portion's wetlands…that runs along Alligator Creek. However, during big rains, two or three areas flood, and that water ends up covering quite a few acres in size."

Percy then asks, "And how many employees do we have operating the fields?"

"Well, we have five full-time, and then we just hire whatever we need for harvest or planting."

"Do any of them live on our property?"

"We used to have employee housing, but the buildings are all rundown and unusable now. The cigarette factory has 15 full-time employees. They all live in Bixby and come to work six days a week."

John T. points the van back toward the mansion and drops us off saying, "Y'all call me anytime and I'll show you any of the operations you'd like to see."

Percy then replied, "Please call us a few days in advance before harvest or planting, or before any major decisions are made at the factory. We may wish to be present."

After he leaves, we head toward the trailer, discussing what we've seen and heard about the operation so far.

Bill shakes his head a bit, saying, "From what I learned from either

Jackson or in the local bar, the work force is poorly supervised. The word is they also don't like John T. No one shows up for work on time, and when they do, the daily work has not been set out for them. They all feel they're underpaid, which apparently factors in to their lack of diligence in doing the work."

Percy, says, "Hmmm, it looks like there's some potential here to do other things and to definitely better supervise this operation. I wonder how we can reclaim the 3,000 acres of rundown land? Should we rebuild the worker's housing units? That area's out along Alligator Creek which floods, so maybe we could have some communal gardening in that spot. Seems to me there's several possibilities."

"Speaking of Alligator Creek, what are we going to do with Pegleg Joe? He apparently lives in a bunkroom off the pool service area. He's been a fixture 'round here for more than 40 years. We can't just get rid of him, can we?"

Percy shakes his head, "Well, I guess he is kind of a watchman, but he's dressed in rags and always looks so grimy. I don't know if he does anything useful, he's actually kinda strange. He has that staff which he continually waves around while jumping back and forth. I guess he's a little touched in the head."

Bill then says, "Ok, let's have Barney fix up his quarters and get the bathroom repaired so he can bathe and stay cleaned up."

"I like that. We could also pay to get his wooden leg replaced with a more realistic leg. We might get him some kind of a uniform, say a doorman, a coachman, a butler, or whatever. Actually, I kinda like the idea of dressing him up as a pirate—like Long John Silver from Treasure Island, but let's ask him what he'd like to wear."

We call him over as he's always around us somewhere close by. "Hey, Pegleg Joe, what do you want us to call you?"

"Everybody just calls me Pegleg, so I guess that's ok."

Percy tells him, "Listen, we want to keep you here on the plantation as you know more about it than anyone else. We're going to fix up your quarters, especially the bathroom. What salary were you given by the

Taft's and what have your duties been consisting of?"

"Ahs s'pposed to look over things around here. Pickup things like trash that was lying 'round. They gives me money when I asked for something that ah needed."

"Well, we'd like to get you some clothes, Pegleg, like a uniform for you to wear. You look a little ragged, m'friend. What would you like to be, a pirate, a doorman, a butler, an admiral? What's your fantasy of who you'd like to dress up as?"

"Well, sir, Ahs always liked to be Robin Hood. Maybe a green tunic uniform would be nice."

Hearing this, a burst of light rings my bell. It dawns on me what Pegleg is doing with his staff. He's acting out scenes from the movie having the staff mimic his sword. "Pegleg, are you Little John or Robin with your staff?"

"Sometimes, Ah is one and sometimes Ah is the other. It's great fun."

"When did you see the Robin Hood movie last?"

"Well, it has been a long time ago now, I guess. It was one of the first movies that I ever did see."

I immediately think to myself I'll get a DVD of the Errol Flynn version of Robin Hood for Pegleg. "We can fix that so you can relive it with a new DVD of the movie you can watch on a new player, how does that sound?"

"Ah thank you so much, Lady Marian—I mean Miss Gee."

"Ok, Robin, you can call me Lady Marian. Actually, I rather fancy that. Any other requests?"

"Yes, Ah's like to be able to shoot a bow and arrow like Robin Hood's merry band. Can any of you teach me to shoot arrows?"

"Yes. I can, I'm an archer and will get us some equipment. I need the practice anyway and it'll be fun to teach you how to be an archer."

Percy laughs, "This is too terrific a fantasy. Maybe we all need green outfits. Putting up with Karen is one thing, but now you're Lady Marian?! I guess that means I must be Little John and Bill's Will Scarlet."

Pegleg replies, "Hey, how'd you know what Ah had named y'all?"

(I wonder about Percy's comment mentioning Karen—I thought he knew nothing about Karen. Have I not been as secretive as I thought I was? I must ask Bill if he has ever let mention of Karen slip out during their conversations…?)

The next day Bill and I fly back to Boston as Ma Mah needs to be flown to Chicago for an event. I have several events planned myself in the next couple of weeks. Percy has lots of supervision to do at the Taft Plantation and wants us to come back in a few weeks or less. I call my designer, Pierre, and charge him with creating green tunics for Pegleg. I order three different vintages of Robin Hood movies and have them sent to Percy. I have UPS deliver bows, arrows, and targets to Percy too. I'll bet Pegleg will want Percy to begin his archery lessons. I know that Percy could shoot once upon a time, but of course he was not of my caliber.

CHAPTER 6   A night like no other at the Boston Pops

Back in Boston for only two weeks and it turns out much has happened in our absence. Maybe I should've stayed in Mississippi at the Taft Plantation. Dealing with restoration of the mansion and the incompetence of workers, not to mention the graft of those in charge, seems like child's play compared to what I went through in 40 seconds!

I'm leading a lecture on gun violence to examine what our community has suffered. The papers and news channels have hashed it and   rehashed it every single day since the event which just happened two weeks ago. Reporters continually call me and stop me whenever I'm spotted in public. They call me a hero—and maybe I am—but I did what needed to be done at the exact time it was needed, that's all.

Following a nice introduction from the Assistant Mayor who's an advocate of removing automatic weapons from the public domain, I begin my lecture.

"Thank you for having me here tonight, as well as this generous introduction branding me a hero. However how I did what I did and how it all happened, I'm frankly still having difficulty processing in my mind. I've never killed anyone before, and never thought that I would. I'm very much against gun violence, and especially against there even being fully automatic weapons in any of our hands—other than the military and the police. I even wonder if the police should have such weapons at times. How do we get them off our streets?

Let me begin by reviewing my history with guns for you. As a young teenager, I learned how to shoot with a bow and arrow. And, after awhile, I got pretty good at it. My archery coach was the one who then introduced me to the rifle range. After some practice, I then got good at hitting a target with a rifle. Pistols came next, and then shotguns. My father was a hunter and took me duck hunting, and finally deer hunting. I shot a couple of ducks, but could not bring myself to shoot a deer. I understand that there are a lot of hunters out there. And I'm alright with that, but for myself, I cannot kill animals. So how could I kill a person— no matter how bad he is?

I still go to the rifle and pistol range at least once a month, sometimes more often. Shooting at a target, be it a bullseye or an outline of a human head or body, somehow gives me a release from the stress of life. If I fantasize about killing an evil person, or even someone I don't like, it relieves that internal tension for me. If I meet that person later on the street or in a restaurant, I smile and greet them warmly. My fantasy has washed the event or problem with them out of my mind. However I cannot conceive of actually killing that individual…or anyone. So how did this happen?

It was Friday night and I was attending the symphony at the Boston Pops. Some of my favorite Beethoven and Mozart pieces were to be played that night and my friend, Mary, and I had tickets for seats in the fourth row. We arrived at the event just a few minutes before the performance was to commence. I told Mary to get our seats as I wanted to visit the ladies' room beforehand as it'd be too crowded during intermission.

The timing of all the minor occurrences and how they came together is the mystery here. Was it by chance, good luck, bad luck, or perhaps an act of God? We'll never know. I nodded and said 'hello' to Clarence as we entered the lobby, he was the off-duty policeman covering security for the event.

He replied, "How are you, Miss Lowell?" I said another few words to him about the musical selections scheduled for that evening. "Watch the crowd, Clarence. Tonight, they're playing a Wagner piece as well as Beethoven, and you know how wild that is!"

I keep wondering after the fact if I had distracted him with my brief conversation, causing him to miss the perpetrator preparing to do the evil deed. . . ? Clarence was nearing retirement age and liked the money from these events where there never seemed to be any problems or disturbances whatsoever given their tony attendees. In retrospect, maybe we need to examine the police officers who perform these duties. Possibly a younger officer with more rapid reflexes is what's needed, one with more training in looking for shooters and terrorists, perhaps he'd be better able to protect us.

So, back to the event, I was having difficulty with the towel dispenser in the bathroom and spent maybe three extra seconds getting the paper out. I proceeded toward the door and met another woman, Doris Lerner, an acquaintance of mine, just as she was heading out. I stepped off to the side, held the door, and allowed her to precede me, which condemned her to death as I was two steps behind her when the shooting started. Clarence and poor Doris took the first shots as a lone assailant and obviously a madman suddenly opened fire on the symphony attendees, beginning his lethal sweep of the lobby.

From this point on, everything seemed to be in slow motion, with my mind racing but my body slow to respond. I dove behind a large plant just out of the killer's view. "Poor Doris, she took my bullets. I should not have let her go first!" I wailed inside my own head. The gunman marched forward in a measured fashion and flung open one of the heavy doors of the auditorium. "Someone must stop him. Poor Clarence is dead. WHO can stop him? I guess I'm the only one here." I dove for Clarence's crumpled body and wrestled his gun out of its holster from my awkward angle. "I wonder if it's actually loaded? Is there a bullet in the chamber?" I pumped a shell into the chamber and took off the safety. By now, this shooter had burned up the 30 bullets of the first clip, and in two or three seconds he put in a new clip and resumed firing into the crowd. "I must get to him, and quickly." I gingerly stood, quickly sprinting to the auditorium's opening, bypassing a couple who'd been mown down, and I then stepped over a body partially holding the door open. Twenty feet in front of me was the killer, firing what I think was about his twentieth round of that clip. I'm astonished to now see he's wearing body armor from head to toe. "Where can I shoot him? If my bullet doesn't stop him, he'll turn his weapon on me." There seems to be no place to shoot him that will be effective. "I could wait until the clip is empty and charge him, but I only weigh 115 pounds. I could empty the gun into him, which possibly would throw him off balance allowing me to tackle him. He might drop his assault rifle and others might help me. No…I must TRY to take him out before he finishes emptying this clip and killing more innocent people.

What'd I do? I spotted a crease between his body armor and his helmet. A bullet right there would be deflected straight into his spine." All this went through my mind in three or four seconds as I took aim on that half inch spot on his neck. One shot and he was dead. However, his gun actually continued to fire into the floor as he fell. The whole incident had taken but a mere 40 seconds. Two clips of ammunition fired, with the discovery of four more clips unused. Twenty people were dead, and nearly 30 others were injured, many severely.

Someone next to me dialed 911 on their iPhone. I said, "Let me have that!" and yanked it out of his hand, telling the 911 operator that a mass killer's dead and to get a fleet of emergency vehicles here a.s.a.p. as there are over two dozen wounded among the dead. "Get them here NOW!"

After quickly handing the cell back to the bystander and asking him to stay on the line with her, I yelled at the people near me to help the wounded and put pressure on spurting wounds. Within minutes the first emergency vehicle arrived, but it had to remain outside until the police secured the scene. I dropped Clarence's gun in my purse so I wouldn't get myself shot by the swarm of police arriving on the scene. About then I think I went into shock as I remember little from that point on."

After I finished recounting the episode, I then took questions from the audience. "How did you process all that and then respond so quickly? Most of us would've just stayed down on the floor or run out the front door if we could."

I answered, "When I was a child, I had a friend named Karen. We played all kinds of games. Many of these required fast thinking so we could outdo each other. We endlessly analyzed events that happened around us or that dominated the news. We could always come up with a better way or a different way to deal with a situation. That background developed a skill in me for thinking quickly on my feet.

Next question: "What do you think about the police response to the tragedy? Did they help with the wounded?"

I replied, "The police and emergency medical teams were there in two minutes but remained outside directing and helping patrons exiting the hall. A few slightly wounded folks made it outside on their own with the help of their friends. We were still on the line with 911. I told them we needed medical help now as people were bleeding to death. They responded that the scene was being secured by the police before medical help could enter the auditorium. I told them the scene is secure and the perpetrator's dead. Get us help NOW!"

After about five minutes, the SWAT team arrived. They charged into the auditorium with automatic weapons drawn, and ran rapidly down every aisle, doing a quick but thorough sweep of the auditorium. Many people screamed as the SWAT team were dressed much like the perpe-trator. "Don't shoot us! Don't kill us! We need help. We've already been shot!" The SWAT leader yelled "all clear" loudly and their group then withdrew for the most part. The medical teams then swarmed in and the victims started being attended to. More than 15 minutes had passed, and several more people had died of their wounds in the interim.

I was in a dialogue with the team leader. He'd first asked me, "Where's the perpetrator?"

"It's obvious, isn't it? He's right there—the guy with the AR-15 still clutched in his hands."

He said, "Why didn't you remove his weapon?"

"And, what, get killed by you guys because I have a gun in my hand?"

"How did you know he was dead?"

"Well I got a clean shot and he didn't move after I dropped him."

"YOU shot him? Where? How could you? He's completely encased in body armor."

I replied, "I shot him in the one venerable place in his armor."

"I don't see any holes in the armor or any vulnerable spots."

"Take a look at the base of his neck, there's a crease there between the armor and his helmet. The bullet entered his backbone and severed his brain."

He looked at me rather incredulously asking, "How'd you know that?"

I responded sarcastically, "Well, Officer, I took high school biology, didn't you?"

He bent down and examined the body. "Well, there is a small hole right where you said you shot him. How far away were you when you fired?"

"Maybe 20', I was just inside the door."

"Wow! That is some pretty good shooting, lady. Do you have a permit for the gun?"

"No, the gun belonged to Clarence."

"It doesn't matter who it belongs to, you still have to have a permit to carry a concealed weapon. Who's this Clarence?"

"Clarence is the dead cop you had to step over to get in here. He was my friend and the first one the perpetrator shot. I was in the line of fire for the next rounds, but this woman stepped in front of me and took those bullets. In less than 10 seconds I dove for Clarence's gun, pumped a bullet into the chamber and took off the safety. In less than 15 seconds I stepped over the bodies and shot the killer dead."

"Where's the gun now? We need it for evidence."

"I dropped it near his body, or maybe into my purse. I think it's back there, maybe about three feet behind you."

Next audience question is asked by someone I don't readily see: "What happened next?"

"The medical teams came in and relieved those of us who were tending to the wounded. I needed some air and asked the policeman if I could go outside. I was covered with blood from a victim I'd been trying to help. The cop picked up my purse, opened it, and saw the gun. He said he'd just keep it in the purse until they got the fingerprints off it. I told him those fingerprints are mine. Please be careful of that purse as it's a very expensive designer handbag. Don't get any blood on it!"

He asked me again. "How did you get this gun in here? This is not a policeman's gun as you claim. This is a 38 caliber small pistol. Boston Police carry larger 45 caliber standard issue pistols."

"No, I got it from Clarence's holster. It was *his* gun!"

He then smirked, "maybe!" and carefully dropped it into an evidence bag.

Next question: "So what happened when you went down to police headquarters?"

"They had me retell my account of the events, so I repeated everything over again, actually multiple times. They couldn't believe my account of the timeline involved. Surveillance cameras verified this for them, that the entire incident only lasted 40 seconds. After two hours of rehashing, I called my lawyer to get me out of there. He had seen TV coverage including me coming out of the hall covered with blood. So he'd already arrived at the police station shortly thereafter and demanded my release. He was informed they might have some more questions for me, but he insisted, and he accompanied me out the door a short time later."

"He took me home where Ma Mah was anxiously waiting, glued to the TV. Accounts of the wounded and dead were coming in as breaking news reports in the metro area as well as nationally. Once again, the pundits were immediately discussing gun violence and the use of fully automatic rifles. Ma Mah helped me get out of my blood-soaked clothes. I took a very long, hot shower and then downed a large glass of whisky. After that, I slept for 18 hours. The phone rang continually, and reporters were gathered outside on the front steps. Ma Mah chased them away and answered all the calls."

Next question: "How did you deal with killing the perpetrator and the whole bloody scene?"

"Yes, that was and is the most difficult part. That's one reason why I am giving this talk today. Since this event, I've been to a therapist every other day for two weeks and occasionally have additional sessions too.

I had never killed anyone before and hope I never witness anything like this ever again in the future. We must deal with this gun problem, in spite of the NRA and the gun manufacturers. Our elected officials must develop some spine to deal with this serious issue in our society. Please, no more questions now as I'm feeling a bit overwhelmed. Thanks to each of you for coming today—and please contact our legislators and keep the pressure on them."

As I leave the podium and exit the stage Bill meets me in the wing and steers me out of a back door of the auditorium to his car where I collapse into the passenger seat in a semi-conscious state. I hope the next time I have to discuss the shooting it will be easier. After all, "time is the great healer." But, right now, what I need is to go to sleep again............. zzzz.

CHAPTER 7   Escape from Reality

I awake with a start. Why does this happen so often? Awaking with a start, still partly immersed inside one of my fantasy dreams? Where am I today? I look around and see I'm in a cabin in the woods, constructed of logs. Am I back in the Catskills at the lodge where Cassie was killed? As my gray cells snap like a rubber band in that direction, I realize I must get back on that case. The killer cannot get away with killing one of my friends. But, no, this cabin is different. A fire is still burning in the stone fireplace. Deer horns are hung on the wall. I wonder to myself… who killed the deer? A homemade quilt covers the bed I'm lying on. I look out the window and see the cabin's nestled inside a deep pine forest.

Glancing down, I see I'm dressed from head to toe in a tan doeskin outfit. Is this getup real or fake? I then notice I'm wearing moccasins. What the heck—am I an Indian princess? Not with red hair and white skin! How did I get red hair? Yes, ok…now I remember—I had it dyed a couple of days ago to change my appearance and help me hide out from all those reporters who've been pestering me.

The tapping at my door continues. Apparently, that's what awakened me. I call out for whomever to come in. The door opens and a man slowly enters.

"It is I, Prince William, Sir Lovesalot, Robin Hood, or whoever you want me to be. Who are you today? Gee? Karen? Cinderella? Maid Marian? I am your friend, your confidant, your would-be lover. You need a kiss to awaken you, sleeping princess." He crosses the room and gives me a gentle but firm kiss on the lips. Something stirs within me, recollecting times past.

"Ok, Princess, do you want me to caress the savage beast within your chest "It is a very luscious pair of breasts as I recall…"

I look over in the corner of the room where my bow and a quiver of arrows are leaning against the wall.

Pointing to them I say, "Do you want me to shoot our dinner, or keep the Sheriff of Nottingham and his men away from our castle? But this is not a castle, is it?"

"No, but it is a refuge for as long as you need it, m'lady. Come, take my hand, and we shall go down to the lake and toast the incoming day."

I ask, "Where the heck ARE we? And what time is it anyway?

"No, this is not Sherwood Forest, we're in Minnesota, and this is Lake Almost-Begone. It's late afternoon and gorgeous outside, Come down and see the lake with me."

Bill, my Prince William today, pulls me to my feet and we head out the door and stroll together leisurely down to the lake. He spreads a blanket on the ground and takes food and wine out of a large basket he's brought along. Ooh, one of my favorites—Navarro Pinot Noir. Two loons wale to each other along the lake. I listen for a minute and then say, "Isn't that a sad song they sing? I wonder why they're so forlorn sounding. They aren't the ones who've just killed a mad perpetrator."

"Don't think about that, m'lady. You're far removed from all that now. This is a different place, a different time, a different life. It is what we make of it…here and now."

"I know this is not a fantasy, although I want it to be. I saw the oil lamp in the cabin has an electric bulb. I looked at the windows and the glass was not rippled but was dual pane insulated glass. Therefore, we are in the 21st century."

"G.W. you certainly are a killjoy. I was enjoying being Prince William, rather than just good old Bill, the pilot!"

"Oh, I am sorry. Please…be my Prince Charming and sweep me off my feet and make love to me. Maybe I'll run away and no longer be Gee and will instead morph into Karen the recluse and hide out in a castle, or maybe on a deserted island. I don't know what the future will bring, but I know I want you to be part of it."

We kiss, then have some cheese, and more wine. Then we take a long walk at the outer edges of the lake, and finally head back to the cabin. There we make long, tender love far into the night until we each drift off into sleep, nestled together in our nakedness. My last thought before I drop off to sleepland is hoping I'll still be inside this delicious fantasy when we awaken.

The next morning, as I regain consciousness, I smell bacon cooking. Bill, my Prince William, is obviously busy in the kitchen. He comes into the bedroom, reaches down and raises my hand to his lips, and kisses it gently.

"Breakfast awaits us, m'lady, in the dining room." We chat as we eat and I realize how famished I am as I gulp down my bacon and eggs with gusto.

"Bill, whose cabin is this?"

"Don't you remember? It belongs to your cousin, Reginald—Reggie, I guess you call him. Why does your family have all these names that no one seems to like?"

"Old English tradition, I guess—I don't know why they brought it to America! So, what do you have planned for me today?"

"I brought the bow and arrows with a target we can setup. No, I know you don't kill animals. But I do know you use shooting as a release for your tension. I thought guns were out at this point, too close to the event. But let's have you try the bow and arrows, ok? Force yourself through 180 shots—the number of bullets the perpetrator had. If he'd used them all, just think of the carnage. What you did **saved** all those people, Gee. The target is also a bull's eye not a human form. What you do in your head will provide you the decompression you need. I have seen you use this method in the past as a cure for built-up stress. This'll work, so let's get going…I'll fetch the gear for you."

I knew Bill was right so I did the 180 shots—and I know within minutes of beginning my arm will be telling me about it for the next few days! I completely destroyed the target and the thick straw bale supporting it. With each shot I saw a person fall. After the 55 he had hit or killed, I saw him fall on each shot. If someone could have gotten him help before the shooting, that horror might have been prevented. Once he pulled off the first bullet, there was only one way to stop him though. . .and that was to kill him. I killed him over and over and over again that morning. Bill told me when I reached the 180 point, and then I just collapsed in his arms. He opened a small flask and then pressed a shot glass of whisky to my lips which I slugged right down, the caramel-colored liquid burning all the way as it slid from my throat into my stomach. Then I cried, and cried, and cried—but this horrific attack was over, finally over…inside my mind. From now on, I could talk about the incident without breaking down, and could also use this nightmare as a platform for speaking out against gun violence, and especially the use of automatic weapons.

For the next two days, Bill and I did everything together. We talked endlessly about each of our pasts, about Karen's detective business, Gee's fundraising projects, with some maybe-flavored discussions about what we thought the future might hold. We listened to music, drank wine and whisky, and made love at all times of the day and night. On Saturday, I had scheduled Jackie to come to the cabin on short notice, and Bill went to the airport to pick her up. She and her detective, Charlie, tumbled in just after noon, escorted by Bill who was also loaded down with bags of groceries, and a replenishment of wine.

I give him a quick kiss on the cheek and ask, "Bill, did Jackie tell you she was one of my Vassar roommates? I guess I never really told you all the details about the reunion and Cassie's murder. Jackie and I have avowed to catch her killer. It seems the police have no leads though, and it's becoming a dead case for them now."

Jackie drops her purse near a chair and says, "Listen, let's have a drink and some lunch. We brought lots of food." She then does a quick double take when looking at me, "Say, when did you become a redhead like me? Maybe we could dress like twins. Think of the next big social event… we could bounce in wearing the same outfits! That should certainly get some comments from our friend, Mary, the fashion writer. Hey, what's this 'Leatherstocking tales' outfit you're sporting, girl? Is Bill maybe the Uncas of James Fenimore Cooper?"

"Nope, today he's Robin Hood, and I'm Maid Marian. Who do you want to be?"

Jackie immediately grasps our joke and replies, "Well, as I recall, Robin Hood didn't seem to have any women in his 'band of merry men,' so who can I be? I guess we'll have to go to a different venue. Wasn't there a Jacklyn Cochran, a famous woman aviator?"

"Jackie, good grief, please introduce us to your friend Charlie. We've been rambling on and we haven't even dispensed with the niceties. Where did you find him? He certainly is handsome. I love his tall, athletic figure and that square masculine face of his."

Charlie blushes and stammers in reply, "Jackie hired me to look into the Cassie case. The 'what if' conversations became long and complicated. We've both survived recent divorces, and when several meetings then led to dinner and wine—well…love happened! Now I believe Jackie's my soulmate."

Bill exclaims, "Wow, that's beautiful, you two. I like the term soulmate…in fact, I believe Gee and I are soulmates too. Sometimes we even know what the other is thinking. It's like we communicate telepathically without even speaking aloud."

The four of us then enjoyed a lively lunch together, quickly killing a bottle of wine. To bring Bill up to date, Jackie goes through her version of the reunion week and Cassie's murder.

"I told you I hired a private detective to delve into Cassie's past for the last 15 years since we were together at college. Well, Charlie discovered things are not as she led us to believe. For one thing, her husband, Glenn, deals with several drug dealers in South America. He's made numerous trips back and forth to several different countries, and Cassie often accompanied him on these trips. Remember she claimed to know nothing of their (his) finances? But she took business courses at Vassar, and guess what? She was actually the bookkeeper for more than one of Glenn's companies—so she *had* to know if he was laundering money. Hell, she had to be a big part of it, and certainly would have needed to create the paper trails to hide anything along those lines and ensure the books could withstand scrutiny from the IRS."

"So, do you think Glenn had her killed to cover-up what she knew? But if Glenn had been the one to shoot her, we would've seen him- but there weren't any other men around except for the bartender and a couple of short Mexican guys working in the kitchen. Oh, and I just remembered, there was also the cleaning crew of around half a dozen women, but they only showed up in the mornings. But didn't we see one of them there that evening cleaning up after our party at the lake? I won- der why was she there at that time of day?"

Jackie replied, "The bartender and the deputy sheriff immediately came out of the lodge at the sound of the shot with Debbie screaming about Cassie being hit and was dead. They would've seen anyone, espe- cially a man, amongst all us gals. But no one reported seeing a man, so it must've been one of us who killed Cassie."

"Cassie told me she thought Glenn was having an affair, but she didn't know who it was with. Do any of our girls live in their same region as him?"

"No, Charlie confirmed that no one from our group lived near them. However, Glenn traveled around to a lot of different cities, much of the time without Cassie. Therefore, he had opportunity to meet up with any one of us. We must figure out which of us is associated with a business Glenn could have had financial dealings with. It's hard to believe that any of us could kill anyone…let alone someone we know!"

After hearing that comment, I burst into tears saying, "I killed some- one!"

"I'm SO sorry, Gee. I didn't mean to hurt you. Or upset you, hon'. But please remember you made it through that horribly tragic event, YOU are a hero for what you did! I think I would've just laid still on the floor and waited for it to all be over. How many more clips of ammo did he have anyway?"

Bill replies, "He had six clips of 30 shots each, so 180 bullets. Gee stopped him at bullet 55. Listen, gang, let's open another bottle of wine."

We finish what turned into a very long lunch, including us polishing off that second bottle. Everyone's up for a walk by the lake which we all agree will be just the ticket for clearing our collective minds. Jackie comments about the two wailing loons we had heard earlier.

"Why do they sound so woebegone? There are only two of them and no rival in sight to create a problem. Do loons mate for life? Maybe they don't like each other and that's why they're a couple hundred feet apart and making those forlorn sounds at one another."

Bill says, "Well, instead, maybe they're both females and their mates have flown away."

I reply, "Here's a thought, maybe we all have had too much wine, folks! We're getting way too philosophical and analytical about a pair of birds! I know what will cheer us up, let's go into town for dinner tonight."

A bit later, Jackie tells me she's planning to leave the next day. She says she wants me to give a couple of talks in Chicago about my experience and the topic of gun violence. I agree to her request and she's going to set something up for the end of the following week. She also says she will have Charlie, her detective, continue to investigate us girls in searching for possible motives and/or any history of contact with Glenn. Bill and I decide we will stay here at the lake until we leave to meetup with Jackie for the anti-gun meetings next week. I call my designer and arrange to have him send two outfits to Jackie's house for me to wear to those. I want my attire to appear modest and professional but need clothing in a hue that will compliment my now-dark red hair. I'm already thinking of possibly switching back to black at one of my next hair appointments though.

It finally occurs to me to phone Ma Mah and assure her I'm doing just fine and am recovering from the trauma of the shooting, and also inform her of my two upcoming talks on gun violence. Ma Mah tells me the District Attorney has been calling. "He wants to know where you are, Gee, but I didn't tell him. He wants you to come in and talk some more about the incident. I told him you had talked for hours with the police and that you also gave an address on the topic at a public meeting on gun violence, and told him every word you said had been printed in the newspapers. If the D.A.'s forgotten the details, he should just read your speech in the papers!"

But he then said, "Well, there just might be something else that's unanswered!"

"I told him he needed to get these fully automatic weapons and 30 round clips off the streets. If he can't or won't do something about it, I'll be supporting someone else for D.A. in the next election. Get some spine and do something, and please also quit bothering my daughter!"

"And then I hung up! If he calls you again, you tell him to talk to our lawyer. I'm tired of this fellow."

With Bill taking care of my emotional state and Ma Mah defending me against the law, I may just recover from this ordeal.

CHAPTER 8   An unexpected crusade...and rescue

Our delicious and relaxing week at the cabin passed, and now it was time to fly to Chicago for the two talks Jackie had scheduled for me. For such a short lead time, the publicity was intense, and crowds were expected. The NRA was actively opposing any new gun legislation, as usual. A large group of protestors was also expected at the talks. Much to my surprise, reporters were lined up en masse along the sidewalks, waiting, just outside our hotel.

"Ms. Lowell, how are you going to deal with the gun defenders and the NRA?"

"I am not opposed to guns. When I was younger, I was even a hunter myself for a brief period. Since I don't like to kill animals though I gave up hunting and just restrict my gun usage to the firing range."

"Then why are you labeled as anti-guns?"

"I oppose the use of fully automatic weapons and the large clips of ammunition. Certainly, hunters don't need 30-round clips. If you miss the animal on the first shot, it's gone. If you spew 30 shots after it, you'll just hit a lot of trees—and hopefully no nearby hunters."

The first event was packed with people both pro and anti-gun proponents. I was introduced and crossed the stage to the microphone. Several people boo'd and others hooted.

Looking out into the crowd, I said, "It's too early to boo me. You haven't even heard what I have to say yet. If you don't mind, I'd rather you turn your boos into questions after I've shared my thoughts, and maybe we can have some genuine dialogue on this issue, ok? To begin though, I want to tell you about my firsthand interaction with the killer at the Boston Symphony. The whole horrific event took place in just 40 seconds, ladies and gentlemen—that's all it took for 20 people to suddenly lose their lives on a night that was supposed to be filled with the beauty of classical music. Secondly, I would like to hear your views on how this kind of senseless violence can actually be stopped. I believe there must be ways to stop or prevent these sorts of incidents from happening. The NRA should be supportive of these efforts and help us find common-sense solutions."

I then gave my account of the terrible event and the questions from the audience thereafter went on for nearly an hour. Of course, their Second Amendment rights were the primary point cited by the NRA and their ilk. However, no one succeeded in making a case as to why anyone other than military personnel need the big clip magazines. The NRA's stance is they don't even want to limit the number of clips a person can carry.

"When do you ever need more than 30 shots in rapid succession?" I suggested the rapidity of the change of clips was also a real problem. If it took, say, 20 seconds to change clips, then people would have a chance to escape, or to tackle an armed perpetrator. And this shouldn't be a problem for the police.

"Think of the number of bullets a SWAT team of six can fire from one 30-shot clip each! If they can't take down a gang of perps with one clip apiece, they need to go back to the firing range and practice some more!" The conversation degenerated from there. "How many bullets should be in a clip?" "How many clips can a person carry?" "How rapidly can one change clips?" "What types of guns, if any, should be banned from sale?" "Should all guns be registered?" "What about vintage guns?"

At this point, I asked the crowd if we could form a committee consisting of the NRA, the police, both pro-gun and anti-gun advocates, and legislators to meet regularly and discuss these issues. People from each group were identified and promised to organize an initial conference in the near future. The meeting ended, and I was glad to get out of there. Bill said I did a good job.

The second talk was held in another part of the city with a slightly different cross-section of people. The constructive part of the meeting was led by a couple of doctors and psychiatrists who deal with mentally disturbed individuals, including criminals. Certainly, these professionals need to be heard and participate in the committee as well. Questions from the audience: "Why do mass shootings occur? Who are these per-petrators? Can we predict who will become a mass killer?"

I respond, "These are great questions, yet no one seems to have the answers. The NRA and the gun industry tell us guns are not the problem—people are the problem. People kill people and always have... with a gun, a knife, or a rock.

"The question is why? Does the perpetrator just become over-whelmed in a fit of anger and go on a killing spree? Studies indicate these mass killings are instead often planned well in advance. This may be an important clue to examine.

"Domestic violence is usually a 'fit of rage' that goes out of control to the extreme. Rarely does this motivation lead to a mass killing, but it makes good sense to stay out of the range of one of these kinds of of-fenders just after an incident occurs. They may kill people stepping in to prevent the violence, or they may commit suicide themselves.

"Are all mass killers crazy? More than half of them have had some psychiatric help in previous years to deal with their 'demons.' Rarely have psychiatrists identified a person on the brink of committing a mass kill-ing though. I guess it's hard for even a trained mental health professional to recognize a potential mass killer! Maybe they recognize a potential lethal action exists but think they can effectively head it off, or succeed in curing them. However, the facts indicate few of the killers are actually receiving help at the time of their killing spree."

Next question: "Are there different types of killers?"

I answer, "It seems to me there are three types of killers. First, the psychotic killers who have little regard for others and just unilaterally hate people.

Second, the psychotic individuals who are paranoid and obsessed with delusions about others. They may hear voices that tell them to kill.

And, lastly, there are traumatized individuals coming from a back-ground of child abuse, drugs, and being bullied. Some of them become bullies—or worse—themselves.

Most of these individuals who eventually become violent have poor social skills. They tend to be male loners but may have a cohort they fanaticize with about getting back at society—or the school, workplace, or family, etc. They have a sense of wounded masculinity which may lead to their rage against the world. They typically feel that life is unfair, and everyone is against them."

Comment from the audience, "Wow! That is a broad explanation. I'm still not sure that I would recognize a potential killer myself though. We all see people who are 'loners.' They don't socialize well. They are the 'grey people'."

Another question, "Do they join gangs?"

"I don't think so. People who join gangs are seeking socialization and identity.

"These people—killers—are like what you mentioned, the 'grey people'. They don't wear brightly colored clothes. Maybe they wear trench coats or dark-colored hooded sweatshirts. But many of us are just poorly socialized, suffer from feelings of inferiority, and may have an 'inferiority complex.' That doesn't make us, or them, potential killers.

Ok, that's all for now as I'm a bit overwhelmed at this point, I must admit. Thank you for coming. Please give some thought to these matters we've discussed today, ok? Keep contacting and pressuring our legislators. Maybe there are things that can be done if we can just come together on this pressing issue."

Karen gnaws at me in private, "Gee, Your anti-gun talks are leading to confutations with the NRA. As a result, you're not only being pursued in public, but you've even had rocks thrown at you. A couple of shots have even been fired over your head as a warning. You must protect yourself (and ME!). You need to carry a gun in your purse!"

"I can't do that Karen. You know that I hate guns. In fact, I have never fired a gun since I gave up hunting with Pa Pah. You are the gun person in the family. You go to the shooting ranges while I hate the smell of gun oil and that acrid smell of gunpowder. After your shooting matches, I have to take a shower twice just to get that awful smell out of my hair!"

"You know what? You're crazy, Gee. I actually enjoy both those "fragrances." But, whatever your feelings, you simply *must* protect yourself. If you can't personally carry a gun, get Bill to always carry one for your protection. That may work for now but, believe you me, I *will* bug you about this again later."

Bill then whisks me away back to the hotel. We eat in the room and have a couple of drinks. I then collapse after the strain of the back-to-back talks. He helps me out of my clothes, and I plunge into a deep sleep. Next morning, I'm still in a drowsy stupor so he steers me onto the plane, and we take off for Salinas, California, where I'm to meet Hollie and tour her animal rescue ranch.

Phoning her from the plane, I provide her with our arrival time. She meets us at the airport, and we share warm, happy hugs, and she is then introduced to Bill, my pilot, confidant, and lover.

Hollie says, "Before I take you to my ranch to see my rescued critters, I have a treat for you, Gee. Tonight and tomorrow night you'll stay in a tent house at Vision Quest, which is located just south on River Road. You'll see their rescued big game, including elephants, lions, and tigers. To hear them at night is a wonderful although slightly-terrifying experience, but I think you'll enjoy it. I'll pick you up about noon on the second day."

We catch an early dinner with Hollie in Salinas, and she drops us off at Vision Quest afterwards. We check in and are escorted to the promised tent house. An elephant then brings our luggage to the tent! And we had been told at the front desk, he'll bring us breakfast in the morning as well. Having this gentle giant wait on us is beyond belief, but we soon recover from our astonishment and settle in. The sky darkens, and we detect a thunderstorm is brewing. The rain begins to fall. 'Tis a warm and stormy night.' I wonder what fantasies this nocturnal rainstorm will generate in my head!

It's now dark, except for sudden flashes of lightning. These illuminate the dark furry hulks pacing back and forth in their cages, less than a hundred yards away. Just shortly, I find I'm still feeling wrung out and quickly drift off to slumber land.

What seems like a short time later, I awake with a start. "Where am I?" A lion roars, and it seems he must be right outside our tent and ready to attack.

Bill smiles and cocks his head, "Isn't that just a marvelous roar?" Soon, another lion joins in with his own throaty growl.

"Yes, they are marvelous, but don't you think they sound rather melancholy too? Maybe they're lamenting they never lived in the wild and have always been stuck in captivity!"

Bill replies, "Just relax and try to enjoy this guest appearance on Animal Planet, Gee…or are you Karen tonight?"

"No, Dr. Stanley. I'm Dr. Livingston, I presume! And I've been looking for you, it seems, all my life. I've wandered the Congo, the Amazon, and even crossed the Sahara in tracking you down. In the process, I searched for Prester John and even Amelia Earhart while I was at it. It's so difficult to keep on-track and confine one's life to just a single target once in full blown search mode, y'know."

"Maybe that's why you invented Karen. It must be difficult to keep two or more lives going. Does that make you a schizophrenic, m'dear?"

"Sheesh, I hope not. You know I was raised as virtually an only child though, right?"

"What about your brother, Percy? Didn't you grow up with him?"

"Percy is a year and a half older than me. But when he was seven, and I was only five he was sent away to a boy's boarding school. Thereafter I only saw him when he came home for holidays. Even then, Daddy doted on him—because he was a boy. Therefore, I only received the full attention I wanted when he was away at school. I actually hated him for that in my early years, but we've become closer recently. At long last."

"So, you created Karen, a girl rather than a boy, because you needed companionship vs. competition for your parents' love? Is that it? And yet, it seems you and Karen developed a very competitive relationship after all. How do you explain that?"

"In school, I took up sports. I wanted to outdo Percy as he always did well in those competitions—and Dad complimented him— endlessly, it seemed. Karen and I became competitive to sharpen my sports abilities, and my wits to outsmart Percy—a.k.a. Mr. Smarty Pants!"

"Hmmm, I guess you carried—maybe still carry—a little streak of jealousy toward your brother, 'eh?"

I'm mum in response to this question and instead cross the room to the clear vinyl section serving as a window in the tent.

The rain is finally letting up. The lions continue to roar periodically through the night. Bill exclaims, "I think they're telling us they're the 'kings of the forest.' They don't sound sad to my ears! Maybe they are...........zzzzz." We quickly drift off to sleep.

The next day, we slowly rise from our deep slumber to the tinkling and clanking of bells. An elephant is lumbering our way with our breakfast! He's wearing a chain of bells around his neck—I think it's a "he" anyway, and am frankly too scared to peek! The rain hitting the tent again this morning and the delight of our food arriving via a giant pachyderm has left us in a buoyant mood, the altogether exotic new day gently pushing aside the recent past, causing the trauma of the shooting to retreat further into the deep recesses of our minds.

"Ah, Romeo, how art thou this morning?"

"Juliet, you are my sun, my moon, my love." We banter on in our silliness. Bill becomes Anthony and I then morph into his Cleopatra.

"Bill, aren't fantasy worlds wonderful places? Do you think very many people use them as I do for escape—or adventure?"

"Maybe more people should use them or at least visit them—maybe even try to live in them on occasion as you do with Karen. Many men work their whole lives toward retirement, but once they make it there, they're totally bored or can't find any new mountains to climb, or oceans to cross. They drive their wives crazy, and many of them don't live long enough to even enjoy the "rest" they've earned. So sad."

"Hey, Bill, you're the one who said we should dwell on the positive and not the negative. So, changing topics, what are we going to do today, mister?"

"First let's finish this scrumptious breakfast and this Darjeeling tea and then we'll follow the elephant down the hill to the animal complex. We'll see what they have here and note how they care for them. I'm interested to see what your friend, Hollie, does differently, although I know we won't be meeting up with her until tomorrow morning. Maybe this afternoon we can cruise down River Road and visit a couple of wineries too. There are a number of them down that way."

"How do you know that? Have you been here before?"

"No, but I was looking at a brochure on the nightstand after you drifted off into the 'Magic Kingdom' last night."

The gentle giant "waiter" has been biding his time patiently outside our tent and we now follow him back to his paddock. "Well, Vision Quest is certainly a 'Magic Kingdom' too, although Mickey and Minnie are missing." We then spend some time marveling at the array of animals and talking with them through their fenced enclosure.

"Anyone can talk with animals or birds, right?" I know my author-in-the-background, Tom, even talks with trees, especially redwood trees. *(Why does he keep butting into my book?)*

After spending an hour or more savoring this primal interaction with a host of four-footed creatures, we leave the compound and head off, finding some marvelous vintages at some wineries just down the road. After a satisfying round of tasting, we purchase a mixed case as we know Hollie cannot afford to buy wine.

Returning back to our tent room, we settle in for the evening, order a pizza, and open a bottle of Zin. It's a full moon tonight and we can see many of the animal pads or cages just down the hill from us. But the roars are back, maybe more in tune with one another tonight without the backdrop of the rain. Perhaps it's their full stomachs. Or maybe it's the Zin which has mellowed us out. Our appetite satiated, we make passion-ate love to the sound of the roars of the beasts.

"Hey, I guess tonight we're Tarzan and Jane!"

The next day, Hollie arrives mid-morning and we reluctantly check out of this peaceful animal kingdom and proceed to Hollie's version. Bill and I are growing more and more in love each day; soon we must have a serious talk about our future. For right now though, we need to review the situation with these animals and find a way for Hollie to continue doing what she loves.

Turns out her ranch was once an old stagecoach station in the Salinas Valley. The main building was a ramshackle hotel. Now it houses Hollie and her two children along with other helpers who do much of the heavy work on the farm. Fences always need fixing as wildebeests are hard on them. Most of her animals are grazers and distributed in different fenced fields over the vast 200-acre ranch which is also home to three small ponds with different types of fish. One area is a turtle pond with some giant turtles surrounded by a short concrete wall. Recently she has acquired three small alligators too.

"What am I going to do with them as they grow larger?"

Hmm! I think of Percy and the bayous on the Taft Plantation—and more than 6,000 acres not yet in cultivation, however I mention none of this to Hollie. I'm going to get Percy out here to meet Hollie. In my mind I then suddenly think, "Hey, wouldn't it be lovely if they hit it off and could do something jointly?" Both Percy and I would like to decrease or eliminate the tobacco production, but to replace it with what? Percy wants to turn the mansion into a getaway for the rich. Wild animals could fit into that scheme. If we can't get any lions, maybe we could record their roars at Vision Quest and play them at night...? That would be a treat for the guests, but maybe frightening to the antelopes and other grazers. Will my mind never cease its generating of "out there" new ideas?

After she provides us with a brief overview, we plunge into the day's work alongside Hollie and her staff of children and helpers. Together we build a fence, and then plant some trees. Most exciting though is witnessing the birthing of a baby zebra. After that, a waterline needs replacing. I suggest we rent a trencher to get it underground. Bill takes Hollie's old truck into town, has it serviced, and brings back the trencher. The line is laid and connected to two new water troughs for the grazers.

The delightful week comes to an end and we must return to Boston. We promise Hollie we'll be back in the near future. And I again think to myself I intend to get Percy to come here for a visit. My nails are destroyed after all this outdoorsy manual labor and next week I'm scheduled to have a role at a cancer fundraiser. I better get the to manicurist or I may have to wear gloves! But it was worth it—and Bill, I might add, seems to love this kind of activity also. He certainly is a lot more than "just a pilot." And I must admit…he has me flyin' high!

CHAPTER 9   Becoming political

Well, it's back to reality. So, you might ask, what's the reality of a socialite's life anyway? Gad, I have been involved in this scene ever since my Vassar days. Giving talks at fundraisers, attending social events, new clothes, endless small talk, handshaking and air kissing…and, believe me, it never ends. Shoot, I suddenly realize I totally forgot to talk with Hollie about Cassie's murder during our visit. I wonder if she has any new ideas for Jackie or me to follow? By the next time I see her, maybe Jackie's private eye will have turned up some new leads.

Back only two days and I'm already missing Bill. The last three weeks have been beyond belief, resulting in me really leaning on him for support. The lovemaking wasn't bad either.

He's back at his apartment at his sister's house near the airport. The plane is going through a vigorous inspection and maintenance update. He told me he has some paperwork to do, including studying to meet his pilot's license renewal requirements. Of course, Ma Mah knows nothing of our relationship. She probably thinks that Bill is beneath our class. I hope not though.

I attend the cancer fundraiser and add a short paragraph of support to the organizers of the event in my speech. A reporter there tries to ask me further questions about the symphony massacre, but I brush him off and try to steer his focus toward a discussion on cancer research. As I'm leaving the hall, a young woman approaches. She stops in front of me and presents me with an envelope with my name on it.

Without providing her name, she says, "I am a staff member of Bernie Sanders and the senator would like you to come to Vermont and talk with him. Will you, and if so, can you please come next week—say on Tuesday or Wednesday?"

Slightly astonished but recovering myself I reply, "What would Bernie want of me? I'm not political whatsoever."

She answers, "What do you mean you aren't political? I read your speech in Chicago. If that wasn't political, nothing is! Well, I think virtually every aspect of life is political at some point. Welcome to the gun regulation fight, Ms. Lowell."

I reply, "Ok. I can be there Tuesday by noon. If our plane's not available, I'll just drive up, as it's a lovely route." After shaking hands, she hands me a card which I tuck in my purse.

On the drive home I wonder what Bernie is wanting to get me involved in? I suddenly realize I must have Bill with me. Karen, of course will help me process it, but any whiff of politics could definitely have an impact on Bill, and our relationship. Well, first, we must discuss what our relationship actually is and what it's going to be. I won't make a decision regarding this involvement with Sen. Sanders without discussing the matter with Bill first.

Well, Monday rolled around, and Bill was scheduled to fly Ma Mah to Ireland. I had hoped he'd be available to come with me for the Sanders meeting, but no, looks like I have to meet with him on my own. I decide to drive the Tesla up to Vermont, wanting to appear green and doing my bit in fighting climate change.

Upon arriving, I was promptly shown into the senator's office and introduced as G.W. Lowell. Bernie crosses the room, shakes my hand, and asked, "What does the G.W. stand for?"

I replied, "I won't say, but you can call me G.W. or Gee as my friends call me. Isn't it interesting that hardly anyone goes by their name as listed on their birth certificate these days? Is it too casual for me to address you as Bernie, Senator? I'll bet most people don't ever refer to you as Bernard! Anyway, why did you request this meeting? I'm duly mystified."

He chuckled, shaking his head for a minute and then, gazing intently at me, he exclaimed, "Gee, I'll get right to the point—my team's researched you thoroughly and we see the truly stellar scope of public service you've rendered for many years now in your broad philanthropic endeavors. Building on that foundation of giving back and supporting humanitarian causes, I want to convey to you in the strongest terms that we need people like you who can take on these gun supporters. Not only have you masterfully stood up to them in speaking your mind so eloquently in a public forum, but you're actually a hero for taking out that crazy shooter. How in the world did you act so quickly?"

"I don't know, Senator—chalk it up to some kind of natural reaction, along with my familiarity with guns and training on shooting ranges during the years. There was just no time to wait for someone else who might be carrying a registered weapon to come to the rescue. I was less than 10' from the policeman's fallen body and had his gun in my hands before the perp got through the lobby door."

"Well, that's a truly amazing story. The way I see it, you should begin your political career on a local level or you could go straight to the State level. I'll be glad to steer you along to the right people, to some folks who can be of help to you."

"Wait just a minute, Senator. I have not agreed to a political career. In fact, I have a basic problem I see no way around. I just learned the Boston D.A. is actually trying to serve me with a subpoena—something about using an unauthorized police weapon, taking justice into my own hands—maybe even labeling me a vigilante. If I'm arrested, they'll want to fingerprint me. I have never been fingerprinted, but my fingerprints are actually already on record under another name."

"Wow! How is that possible?"

"My mother had identical twins, although that fact's not recorded on my birth certificate. Karen was born a day and a half early, with severe physical problems. She was sent to another hospital better equipped to deal with neonatal issues. As you may well know, Ma Mah leads a very busy social life, and she promotes many worthy causes. She just couldn't deal with a sickly baby who needed continuous care at the time. Karen spent two months in the hospital and the doctors informed her she would still need lots of care for several years. Good friends of Ma Mah offered to take Karen as they were childless and offered to raise her as their own. Somehow, they were able to get Karen's birth certificate altered to read Karen Hunt. When Karen was 25, her adoptive parents were killed by a drunken driver. Karen decided to become a private detective and hunt down drunken drivers and others who should be purged from our society."

"Well, I certainly agree with her. We need to get drunken drivers off the road. Did you know that if they catch you once in Norway, you get your driver's license taken away for life?"

I shook my head, "So it then turned out that Karen discovered in going through her adoptive parent's papers who her birth parents were, and their background. She became aware of me at that time, about seven years ago now, and she got in touch with me. You can imagine my astonishment as I knew nothing of this bizarre story. She and I subsequently became good friends and spent a lot of time together. Two years ago though, Karen died of respiratory problems, as she had only one well-developed lung. I decided to lead a double life and continue her fight on crime. Karen's work was completely legitimate, with permits, her fingerprints on file, a concealed weapon permit, and she was also a member of several crime-stopper type organizations including M.A.D.D. (Mothers Against Drunk Driving). She ran ads for her services, kept a bank account, had a post office box in Concord, and had an old Toyota Corolla with a secret compartment designed to house her gun. We both have (had) the same fingerprints. If I, G.W. am now arrested and fingerprinted, all this backstory will come out. The D.A. will then have strong data in coming after me with his outlandish claims. So…what am I to do?"

Bernie paused for a minute, looked down, and then leveled his gaze at me, "Maybe you should come out with this disclosure yourself before the D.A. gets wind of it?"

"Frankly, I just don't want to have the story made public while my mother is still alive as I think she will be open to lots of criticism for not having devoted herself to Karen's care. Ma Mah is a wonderful woman, Senator. Karen even specifically expressed to me she was alright with how life had turned out for her. She loved her adoptive parents and didn't think the social whirl of the Lowell's was something she would have felt comfortable living inside of."

Bernie responded, "Too bad Karen can't run for office, but I guess that would also let the secret out. I do hope that you, Gee, will continue speaking out and giving gun-regulation talks though. The more people we can convince to take a public stance on these problems, the better chance we have to fix them as a society. How about if I talk with your D.A. and try to get him to back off? If not, we'll see about supporting his opponent in the next election. Thank you for coming to see me and sharing all this with me today. You're a truly fascinating woman, Ms. Lowell, on several levels." At this, we shake hands as he beams his high wattage smile at me. I give him a calling card of mine, and the meeting concludes.

I decide to spend the night in Vermont before returning to Boston. After finding a hotel with a charger for the Tesla, I treat myself to a nice dinner, and then retreat to the room to contemplate the day's events. I call Karen out of my psyche to discuss the story I gave Bernie.

"Well, Karen, you are no longer just a figment of my imagination, but a real, suffering person who also recently died. We may need this story again in the future. We will have to leave a paper trail to validate my assertions at some point though."

"Gee, you certainly have an active imagination and can apparently crank out a wild new anecdote at will. Maybe you should become a writer?"

"I am a writer! I am the author of this book, in spite of what Cochrane says."

The following day I drive back to Boston. En route, I call my lawyer to see what progress he's made with the D.A. I then tell him about Bernie Sanders wanting to talk to the D.A. on my behalf. My lawyer responds, "Sounds good. I hope he has more clout than I have. My suggestion is for you to lay low for a few more days and avoid the process server."

Upon hearing this, I decide to take Karen's car and head up to the family cabin on Lake Tulossa, located just over the border in Maine. Being outside of Massachusetts puts another buffer layer between me and the law.

There's a strange car parked down the street and I'm sure someone saw me drive in with the Tesla. I quickly grab some clothes and am out the back door before the doorbell rings. As I'm hurrying to the car, I pull up and stuff my hair into a man's cap and am now quickly out the back alley and into the Corolla. I purposely leave my phone in my room in Boston so my location cannot be traced. None of these people should know about Karen's phone number. I leave the number for that cell in a note for Ma Mah, but tell her not give it to anyone. No one seems to be watching the back entrance to James's garage, so it appears I'm safe… for the moment.

I have not been to the family cabin for the past five years, so it should be a nice relaxing time for me to read and think, and maybe to plot. I have no inkling about what I am walking into just shortly! For now, I am simply heading off to my rural hideaway…………zoom, zoom, zoom.

CHAPTER 10   Hiding out in Maine

So far, so good. I have escaped the "long arm of the law," at least for now. I will only use Karen's phone as I don't want Gee's phone traced. It's a good thing I left it in Boston. For the time being, I will only appear in public as Karen, even a more-dressed-down Karen with a cap pulled low over her brow. Hopefully, no chance exists of me showing up on TV here in the boonies.

What does one do with the long days when on the run? I thought that we (I) was hiding. Isn't it interesting how I always think of "we" instead of me? I think of myself as Karen and Gee, yet I am one person. Does that make me a schizophrenic? When it's discovered I have two separate identities—and sooner or later it will happen—then how can I roll these two characters back into one person? Maybe Bill, who's dealt with the two of us, both mentally and sexually, will help me succeed. Or should I even have to?

Oh, to hell with the D.A.!

I call Hollie to see how the animal rescue farm is doing and she reports she has a new bunch of animals showing up in two weeks. She says she doesn't have enough room for them though, and wonders if she can rent some of the neighbor's land. I tell her I will help with the cost. After clicking off my call with her, I ring up Percy, who is just home from the Taft Plantation. He reports the restoration there is progressing nicely. I tell him he must see Hollie's rescue farm and inform him she's running out of room for some new arrivals.

"Do you think the Taft Plantation could house some of her antelopes for a while? Get Bill to fly you out there, Percy. He's taken me there and will introduce you to Hollie. You'll like her, I hope."

He agrees to fly out tomorrow with Bill, who's just returned from ferrying Ma Mah back from Ireland

I reply, "Great. Keep me informed on this number as the D.A. doesn't have it. I left in a great hurry as someone was banging on the door. Was it the process server?"

"Yes, it was. The D.A. has also called and talked with Ma Mah. She gave him holy hell and told him, and I quote, "If you continue to harass Gee, I will see if I can get you fired. G.W. has already given evidence for more than five hours to both you and the police. What else do you need to know? Maybe what color her underwear was? Incidentally, they were ruined after being soaked in blood during the many hours she spent at the police station. I think someone should compensate her for a whole new outfit after she performed such a lifesaving civic duty!"

We laughed at this, and then hung up. I hope Hollie and Percy hit it off. I know Bill thinks the plantation land might be good for an animal preserve.

I call Bill. "Hey handsome, this is Gee, and I miss you."

"Why are you using Karen's phone?"

"The D.A.'s hot after me, so I skipped town in Karen's car. My phone is off so they can't track me. I just talked with Percy and got him to agree to go to Hollie's ranch. Please help talk him into using some of the plantation lands for her wild animal rescue, ok? I haven't told Percy about Karen. Do you think I should before the D.A. arrests me and it becomes public knowledge?"

"Gad! It looks like a real mess. Maybe you'd better quit killing terrorists! That kind of activity seriously raises one's profile! I don't want you in danger of being harmed. I love you—both as Karen and as Gee. If you merge the two, what will the composite look like?"

"Wow! I guess I have a lot to think about. Right now, I'm going for a long run and then a swim in the lake. Then back to a nice fire, a little whisky, and some deep contemplation. I wish you were here to help me, Bill."

Heading out a short while after we hung up, I decide to take the path around the north side of the lake. A half an hour later I meet another runner on the trail, an old friend, Carlton Van Slooten, who I often saw at the lake when we were children. He recognized me although I was dressed in rougher clothes than normal.

"Hey, Gee. Long time no see!"

Whoops, I had hoped not to see anyone who knew me while here.

"Hi, Van." (Everyone called him Van. Carl seems like a normal handle, but for some reason he was always Van.) "Please, Van, don't tell anyone I'm here. I'm actually hiding from the law, not to mention reporters. Why don't you come over tomorrow at noon and I'll cook you lunch and tell you all about it. In the meantime, please don't mention to anyone I'm here, ok?"

I take a quick, cold swim in the lake as autumn is here and the water temperature is losing the summer's heat. Back inside I build a fire, pour a shot of Glenlivet, and heat up a frozen dinner in the microwave. What should I tell Van about recent events? I'm not sure he reads the newspapers or watches TV and actually even knows about the shooting. I then recall he's a hunter, so it occurs to me I should get his views on guns, large gun magazines, attack riffles, etc. I snuggle up in bed in front of the glowing fireplace. The warmth feels so good and I...........zzzzzz.

Dawn breaks and I awake with a bang. *(Why do they always say that in novels? How does dawn break? Who actually awakes with a bang?)* Van is scheduled to show up for lunch so I'm back to wondering, what shall I disclose to him? Although, admittedly, I was too forthcoming in what I already said, bumping into him like that caught me totally off-guard and I obviously went into babble-mode. I sure hope he doesn't try to make any romantic moves. When I came up to the cabin in my late teens and early twenties, Van and I had several slightly flirtatious and definitely sexual encounters. He was more taken with me than I was with him though. I don't even know if he's currently married. Anyway, I am now in love with Bill and committed.

At precisely noon, Van drives up in his muddy Ram pickup with 4WD and a rifle rack in the rear window housing two rifles. He's nicely dressed and not in camouflage gear as I kind of expected.

"Good afternoon, Van. It's been so many years since I last saw you. I don't know anything about your current life. Are you married? What are you doing for a living? How often are you up to the ranch?"

He grins and replies, "I guess I should ask you the same questions.

However, I am aware of the shooting at the Symphony. That must have been horrible for you."

"I promised lunch, so let's sit down with a drink, a plate of spaghetti, and a salad, and then start our catching up. What will you have? Beer or wine, or something stronger?"

"I'd like a beer, thanks. What kind do you have, Gee?"

"Your choice: Bud, Coors Lite, or a local beer I picked up in town." Van picks the Coors Lite and I take one of the local brews. It turns out Van is married. They have one child, a girl named Suzie. They live in the capitol, Augusta, and wife, Jill, works as a secretary for a state senator. Van's parents have both died so he's inherited the 700-acre ranch here. He has 200 head of beef cattle. During deer season, he runs hunts for city folks, many of whom are legislators. I guess Jill is his de facto agent. He claims he is a recluse hiding out from the world on the ranch.

He asks, "Why did you tell me you were hiding out and not to mention you were here?"

"Since the horrible shooting, the Boston D.A. has been on my case. He has sworn out a warrant for my arrest on charges that I did not have a permit to carry a gun, that I was not authorized to use the dead policeman's gun—if it was even his gun—and that I was possibly a vigilante taking the law into my own hands. My lawyer is trying to deal with him—not to mention my mother is threatening charges of harassment toward him in return. So here I am, until the threat goes away."

"I hate it when these crazies flip out with these mass shootings. They give us gun owners and hunters a bad name. After these incidents, all the do-gooders want to take them away from us. Again. We have our Second Amendment Right to bear arms!"

"Wait a minute, pal! Yours truly is one of those do-gooders. I don't want to take away your guns though. But I do want to get rid of 30-round clips of ammunition and fully automatic weapons. What hunter or sportsman needs 30 rounds, or six clips of 30 rounds each, like my perpetrator had?"

"Hey, missy, if the government's coming to get my guns, I need lots of fire power."

"Well, that'll get you killed, for sure. I don't think the government will come after your guns. What politician could get re-elected if that ever happened?"

"You don't know, Gee, since you don't hunt or shoot."

"Actually, Van, yes I do know. I was raised by a daddy who was a hunter. I learned to hunt at a young age, although I have given it up since as I don't like killing anything. But I do believe you have that right. I am not a vegetarian and would eat venison or rabbit if you invited me for dinner."

"So how did you learn to shoot? You're clearly very good at it."

"I visit the shooting range once a week and fire off 40 or 50 rounds in pistols and rifles. You know that totals about 2500 rounds of ammunition per year? So what's your stockpile of ammunition? And WHY does anyone need more than 5,000 rounds of ammo?"

"Well, I guess I have about 6,000 rounds currently, but my AK-74 and my M-16 use lots of bullets."

"Gad, Van, how many guns do you own?"

"Well, I buy and sell them as a kind of a hobby. I currently have ten guns."

"Who do you sell them to? Where do you sell them?"

"Most of them I buy and sell at gun shows, although I have sold a couple online."

"How do you know you're not selling to a mentally deranged person, or a criminal?"

"Well, I just talk to them and kind of assess them as to their suitability."

(Wow! I think this kind of casual practice by untrained individuals is why we have guns in the wrong people's hands.)

"I'll tell you what, Van, I will challenge you to a shooting contest. You use one of your fully automatic assault rifles and I will shoot a semi-automatic rifle with a 10-bullet clip. We'll setup 10 targets of people coming to get you. We both get 25 seconds to hit the targets."

"Sounds like a good game. But you have to know I'm an expert shot and can beat any of our group of 30 in target practice—not to mention I'm an excellent hunter as well. I have a first-rate shooting range on my ranch."

At this point, I think to myself that Van must be involved in one of these survivalist paramilitary groups. After all, he let slip that there were 30 of them in some group.

We finish lunch and switch topics, talking about the old days when we first met. Van invites me over the next day to see his ranch and what he's done to it since I was last there so many moons ago. That evening, I mull over the conversation we had. Think of it! A group of over two dozen of these paranoid types living up here in the woods with their gaggle of assault rifles in tow! I'll bet they think that the law and the feds don't know about them.

After awhile, I feel antsy and decide to run down into town and check out the local bars. The small town has a population of about 6,000. There are five bars, so I pick the one with the most mud-covered pickups out front and pop in for a drink. Lo and behold! Van is there playing pool with some of his pals.

He motions me over. "Hey again, Gee, come meet some of my friends. Can I buy you a drink?"

"You bet, I'll have a local beer. I had to come into town anyway, so I decided I'd stop in for a drink. It didn't dawn on me I'd find you here." I'm then introduced to Rusty and Buck, who are obviously part of the paramilitary group. Rusty's saying he can't wait for the upcoming game next week. I wonder what he's talking about, but I don't ask any questions. Van mentions I used to be a hunter and that I like to shoot pistols and rifles.

"Can you imagine? She's actually challenged me to a shooting contest tomorrow at my place."

Buck says, "Good luck with that, little lady, Van's a great shot. I have only beaten him once. You might want to stick to your indoor gun range."

I smile and thank him for his encouragement. Finishing my drink,

I savor the last of the bitter froth at the bottom of the mug, and take my leave, heading out into the night. In the parking lot, I whip out my iPhone and take a shot of each of the license plates of the mud-covered pickups. No telling if this bit of intel might prove useful in the future.

Well, another day, another dollar! *(Where do all these idioms we all spew actually come from?)* I drive over to Van's farm. Two vicious dogs race out, barking and baring their teeth to meet me. I slowly get out of the car and speak softly to the canine welcoming committee. They continue to growl but keep a few feet distance between us. I slowly walk toward the house with the dogs flanking me. Van comes around the side of the house, it appears he'd been working in the barn. He's amazed to see the dogs hadn't attacked me or that I didn't appear to be afraid of them. He shows me around the place, including touring a new hay barn he recently constructed with his friends. Turns out there's an indoor shooting range in the old cow barn. The milk house has been converted into a slaughterhouse for butchering animals and hanging meat. It also has a walk-in freezer, in which Van tells me he's stored more than a year's supply of food—in case of a disaster...or meltdown of the country(!).

Since yesterday, he's prepared the 10 targets of men carrying guns (coming to get us). We place two of the targets 45° west of the house at 175' in distance. We then place five targets north of the house varying from 225' to 250' away. One was partially hidden behind a tree. The final three targets are placed 45° to the east at 245' distance. Van has chosen an M-16 assault rifle with a bump stock and a modified 30-round clip. He has chosen a semi-automatic rifle with a 10-round clip for me.

"Gee, this rifle's sights are very precisely adjusted to 200' distance. You'll want to compensate for the different distances to the targets. Do you want to try it out on one of my normal ranges first?"

"No, I'm familiar with this particular caliber rifle. How many grains of powder are in the load?" I note his eyebrows arch at my question.

"It's the standard load I purchase here at the local hardware store." This response causes me to think to myself I must check out this place. Maybe I can scrounge up some more information on Van's group and what type of guns they own.

So, we are ready for the test at this point. I say to Van, "We will fire at the same time and try to complete the firing in 25 seconds. Since the calibers of the two guns are different, we should be able to determine where each of our bullets hit the target. One of us will shoot from the downstairs porch and the other from the upstairs porch. Which one do you want?"

Van picks the downstairs porch so I go up to the one on the second-story. About this time, Buck drives up and jumps out of his truck. He pets the dogs and comes over to join us. "I came to witness and monitor the contest. I brought two stopwatches, so we'll have one of them set on each of you." He then turns and heads back, parking himself on the edge of the downstairs porch where he has a clear view of both of us, sitting side saddle atop the wooden railing.

"Ok, you two, load your guns. Alright…get ready, get set…fire!"

Van hits the group of five with his first burst of firepower. I shoot the two to the left and swing to the right group. Van swings to the right group but forgets to let off the trigger during the swing of his gun. He wastes more than six bullets. I swing to the group of five and take down four of them and step to the right to get a good shot at the one behind the tree. Van swings back to the left two targets buts fires too early in his swing, and his bullets are now gone. He misses both of them. We both finish in 23 seconds, Van having fired 30 rounds and me having fired 10.

The three of us proceed to the targets to see what's what. The first two I shot in the center of their chests. Van missed both as he had fired too early. The center group Van had hit 16 times, but the guy behind the tree was only hit in the leg, whereas I had moved over and hit him straight in the chest. On the other four, I had hit two in their chests and two slightly below in their main body torsos. On the three targets to the east, Van had hit two of them with five bullets, but one of them with only a bullet in the leg. I had hit all three in the centers of their chests.

Buck shook his head and smiled, exclaiming, "Van, boy, you are dead. You missed the two closest targets and only wounded two others, so you have four people left to get you. Gee has shot all 10 of them with only 10 bullets! How much are you going to pay me to not tell the group about this one, pal?"

"Well, maybe she's right and fully automatic weapons make it harder to hit the target. Of course, maybe she's Annie Oakley reincarnated. I guess I'll call her Annie from here on."

"Hey, thanks, Van, for being such a good sport," I say to him while giving him a friendly pat on the shoulder. "Tell me, what's this game your group's going to have next week?"

"How did you know about it?" Buck snaps, a little too harshly.

"Well, you guys were joking about it at the bar. If 30 people are in the game, then obviously that whole group and others know about it."

"Ok, well, the game is war with paintball guns with all of us playing. It's on Rusty's 740-acre ranch. We have 30 starting points and the game begins at 8:00 a.m. and goes until there's only one of us left standing. Tom has just been called out of town though, so we have one spot open. Would you like to join us and play in his stead?"

"Hmmm, I've heard of these kinds of games, but never seen one, much less participated in one. What are the rules?"

"The rules are simple. The paint guns are only good for less than 45'—the closer the better. If you shoot someone, they're out of the game and return to the farmhouse. If two people shoot each other simultaneously, then both are out. However, if one person is only slightly wounded—say a little paint on the arm or leg—then they can continue. However, they must leave a trail of blood—red spray splotches, every 5'-10' apart, maximum. They're considered wounded and cannot travel more than 100 yards. It is possible to be wounded and still win the game."

"Alright, I'll play…but I'd like to try out the paint guns beforehand so I can see how they work, their range, etc. ok?" The guys both nod in agreement.

That night, I decide to stay at the cabin and not go back into town. Van and Buck will have to tell the others about me. No doubt Van will receive a lot of ribbing over having been beaten by a girl. I wonder if any females have participated in their games before? If the D.A. ever hears about me participating, it will likely give him more fuel yet for his vigilante, gun-happy charge. Maybe I shouldn't do it?

"What do you think, Karen?"

"I think it sounds like fun. But these people keep telling everyone they have these guns to protect their families. This game is *not* about protection! It's a rehearsal of an actual attack force. They are not protecting their homes! They're honing their skills—maybe for attacking authority. How can you participate in such an activity?"

"Well, you might be right, Karen, but I want to be in the game anyway. Here's how I'll approach it. The starting point of each participant represents their home, but they don't stay there. What I will do is to stay within 500' of my home starting position. My game is to protect my home, and not practice to become part of a military attack unit. If no one comes to get me, then I will not go hunt them down. When they come to get me, I will not shoot them in the back but will always call out to them that they're done. When they turn towards me, then I'll shoot them full frontal in the chest."

The next day, Van stops by to drop off a paint gun, taking a few minutes to show me how it works, and explaining the best ways to shoot someone with it. He admits he took a lot of joshin' by the guys over losing the shooting contest to me. They were so enamored of my performance he said they all want to meet me at the bar tonight. "With that record, they all want you in the game now," he says with a smirk...

In town that evening, before heading to the bar I check out the hardware store and run into two other members of the group whom I hadn't met yet. For some reason, they know who I am.

"You must be Annie Oakley! We heard all about you beating our buddy, Van. What brings you to the store here?"

"Oh, I was just checking on what kinds of ammo are available locally. I have an old WWI weapon at the cabin and want to see if it still works, so I need to get some bullets for it."

"Let me introduce you to George—he owns this place and is also one of our group. He can fix you up with anything you need, for a price, of course."

"Hi, George. They have branded me Annie Oakley, which is a great compliment. I hope I do well in your upcoming game. Looks like you have a very sizable inventory of guns and ammo here. Can you turn it fast enough to make a profit?"

George nods, "Well, we actually do quite well. Seems like I'm always ordering bullets for someone. Everybody seems to be practice shooting a lot 'round here. Maybe we are all a little paranoid about the government."

I answer, "I'm a little surprised to hear that. President Trump is very pro Second Amendment and apparently has no plans to get tougher on gun laws."

After this brief exchange, I take my leave after ordering some ammunition for my old 303 Enfield rifle, and head on over to the grocery store where a couple of ladies stop and introduce themselves to me. I learn their husbands have each told them the story about me beating Van and being invited into the boys' game.

"You have to watch out for Carl though, hon'. He has two blankets with leaves attached and can pop out of the underbrush when you least expect it. He's already won three of these paintball matches."

"Wow! How many years have these games been going on here?"

"Let's see. They started two years after we moved up here, so I guess we're talking maybe a dozen years. There have been no women allowed to enter before now though—Ever. A couple of us could beat them, I think. I hope you do well hon', we're so pleased you made it into their ranks."

That night and each night thereafter I go to the bar and meet more members of this little gun-happy fraternity. All the interaction is first names only, and they do seem a little paranoid about giving out their last names. Turns out some of them also deal only in cash. However, UPS seems to make a lot of trips out to these rural areas, so they must know their names, addresses, and they must each have credit cards to facilitate purchases online. I continue to take pictures of all their license plates nightly. While in the post office getting some stamps, I notice Buck is sorting through a stack and throwing out junk mail. After he nods at me and heads out to the parking lot, I saunter over the trash, glance around, and nip my hand into the barrel, quickly retrieving an envelope he discarded with his full name and his farm's address. In a small town everyone knows everyone else and where they live, so what's the point of being secretive about it to outsiders, I wonder to myself as a I fold my find into my coat pocket.

The Game

The day of the paintball war arrives. I pack a lunch, a thermos of coffee, a bottle of water, and some candy bars. In my brown tote bag, I also tuck in a dark brown cap, a string mophead, a red bandana, a white handkerchief, a large can of mosquito spray, a small bottle of perfume, a metal mirror, some brown string, some tiny bells, and my trusty Swiss Army knife.

Upon joining the men who've already gathered, I'm given four paint gun reloads and a small can of red spray paint. If you kill someone, you get to take their remaining paint reloads. My outfit was put together with Van's help. It's a forest-colored Army camouflage shirt and pants with several pockets. A little additional brown paint creates some nice-looking branches in the pattern. We cleaned our guns and quickly brown painted the shiny metal parts with spray paint.

At 7:00 a.m., I'm led to my home starting point. I have an hour to survey the area and prepare for attack. A power line runs past the site approximately 500' from my "home" base. I leave my pack, except for a few items, hidden in a rock pile near my start marker. The area is a mixed forest of pines, maples, and oak trees. Patches of brush are scattered throughout the area. I notice some large glacial erratics are scattered through the forest, a bit of knowledge leftover from my college geology course. A couple of rocks have a tree next to them and offer perfect spots for a sniper to ward off attack. I take a stand near the power line which has a clearing around it that's 100' wide. Once one is out of the game, the fallen hero will walk down this path to the farmhouse.

At 8:00 a.m., the game commences. I can see a long way down the powerline, and soon one person darts across the open space. A little closer and I hear a yell. "I got you, Paul!" In a few minutes, Paul is already trudging down the powerline path. He is covered with a large splotch of yellow paint and is the first loser of the day.

As he approaches, I step out from behind a tree and ask, "So who got you?"

"It was Carl, watch out." He then proceeds down the path toward the farmhouse. I see him stop, apparently talking to someone else behind a stand of trees. No doubt he's told whomever of my location.

I shift into gear and hurry 150 yards parallel to the trail toward the unknown hunter. I stop and hide behind a large rock and crouch in anticipation of an advancing assailant. I hear some very soft crunches of leaves underfoot nearby. George passes stealthily by me, about 15' away.

I call out, "Hey, you're history, sucker." He spins toward me, and I zap him with yellow paint. "Sorry, George. I don't shoot anyone in the back, you'll notice. I'm just protecting my home." I claim his extra paint refills and he leaves, looking sullen. I scurry back toward my home and park myself in a grove of trees, and wait. Maybe I'll snack on a candy bar. An hour passes with no activity in the nearby woods.

Eventually I see someone far off through the trees moving toward the east. He may be coming back so I will set a little trap. I find a small rock in an open space. I have a cup of coffee and set the metal cup holding the lukewarm liquid on the rock in plain view. I take my can of mosquito spray and spray it on the nearby bushes making a "v" pattern toward the coffee mug. I plant myself in a strategic spot viewing the coffee cup but well hidden in all directions. I see Carl coming from far off. I flash my mirror very quickly two times and see him squint and then turn toward me. Soon he catches the smell of the mosquito spray. He proceeds down the "v" and spies the coffee mug.

He mumbles to himself, "I guess that flash was a glint off the mug. It must be Annie because I smell the mosquito spray. None of us would give away our position in such a stupid way. I bet she's right behind that rock or hiding out just in those trees beyond. Too far to hit me and too far for me to hit her from here." He crouches and creeps forward, passing my position.

I step out just after he passes. He hears the crunch of leaves behind him and whips around. "Carl, you're dead!" I crow as I hit him right in the face and chest with red paint.

He yells, "My eyes, my eyes!" and begins rubbing at them, smearing the paint.

"Lay down, Carl, and let me wash them out." I pour water into his eyes and sponge them out with my white handkerchief. "Why weren't you wearing your glasses?"

"The reflections always give you away. Did you sucker me into a trap or was it an accident?"

We talk for a bit and, now that he's calmed down, Carl is quite magnanimous about losing. He reports he's killed four people so far. "How many have you gotten?"

"Well, only two. I'm staying close to my home base and playing a defensive game."

"Your little trick wasn't very defensive."

"How many people do you think have been eliminated?"

"Well, I got four and they each had two, and you've gotten two. So that's 14, and I've also seen four others walking back the trail. So that means over 20 gone. It's now four o'clock, so this might go on into the night. Do you have a flashlight?"

"Nope, I don't. I didn't think it would last so long."

"Then, here, you can have mine. G'luck, "Annie." He leaves and I thought to myself it sure was nice of him to give me his flashlight.

I follow him out to the trail, lagging well behind, and look for others who might have been eliminated. Soon Van comes along the footpath, covered with red paint.

"Van, it's me. Who's left? And who got you?"

"Well, I think Frank, Bill, and Carl are still active."

"Nope, I got Carl a bit ago."

"Wow. I can't believe you nailed Carl. How'd you do it?"

I then told him of my trap. "Van, leave me your paint gun though, will you please? I don't think mine's working well."

I return to my home spot, break out my sandwich, toss out the old and then refill my coffee mug with steaming brew. There's a hidden path on one side of the house site. I set up a string and the bells in an area I can't readily view, and then deposit a little spritz of perfume in that area. I set up another site at the base of a patch of trees with the mophead, the cap, and the red bandana tied a bit further down in mimicking a person's neck. The fading daylight should make it look like pretty realistic. I pick-up Van's gun and lean it against a tree. I climb into a tree just above the decoy person. It's growing darker, but there is still enough light to see. I hear my bell trap tinkling and the crunch of leaves. He circles around the trail and comes at the mophead man from a different direction. I get my paint gun ready and Bill arrives near the trees, advancing on my decoy.

I yell out, "Hey, I got you!" We both fired at the same time, but I was almost completely hidden behind the tree. I hit him straight on, but he did got some red paint on my leg.

"Shoot, I didn't nail you thoroughly enough, I guess you're considered a wounded person and cannot move more than 100 yards, right?"

"Is there anyone left?"

"Yes, Frank wasn't far behind me and I was looking for a good place to ambush him. I think you and Frank are it. Good luck to you. Do you have the red spray paint for blood?"

I climb down out of the tree and begin my trail of blood across the landscape. I make the trail go between some bushes in a straight line. I come to an area where I can turn either right or left. Which way to go? When I met Frank in town, I noticed he was right-handed when playing pool. He'll have his gun ready pointed forward with his right hand on the trigger. He will most naturally swing to the left, so I turn left with my blood trail. After a few feet, I back up along the blood trail and step six feet further to the right, placing myself behind a tree. By this time, Frank has seen Bill and knows I'm wounded. He then spies the blood trail and carefully follows it, knowing I must be waiting nearby. He searches each side of the trail and I fear he may come up behind me. But he goes back to the trail knowing I must be further on. He comes to the turn and then swings to the left.

I softly say, "Here I am, Frank, and you're now DEAD, buddy." He turns toward me, but his gun hits a bush. Bang, I cover him with yellow paint.

I can't believe it. I've only gotten four of them and they eliminated each other. We gather up my stuff and head for the farmhouse. Wow! I can't believe this first-timer has beaten all the boys at their own game!

Crowning of the winner

The next night, there's a celebration and coronation of Queen Annie as this year's winner held at the local high school auditorium. All the wives and children of the participants are there, as well as many interested folks from the nearby community. It seems these people take this annual game of theirs seriously.

Carl, the previous year's winner, gets up and makes an opening speech, presenting the crown of victory to me. The local TV station is covering the festivities. Well, crap, this'll certainly blow my hideout from the Boston D.A. Carl had wanted to know my real name, but I asked him to just call me Annie Oakley.

I tell him I will reveal my real name at the presentation. Carl is very gracious and tells the story of how I tricked him. "I thought my leaf

farms, I note that the No Trespassing signs delineate your farm's boundaries. Most of you have mailboxes, but a few have post office boxes in town. I saw Rusty dump his junk mail in the post office trash can. I was easily able to note his full name when retrieving mail he tossed. The locals outside of your group know you all, as well as some of your past. I checked your names against recorded state documents. I found out your dates of birth. I checked hospital records and found out your children's names and ages. I was able to run down most of your social security numbers. I ordered aerial photos of all of your properties. I can tell you how many marijuana plants each of you is growing, and how many cows and horses you each have. I notice that UPS and Fed Ex make lots of trips to your houses so, again, you are well known.

I was also able to find most of your recent tax returns. If you haven't filed returns recently—and I note that applies to at least three of you—then you're also in the crosshairs of the IRS. I determined through my research that you all also homeschool your children, which again requires paperwork which can be accessed. You think that you are hiding, but you're not. The government knows where you are, and all about you. With a name like the Maine Wolverines, how long do you suppose it will be before they come looking for you, potentially to set an example? Incidentally, I ran all of George's records and know how many rounds of ammunition the community purchases each year. Last year over 400,000 rounds were sold, and this year the numbers are up, with over 500,000 rounds projected for the year. Those kinds of numbers should spark some kind of notice by the government's domestic terrorism surveillance, don't you think?

As the crowd murmered and turned repeatedly to one another, I pressed on, "I have two suggestions on the gun problem. First of all, you need to be involved in politics, people. Start at the bottom: school boards, city councils, planning committees, state legislatures, and finally the federal government. I just met with Bernie Sanders and he tried to get me to consider running for office. I said no, but told him I'll continue to support politicians who think like I do. You should know by now everything is politics. After meeting the people in this group, your families and your friends, I would like to spend more time in rural America and less time in our country's big cities.

"But why do you have your children outside the public schools? You don't like their quality of education? Maybe you want to teach them your own version of history? People, you are harming your children. They need socialization with other kids. Maybe you want them to remain on your farms and become as paranoid as you are? Another problem is that being isolated makes someone, especially children, more susceptible to disease, as they're not developing the antibodies their systems need. Interaction with other children will expose them to other bugs and their immune systems will develop robust responses and better protect their health.

"My second suggestion is for you, and all of us really, to rid our local communities of these 20 and 30-round magazines. We can't eliminate the mentally ill who may indeed get hold of a weapon and go on a shooting spree. But we can eliminate these large shot magazines from our homes.

So, listen up, I personally will pay $100 for every magazine over 20 shots. My guess is that the 30 of you have 100 of these magazines between you. I'll be here till next week. Bring them by my cabin and I'll pay you $100 cash for each one of them. I'll then find a welder who can melt them into neat little piles I can display in other communities. We also need George here to quit selling these types of magazines. But this is your community and I'm only a visitor, so you must make these decisions yourselves. I am only making the offer to take them off your hands.

"If you are still paranoid about being invaded, set up surveillance cameras around your houses and the town. They know where you are, and who you are, and what your politics are. Many of you go by first names only. I think that is kind of friendly. Your junk mail discloses your identities though. UPS and Fed Ex know your precise whereabouts. Your magazines and books tell me about your beliefs. Since the government is watching you and knows you, you must become part of the government if you want to maintain control. Politicians are supposed to be representatives of the people, which is all of us. Many of them instead make careers of being politicians and forget where they came from and who they actually work for. Let's get rid of them and get real people in there. Rejoin the community, collectively protect your homes, and vote your values. I note that many of you are not on the voting roles. I guess that means you want us to make the laws which could potentially take your guns and control your lives.

"Thanks again for letting me into your group. I don't like the name of it though. Since the name of this town is Liberty, Maine, it would be wonderful if you were called "The Sons of Liberty" instead. However, unless you rejoin this town and have their blessing, I don't think they'd like to be associated with your organization. I have learned a bunch from you and I hope perhaps I've given you something to think about in return. Please take some future actions. Our country needs you to be part of it…of us."

Those inside the auditorium then gave me a round of pretty enthusiastic-sounding applause, even amidst a fair amount of head shaking and shoulder shrugging. Van then took the microphone and thanked me for my speech, although the expression on his face was tinged with bewilderment. "Gee, you've given us a lot to think about here. And, right off the bat, let me be the first to give you my 30 and 50-round ammunition clips."

The celebration then began in earnest, and it seemed everyone wanted to talk with me. A couple of people brought their recent NRA magazines and asked me to autograph the cover. Maybe I should write a rebuttal to their article? After what I considered a decent interval, I slipped away, climbed into my Corolla, and headed for the cabin.

CHAPTER 11   Tangling with The Law

The following day, I called my lawyer in Boston to see if he had made any progress yet in dealing with the D.A. He wanted to know where I was, and I told him of my previous two weeks' events—including last night's talk, and it being taped for presentation on the local news tonight. I feared my winning of the contest and televised gun-related speech would now give the D.A. further evidence of views he might construe as pro-vigilante.

"What can I do to prevent my arrest?" He replied, "Probably nothing. Maybe you should turn yourself in to the local authorities and I'll see if they will keep you there for some time vs. transporting you back to Boston. Do you think a local judge there will release you from jail on your own recognizance? Do you know him?"

"I don't know him, but I understand from one of the guys he was at the talk last night. So should I speak with him, or should you?"

"No, I'll talk to him. Let me have the phone number you used to call me just now and I will provide it to the judge directly."

Much to my surprise, the TV segment was actually a great piece discussing paramilitary groups, the local Maine Wolverines, and of course included me and the Boston Symphony shooting. The national news services soon picked up the story and reporters from parts elsewhere were suddenly dispatched to Liberty, Maine to follow up. I knew by the next day they would be at my door.

At 8:00 a.m. the next morning the judge called me and reported he had been contacted by my Boston lawyer and informed of the yet-unserved warrant for my arrest. The judge said, "Legally, I should not be talking with you, but this is a small rural community. Since you are in my jurisdiction, I have arranged for a lawyer to contact you. He should phone you in a few minutes and will explain your rights here in Maine to you, plus will work out a plan of action with you. I will reserve a spot for you to appear at the beginning of my docket tomorrow."

A few minutes later, there's a knocking on my door. I am panicked as I immediately worry it might be a process server, thanks to my whereabouts being a news topic once again.

A male's voice outside says, "Don't panic. I'm Buck's father, your newly-appointed lawyer. Let me in please."

I open the door gingerly and peer out before letting him step inside—once in the living room he extends his hand, introducing himself as Harry Piel. "I didn't attend the game crowning last night, but I did hear your speech on TV. In no time flat you have turned this town upside down, little lady. It's amazing. My son Buck and two other Wolverines have plans to run for the school board. Buck's wife, Jena, is going to be bringing the children to school and registering them to begin attending immediately. I hear all the No Trespassing signs are coming down. Rifle racks are coming out of the pickups. How did you do it?"

Just then, Van pulls into the driveway in his pickup. Glancing at Harry and nodding, he bursts in to our conversation saying, "Alright, Gee, this is going to cost you. I have already acquired 20 large clips of 20 or 30 rounds each. I am keeping a list of who turned them in and how much each person is owed. Tell me, what you want to do with them?"

"Well, I would like to weld them into a giant pyramid. Can you do that?"

He replies he's a welder and will be happy to oblige. "You'll also be glad to know I have already registered as a Republican so that I can vote in future elections. I am also giving up selling guns online or at gun shows as I realize I can't really assess the fitness of the customers."

After Van departs as quickly as he came, Harry Piel and I sit down at the kitchen table so he can hear my story and plot strategy. He recommends I turn myself into the local sheriff early tomorrow morning, post bail, and appear before the judge at 10:00 a.m. when the court is called into session. He says, "I'll recommend to the judge that you surrender your driver's license and stay in the area until some resolution is made in Boston. The judge will do his best to try and block your extradition back to Boston."

"Why do I have to turn myself in to the sheriff? I have not been served the supposed warrant, so, as of now, I am not under arrest. What are the charges? We have heard the D.A. on the TV listing possible charges, but what does the warrant actually say?"

Harry says, "Hmmm, maybe we could just register you at the police station and petition the judge for a restraining order to prevent 'bounty hunters' from coming after you."

"Harry, I have a long story to tell you that deals with the problem taking my fingerprints will cause." I then quickly shuffle some mental cards in considering which story I should tell him: the one I told Bernie Sanders, or the real truth with my illegal name and false licenses. If I stick with the sickly twin that died, I'll bet Ma Mah would go along with it to protect me. However, if the real story comes out, then the D.A. will have actual grounds for prosecuting me.

After pausing for a minute and then taking a deep breath, I say to him, "Are you ready for this one? I will give you two versions and you tell me how we can deal with it. First, I am leading a double life: as socialite G.W. Lowell and also as detective Karen Hunt. Here are my driver's licenses, one for Karen, and one for Gee. Note the birthdays, Karen on December 30th and Gee on January 2nd, you'll see they're days apart although in different years. One story is that we're identical twins with Karen born prematurely with very serious health problems. She was raised by foster parents, who later died in a hit-and-run accident caused by a drunk. She subsequently became a private detective to run down the perpetrator. Karen then died not long after reconnecting with me, and I then took over her business. The second story is that Karen is a figment of my childhood, one I created to ward off loneliness as my parents were always away. My father raised me as a hunter, and I became very familiar with guns. I have a concealed permit under the name Karen Hunt. It has taken me years to develop these two personalities—which I have kept from nearly everyone. Only my love, Bill, our pilot, knows about Karen."

"Wow! That certainly is a complicated story. You are hung out on several serious breaks in the law. I wonder if we could have you register with the Department of Equalization and file a d.b.a: G.W. Lowell doing business as Karen Hunt, private detective. Where do you have an office?"

"I have a post office box in Concord, but no physical office."

"Hmmm, that's too close to Boston. We want something in western Massachusetts where we can publish the required ad for the registration in small town newspapers not likely to be seen in Boston."

"Let me call Bill as I think he has a cabin located west of Pittsfield. I'll get him to set up a P.O. box for Karen there. Maybe we can list his cabin as my office. I could also rent or buy one, but that will take some time. Do you think this will save us? Or just cause the deception to grow exponentially larger still?"

Harry says, "I think you should try it. By the way, how many case files do you have and where do you keep those files?"

"I guess I have around twenty cases. I keep all the paperwork in a small two-drawer filing cabinet in my bedroom closet."

He replies, "If Bill is willing to go along with this scenario, have him take the file cabinet to his cabin. Draw up an agreement with him for rent, or quid pro quo use of the cabin. Back date it a couple of years or more. You can file with the Board of Equalization going back for two or three years and pay a penalty for not having done the proper paperwork at the time. You need to get this done before the D.A. gets his nose into it."

I phone Bill straightaway to see if he will go along with this plan. "Gee-Karen, I am so glad you came up with a strategy for handling this mess. I know that if the D.A. gets wind of Karen it'll make things more difficult yet. Ok, I'll swing by and grab the file cabinet tomorrow as I actually have already been planning to spend the weekend at my cabin. I'll set you up a box at the contract post office where I receive my mail. We can always say you have used my box number in the past to receive mail. Hey, I saw your winning speech after the paintball contest. Congratulations on beating all those rednecks, lady! I can't believe it! How'd you do it?"

"Bill, let me tell you what is happening on that front. The Wolverines have suddenly become tame, decided to mend their anti-social ways, and are rejoining local society. My buy up of the 30-round magazines looks like it'll cost me over $10,000, but it's worth it to me. If we are going to solve the gun problem, the situation must be turned around from the bottom up, and that means getting through to the enthusiasts themselves. Will Ma Mah give you time to come up here? And HOW am I going to tell her about Karen?"

"Don't worry about that right now. I'll think of something. Love you. See you soon—next week I hope."

Bill meets with Ma Mah

Bill thinks to himself he must tell Ma Mah about Karen, but he knows he needs to do it in a very low-key way that does not put the blame on the parents for their lack of personal attention toward Gee and Percy. Gad! I had forgotten I have to pick up Percy next week from Hollie's animal rescue farm. Maybe I can get him to fly to Maine and be with us.

After checking with Ma Mah's personal secretary, Bill asks if Mrs. Lowell has time to meet with him. She calls back shortly, saying, "Mrs. Lowell says she always has time for her employees. Meet her at the pool patio bar for tea in twenty minutes. She has one phone call to make and then she'll be free."

When he arrives at the designated spot, Ma Mah is seated with two cups of tea on the table—along with a bottle of brandy and two shot glasses. He shakes her hand briefly and sits down poolside, saying, "Mrs. Lowell, I would like to talk with you about Gee."

"What's this formal "Mrs. Lowell?" Just call me Ma Mah like the kids do. What's on your mind, Bill? I would like to hear your thoughts on this D.A. and how we get rid of him. Please have a cup of tea with me."

"Well, Mrs. Lowell, er, Ma Mah, I'm afraid there's a long story I have to tell you about your daughter. About six years ago, I caught her leading a different life. Gee either has a split personality, or maybe this behavior of hers all began as a lark, or a game. You see… she talks to herself as Gee…but at times answers herself as Karen."

"Yes, Bill, I know about her imaginary friend—she showed up after Percy was sent away to boarding school. What's the harm in that? She apparently was lonely for someone her own age and developed this friend—you call Karen. I was not aware of the name till now though."

"Well, you see, it's actually gotten much deeper than that. Gee, although she is a great fundraiser and socialite, has railed against the superficiality of your social group as she sees it—instead, she's wanted to do something for the more needy people in our society."

"I understand that feeling, I often become angered by the games which are so often played by my "elite" peers myself."

"Ma'am, you would hardly recognize Karen—she dresses differently, wears her hair differently, even walks differently. On top of that she has a business, a private detective business! She advertises as Kevin Hunt, Private Detective, but then meets clients as Karen Hunt. She has a license, a concealed weapon permit, and has been fingerprinted in the process—as Karen Hunt. So now you can see the problem that'll arise when the D.A. discovers this."

"Hmmm. Well, I have noticed that Gee is called away at odd times on some lame excuse or another. I thought possibly she might have a secret lover, or might even be gay."

Bill shakes his head, "No worries there, I'm her lover, Ma Mah. Actually…I'd like to ask you for her hand in marriage. I haven't proposed as yet, but I want to, and I think that she wants me to ask her. I worry about the difference in our social status though, with me being far outclassed by your lovely daughter. However, Karen operates in a different stratum. It's interesting that I love both Gee and Karen, and sometimes don't even equate in my mind they're actually the same person. Maybe I've developed a split personality too!"

Smiling and nodding, Mrs. Lowell replies, "I may be old, but I've seen how you look at her, and occasionally I've seen her gaze at you at length as well. Maybe the loneliness she experienced as a child caused her to hide her feelings from outsiders, except for Karen?"

Bill skims past this touchy topic though and presses on, "Gee and her Maine lawyer have two different stories they're working on. Did you know Bernie Sanders got her to visit him in Vermont recently? He asked her to meet with him because he wanted Gee to run for political office, can you believe it? But apart from that unexpected notion, she told him in reply of her fingerprint problem. However, she gave him the wildest story—saying she was born a twin, Karen was premature and sickly, so you arranged to have her raised by a couple who could devote all their time to caring for her and helping her try to fully recover. Then she said this couple was killed in an auto accident and Karen subsequently became a detective in order to track down their drunken killer. She said Karen then died six years ago after having searched out Gee and the family. Gee promised Karen she would take over her detective business and continue searching for the hit-and-run driver who cost her adoptive parents their lives."

"Wow! That is a wild story. Can she sell it?"

"Not without your help in going along with this story of hers. However, if it gets out, you may be branded by the press as a heartless mother who gave up a sickly child as caring for her would interfere with your social life."

"Hmmm. Well, I certainly don't like that spin on it. I can anger plenty of people on my own, thank you kindly. However, if it'll keep Gee out of jail, I suppose I will go ahead and support this version of the truth she's cooked up. Tell me though…what's the second story?"

"I like this one the best, myself. Gee is filing with the State Equalization Board for a DBA to operate as Karen Hunt, Private Detective. We are moving her office from here to my cabin, just west of Pittsfield. I will open a post office box for her and lease my cabin to her for use as a part-time office. Hopefully, she can avoid being fingerprinted until we get legal authorization for the business. I don't know what we can do about the wrong name on the fingerprints. It works for identical twins, but this scenario is different.

"Ma Mah, I would like to take next week off and have Percy come with me to Maine. You wouldn't believe it, but Gee referred Karen to Percy and he used her for some type of investigation. However, Karen never met Percy in person, or he obviously would have recognized his own sister. Believe me, we'll have some laughs when she tells him she is Karen."

"Alright, Bill, you have the time you need to go to Maine. I will call Percy and recommend that he accompany you. You also have my permission to ask Gee, Karen, or whoever they are for her hand in marriage. You really don't need my permission though, this is the 21st century, after all. Please do your best to straighten this whole thing out, will you? My goodness, I think we each need a brandy now. Pour us two shots, will you please, Bill? But we may need some refills shortly too!"

CHAPTER 12   A question is posed and a timely escape

Bill called me, saying he and Percy would arrive in the evening. "We have much to talk about. It's time you clue Percy in about Karen and her past activities. I talked with Ma Mah and she already knows about your imaginary friend, although she says she never heard her called Karen. Apparently, your conversations with her became so involved you just continued them in front of everyone."

The day crept on with my growing anticipation of being reunited with Bill and Percy. Several of the Wolverines came by with gun magazines and I paid them in cash, totaling over $2000 for the day. I had now paid out nearly $10,000 for the gun magazines I'd collected. A couple of other benefactors in both Liberty and nearby Hornby were also paying for magazines now as well. Turns out the pyramid of welded clips in our town had inspired a similar pyramid being constructed in Hornby.

Van came by to pick up the clips to take to his barn for more welding. "Listen, Gee, keep a low profile, will you. There are two suspicious looking guys hangin' around in town with a van which has metal screens inside the windows. I fear they're bounty hunters looking for you. Keep your shotgun handy, girl."

"Suppose I shoot them and they have a warrant, won't that make me a real vigilante or terrorist? The D. A. would love that."

Van quickly replies, "Maybe you had better not shoot them. I left my power boat down at your dock on the lake. Here's the key to the motor. If you need to run, take it down to the fish dock at the other end of the lake. Call me, and I'll come pick you up, and then we can re-strategize."

"Ok, thanks. Percy and Bill are coming tonight and we three will develop a plan. I'm supposed to see the sheriff and go before the judge. It was supposed to be today, but I delayed it until tomorrow so Percy and Bill and I could put our heads together first."

After Van left, the afternoon wore on as I was feeling at loose ends and a bit out of sorts. Suddenly, I heard the crunch of gravel in the driveway and knew it must be Bill and Percy. The bounty hunters would no doubt creep up on me with little warning. I bounded out of my chair and flung the door open, rushing out to see them. I wave at my brother before Bill enfolds me in his arms, giving me a very long, passionate kiss.

Percy exclaims, "Wow, Gee! When did all this develop? I must have left you two alone too much when we were at the Taft Plantation."

He laughs and says, "It actually has been going on for a long time. In fact, yesterday when I was talking with Ma Mah about Karen, I asked her for your hand in marriage. Gee…will you marry me?"

"Bill, What? The answer is no, a very strong and definite no! What kind of a proposal was that? No lady in her right mind would say yes to a flippant offhand proposal of marriage like that! What happened to the romantic Prince William or Prince Charming? Did you lose them on the flight?"

"Gee, I'm sorry. Hey, there's a full moon tonight. Will you come down to the lake with me later this evening?"

We three soon have dinner and a long discussion commences during which Karen is fully revealed to a duly surprised Percy. Bill had also not heard of several of Karen's adventures which are now disclosed as well. The plan was to talk with the sheriff first thing tomorrow morning and then see the judge. With the publicity of me being in town and winning the contest and all that, we all concurred I now need to get away from here. The decision was made to go to Taft Plantation and continue working on the remodel. Percy had also recently made a deal with Hollie to move her wild animals to the property. Percy also confessed he and Hollie were becoming more than just good friends—as he put it.

The time passes quickly given the variety of topics being covered, and soon it's nine p.m. and the full moon is spilling its shimmery light over the lake. Bill takes my hand saying, "Please come on our little evening stroll now, darlin'." We walk hand in hand down to the lake where I see two Adirondack chairs have been set close together looking out over the still water. A bottle of champagne with two glasses and two roses adorn the small table between the chairs.

When I see them, I exclaim, "Hey, how'd you get all this down here? I didn't see you slip out after dinner."

"I guess you were so involved in the conversation with your brother you missed me nipping out for a few minutes. Will you have a glass of imported bubbly, my princess?" He then pours two glasses of champagne and kisses my hand. After which he ceremoniously places a small ring box on the table between us.

Glancing up, his face breaks into a sudden grin, "Gee, will you give me the great honor of being my wife?"

"Are you proposing to Gee? What about Karen, will you propose to her also?"

"Yes, I love you both. Will you continue to be both Gee and Karen?"

"How can you propose to two women at the same time? When we make love, which one of us is in your mind?"

"Well, hmmm, I suppose that's a fair question. I have made love to you when you were Gee. I have made love to you when you were Karen. I guess I only call you love or darling while we're having sex. But then, all men do that—suppose another name like Jean or Sharon slipped out!"

"So, wait a minute, who are these other women please? Are those names of your past conquests?"

"Don't be silly, I was only giving an example. I don't know anyone by either name. How interesting that you instantly responded with a streak of jealousy though."

"Which one of us makes love the best? Gee or Karen?"

"Initially, I noticed a slight difference. You have a different persona depending on whether you're Gee vs. Karen. Now it seems you are both the same. That's why I don't have to make a choice. I contemplated that I could marry one of you, and that the other could still exist outside of the marriage. But no, I don't think that's actually possible, so please don't suggest it."

I think about this exchange and am quiet for a bit…and I have yet to reply to him.

"Once again, I would like to marry you—Gee, or Karen, or both of you. I love you and want to spend my life with you. We will have to work out where our lives are going and what we want to do with them—but we must be together. So…what's your answer?"

"My answer is *yes*. We will have to deal with all the other complications later. But for now the answer is yes, m'love!"

Suddenly, two men in black bulletproof outfits jump out of the bushes wielding automatic weapons with large clips, and yell at us to hit the ground. We just sit there petrified and in disbelief at what's happening. We each raise our hands in the air, the sign of surrender. I cry out, "Don't shoot, we're unarmed. What do you want? Please don't kill us!"

"We are process servers, Ms. Lowell. I have a warrant here to serve you."

"What kind of process servers come dressed in armored flack suits with automatic weapons?"

"In view of your past history of killing a terrorist and, more recently, killing over 20 paramilitary terrorists, we came prepared. Now hit the ground as I ordered."

Two more dark shadowy figures then jump out from behind the brush. One hits one of the other two with the butt of his rifle, causing him to fall face first, apparently unconscious. As he thumps the ground, his headgear rolls off his head and toward the lake. For a minute, I think it might be his head and I let out a scream. The other newly-emerged figure is startled and suddenly swings around in response.

Two guns are instantly pointed at him. "Drop it now or you're dead! We're sheriffs' deputies and you are both under arrest."

The perpetrator drops his automatic gun to the ground. "We are officers of the court and have the right to serve this warrant."

Van replies, "You are not authorized in Maine to my knowledge. I have never seen process servers dressed like this and armed with automatic weapons. I suspect you are friends of the Boston terrorist and are actually here to kill Ms. Lowell. We will take you down to jail and introduce you to our local way of dealing with the likes of you. We are understaffed, slow but methodical. You will be given full due process of the law, but it'll take awhile, boys."

I jump into the conversation, "Buck, run up to the house and get my first aid kit from the kitchen counter. Tell Percy what's going on. Keep an eye open in case there are any additional thugs around."

My mind is racing. Karen is in full charge of the situation now. Bill has picked up both the automatic guns from the ground. Van is cuffing the conscious perpetrator. He stands up and I wrap my arms around him, kiss him, and whisper in his ear, "Thanks for saving us, Van. Turn your head so you will not see me and talk to Bill. I want to make a quick search of these guys. I want them to have no identification when you take them in. I don't want you involved. Let the sheriff take it from here. Leave their van and have the sheriff look for it in the morning. Thanks again for coming to our rescue so bravely! I think we'll be leaving town tomorrow. Geez, I'm SO grateful you showed up when you did!" And, with that, I give him a heartfelt squeeze of his muscular arm.

In a short while, Buck and Percy come down to the lake with the first aid kit. They stop the bleeding and the perp comes around, exclaiming, "What happened? Who hit me? I thought this was going to be a 'piece of cake' operation, what went wrong?"

Buck replies, "You came to the wrong neck of the woods, fella. You've met up with the Wolverines."

Van replies, "Buck, the Liberty City Council just voted to give us our new name—The Sons of Liberty. We're no longer the Wolverines."

I pipe up saying, "That's great news, Van. Get these guys outta here, please. We have a few things to do before we head out of town in the morning."

Van and Buck march them off to their SUV and drove them to the jail. Percy, Bill, and I return to the cabin. "Ok, gang, I'm calling Joyce Jones, the local newspaper reporter to come out here right now for an exclusive for tomorrow's papers—I hope the story gets picked up by a wire service."

Bill asks, "What do you have in mind, Karen? I know you're in Karen mode right now."

"Bill, you will search their van for any paperwork, including insurance card, license, and registration. Look behind the visors. Make sure you wear gloves. We don't want your fingerprints in their vehicle. Here are the keys. Leave them behind the visor and leave it unlocked. Get this done right away before Joyce gets here please. And don't let her see you on the road."

"Wow! That's a real plan. Anything else come to mind?"

"Yes, take this coffee can full of ammo we took out of all the clips I bought back from people and leave it in their van. The headline of how much ammo they had with them will discredit them even further."

My newly-minted fiancé heads off to follow my instructions. I call Joyce and tell her she must come now for the story as we are leaving town. We don't want it to appear we are sneaking out of town as guilty persons, seeking to hide from the law.

Bill is back in half an hour. Joyce pulls up just after he arrives. She races up to us asking, "So what the heck's so important that you dragged me out of bed?"

I reply, "We were just attacked by two armed terrorists with automatic weapons. Do you think that it might be because of my talk and our stance against large magazine automatic rifles?"

"Wow! Really? What happened?"

"Bill and I were down at the lake having a glass of champagne. In fact, he just proposed to me. It was so sweet and so wonderful. I had just said yes, and before he even took the ring out of the box, it happened. Oh no, Bill, do you still have my ring?"

"What happened?"

"Well, these two terrorists jumped out of the bushes and drew their guns on us. They yelled for us to hit the ground. I asked them what they wanted. They replied they were process servers, but they were dressed for war and not for just delivering a legal document. We never saw any papers or identification. And then two of The Sons of Liberty—newly-appointed deputy sheriffs, as it happens— came to our rescue. Carl Van Slooten and Buck, I mean Harry Piel, Jr. had seen these two guys in town asking questions about where my cabin is located. Buck snuck up and hit one of them behind the head with his rifle butt and he fell to the ground. Van jumped the other one and he dropped his automatic weapon. We patched up the one injured terrorist. Van and Buck searched them but found no wallets, papers, or identification. We didn't find their vehicle, so the police will need to look for it in the morning. It can't be far off though. Van and Buck took them off to jail in handcuffs and we came back here to the cabin."

Joyce shakes her head and is quiet for a moment, then says, "This certainly is an exciting story. I wonder if they were friends of the Boston Symphony terrorist you killed."

"I don't like the word killed, can you use something else—maybe put down or stopped. I don't like to think of myself as a person who has killed anything or anybody. I sometimes think back with great sadness over the wild animals I killed when I was younger while hunting with my father. I gave up hunting man-n-y years ago."

Bill chimes in, *(why do we say "chimes in"—when do people speaking sound like the ringing of chimes?)* "Well, in addition to spiking my heart rate off the chart, they certainly ruined my proposal to Gee. Whenever we think back on it in future years, it will have this moment of terror attached to it. Maybe we should cancel the proposal in our minds—I have not given Gee the ring as of yet. I will re-propose in a couple of days in a more romantic place…we need to forget this evening and its upsetting events."

Joyce exclaims, "That is so sweet. Gosh, I am *so* sorry this happened to you two. I will put the word out for terrorists to stay away from Liberty. I'm sure our sheriff will determine their identities and I hope our judge will give them a maximum sentence for this assault with a deadly weapon!"

The journalist leaves to write her piece for the newspaper. She also alerts the networks about this terrorist attack, and "how we deal with these things here in Maine."

Bill chides me, "Karen, you really led her down the garden path. Now she'll play up my proposal to you and the whole world will just be touched by our romantic moment turning into terror."

Percy replied, "Gee-Karen, what did you find on them and what did you find in the van, Bill?"

"Why would you think we found anything? Surely, they're terrorists, don't you think?"

"Gee, you are haughty and, Karen, you are devious. Remember, I'm your brother, ladies. I can see you both laughing at the same time. Do you think this is a game?"

"Well, we think it certainly is. But they ruined Bill's proposal to me (us), and they deserve to pay for that, not to mention scaring the livin' daylights out of us. Now let's pack and get out of here early in the morning. The Taft Plantation needs our attention, and I'm looking forward to leaving Maine at this point, I have to admit."

We start to pack and then stop after awhile to get ready for bed. It is now just after midnight. Karen's cell phone starts ringing. "Who can that be? Hardly anyone knows this number—well, it is in Kevin Hunt, Private Detective advertisements." I click to answer the call, "Karen Hunt here. How can I help you?"

"Well, this is Senator Thaddeus Throckmorton, U.S. Senator from Louisiana. Bernie Sanders gave me your name. I need your outfit to set up surveillance cameras in a subdivision of 50 homes here in northern Louisiana, just outside the Hurricane Henry disaster zone. Robbers are moving into the area and we need our resident's homes protected, or what's left of them at any rate."

"I might be able to help you, Senator. We are leaving in the morning for our Mississippi plantation home. I understand you want your homes protected, but aren't most of these looters people looking for food who have no work as their homes and jobs have been destroyed?"

"Well, yes, I guess that may be true...at least partially."

"We are taking some of these storm victims on the Taft Plantation, which we have also just converted to an animal rescue farm. We are setting up temporary tents and trailers to handle maybe 1,000 people. Is there room in your enclave to set up any temporary shelters for displaced persons? Is there any work you could hire them to do? A lot of these people will likely move to other areas and not even return to their damaged homes. I would like to help as many of them as we can. What can you do?"

"Well, little lady—Bernie told me you were a real cracker, and to watch out for my wallet. Yes maybe, we can come up with some jobs. Several of our workers have gone to help relatives rebuild. Each house in our 'Mayflower Division' has yard people, cleaning people, repair men, and painters plus all the other repair folks from the local town."

"That sounds great. Ok, we can do the job for you. I will be there in two days. Can you get some tents delivered there? We will put up a tent city. We will also need some port-a-potties, portable showers, and a portable kitchen. Can you supply those?"

"Bernie was right. You don't mess around. Ok, I will arrange to get all the stuff there by the time you arrive or shortly thereafter. I will call up my friend, John Clampton, who lives there full-time—he will pick out a location for the tent city and be your contact. I will have him call you in the morning."

I call out to Percy and Bill, "Hey guys, we have a new job. Tell you about it in the morning. Good night."

The sun breaks *(how can that happen?)* and it's a peaceful morning following the unexpected drama of last night. Breakfast first, then we finish packing, and soon we're ready to head to the airport. We call a cab as I'll have to leave Karen's car at the cabin, but I recover my gun and the surveillance cameras from the trunk as it occurs to me I may need those in Louisiana. On the way to the airport, I relate my conversation with Senator Throckmorton and my plan for the displaced hurricane victims.

The plane has been fueled and checked out by the local airport mechanic. We are about to board and are checking our gear, when a group of 12 people led by reporter Joyce shows up to see us off. Individuals from the assembled group share they're sad to see me leave, but promise to continue the gun magazine reclamation program. They are also raising money beyond the $10,000 I paid out.

Joyce exclaims, "My piece has hit the newsstands here locally, CNN and ABC called and are each running pieces on the terrorists even though, so far, the sheriff has still not identified them—but he has found their van. Last I heard it's being worked on now by a fingerprint team. The sheriff reports the two terrorists had five guns and over 700 rounds of ammunition with them and in the van. Truly, they are bad guys. You're lucky you weren't both killed!"

We thank them all for their good wishes, and for Joyce's quick work, and we give a final wave to the small crowd. The door to the plane is closed, and within minutes, Bill is taxiing down the runway. Percy says, "Karen, you certainly knew how to program that one. It should take them several days at least to get out of jail and prove their 'innocence.' Maybe they should find a different line of work!"

"Well, if Gee can write this novel, maybe I can get it made into a movie. I wonder which star we should get to play us?"

CHAPTER 13   Helping hurricane refugees

After a few hours in the air, we arrived at the local Bixby airport, found our parked van, loaded our gear, and are headed off to the Taft Plantation. It was only a week since the pair of hurricanes had decimated both Texas and Florida. People had checked their wrecked homes, and many had decided to go north to seek shelter and make plans for rebuilding. Many people live from paycheck to paycheck in these regions and the storm put them in dire straits as a result. Banks had been damaged, and it was obvious many businesses would not re-open for some time. If you weren't in the construction business, your job would not resume for an uncertain amount of time. Given what often happens in a severe storm's aftermath, surely some businesses would never reopen.

On the flight down, I tell Percy and Bill about Senator Throckmorton's job for us, along with my proposal to set up a nearby tent city to provide temporary homes to storm victims. "The Mayflower enclave is 50 homes on 100 acres. Adjacent to it is a 200-acre field belonging to the senator. He has agreed to setup a tent city there similar to the one we are putting together on the Taft Plantation. The materials supplied by FEMA will land there the day after tomorrow. I have ordered surveillance cameras for the Mayflower homes and the tent camp area. "We need to get our boys here at Taft to go there with us and set up the system and help with the tents. Bill and I will go and you, Percy, should direct the setting up of the camp here at Taft Plantation."

"Wow! Sounds like Gee's in charge! Yes ma'am, we can do it."

"Sorry, Percy. I guess I just got carried away with the project."

"Thinking more about the long term plus the development of Hollie's Animal Rescue Farm, it's obvious we will need quite a number of full-time workers. We should rebuild the old slave quarters and convert them into permanent apartments or condominiums. There's also one empty warehouse which we might set up as a distribution center for food, water, and supplies for these poor displaced families. I will call

FEMA to see about helping make it happen. With two senators endorsing us, there should be no problem in getting rapid relief."

Upon our arrival we see Hollie is waiting for us at the mansion. Over half her animals have been delivered to the plantation prior to the rains produced by the hurricanes. She has been busy, having already hired 15 locals to build fences and construct shelters for the animals. A smaller building at the tobacco factory is also being converted into an animal hospital. Two local veterinarians have agreed to spend time with Hollie and help treat her animals when needed.

We bring her up to date with our plans. Percy asks her, "When will the construction of the animal shelters be completed? We need those workers to start on the tent city and the remodel of the old slave quarters."

"The crew is just finishing up, so by tomorrow night most everything will be done on this phase. The rest of my animals can remain up north until we get time to prepare for them. Percy, come here and give me a kiss."

The evening is spent with all of us on our phones. We have many workers to hire and supplies to arrange to be delivered. Our travelling crew will be packed with their tools and supplies by noon the next day. Three vans will carry seven of us to the Mayflower Addition in Louisiana. Senator Throckmorten invited us to stay in his mansion as he's currently at the capital. It has five bedrooms and a cabana by the pool.

We arrive at Mayflower about six p.m. Flashing lights from three police cars greet us as we pull up. The senator's friend, John Clampton, is there with the police who've stopped two vehicles with eleven adults and children. These people were trying to break into the main gate in search of food.

A man replies, "Officer, I'm sorry but we're just so desperate. Our children are hungry, and we have used up all our cash. Our credit cards are max'd out and were refused when we tried to use them earlier   today."

I address the officer in charge; "Sheriff, my name is G.W. Lowell and we have been hired by Senator Throckmorton to patrol this area and to set up a temporary refugee camp. Will you release these people to us? We will take care of them tonight. In the morning FEMA supplies are supposed to arrive here. Please also send other people in a similar plight to us and we will help care for them as well."

The sheriff nods and after a further brief exchange and tip of his hat, he leaves, and we are now on the spot. *(What does that mean? Where did this 'on the spot' phrase come from?)*

"John—Mr. Clampton—the senator told us he would talk with you and that you would help us in planning and setting up the tent city. Supplies are supposed to be here in the morning. We are staying at the senator's house, but there's room in his cabana for one of these families. Can you take the other family?"

John thinks for a minute and then responds, "Yes, I reckon I can take one family. And it's nice to meet y'all. The senator said you could deal with any problem that arose, I have no doubt he's right about that."

"Is there a nearby restaurant where we could get these folks a meal?"

"Sure thing, there's a nice family style restaurant just a half mile down the road."

"Well, let's go. We all need some food. Tomorrow will be a busy day."

At the restaurant, we enjoy a great meal together with our group spilling over into several neighboring booths, and introductions are hurriedly made as we each pour over the menu. The children are obviously exceedingly hungry as they gobble their food voraciously once a plate is set down before each of them by our friendly waitress. I ask the parents if they want to stay and help setup the tent city…?

The mom replies, "Sure, we have no place to go our homes were destroyed."

I ask, "What skills do you each have? We need experienced workers to help make this tent city work."

"Well, ma'am, I am a plumber and, Ted, here is an electrician. My wife was a secretary to an accountant. Ted's wife has had a lot of experience with fundraising for good causes."

"Ok, good, we can use all of those skills. Ted, please report to Mel, our electrician, and the two of you can figure out how to wire the tent city and after that's done, we need help setting up a surveillance camera system. George, you can help plan where the bathrooms and portable sewage reclamation plant are to be located. The women can setup a welcoming committee and keep records of all those folks who need housing and are being admitted. We will also need them to notify the various agencies who are keeping track of people so their relatives can find them. We also need to set up a phone system to the tent city. The phone company has to be called and we need to find a phone repairman to handle the installation of equipment and lines."

By 10 a.m. the trucks begin rolling in. The sheriff had already sent ten carloads of people and children out to the Mayflower development. He dispatched two food trucks to us, and these were also stocked with hot food in warming ovens.

Bill, Mel, George and a newly-arrived architect meet together and work to plan the layout for the new tent city. Soon they are chalking out the major streets, setting up a parking lot area, two playgrounds—one for younger children and one for the older children. There are already more than 40 children running around the area—and not a single tent setup as of yet.

Chaos reigns and people are milling around looking rather understandably disoriented. I give five older children whistles and ask them to blow them in various parts of the camp in helping round up the adults, telling them a meeting will occur in twenty minutes. The adults soon gather and it's up to me to lead this ad hoc gathering.

"Hello to each of you, my name is Gee Lowell. This land which will be used to setup the tent city belongs to Senator Throckmorton, who owns a home here in the Mayflower Addition. We will be tapping into the infrastructure of that addition—for water, power, and phones. No doubt there will be problems as more and more people arrive here. There's obviously no telling how long this tent city will be in existence. You will build it and you will run it. Today we will set up the infrastructure to create a City Council with departments governing water, electricity, phone, sewage, bathrooms, food kitchens, playgrounds, schooling, counseling, and religious services.

"What have I forgotten? Medical and dental treatment. We will also need a security force and a grievance board to settle problems that will no doubt surface.

"My suggestion today is for you to volunteer for one of these positions. In one month, you will have gotten to know each other, and we will then have an election for these positions. I will continue to deal with FEMA and others for the funding of this operation. You need jobs and what we do here in the tent city (you need to pick a name for it) will be voluntary with no pay, at least at first. I'm working on arranging funding so that we can provide some paid positions."

"In the meantime, the Mayflower Addition requires workers to maintain the 50 homes there. Mr. John Clampton is a resident in the Addition and is your contact for paying jobs there. I don't know what's currently available. There may be positions open in the surrounding towns. You all should prepare a resume of your previous work positions and skills. A computer, printer, and a paid secretary to help you with your resume is available at the Mayflower Gatehouse. Set up a time to meet with her."

Bill and Mel then each address the group and first arrange for the majority of the men present to help setup the tents. One larger tent is identified as the city office building. Tables and chairs are setup and four women take charge of receiving applications for positions in the tent city work force. Two other women register everyone who will be staying in the tent city. Two additional women interview all the children to determine what grade they belong in. A call is put out for teachers. A library tent is picked, and shelves will be needed for books.

In two days, all the tents onsite are erected, and more tents are ordered. The basic glitches are worked out, and maybe life will be better before long for these hurricane survivors. On day four, the new temporary city council meets. It was put together by the two women who were taking applications and interviewing applicants. Everyone introduced themselves to the audience and stated their qualifications. The audience then came up with several suggestions for the ongoing tent city operation. Items voted on were: 1.) to raise all the tents off the ground onto wooden platforms 2.) to provide a tarp awning adjacent to the entrance of each tent so people can sit outside and be protected from the heat. 3.) The children need playground equipment for the two playgrounds.

I note the tarps are easily acquired and we will look for money needed to construct the wood platforms. I suggest that some of the men might construct playground equipment. "Give us a list of the materials required," we tell them.

By day seven, we are ready to take our crew back to the Taft Plantation. Percy and Hollie have our tent city well into operational mode. They have fewer people initially than expected, and therefore there is less confusion. However displaced people with families are now arriving and filling the tents.

Construction is still in the planning stage for the old slave quarters. The children love the animals and Hollie is setting up tours and educational talks to introduce them to background information on her rescued wards. She also sets up early evening video sessions on different kinds of animals—these are to be shown on consecutive nights and we hope will be well-attended by both young and old.

We are settling in nicely ourselves. The restored Taft Mansion is a marvel and takes one back in time to an earlier gracious era, and a truly different way of life. Of course, we had no slaves, but among our staff we did have black cooks, maids, butlers, and handymen. Today's South is now a different place but there is still some inequality in the pay of women, African Americans, and Latinos, however we make sure everyone in our employ is paid on one standardized pay scale.

The back-porch swing is one of my favorite places to rest, contemplate, and plot. Bill prefers the hammock and often falls asleep in it, while it gently sways.

He and I had not yet seen Pegleg Joe's new uniform which I had made for him by my designer, Pierre. In styling, it was close to the costume Errol Flynn wore in the old original movie from the 30s. He strode in proudly to see us shortly after we arrived. "Welcome back, Lady Marian. I see you have Will Scarlet with you. We will have to get him some new clothes though. He definitely does not look like one of my Merry Men."

"I have been practicing with the bow and arrows. Little John—Mr. Percy that is—has been training me, but ah needs some of your special instruction."

"Certainly, Robin, I'll be glad to help you this afternoon.'

It's unbelievable. His whole demeanor is changed. I remark to Bill, "I can't wait to tell some of my socialite friends of this terrific transformation. How do you suppose he developed this fantasy?"

Bill replies, "You, Gee, should be the last one to wonder about people's internal imaginations—you have Karen who follows you, or proceeds you, everywhere you go. For years now!"

"I wonder if everyone has a fantasy life? Maybe it begins inside our dreams."

Percy joins in, "Often people awake from a bad dream, in which they are the victim. If they are not the victim, then they are instead the hero, the savior of the victims. I doubt if anyone dreams they're actually a bad guy or the killer."

"Do you think people dream in color, or in black and white? Are the settings for dreams in bright light, or in dark places?"

Bill cocks his head to one side and then says, "Sigmund Freud studied dreams and determined many symbols inside them are sexual in nature. Actually...I remember my mother often told us of her dreams. And, after reading Freud, I interpreted those dreams for her. I told her of all the sexual symbols they represented and said maybe she had repressed desires."

"Yikes, I'll bet that discussion ended well!"

"Well, perhaps it's no surprise that for the rest of her life, she never related another dream to me. I guess I shouldn't have told her about Freud's take on this topic!"

At this remark, we all just break into a laughing stitch. "But isn't it wonderful how Pegleg Joe is living his fantasy now?"

"Yes, and you are living yours," Bill says. "And how do I fit in? With Gee, or Karen, or now Lady Marian?"

Just then, Karen's phone rang. Remember, I had left mine in Boston so it couldn't be traced. Van and a couple of others, including the three senators, had this alternate number, but no one else had it to my knowledge. The phone indicated Joplin, Missouri. I answered, "Karen Hunt here. How can I help you?"

"This is Jackie. I'm looking for Gee—you sound so much like her. Who's Karen?'

"Jackie, yes, this is Gee—but I'm also Karen. I guess I need to tell you about Karen as it'll come out one of these days. I'll explain when I see you. So why are you calling me? And where'd you get this phone number?"

"From your mother, who also informed me the Boston D.A. was not tracking this number, to her knowledge. I'm calling because I need you to come to Joplin, Missouri right away, please, Gee. I'm right on the verge of finding out who killed Cassie. But, probably as a direct result, my private detective, Charlie, and I are each being stalked and also threatened—I feel we're getting too close to the drug cartel, or mafia, or whoever they are. Maybe it's even Cassie's husband. I need your help. Can you come out here right away please…say, tomorrow?"

CHAPTER 14   Stalking a stalker

Soon thereafter Bill and I are in the air and headed on our way to Joplin. I'm sitting in the copilot seat next to him. He starts the conversation once we've leveled off at our cruising altitude, "I'd hoped we might get a little more down-time at the Taft Plantation. I was loving that hammock, and you looked pretty darned relaxed in the swing. I was planning on a new proposal to you to make up for the ruined ending of my first one—now it seems like that happened months ago, but it was actually less than three weeks."

"Oh, Bill, it was beautiful in spite of the ending. I wonder what happened to the bounty hunters? Should I call Van for an update?"

"Sure, go ahead and call him. I'm curious too. I'll bet they regretted that job!"

I grab my phone, dial the number, and the call's soon answered, "Hey, Van…it's Gee…so what happened with those guys?"

"They spent five days in jail until their identifications were officially authenticated. We're awful slow here in Maine! They were charged with operating without legal authority in this state. Also, they had no hunting licenses and fired a gun out of season at a duck in the lake. I think maybe Buck fired the gun, but I didn't see it. The judge let them off though, but they had to promise to give us the 30-round clips for their rifles. He also confiscated all their guns and the 700 rounds of ammunition we'd seized in their vehicle. He also admonished them for dressing like terrorists. Their van was in impound and they had to pay storage fees for the week. Something smelled BAD in that van, I can tell ya. Apparently, by chance or mistake, one of them—or somebody—had dropped one raw shrimp inside. A week spent ripening in the closed vehicle produced an awful stink. I'll bet their ride back to Boston was spent with them hanging their heads out the windows!"

"Well, I guess they tangled with the wrong gal, in the wrong town, who had the wrong friends. Or I should say…the right friends. Thank you so much, Van. I won't stay away so long next time and am already planning to spend some future vacations at the cabin there in Liberty. Love ya. Bye for now."

After I clicked off the call, Bill and I laughed over the mental image we each had of them finally being sprung from their cells—only to then be greeted by the interior of their smelly ride. "I thought Van was planning to leave two fish in the van and charge them with no fishing license. Shrimp produce a far worse stench for such a small overlooked piece of seafood!" At this we grinned devilishly at each other and laughed some more.

Arriving at Joplin, Bill parked the plane, and we then rented a car and proceeded to the Ramada Bar where Jackie and her detective said they'd be waiting. As we enter, she sees us and waves us over. "Glad to see the two of you. Charlie, my sleuth has been tracking down some of Cassie's past activities. But before we get into that, tell me about Karen. Who the heck is Karen, pray tell?"

I pat her shoulder as I take my seat, "Well, it's actually a long and convoluted story, missy. Bill, can you give her a broad outline of it please? It might be interesting for me to hear it recounted from someone else vs. just inside my own brain."

"Alright, I'll try. Well, quite simply, your friend, my sweetheart here, has led—leads—a dual life. She is Gee, the socialite of Boston you know…and also Karen, private detective. Karen, show her your credentials and license." Out of the purse come the requested materials which Jackie examines briefly.

Bill then continues, "Gee and Karen both maintain separate identities, and lead completely different lives. Except recently, when they started to converge and overlap. This dual identity began when Gee was a child, having been raised by a series of hired nannies and governesses. Percy was sent away to boarding school at a young age, and Gee was left all alone with no one to play with. Karen began to talk to her to fill the vacuum of her brother's departure, and soon they became inseparable. They played together and schemed together. They made up situations and adventures they had to solve and overcome. It was a glorious game. No one really knew the extent of this private world of "two" at the time though. Ma Mah and Percy heard Gee talking— apparently to herself- but excused it as just a slight oddity.

"Gee later fantasized that Karen was her identical twin, born prematurely and raised by foster parents. She invented a story that the foster parents were killed in a car crash caused by a drunk driver, and Karen was then motivated to become a detective and search him out. Much of this is actually real in Gee's mind. Is she crazy? I don't think so. Gee is a terrific philanthropist and socialite, and Karen's a whip-smart detective. I guessed at the presence of Karen when Gee asked me to fly her to San Diego and she arrived dressed as Karen, a completely different look. In her business, she's tracked down murderers, lost persons, and even kidnapped children. However, if the Boston D.A. arrests her and takes her fingerprints, this dual identity will come to light. Gee has never been fingerprinted, but Karen has in order to obtain her investigator's license."

"Wow! That's sure some tale I knew absolutely nothing about! Maybe Karen and Charles will make a great pair in partnering up and solving this Cassie murder mystery, 'eh?'"

Changing the topic, the next question switches to, "Jackie, what did you ask us here to do?"

"We're here to meet with Cassie's sister, Lisa, at her home. She has a safety deposit box at a local bank in which Cassie kept documents. Charlie and I have met with Lisa, and we convinced her we were Cassie's friends from Vassar and looking for her murderer. She is cautious and not as outgoing as Cassie was. She wants more proof of our identities, so I told her you had additional pictures of all of us at the reunion."

"Hmmm, well, that'll be a problem in that my—Gee's—phone is back in Boston, so I don't have any pictures with me. Do I appear in some of your pictures?"

"Yes, you do, so maybe we can convince her that way."

Bill jumps in, "Gee can sell anything. She recently convinced a group of survivalists called the Maine Wolverines to give up their automatic rifle bullet clips and to rejoin mainstream local society versus hiding out in the woods in their the-world-is-ending mode. She beat them at their own game, on their territory, and came out the winner in a mega royal paint gun battle of theirs."

Jackie's head swivels as she smiles briefly at her friend and then replies, "Ok, I'll call Lisa on a cell phone I bought for her. She's actually become quite paranoid and thinks her phone is tapped and that she's also being watched. As I mentioned, both Charlie and I have also been under surveillance by someone in the past couple of weeks. Therefore, I purposely left my cell phone in Chicago." Jackie turns away from the table and calls Lisa, instructing her to park outside of Sam's Bistro downtown, and then to walk straight through the place, and out the back door. She tells her we'll be waiting for her.

As planned, a short while later Jackie and Charlie pick her up behind the restaurant and head for our rooms at the Ramada Inn. Lisa is a petite blonde like Cassie, with a longer lean face. She has two teenage children and recently became a single mother as her husband was killed on active duty in Iraq.

Knocking on the door, it opens before she can say anything, the exchange begins with, "Hi, Lisa, my name is Gee Lowell. I was one of Cassie's roommates at Vassar as was Jackie. Sadly, it was my idea to arrange the reunion for fifteen of my best friends at Vassar. I had dinner with Cassie just before it happened. She had been pretty downhearted during the whole reunion week though. She had a couple of accidents, which some of us thought afterwards were actually suicide attempts. She told me at dinner she was sorry to be such a downer. When I expressed my concern about her mental state, she assured me she wasn't wanting to end her life—she also was very adamant in telling me if anything happened to her, the culprit would be Glenn. Her last words to me were, 'Tell my sister I love her.' She didn't mention your name or tell me you had anything of hers though."

At this disclosure, Lisa breaks down crying, putting her head in her hands—Jackie and I quickly join in with a few tears running down each of our faces as well. Jackie fishes around in her purse for a Kleenex.

After she starts to calm herself a bit, Lisa then tells us, "Cassie had me open a safety deposit box in my name in which she put both money and papers of some sort. She said if anything happened to her, the money was mine, and the papers were to go to the right people looking for her murderer. I have been asked by a local police detective and a lawyer if Cassie had left any papers with me. I said no, she hadn't. I knew I should give up the contents of the safety deposit box, but I wanted to first meet with my lawyer to examine what it contained. She left me a couple of magazines which I gave to the police detective, but there was nothing in them that pointed in any specific direction to my knowledge."

Bill then asks her, "What makes you think you're being followed or watched, Lisa?"

"My phone clicks when I make a call or answer one. I've never heard that clicking before and I've had this cell two years. Also, a black car with very dark windows is parked down the street every single night. I see the glow of a match or cigarette through the glass, so I know someone's sitting in there. During the day, every time I check, I see the same car following me wherever I go. At first, I didn't notice, but each time I looked in my rearview mirror I could see the same black car back following me, always about a block behind."

"Have you opened the safety deposit box yet?"

"No, I haven't, not yet. I want my lawyer to be there when we open it. He was my father's lawyer and is an old family friend."

"Call him and set it up for tomorrow morning please, Lisa, and we can meet you at the bank. Bill will pick him up in another rented car. We will come get you the same way as today, but from a different place. Does your hairdresser have a back door not visible from the front?"

"Yes, she does. Is this a little paranoid? Do we need to be going to these extremes? Although I admit I like your strategy."

"Yes, we do. These people likely have billions of dollars and kill people for any slight. I am indeed a little suspicious about this whole thing. I don't mean to get you upset though, Lisa—I only want you to be careful and take precautions."

The meeting is soon setup for the group to head to the bank and see what's in the locked box. Heading out into the night, Bill drives Lisa to the back door of Sam's Bistro and drops her off. He instructs her, "Leave through the restaurant's front door and appear to be sick. Pretend to throw up in a potted plant just outside the restaurant and again near your car. Anyone watching you probably would have checked the inside of the restaurant to see if you were there. This way it will create some cover in appearing you were sick in the restroom for some period of time."

We head back to our hotel and eat in our room, barely noticing our food as we discuss the case. Charles brings us up to date on what he has discovered thus far.

"Ok, gang, here's the scoop: Cassie and Glenn lived in Kansas City, Kansas and have businesses in both Kansas and Missouri, as well as a number of other places across the country. Glenn also owns a condominium in Kansas City, Missouri, which he takes his girlfriends to. Probably Cassie knew about this little love nest of his. And Cassie flat out lied to you girls about knowing anything about Glenn's businesses because it turns out she's the officer of record, the chief financial officer, the president, or the vice president, but most often the secretary-treasurer of more than a dozen corporations he's setup. As a result, she was also the signatory on every tax return I could find for the corporations.

"The feds are trying to get him on money laundering for the drug cartels—probably not the mafia. Some of the monies were going into three real estate corporations in California, Nevada, and New York—all with very similar names. It was easy to write checks to one corporation and deposit it in the bank of another one in a different state. They stamped the checks with a rubber stamp—for deposit only in account No. 231245 or whatever the account number was at that bank. They had several check-cashing exchanges in various cities that deal in lots of cash.

Turns out they also owned pawn shops in Nevada, again lots of cash transactions.

"Large loans were made between various corporations. Large loans were made to Glenn—none to Cassie. Guess what? Glenn never shows up on any corporation paperwork as an officer. He only shows up as a large stockholder and sits on the corporate boards of several large corporations. Many of these corporations appear quite clean with no ties to the drug cartel or any of Glenn's corporations. They may just have taken loans from what they supposed were legitimately operating corporations. Cassie also appears as the signatory on most of these loans, by the way.

"The feds must know all of this and either have made a deal with Cassie or were about to arrest her and prosecute her. Glenn must have felt safe as Cassie wouldn't be compelled to testify against her husband in court. However, I also couldn't find any divorce documents from Cassie and her first husband."

I then asked, "So what's the legal implication of that?"

"Glenn travels a lot between all these businesses. He has a girlfriend in every port, and he's not even a sailor. One place he flies to every two or three weeks is Pittsburgh, PA. However, he has no businesses there that I could find. He also never rents a car while there, which is very strange. So, someone must pick him up at the airport on each flight. I haven't been able to find out who that is though. Maybe we can hire someone to watch incoming flights and photograph him with whoever picks him up. By the way, get this, he always takes the same airline and same flight—although there aren't too many flights from Kansas City direct to Pittsburgh."

"Ok, thanks for the update, Charles. We didn't know any of this. Wow, it's really revealing, seems to me. So, I guess Cassie's business degree from Vassar has led to an empire of crime. She must have been good, or the enterprises would have been detected years ago. Charles, how far back does this history of hers and Glenn's stretch with all these corporations?"

"It appears her first meeting with Glenn was 13 years ago, just two years out of Vassar and a year and a half into a bad marriage. She was a good target for Glenn, who's more than a decade older than her."

As the meeting breaks up, Bill and I get ready to retire. I suggest Jackie and I room together, and Bill and Charles take the other room.

Jackie replies, "No, Charlie and I'll take the other room, and you two lovers have this room."

At this point I'm remembering Charles is more than just an employee. (She introduced him as Charles but refers to him as Charlie.) Jackie just came through a long and contentious divorce less than two years ago. Hmmm, time to play…or time to look for a serious relationship?

Once again, morning rolled around. Thankfully there don't seem to be any lurking hulks watching the hotel. (No foreshadowing this time. I've had no bad dreams when sleeping with Bill.) As I pull back the curtain in the hotel, I see it's a beautiful autumn day outside and leaves colored yellow and red line the street. We meet up with the other two, have a quick breakfast, and then Bill heads off in the new rental car to pick up the lawyer. Jackie, Charles, and I head for the hairdresser's shop to pick up Lisa. As arranged, we park in the alley behind the shop, turn off the ignition, and wait quietly in the vehicle. Ten minutes later, Lisa pops out of the back door.

As she gets in, she exclaims, "Listen, I think I was just followed from my house. Hopefully he thinks I'm inside having my hair done."

I'm behind the wheel and, upon hearing this, immediately instruct everyone to duck down out of sight in the van and I will pull around the block and see if anyone is watching. Two minutes later I pass the front of the hairdresser's shop and, sure enough, the black van is parked down the street. They of course, must see me, but hopefully don't recognize this vehicle. To play it safe, I drive downtown and call Uber to pick us up near the Third Street parking lot. Just a few minutes later, we get into the Uber driver's car and are delivered to the bank soon thereafter. I place an order with Uber to return in one hour and pick us up at the coffee shop next door to the bank. Upon entering the bank, we proceed into the back where the safety deposit boxes are located. Bill and the lawyer join us there. We're then shown to a small room inside the vault. Lisa and the teller use their keys and proceed to retrieve the box and bring it to us.

The safety deposit box itself is a large drawer and quite heavy. The teller and Lisa each hold one end of the drawer. The teller mentions she doesn't recall Cassie coming to the bank more than once a year since she opened the account for her maybe ten years ago. She then excuses herself and leaves, and Lisa opens and unloads the contents onto the table.

"Yikes! Look at all this stuff!

We begin to inventory what's there: one hundred huge stacks of $100 bills, thousands of shares of various stocks made out to Lisa, titles to various real estate lots as well as a couple of houses, some rare gold coins, and even a couple of loose high grade diamonds.

The most important items are the papers: a ledger of the first ten years of operations of Glenn's variety of business entities, a spreadsheet of monies received from various individuals including an indication of which were cash, and which were checks or securities, along with microfilm of all the tax returns. The most recent eight years were labeled and on CDs and flash drives.

The lawyer says, "This is really critical evidence which the feds will need to shut down this operation. We should make copies straightaway—three copies of all the paperwork, I think. I'll keep one copy in a new safety deposit box here in this bank. Gee and Jackie, you take two copies and place one in a safety deposit bank out of this state. The other copy needs to go to the federal prosecutor referenced on Glenn's indictment."

I have brought a small laptop with me and set about quickly making flash drive copies of the CDs and flash drives onto my hard drive. Jackie checks with a bank employee and then begins copying the paper documents on a nearby copier. The lawyer exits the vault and meets back up with the teller, making arrangements with her for a new safety deposit box in his wife's name. He then phones his wife and asks her to come down to the bank with her ID which shows she retains her family name.

The lawyer comes back in soon thereafter and tells us about the arrangements involving his wife. "We will take all the cash out of the drawer. And I want to hire 'round the clock security for Lisa until this matter is resolved. I'll open an escrow account in my name and pay expenses needed from that account. Lisa is a family friend and I will not charge any fees for my services."

The bank's chief teller then comes and picks up the money, which is scanned to see if the numbers appear on a list of dubious currency, however the bills have a variety of random numbers and no successive sequences, so that's good news. Cassie must have worked hard to replace the drug money with clean, unlisted cash from whatever sources. By putting all the cash into an escrow account, we now have a good record of how much was there—in case it's later proven to be drug money.

We finish our inventory of the contents and the drawer is returned to its place inside the vault. Lisa worries she may be kidnapped or forced to bring someone down to the bank who'll want to clean out the box. Upon hearing this remark, Bill replies, "I know how to fix that. Give me the key and I'll hide it. Uber should be here by now, I'll meet you out front."

We all leave the inner room and Bill joins us a minute later. "That was fast. What'd you do? Swallow it?" He told me weeks later he'd taken an electric cover plate off in the vault's interior room and taped the key behind it, using a small roll of adhesive he had in his pocket. "Since Lisa and no one else knows where I put it, its location cannot be revealed."

The Uber driver takes us to our car. The lawyer departs first, heading home with his wife. Next, we drop Lisa at the hairdresser and she then returns home, with her tail out front quickly in tow. Apparently, they had not followed us to the bank.

Back at the hotel, the same man we had seen the day before was loitering in the lobby, watching us. He appears to make a notebook entry of our comings and goings.

Jackie says, "He looks like the same guy who's been stalking me back in Chicago. What are you going to do about it?"

I reply, "Charlie and Karen can take care of this guy. Jackie—you go out to the van as soon as it gets dark. Appear to be getting some papers from inside the vehicle. Charlie and I'll jump this guy and see if we can scare him off the job. I have Karen's 38 with me—but, hopefully, we won't have to use it."

Back in our room, we call Room Service and arrange to have dinner sent up. While we wait, we continue looking over Cassie's trove of documents. Tomorrow we will fly to Cleveland and open a safety deposit box for one set of the copied documents. The other set will go back with us to the Taft Plantation until we can figure out how to get them into the right hands in D.C.

Later that evening, Charlie and I slip out separately and head off in different directions. We place ourselves on different sides of the van, taking care to stay in the shadows. Jackie meanders out to the van with a casual stride, opens the front passenger door, and picks up some papers from the seat. The perpetrator looms out of the darkness and suddenly points a gun at her. "I'll take those papers…and you won't get hurt."

I pounce out of my concealed spot and whip out my gun, telling him, "Drop your weapon or you're dead, pal."

He turns abruptly in my direction, sees me, and then laughs, "You are not going to shoot me with that little gun!" Then Charlie quickly moves up behind him and hits him on the back of his head with the butt of his gun. The perp quickly collapses to the ground with a quiet thud, unconscious. We truss him up with plastic ties and search him for i.d. and whatever other papers we might find.

After some quick checking with a contact of Karen's on her phone, it turns out he's a small-time hood from Chicago with a bad record including being a suspect in a death or two. I collect all his credit cards, money, and identification, so he'll now have a hard time getting back to Chicago. After a bit, he begins to come around. We blindfold him.

I lean in close and whisper in his ear, "You don't know who you're dealing with. You have followed Jackie here from Chicago. My question is why? But I am sure you will give me no answer. Maybe you need a couple of broken knees? The point is we now know who you are and where you live. If my friend Jackie or anyone we know or have talked with on this trip informs us you are tailing them again, we'll take action and then you'll be out of action permanently. Do you understand what I'm saying?"

He mumbles something. Just to be sure my point's been made, I hit him across the face with my pistol and his nose explodes with blood.

"I did not hear what you said! Do you not believe I will kill you…do you not think I'm serious?"

"Yes, ma'am. I hear you!," he wailed. "Believe me, I am now off this case. You will never see me again. Will you untie me?"

"No, you can get them off yourself. They're just tied in front. Just chew 'em off. Now get outta here!"

He stumbles up onto his feet and walks off rapidly, a trail of blood oozing from his nose and down onto his chin.

Once again back at the room, Charlie weighs in on my performance. "Wow! You are one tough lady. Sam Spade or Phillip Marlowe could not have done it better! How long have you been doing this?"

Bill and Jackie are having their own discussion, and both seem to agree that we should move. "These guys have guns and may do anything. Let's check the cars back in and get a hotel near the airport. Maybe we should leave tonight, especially since we have all this evidence in hand."

"Can you fly us out of here tonight, Bill?"

"Yes, I can. The plane is serviced and ready to go. I'll file a flight plan to Cleveland, and we can be there in an hour."

We pack up, check out, and proceed to the airport without delay. Glancing back from time to time en route, no one appears to be following us. Soon we're on the ground in Cleveland and check into an airport hotel. Tomorrow morning, we'll arrange for a safety deposit box in a bank I used a few months ago as Karen Hunt.

The next morning, we meet for breakfast, then head to the bank with our dangerous documents. Bill and I open the box in Karen's name, but with keys for both of us. Then it's back to the airport. We fly to Chicago and drop off Charlie and Jackie, and then head back to the Taft Plantation. It was actually an exciting trip and we've now discovered much about Cassie we hadn't known. We still have one set of the documents to get into the right hands at the federal level. I'll call Senator Throckmorten, who sits on the Homeland Security Oversight Committee, and seek his advice about what we should do with the information that's come into our possession.

CHAPTER 15   Homeland "security"?

Back again to the Taft Plantation. It was like awaking from a pleasant dream. The stalker and the people watching us at Joplin were real though—not figments of my overactive imagination. They were actual hulks skulking in the dark outside the window. I must call Jackie in a couple days and see if they're still shadowing her. I know she has complained to the police, but they'll do nothing until she's attacked. Then of course it'll be too late—I sure hope she keeps Charlie close.

Bill and I would each like to go back to the swing and hammock on the porch, but work calls. Taft Tent City is still under construction and we learn more people are arriving every day, having learned of the refuge. Much of the work is still being accomplished by volunteers, but we're only getting a little money to pay for services so far. Ma Mah has a major fundraiser happening in Boston to help aid the hurricane survivors and has arranged for us to receive a portion of the money raised to help with the costs being incurred for Taft Tent City.

Percy and Hollie have now completed this first phase of the Animal Rescue Farm. Ten people are kept on the staff full-time to take care of the animals. Their pay comes from monies donated to the Taft Animal Rescue Farm, a nonprofit organization. Percy has three full-time employees back in Boston who work for the Lowell Foundation who are now working full-time on fundraising activities to support the animal farm.

Percy is directing the rebuild of the old slave quarters. The buildings are all beyond economically feasible repair with questionable foundations, so all except one are being torn down. One unit is being restored as a historic remembrance of what things were like before the Civil War. Old photos have been found, copied, and enlarged for an exhibit. Rustic and crude period furniture like what was used in the slave quarters has been found or replicated as seen in the old photos. Percy found a couple of woodworkers among the hurricane refugees, so they've now been hired to build as well as repair furniture.

The area has been reconfigured with the reconstructed slave quarters situated at the edge of a new park and playground area. Two small apartment buildings are also under construction on two sides of the park area. An affordably-priced workforce housing condominium of six units is planned for sale to refugees who decide to remain in the area. The permit process is slow in the South—maybe slower than other areas. It helps to have a senator's office making a phone call to speed things along though. Laura Lee simply drawled out in her sweet Southern-tinged voice "The senator thinks this is a good project. It puts people to work who have lost their jobs as well as their homes. It also produces new tax monies for the county. Could you personally ram-rod this project on through to completion please? We will all be so-o happy to have your gracious assistance!"

Our tent city is also being setup with a city council and various departments. Percy has insisted that the housing will not cluster various ethnic and racial groups in various small enclaves, like what's happening at the Mayflower Tent City. Later I will meet with their city council and discuss their segregation there—intentional or accidental, as I don't believe this as the best way to integrate these refugees into a cohesive body.

At dinner later that night, Bill and I bring Percy and Hollie up to date on our adventures in Joplin. "It appears Charlie and Jackie have uncovered a dangerous hornet's nest indeed. Charlie's poking around to find Cassie's murderer has put him and Jackie under surveillance, and Cassie's sister, Lisa, is now fearing for her own life. We were followed while we were in Joplin, so it's reasonable to assume we too may also be watched—possibly soon. Although there are so many people around here that someone who's lurking and watching us will probably be difficult to spot. Have either of you noticed anyone just watching, possibly taking notes, or looking like they're standing around idly near the mansion?"

Percy replies, "No, we haven't seen anybody fitting that description or sitting around idly. Remember though, we have surveillance cameras everywhere. We'll make a point of checking them daily to see if a pattern emerges of someone being near the mansion, or we observe a person following any of us…see if we turn up anyone suspicious."

Hollie joins in, "We've been busy here too while you were gone. Various organizations seem to visit each day—the Red Cross, Doctors without Borders, FEMA, and Homeland Security just yesterday. We have supplied all of our lists of refugees to FEMA and the Red Cross, so the refugees may contact or connect with relatives through their resources. Homeland Security wanted the lists to check for anyone who might also be wanted by law enforcement or possibly illegals. I put them off and told them that both FEMA and the Red Cross had the lists, and that I didn't have time for them to go through them. I resent the idea they would want to deport some of these poor refugees who've already been through such a harrowing natural disaster."

Bill then asked me, "Hey, when are you going to call Senator Throckmorten? He ought to provide us with some guidance on how we should route those documents to the feds."

"I know, I haven't forgotten, but we were just so busy today that I haven't gotten around to that yet. I have his home number though, and it's only 9 p.m. in D.C., so I'll give him a quick call now."

I use Karen's cell to phone him, remembering I had already given that number to the senator. He answers immediately, "Gee, how is the Mayflower Tent City project going?"

"It was going nicely when I left, Senator, but I had to be away for the last four days. I hope you can come down here and see both the Mayflower project and our similar project at Taft Plantation. I have another bit of information which will spark your interest though given your role on the Homeland Security Oversight Committee. And, frankly, we need your advice on how to proceed with this sensitive information, please. Can you come down here, or do we need to come to see you in Washington?"

"It sounds like you think it might be urgent. I had already been planning to head down to Mayflower. John Clampton has been keeping me up to date and is quite impressed with the progress there. Maybe we can use this tent city as a model for other refugee areas. Maybe it can be replicated overseas. I will get some newspaper and magazine reporters to come down there. Their coverage can generate some private donations or help from other nonprofit outfits. Have you thought of setting up these two tent cities as 501(c)3's? How about if I move my plans up and get down there this coming Sunday? Is that soon enough?"

"Yes, Senator, thanks so much, that'll be great. We'll see you at Mayflower on Monday morning and then we'll fly you over to Taft to see our operation there afterward."

That night, I retire to bed with a little nervous feeling of apprehension. Were those two bad guys in Missouri the only ones watching us? It suddenly dawns on me we didn't really cover our tracks when we left the hotel and picked up our plane. After all, the plane manifest could easily be checked and our destination here at Bixby found out. Even very casual questioning at the airport could then readily produce our location at the Taft plantation.

About two a.m., the red light next to our bed blinks rapidly. The flashing light caused Bill and I to both awaken. "We must have visitors, or maybe it's just the old gator that got Pegleg Joe's right leg."

I buzz our security station and ask them what they see on the cameras? One of our FBI agents has also seen the red flash and proceeded to look at the camera's screen images. We're told, "There appears to be two figures just inside the fence to the bayou and also near the back gazebo."

"What are they doing?"

"It appears they have some bags with them and are putting something together."

"What could it be? Maybe a bomb or something?"

"That certainly is a possibility, since we understand you had two dangerous perps after you in Joplin, which is why we thought we should alert you. There's also a third figure moving out of the pool house area. He must be one of our people though. Do you have any other security persons on duty tonight?"

"No, we didn't instruct anyone besides the regular fellow who monitors the cameras. Pegleg Joe stays in that building. I hope it's not him, he might get killed! Turn up the level on the audio monitoring equipment please, and let's find out if we can hear them talking."

We hear the third man speaking with a gruff voice saying, "Alright, you two. Drop your weapons or I'll shoot."

"Who do you think you are, buddy? That bow and arrow won't stop anyone. Buck, finish him off with your knife. He's making too much noise. I could shoot him, but we want to get this bomb in place."

"Ah told you to drop your weapons. Ah could just shoot that knife right outta your hand. Don't you know about the masterful capabilities of Robin Hood?"

Buck laughs and says, "Isn't he funny? Look, holy cow, he really does have on a Robin Hood outfit. Well, I will dispatch him back to Sherwood Forest...and fast."

The next thing we hear is a gigantic explosion. It seems Robin (Pegleg Joe) has fired his arrow into the would-be bomber's chest, causing the pin to a hand grenade he had hanging from his armored vest to become dislodged. We rush out to see if Pegleg—Robin— is still alive. As we dash around in the dark, we finally make our way to their location and see all three are on the ground, knocked flat by the explosion. In fact, it's a gory sight seeing little is left of the one closest to the bomb. The second perp is wounded but jumps up quickly and dives over the fence, running toward the bayou.

"Robin, are you hurt?"

"No, Lady Marian," he said, struggling to sit upright and clearly dazed, "but I sure did get 'em, didn't I?"

We next hear a horrible scream coming from the direction of the bayou. We rush over and frantically shine our flashlights every which way, the beams slicing through the pitch blackness. We suddenly spot the second perp, now bleeding and missing his right leg. A big alligator is sliding back toward the bayou, remnants of the leg protruding from his clenched jaw.

"That's *my gator*. See the scarred plate on his head. That's where I stabbed him when he got my leg, so ah knows it's him. Now he has two right legs. He should a took the left one to have a pair. Course this one is white and mine is black. He sure gonna look funny with one black leg and one white leg!"

At that moment, having been so gripped in terror, it was suddenly hard not to laugh. After all, we had just officially been saved by Robin Hood. This perp, if he ever gets to relate his story, will be of little use to his employers for field work with only one leg plus this story that goes with it. We'll just have the FBI deal with him. An ambulance is called and we administer first aid to control the bleeding.

"We need to make sure all the original data we've acquired on Cassie and Glenn thus far is preserved and hidden. Maybe we can find a home for that info and get the heat off of us. I will scan and copy the ledger and put everything on flash drives. They're small and will be easy to hide and will ensure the evidence we have is secure, even if the place is ransacked and our safe is stolen. Oh, I'd forgotten it. Crap, where's my purse? Lisa gave me a letter just as we dropped her off at the hairdressers."

CHAPTER 16   Cassie's letter

Upon hearing this, Bill quickly glances sideways at her and replies, "You never mentioned a letter before. And I didn't see Lisa give you anything."

"Just as we dropped Lisa off, she slipped me this letter and I dropped it in my purse at the time. Apparently, it was in Cassie's safety deposit box, laying on top of some other folders, and addressed to her. She must have slipped it in her purse before we unloaded it. She whispered to me as she left that it might be important, but she was too distraught to read it just then. However, Lisa gave me no instructions as to what to actually do with it though."

We looked at each other briefly and then at the envelope which I promptly picked up and carefully opened. It contained several pages of handwritten text. The copier was already switched on so I quickly made four copies of the letter and handed one each to Bill, Hollie and Percy, so we could each read along together in digesting the letter's content.

The date at the top indicates it was written just two weeks before our Vassar reunion—and her murder. It was written on lined notebook paper with numbered lines indicated on the left side of the pages. This will make it easy for lawyers to refer to specific sentences. Cassie must have thought of that.

It begins as follows—remember, in handwritten script:

To my sister, Lisa,

Use this letter as my side of the story as you see fit in the prosecution of my murderer(s), for I fear I may soon be killed as I know way too much.

I am writing this in longhand so that my words cannot be changed.

Each page will also end in a split sentence, so that pages cannot be omitted from my testimony herein. My signature at the end is witnessed by four people who know me well and can verify I signed this document in their presence.

I am writing this in solitude and am under no pressure from anyone else. My part, my guilt, is all revealed in my ledger and the papers preserved in this safety deposit box.

It all began nearly 13 years ago. I was working for United Fruit Company in Kansas City, which imported bananas and other produce from Mexico, as well as Central and South America. I was working in the accounting department and handling offshore purchases and payments.

I met Glenn there, who also worked for the company. He was basically a travelling salesman and purchasing agent for all points south accounts. Glenn was exciting to talk with and had great stories of his trips outside the country.

My marriage with Joe was going badly at the time with little chance of getting better. Glenn took me out for dinner and drinks, and it became a habit more than once a week. Soon we ended up spending those nights together too.

The drug cartels own many legitimate businesses in Mexico and South America. Drug monies are laundered through these businesses. Glenn dealt with some of these companies and got to know some of the drug lords as a result. Initially Glenn became a money courier with a few thousand dollars slipped to him from time to time to bring back to the U.S., or to take south.

He opened bank accounts in the U.S. and in Central America with these drug funds. I kept track of all these transactions in the first few pages of my ledger enclosed in this bank box. Runners soon came by both Glenn's and my apartments with bags of money for us to deposit. Packages full of money were also delivered to me at the office or sent to my mailbox. All these money drops are shown in the ledger on pages eight thru fourteen.

I became very nervous that someone at work might end up opening one of these boxes addressed to me. So, I decided to quit my job and work from my apartment as an investment banker. It was fun at first and I was my own boss. Soon I was dealing with hundreds of thousands of dollars and completely in charge of where I invested it.

I served papers to Joe for a divorce along with the settlement I requested. But the final arrangements were never worked out nor the divorce legally recorded. Joe knew I was making money now, and every so often he would stop by and I would give him a few thousand dollars.

In January 2000, I got a passport, the first one I ever had. Glenn and I flew to Barbados where we were married. One of Glenn's new friends had a large yacht, and for three weeks we cruised around the Caribbean. Stops were made at many ports and we were introduced to several millionaires or their associates, all of whom were drug dealers. We talked investments and methods of turning cash into solid assets. They told us which cities in which countries they like to do business in, and own homes in.

Egad! It was a whole new and exciting life—rich, adventuresome, and dangerous. There were no threats though regarding money lost in bad investments. They understood risk in ways we never can and had a very different attitude. On page 21 you'll see a list of all their names and the addresses where Glenn and I met them.

After returning home to Kansas City, we purchased our first house. Later, we built several other homes in different states as well as others located in four different countries. Guests continually cycled through these homes—often with little advance notice.

Glenn brought several large new accounts to United Fruit. As a result, he was able to reduce his duties to 'special projects' and take company trips almost at his leisure.

The cash kept rolling in. It wasn't uncommon for us to have two or three million dollars cash at the house just waiting for us to find an investment where we could put some cash. Glenn moved a large safe into the basement for storing money. He personally constructed a wall in front of the safe with a movable bookcase in front of it. It opened with a secret button. The combination of the safe is 6R-7L-2R. All of our houses have similar safes hidden in them with lots of cash and some paperwork. The combinations are all the same as Glenn could not deal with having different combinations. What a dummy!

We had to setup cash businesses. There are now 27 check-cashing shops located in the poorer sections of many large cities. See the ledger for locations and cash flow details. There are many pages of transactions. We also setup money exchanges in 14 different airports. We gave better rates than the competition and moved lots of money through these operations.

We made bank deposits at least three times a week to the same accounts. We tried to mix in checks with the cash and put in odd amounts, usually under $10,000 for each deposit to stay under the Fed's radar. We wrote checks back and forth between our different corporations, and also made loans back and forth.

I purchased and sold stocks in major corporations on several stock exchanges around the world. I might purchase a stock for, say, $100 per share and then transfer it to one of our drug lords for $10 per share. If this transaction was later questioned, I would just say it must have been a numerical mistake. No wonder I couldn't make the books balance!

We setup several real estate holding companies with several hundred employees. We focused on first-time homebuyers with poor or no credit rating. We would slip the new buyer $5,000 or $10,000 to use as a down payment, usually just half of what we gave them. The other half was attributed to them for making some kind of repairs or whatever to the house they were purchasing.

Glenn and I were major stockholders in all the new companies. We assigned 75% or more over to our cartel bosses. We sold off some of our interests for money to hide or to start a new business.

The total assets of all the companies that we started, sold, invested in, or were acquired by other companies must exceed $70B. The cartel's worth must be more than $20B. Glenn's and my joint net worth is around $500M.

On pages 120 thru 152 is a list of political contributions that we or our companies made to U.S. senators and congressmen. Glenn may have also made some secret cash contributions to some of his Washington connections. I never personally met or had any direct interaction with government officials and politicians.

He made many trips to Washington, D.C. Several special stock purchases were made by a few members of our government. Glenn would brag to me that he had senator so-and-so in the bag. We worried about getting caught by Homeland Security. However, I believe Glenn has two or more special clients on their Oversight Committee.

In the last four years, the cartels seem to be at war with each other almost constantly. There've been many murders and assassinations Other investment firms have also been setup that are now in competition with us. We have been threatened and also aggressively cut out of several market areas. Our cartel investors are unhappy with our loss of business.

The Feds are now after Glenn…and I can't be far behind on their list. My name appears more often than his on all the documents for these various enterprises. My lifestyle now is work and more work. Glenn is more flamboyant though, so he's made himself a high-profile target—with either a likelihood of being prosecuted, or killed. He's having numerous affairs, so maybe some possessive woman will get him. Why would they come after me?

But if anything does happen to me, please look to Glenn first as he's likely to be the guilty person behind it. I love you, Lisa. Get Glenn and blow the whistle on the cartels.

Cassie Jones

Witnesses to my signature:

Susannah Wilson	Date *March 31, 2019*
George Myoki	Date *31 March 2019*
Steven Roadhouse	Date *March 31, 2019*
Sharon Benjamin	Date *3/31/2019*

We all finish reading about the same time and are unilaterally dumbstruck by the confession letter, glancing up at each other with eyebrows raised and mouths hanging open. This comprehensive confessional-especially accompanied by the voluminous documentation—certainly explains what we see in the ledger and the other documents.

Bill exclaims excitedly, "I wonder what's IN all of those safes of theirs scattered around the world?"

I reply, "If the cartels find out about those safes, they will soon be emptied. But how can we talk to Senator Throckmorton now if he's on the Homeland Security Oversight Committee? He may even be taking kickbacks. How can we find out? Even if he's not personally one of the bad ones, the moment he brings up this information, the cartels will be notified through those inside moles."

Percy then weighed in, "Let's play it by ear and only reveal to the senator that we think Glenn killed Cassie, your college friend. It's already known Glenn is under federal investigation. Cassie told you she had only worked on the tax return of one real estate holding company and was concerned there were irregularities. Several apparent illegals had been able to buy homes with virtually no appropriate identification. We will quiz the senator to see if he knows Glenn, OR if he knows that Glenn has made political contributions to members of his committee."

Bill then adds "That sounds like a good plan, Percy. If the senator seems to be clean, then we might let drop that Cassie hid papers away on some of Glenn's illegal activities. Since Glenn operated internationally, then it might be of interest to the Homeland Security Department. If we can find any of this evidence, who should we turn it over to?"

I then said, "I like that plan too. If we could get a Special Ops type unit to raid all these homes in the Caribbean, we could collect more evidence before the cartels get a heads-up. With all the hurricane relief happening, these raids might be carried out without bringing it to the wrong people's attention. Maybe we should conduct these ourselves?"

Karen then jumps in, "Gee and I often planned these kinds of adventures. We know how to find hidden safes. We've done it for fun at several of our rich friend's homes. They're so obvious if you just know what you're looking for."

CHAPTER 17   Contagion

After yesterday's astonishing developments, I awake with a start accompanied by an immediate feeling of dread. The sun is shining brightly though, and it appears it'll be a nice day weather-wise. There are no lurking hulks outside my window, so what can be bothering me? It seems every time I awake with a start, it turns out to be a premonition of some sort that something bad is about to happen. Bill and I join Hollie and Percy for coffee and a quick breakfast.

Just as we begin eating, Percy's phone and my own suddenly ring simultaneously, breaking the sleepy morning quiet. Percy learns the two CDC workers who have been assigned to our tent city have stopped a bus of hurricane refugees at the gate. Several of them are sick. They must be confined immediately along with anyone who they have come into contact with.

My ringing phone turns out to be a call from Senator Throckmorton who tells me he must delay his trip for a week until we learn if the busload of refugees at our gate has the Zika virus. I asked him how he knows about this development when we are just this minute finding out about it. It seems the CDC called him when they learned of the situation and determined the bus's destination, e.g. to nearby property that he owns.

Percy then says, "I forgot to tell you, the few days you were gone, the CDC converted our empty warehouse, Number Four, into an isolated medical facility in which to quarantine sick refugees until they're cleared of possible contagion. Wait until you see it! It's split into two sections with multiple compartments: one area for the sick and one for individuals who've only been exposed but don't yet have any symptoms. A National Guard unit has been deployed to surround and guard the facility 24 hours per day."

Upon its arrival the two CDC medical staff members direct the bus to Warehouse Number Four. They then don medical suits and separate everyone into two groups inside the warehouse. Our Security Force stands by with loaded guns until the National Guard arrives later in the day—ensuring no one objects or refuses to enter the facility as required by federal safety protocols.

An hour later, we get a phone call from the CDC in Atlanta. "Can you provide another warehouse for a medical isolation hospital?" Percy replies, "We have a larger warehouse, Number Three, but it's partly filled with tobacco leaves which are in the process of drying."

The caller then asks, "Well, can you empty the warehouse? We'll even pay for the tobacco, if you have to dump it." Percy indicates they'll go ahead and empty the warehouse as requested.

"We have a larger isolation unit on the way. It should arrive there by tonight. We're also sending 20 medical personnel to man the units. Make sure any new arrivals from southern Louisiana are immediately screened and settled into a separate area in your tent city. Have your Security Force keep them separated from the rest of the camp until our medical staff has cleared them."

Percy immediately calls for tent city's city council to meet to discuss the situation and the individuals needed all scurry to comply. When it's held later that day, all of us attend the meeting as well. Percy also quickly arranges the hiring of 20 people to empty the warehouse and take the tobacco to Warehouses Number One and Two. This staff will also cleanup the warehouse and re-assemble it when installing the CDC unit upon its arrival later tonight.

Some members of the city council and others are worried about new refugees who may soon show up at our tent city. The council votes to setup additional tents and facilities in an adjoining 100-acre field. Security guards will patrol the separation strip sandwiched between the two areas 'round the clock until the CDC releases people to join the general population of refugees being housed there. Hollie says, "I think this seems a little draconian, but maybe it's necessary. I sure hope this latest emergency situation gets resolved soon."

By six p.m. the warehouse is ready for the CDC unit, which finally arrives about nine o'clock. The workers have dinner and a little rest, but then they re-gather to work on setting up the facility. By two a.m., four large specially-constructed house trailers arrive for the medical staff. The following morning, the medical staff assembles, having expeditiously arrived from various points around the country.

The next few days are busy ones, with many new refugees arriving as was projected. Over three-quarters of the original busload have now come down with the virus, including the poor bus driver himself.

Many of these new arrivals are fleeing the virus itself, as the media have informed the nation of this growing health concern, and of course the news spreads quickly globally as well. The newly separated part of our tent city is rapidly filling up. We contemplate having to open up another isolated section of our Taft Tent City. However, the numbers of sick in southern Louisiana have not increased, and therefore we're not receiving many more sick people.

The Mayflower Tent City has not received any sick individuals as most of their refugees are from the Houston area which has not been hit with the virus (yet).

Senator Throckmorton's office calls and the staffer informs us he will be at the Mayflower Addition on Thursday and asks if we can we meet him there.

CHAPTER 18   Senator Throckmorton weighs in

The week goes by quickly in attending to this latest round of arrangements, and it is now time for Bill to fly Percy and I to meet Senator Throckmorton at Mayflower as scheduled. The senator has arrived alone, possibly in not wanting to place his wife in danger from the Zika virus, but perhaps because he senses our meeting has an additional serious component which needs to be discussed.

Upon our arrival, he greets us warmly, "Y'all have really taken hold of this contagion problem. I appreciate it. Hell, the country appreciates it. I'm looking forward to hearing about all the things you've gotten done at Taft Plantation since we last saw each other. The press has only had limited access to you of course—as requested by Homeland Security. We don't want to cause a panic. But now let's get down to business, what was it you wanted Homeland Security to know about?

I cautiously begin, "One of my Vassar college alumni friends was killed a few months ago at a reunion we were having in the Catskills, Senator. Her husband is Glenn Jordan. By any chance, do you know him?"

Senator Throckmorton replies, "Well, yes I was introduced to him maybe five years ago. I know he's under federal investigation for fraud, and alleged illegal campaign contributions…including possibly to my fellow members on the Homeland Security Oversight Committee. I personally have never had a long conversation with him. However, two of our members that I know of have received campaign funds through him. And one has also received a large loan for the purchase of a vacation home in the Virgin Islands."

"Well, we suspect Glenn killed or had Cassie killed in order to protect himself, in case of prosecution. Cassie was heavily involved in Glenn's businesses and was often listed on various legal documents as the front person for a variety of his enterprises. Did you ever meet her perchance?"

"No, she wasn't ever with Glenn, but I often saw him around town with several different women. I recall my Senate friends remarking more than once that he's a real player."

I turn to Percy and Bill, "Do you think we should continue with this discussion with the senator, or should we maybe go to the FBI at this point?"

The senator replies, "I understand your hesitancy since we all know the Homeland Security Oversight Committee appears to be compromised in this situation. I don't know how deeply these people are involved, but to my knowledge no one's mentioned Glenn's name in recent months. Give me a brief outline of what you think you know. And do you have actual proof of any wrongdoing that will hold up in a court?"

Bill says, "I concur, let's go ahead and give him a brief overview. Do you agree, Percy?"

"Yes, let's go ahead and lay it out for the senator. We definitely need help with this matter."

At this juncture, I take over the reins, "Ok, here's the story in brief. Glenn handled what turned out to be billions of dollars of drug cartel money. His job was to launder it and do so by investing those monies. We're talking about companies that may be worth $70B, folks. Even if the cartels have no control of these companies, just think what would happen to the economy if they simply sold their mega stock positions!"

The senator is obviously flabbergasted by this revelation. "I can't believe that the operation's THAT big. Why, the resulting effects could stretch into all parts of the government."

"My friend, Jackie, hired a private detective to try to determine the identity of Cassie's murderer. She and her detective report they are under constant surveillance themselves now, and we believe this is being done by the cartels. Since we were recently seen with her, we think there's a good chance we're probably being watched too at this point. One of these perps also pulled a gun on Jackie attempting to get some papers she had. Her detective, Charlie, and I jumped this thug and beat the shit out of him. We have all his i.d., and I hope I succeeded in convincing him to retire, or die. I'll bet he left the country straightaway without reporting to the other two who were watching us. They probably would have killed him for his screw-up."

Senator Throckmorton then drops his chin onto his chest and lowers his voice, saying, "They certainly seem serious. With that kind of money involved, they'll surely want to eliminate anyone in their path. Likely permanently."

"One thing we recently learned, Senator, is that Glenn has secret safes at his home in Kansas City as well as in each of his four homes in the Caribbean. We now have the combination of those safes and their locations, as long as they haven't been changed, that is. We need this data of his to add to our case."

"You are certainly correct. We need to seize the contents from all of those safes in one quick operation. I have access to those coordinating Special Ops. They can arrange a hit that's synced to occur at the same time at all locations. Get your friend Jackie and her detective, Percy, Bill and you, Gee, will each hit one of the safes, with no one else needing to be privy to the combinations themselves. I will have Glenn arrested just before you hit his home. Four helicopters in the Caribbean will be there helping with delivery of supplies or damage assessment. We will fly you to Guantanamo where you'll be picked up by helicopters. The data, money, and whatever else from the safes will be left in your hands to hide and hold in safekeeping. Make three copies of everything. When you have a complete copy of everything you've discovered and obtained, I will then arrange for all of us to then meet with the Attorney General and the Head of the FBI. I will be involved, but we will not inform the Homeland Security Committee. I think you should leave from the base at Leavenworth, Kansas on Friday evening and plan to hit them Saturday evening just before sunset."

We return to the Taft Plantation and prepare for this next adventure. Bill calls Jackie, "Shake your tail girl, we need to make wild passionate love. Call me in two hours—no, I can't wait. I'm craving you."

A half an hour later, Jackie calls from a secure location at a pay phone. "Wow! That was a nice call I received from Bill. I didn't know he was hot for me."

I reply, "We all are hot for you, and a plan has been formed. That message was to give you a heads-up to call us on a secure line. And, good job, you picked up on that real fast. Meet us at Fort Leavenworth Friday afternoon. You need to get a move on. Don't leave with a big suitcase or anything that would make it obvious you're leaving town though. Drive part way there and then rent a car for the rest of the trip. I will clue you in on 'the operation' when we meet. This has got to be quick and secret. Show your ID at the north gate to the base and there you will be directed to us."

Percy says, "We will leave tomorrow afternoon and be there in plenty of time. I'm going to check in with the Tent City Council and see what they need."

I then respond, "Ok, and I'm going down to the children's playground and tell them a spooky bedtime story. You can stay here and just relax if you wish, Bill. How does that sound?"

The sun is setting as I walk to the children's playground, collecting curious little ones on my way. We start interacting to break the ice a bit and I offer to tell them some stories about spooks and goblins. As I get into it, using different voices for the characters and hamming it up, they alternate between laughter and shudders. By now it's dark, and I realize I forgot to bring a flashlight, so I stumble a bit in making my way back along the unlit trail back toward the mansion.

Suddenly a man steps from behind a tree and puts a gun to my head. "Yes, there are real goblins, missy, and I'm one of 'em. Don't make a sound or you're dead! It's time we picked you up and find out what you've been so busy telling the senator. Believe me, you are snooping into things that'll get you killed."

I try to spin away from him, but he hits me in the head with the butt of the gun and I collapse to the ground. Thankfully my prince is secretly on-hand for my rescue. He forcefully hits my attacker in the head with an aluminum baseball bat he picked up at the playground. I crawl over to the man and grab his gun. I check him out quickly and am relieved to see he's not moving. I then check his pulse, but Bill hit him too hard… he's dead.

"Bill, you killed him!"

"Well, he was threatening you with death, wasn't he? I saw a panel van with no windows in the parking lot near the trail. A guy was smoking a cigarette in the driver's seat. We have got to capture him, or the word will be out on us."

We search the dead guy, retrieving his wallet and I now have his gun. We find another gun strapped to his right leg. "Bill, take this other gun of his and that'll give us two guns to use against the guy in the van. We should be able to get the jump on him. I'll walk with my hands behind my back like he had me restrained with the ties we found on his body. Here, wear his cap and we will just walk up to the van like you're him and have me in custody."

We pull the body off the trail and into some bushes to conceal him for now and then proceed toward the van. The perp is standing in the shadows, not inside the van. "Drop your gun, Bill. You don't fool me. I know you aren't Joe."

Gad, he's onto us!

Bill shakes his head and his shoulders slump slightly, "Alright I'll just ease the gun down onto the ground," leaning forward slowly and extending the gun as he speaks. The perp is watching him rather than me at this point. But I can see he is very nervous and, next thing I know, his gun goes off right at Bill. The bullet hits the ground…right between Bill's legs.

I think aloud, "Oh, my god! Bill's been shot." I whip the dead man's gun around from behind my back and shoot the second perp point blank in the chest. He dies instantly, dropping with a thud to the ground. Both guns have silencers so thankfully not one sound of gunshots has been heard inside the camp.

Bill says, "Oh, crap, Gee...I'm alright. He missed me, but you sure didn't miss him. How'd you shoot so fast? I was just frozen when he popped out from behind the van. Let's put them both inside it. We don't need the publicity of two killings right now." We heave the second guy into the van, slamming the door securely, and then head back along the trail to retrieve the first one. Given the darkness, no one sees us drag him along en route to the vehicle. "Let's drive it back to the mansion and get Percy. We'll have to wipe our fingerprints inside the van so remember what you touch."

After we arrive, we fetch Percy and take him out to the van. "My god, you killed both of them! I wonder if there are more of them watching us? I think we'd better get out of here NOW...before either of these guys are missed."

We look at each other and nod in silent agreement, deciding to quickly pack up and drive the van, with the bodies, to the airport. Percy calls our Tent City Security force en route, assigning two women to stay with Hollie and watch for anyone else who might be watching the plantation. The women are both armed with small, discrete handguns. He tells them drug runners are trying to use our camp as a distribution point for moving drugs to other areas. "Stay alert. These people are dangerous," he warns them, just before we turn to depart.

The 10-mile ride to the airport is grim with the two bodies in close proximity to us in the back. We cover them with a sleeping bag of theirs. Bill says, "We need to check the airplane. They may have rigged it, so I don't want to short-shrift looking it over thoroughly before we take off. And probably it's at least bugged, but I keep equipment at our locker at the airport and can do a quick sweep."

We unload and park at the edge of the airport long-term parking lot, under some trees. Percy wipes down the van to remove our fingerprints. Using the equipment, he's just retrieved, Bill quickly finds a bug in the main cabin of our airplane. Descending the gangway, he motions to me, "Look," he whispers, "it's behind this seat." He then turns, steps briskly up the stairs, ducks inside, and lays a cushion in front of the bug. In the baggage compartment we find a transmitter hooked to the bug. A thin wire antenna is taped to the tail of the airplane.

Once back outside, our conversation resumes, "These people want to know what we're talking about and where we're going. I will file a flight plan to Atlanta, but we will violate it."

Percy then said, "Actually…let's not disconnect the bug as that'll alert them to the fact, we know about it. Instead, let's feed them some wrong information. I'll cut the bug wire and stretch two wires into the passenger compartment. That way we can connect or disconnect the bug at will. We can also touch the wires together and form static or breaks in the connection. This'll make them think the device failed when we decide to disconnect it."

As Percy and I wait in the hanger, Bill continues checking the plane and finds most of the hydraulic fluid has been drained from the rudder and landing gear, which would be disastrous upon landing. He refills the hydraulic fluid and checks for any nefarious leaks. He further changes out fuel filters and checks every bolt for proper connection.

Percy gives him a quick pat on the shoulder, "Good job, Bill. I'll bet we got it all. Didn't the perps have a cell phone though? Should we check it or call in on it with a message?"

I pull out the cell phone I'd retrieved from the one I shot. "We can't take this with us as it might be traceable. Maybe we can leave them a message. I could hit redial and see what happens. Percy, tell them in a deep voice, "We got her." Then mumble and have it sound like the rest of the message breaks up. Here, make the call next to this generator so it'll be poor sound quality."

Percy hits redial as instructed and a voice answers, "It's late—did you get her?"

Percy answers, "Yes, we got her." He mumbles and disconnects the conversation. "What shall we do with the phone?"

Bill answers, "I know….there's a small disaster supplies truck going at daybreak to Florida. Let's put the phone in with those supplies. That should confuse them."

By now, it's about 3 a.m. and we three board the plane in silence. We connect the bug to the transmitter. Percy says, "Bill, I am sorry to get you out so early in the morning, I need to pick up those generator parts from Atlanta as it'll be a hot day in Tent City, and we need that generator that's malfunctioned hooked up and running as soon as possible."

Bill replies, "I want to pick up some toys for the young kids too, so I'll take care of that while you're rounding up the parts."

We take off and disconnect the bug. An hour out, we change course and rapidly descend to 500' elevation. We reconnect the bug and Bill yells to Percy, "The plane's not running right. We must look for a near-by airport and land." Percy makes and breaks the bug connection for several minutes and finally disconnects it. "Maybe, they'll think we went down."

After this little charade, the plane climbs back to 3000' and we proceed toward Tulsa. Bill talks to the tower and says we have a mechanical and instrument problem and asks, "Where are we?" The landing is smooth, and we park in the small plane section of the airport. We instruct ground mechanics to check out everything on the plane and inform them we'll be back to pick it up in three days. We rent a car and proceed toward Leavenworth AFB.

Once at the military installation, we're directed to the contact we've been assigned in Special Ops. He informs us four of us will be flown with twelve Special Ops soldiers to Guantanamo. We will have four helicopters, each manned by a pilot and two soldiers, accompanied by one of our small team. As had been determined beforehand, the plan is for us to hit the four homes simultaneously and clean out the safes. I will go with four Ops soldiers to the Kansas City house. Glenn will be arrested and brought back to Leavenworth before the operations commence.

I remember something and mention to the others, "Cassie told me there are two women at the house who are relatives of two of Glenn's clients—no doubt cartel families. Cassie said they watched her all the time. We'd better pick them up too or they'll blow the whistle on us for sure."

At noon on Sunday, we are all in place and ready for action. At the location of each of the four homes in the Caribbean, each chopper lands and hands out some cases of water and food to a few locals who greet the arrivals with surprise and curiosity—seems better to create goodwill vs. suspicion. Four of our group, Jackie, Charlie, Percy and Bill, quickly enter Glenn's houses at those three locales and head for the basement of each. Damage from the hurricanes was minimal as the structures were well-constructed. Each of the safes are quickly found and the one-size-fits-all combination has worked on all. Money and papers were scooped into duffle bags and each crew returned by chopper to Guantanamo without incident.

The Kansas City home posed more of a problem. For weeks, Glenn had been under surveillance by various cameras as well as a couple of bugs in his primary home. Just before our planned raid, one of the female housekeepers told Glenn they were out of eggs and milk and asked him to pick more up at a local convenience store. Two of our Ops guys were watching Glenn and contemplated arresting him when he arrived at the store. I told them to wait and said we would instead get him at the house as there'd be less chance of observation.

At 12:30 p.m., Glenn returns from his errand and we zip in right behind him through the electronic gate. The Ops guys grab him, throw him to the ground and handcuff him. One of the women Cassie had mentioned pulls a knife and the other grabs her cell phone. The Ops soldiers encircle her and tell her to drop her weapon. I tackle the other one as she begins punching in numbers on her phone. "Oh NO you don't, sister. We have a special place for you. And you can kiss your freedom goodbye."

Something about her seems familiar. I ask her, "Do I know you? What's your name?"

She replies, "I am just a housemaid. On this gig my name is Rosa. I have done nothing wrong that you can arrest me for. I have no connection to the drug business, but I suspect that Glenn may have a connection. I can't testify to more than that as I was never introduced to any of his houseguests. The family lawyer will have me out of here by morning."

"But somehow, you seem familiar to me. I wonder why?"

Rosa replies, "You are mistaken. You gringos think we all look alike. We are the invisible people that do the work of the nation. You have a great slogan 'Make America Great Again' but the U.S. is in decline, and soon you will be in the 'dustpan of history' like the Roman Empire. You gringos don't like to work and when you or your government does anything it is incompetent."

I reply, "You don't sound like an uneducated Latina. Are you a citizen?"

"I was born here and attended college at UC Berkeley on a scholarship. I graduated fourth in my class."

"Why are you working as a housemaid?"

"Maybe it is just easier. I am waiting for all of you to become zoned out on legalized marijuana and then we will take over. The only way that you can stop the drug cartels is to give up using drugs. Somehow I do not think that it will happen in your society."

I retort, "You can reflect on all of that in your prison cell, Rosa, or whatever your real name is. And I very much doubt you will be released in the morning. I do think that there is enough evidence to put you in prison. Cuff them and take them away!"

Rosa mumbles softly to me, "You have no clue. Cassie is dead and maybe I will take care of you next!"

I laugh, "From your prison cell? Ha, I'd like to see you try! You will be a guest there for a lon-n-g time. But what do *you* know about Cassie's murder anyway? Maybe we can pin that one on you!"

I then make my way through the living room and head downstairs to the basement, relieved the combination works on the safe I readily find there. Inside, there's lots of money, but no papers. A trash burner is just outside the basement door in the yard. It appears from the remnants inside that Glenn has been busily destroying documents, given the charred remains. "Let me talk to Glenn outside, away from these women."

The soldiers hoist him by each arm and muscle him outside by the pool, swiftly placing ties on his feet. I say to him, "Glenn, you are going away for a long time, pal. Cassie left us all the evidence of your activities for the past 18 years. Obviously, the government wants you, and I want you for Cassie's murder, but we all want to shut down the cartels. If you have any papers around here or will turn evidence against the cartels, possibly your sentence can be reduced."

Glenn is visibly shaken but, looking up, quickly replies, "I burned the papers with the help of those women. However, I do have a flash drive hidden away which contains lots of damning evidence. Listen, I need to disappear to I'm not quite sure where. These people I've been working for will kill me when they find me. Maybe I could get a new face? They will be out to get me, even if I'm found innocent in court. But you need to know I *did not* kill Cassie. I couldn't have—I loved her. I think maybe Kathleen killed her though…she and I were having a pretty hot affair."

"Really, Kathleen? We never found any evidence indicating you even knew her."

"Yeah, I've actually known her for quite a long time. I used her to launder my money into legit investments. I had hoped to retire someday from the cartels…and just disappear with all that loot."

At this I can't resist saying with a smirk in my voice, "Welp, doesn't look like that'll be happening anytime soon now."

"The flash drive is in on the fireplace mantle in the living room. It's hidden in the urn with my father's ashes. Please be respectful of his remains though, will you?"

I had secretly recorded this exchange on my cell phone without Glenn knowing it. I told the crew to take the prisoners to the cars. I went to the living room and found the urn. Opening it, I took a letter opener and gently probed the ashes, trying not to breathe while I mucked around in what little was left of a dead human, and feeling intensely disgusted this was Glenn's chosen hiding process. A small plastic bag surfaced with a flash drive inside it. Opening the baggie and retrieving it, I carefully tucked it inside my bra and went back outside, joining the group in the cars.

Given there's such a staggering amount of money involved and so many players, I now find myself feeling suspicious of everyone. Senator Throckmorton appears alright and he got this Special Ops team together—but can I be sure all these people are actually "the good guys"? The senator seemed to remember Glenn perhaps a bit too readily—especially if he'd never even had a sit-down conversation with the man. Did he also admit too quickly (and too freely) that he thought those other senators on the committee had possibly illegal or at least dicey ties to Glenn?

So…where do we go from here with all this information? Will we be released from Fort Leavenworth, or imprisoned like the three we just picked up? When the group returns, I guess we'll find out what the score is. I wonder what the others found, or if all the safes had been cleaned out by the cartels before our teams got there? I'm sure Glenn will have his passport confiscated first thing while awaiting further interrogation. I wonder to myself if that's legal since he's yet to be charged with anything.

CHAPTER 19   An unveiling

I arrive back at the base before the rest of our group returns. We are placed in a special set of quarters containing eight bedrooms, a kitchen, conference room, and, as I look around, I see there are also computers and copy machines at our disposal here. Along one wall in the conference room is a bank of lockers with combination locks that can be individually set by whoever uses them. I think this is just what we need to deal with this cache of data, but I'm also immediately curious what other operations may have gone on here in the past.

I have brought my own laptop with me and am keeping notes of what we'd collected thus far. My suspicious mind wondered if the base has this area and these computers rigged in order to keep tabs on us and have access to the progress we've made on this matter. I have no papers to copy as Glenn had burned them all at his location. I counted the money from the safe, which totaled nearly $650,000, mostly in $100 bills and some $20 bills—perhaps from ATM machines. None of the bills appeared to have sequential numbers during my rapid perusal. What are we going to do with these mounds of cash?

The group arrived the next afternoon with six duffle bags in tow. We are all happy and mostly relieved to see each other and hugged and kissed our hellos. Jackie pronounces, "The operation was smooth and rapid. The locals thought we were heroes, surprising them with what turned out to be needed supplies. The safes were all intact, and just look at all these duffle bags of stuff we seized!"

Shortly thereafter, their contents and personal gear are taken back with us to our quarters. We put each location's safe's contents in a different locker, with each of us picking our own combination.

We peer inside the refrigerator and find plates of food are on hand for us and discover the oven is currently heating two large pans whose contents are now bubbling. We open a bottle of Zinfandel to have with the piping hot beef stew. As we start to settle around a table, grabbing silverware and plates, I pass a note around to the group which says, "I suspect this area is bugged and likely has hidden cameras. Let's keep our comments about the materials we retrieved and copied very general in nature. Don't mention other people's names, or reference any of our past activities. I am very paranoid about this whole venture." The others each look up from the note after reading and passing it along to the next one, and everyone nods at one another in silent agreement.

After dinner accompanied by wine and our effort at generic conversation, I open the door and ask our guard if he will connect with our Special Op contact so we can have a quick meeting. He leaves to carry my message and another guard instantly appears to replace him. "Yes, my friends, we are being guarded. They have Glenn and his two cartel women servants in custody someplace else on the base—at least they were delivered here."

A knock on the door is heard, "Hello, I am your contact, Captain Blalock. I am in direct communication with the senator (note he did not mention his name). He informs us that the mission went well and that all of you have arrived here safely. Is there anything else you need?"

"Yes, we need a money-counting machine and a way to bundle this cash in different identifiable wrappers, as this is evidence and will be important at future trials."

"I can get you a counting machine from the bank and will see about different wrappers. How's the food?"

Percy replies, "Actually, the food is great, thanks. But how long do you think we will be here, Captain?"

"The senator will be here in two days and is bringing two additional people with him. As I understand it, everything will be worked out at that meeting. Until then, the time is yours to copy and assemble your data, whatever that may be. Mind you, I have not been made aware of what you are doing precisely. This unit has been swept for electronic surveillance devices and I can assure you none are present."

After this pronouncement, he turns to leave us, closing the door behind him. "I don't know," I say to the others, dropping my voice to a whisper, "I'm still feeling paranoid, maybe because he specifically claimed there were no bugs in here. Still, let's be careful in what we say. If you find something, call us over to read it directly vs. reading whatever aloud, ok? We should go through the data recovered from one house at a time. I have already been through Glenn's house. But he burned all the important papers, so we just have money. I hope you two came back with better pickings."

We selected one of the houses, and begin by labeling it House A. I put its address in my laptop, but record it no place else. We then copy, scan, and record the data on a flash drive labeled House A after which I make three copies of the flash drive. In two hours, we have finished this part of our task, except for counting the money, which will happen once the counting machine arrives.

At this point we all agree we're pretty much pooped and ready for bed, Bill and I snuggle down—two murderers entwined together in a fitful sleep. I can't believe both Bill and I had to kill two cartel thugs. My restless mind then wanders to the startling and unsettling fact I've now actually killed two people. How can I live with that? ? How is it that I—Gee—have taken *two* lives? After all, Karen's the one who's the crack-shot detective. And how will this whole mess play out? Will the Boston D.A. ever hear about it? That would cinch my fate in his court!

I awake with a start. What's that? *Gunfire?!* No, someone's knocking at our door and I see as I glance at the clock on the wall it's only 5:45 a.m. I forgot these Army types get up at 5:00 in the morning. As Bill opens the door and stands back, we see it's Captain Blalock accompanied by two aides, one holding the counting machine and the other a money-wrapping machine. How did he get them from the bank so bloody early? Bankers aren't even up yet. It seems we're certainly high on their priority list here.

After they deposit the units, the two uniformed men turn to leave without a further word, the Captain tapping his head and giving a brief nod on his way out the door. Recovering from my state of sudden alarm, I wander into the kitchen, looking around, and soon manage to get a pot of coffee going. As the others awake, everyone takes turns showering, and we're soon dressed and have congregated around the table. I always just have a quick easy breakfast, but looking at the supply of provisions available I see we could enjoy quite a feast this morning. By 8:00 a.m. we're well fed and ready for the day's work ahead. Two of us will deal with the task of counting and wrapping the money. The other three will begin inventorying the papers retrieved from House B.

By seven p.m., we've finished copying all the data from all four Caribbean houses. The money has all been counted and wrapped. Our orderly has arrived with an evening meal of swordfish, asparagus, salad, and dessert. There are two bottles of Navarro Chardonnay to go with the meal. We plunge in as we've worked hard that day and need the break. At 7:45, Captain Blalock arrives. "I came by for coffee and dessert...if you'll have me?"

"Of course, we will, come on in," I say, standing aside after opening the door.

He states, "At 1500 hours tomorrow, the senator and his party will arrive. They will want a brief rundown of what you've found and what you suspect it means. Get a good night's sleep. You will have plenty of time tomorrow to get your story together before they arrive."

The next day, we're up at 7:00 a.m., and thankfully no bad dreams occurred during the night. Too tired, I guess. We begin to summarize what we've found. There is the money of course, which totals $6,753,000, all of which looks to be legitimate cash. There are also stock certificates made out to various cartel members, to Glenn, and some to Cassie. These have an estimated worth of another $6M on the current market. Apparently, Glenn had not yet delivered these stocks to the cartel owners. There were also numerous documents containing a variety of information as well as names, addresses, and phone numbers of contacts located throughout Central and South America. There were lists of bank account numbers, as well as money transfers to banks in numerous countries globally. (Remember Cassie's ledger had amounts and names of many of these transfers. We agree to keep Cassie's information secret until we know what's going to happen next. That's our bargaining ticket, should we need one.)

Each house also had a guest list logging times and dates and who they met at the property. Several U.S. politicians, including two on the Homeland Security Committee, show up more than once on these guest lists. However, Senator Throckmorton is not on the list. Maybe he is a good guy after all.

We will soon find out.

After a somewhat relaxing morning mostly spent just tidying up and collating our multi-property haul, we have a late lunch and await our meeting. Three o'clock approaches and a knock is heard at our door. It's Senator Throckmorton accompanied by the head of Homeland Security, the U.S. Attorney General, and the head of the FBI. Wow! This matter is obviously being taken very seriously indeed!

In preparation for the handoff of our findings we've compiled an outline and I hand them each a copy. Seven duffle bags line the center of the conference table, with original data in the bag and the piles of money and securities placed on top, all neatly stacked.

I begin, "Gentlemen, this is just the tip of the proverbial iceberg. The mega investments by these drug cartels are intertwined inside many of our country's major corporations. If they sold out their stock interests en masse, they could wipe out the stock market in one day's transactions. If you look at the names of politicians they have contributed large sums to, they may even control our government—at least they can potentially bend it in the direction they choose on certain policies. The data we recovered from these four houses in the Caribbean have enough information to secure many arrests and will surely provide substantive fuel for several congressional investigations. On top of this, we have ledgers documenting 18 years of Glenn Jordan's operations including names, dates, and amounts—as well as microfilm proof of the financial and money-laundering transactions themselves.

We have been watched, followed, and threatened. We have had three attempts on our lives. We have returned fire with fire. These results now need to be cleaned up so we're handing off all of this into your capable hands. Speaking for myself and my small team here, we want out of this and need to return to our normal lives. What else do you want from us at this point?"

Upon being greeted with this summary, disbelief appears to collectively reign based on the countenance of the faces of the newly-arrived government leaders.

"How could this happen? You say for 18 years? And you have proof of such widespread illegal activities?

"Senator, how could this Glenn guy get to so many politicians in Washington? Well, how did Bernie Madoff do it for so long? Although I'm sure you're privy to a host of other such large-scale networks; but speaking personally, I guess we're all just a bit too naïve, so this has been a pretty startling revelation to us, you can be sure."

"How do we proceed? We can't arrest several hundred people-especially politicians—all at once. It'll endanger government stability. Remember…this all started three or four administrations ago."

Senator Throckmorton then added, "I have been thinking about this since Gee brought the matter to my attention. No doubt, this is a huge discovery and will produce many shockwaves inside our government, society, and business arenas—not just in the U.S., but around the world. Maybe, we prosecute this Glenn guy for attempted bribery, convict him with little fanfare and salt him away in an obscure prison—OR maybe he just has an accident and is killed. This news then gets out to all his political friends that he's been paid off. We quietly convince them to resign, not run again for political office, and impress upon them their need to make sizable contributions of their ill-gained wealth to charities, or drug abuse programs, or whatever. One or two of the worst ones might want to commit suicide."

At this, the Attorney General jumps in, "I want to prosecute all of them and throw away the key on the worst offenders. These people are a threat to our democracy! I'm going to overlook that last remark of yours about getting rid of this Jordan character, Senator. I realize this is a very shocking and unsettling business we're learning of here.

The Head of Homeland Security then says, "I want to go after all the drug lords and their investments in our companies and businesses. We could hit them once or one area at a time. These modern day "money changers" are a blight on the poor for the most part. New sweeping laws could also straighten these practices out. If any of the politicians on the take oppose the legislation, we could talk to them about the evidence we have on them. They might become avid supporters of a new bill after such a chat."

The Head of the FBI exclaims, "While we've made strong headway on other crime syndicates, we obviously have missed a lot in the last twenty years or so too though. This new cache of evidence you've secured will require much deeper investigation in order to weed out the bad pennies from solid career folks. We need to be strategic in containing the fallout, both in the government and corporate sectors, including the potentially negative impact on morale so we don't become ineffective in our future investigations."

Senator Throckmorton then jumps back into the discussion, "I propose, Gee, that you give these three gentlemen copies of this data you and your team have recovered. The four of us will constitute an ongoing committee and plot channels of operation to shut down the cartels and their influence on our government and country. For the time being, we will keep the money here in the vault at the base. We can later draw on it to pay undercover agents and clandestine operations against the drug cartels. Your group will take the originals of the data and hide it around the country at banks or secure safe places. During certain prosecutions, we will need the originals of certain data for proof in the court cases. Your names and your involvement in securing this trove of information will go no further than this room and, in fact, I have only used your first names in this meeting, although your identifications were noted when you first arrived at the base gate. At this point though, Captain Blalock will make your visit here disappear from the official record."

We thank the group of four, shake hands, and give them four flash drives each. Captain Blalock is called in to gather up the six bags of money. He provides us with four briefcases into which we distribute the original paperwork. After the group disbands, the government officials are flown back to Washington. Jackie and Charley depart for a flight back to Chicago with their two briefcases. They will hide them in safety deposit boxes under the names of some other family members. We are flown to Tulsa to pick up the Lowell airplane. We leave straight from the airport and head to a bank where we put our two briefcases in safety deposit boxes in Tom Cochrane's name. (He keeps sneaking into my novel. I again tell him to stay out of our business and imply we may otherwise let his name slip to the drug cartel thugs.)

Captain Blalock agrees to send a cleanup crew to haul away the van with the two dead bodies, so that problem is eliminated. (I bet that pair are smelling really pungent by now.)

After our task at the bank, we take the taxi back to the airport, pick up our plane, and head back to the Taft Plantation and our allegedly "normal life." I can't help but wonder as we climb to its cruising altitude if the senator will follow through and get rid of several of the politicians we uncovered. And was he actually serious about them "committing suicide"?

CHAPTER 20   Perps nabbed

We arrive back at Taft Plantation and the bustle of dealing with a few thousand refugees seems like regular business now. At this stage, we've now become a distribution point for disaster relief supplies. Trucks arrive and leave daily. Many of our refugees living in Tent City are very involved in the distribution of supplies to their hometown areas in Louisiana and also in Florida, as well as a few to towns in Texas. Some of these folks are travelling back to these destinations with the supplies and returning to their damaged homes to begin the restoration process, although some places were so badly destroyed there's literally nothing to salvage. So, these folks are now walking away from mortgages and property where they had, in some cases, spent a lifetime. How the government, the mortgage companies, and the insurance companies will resolve these horrendous losses is yet to be determined. Will these poor people ever have good credit again? How can they build or buy replacement homes in the future? I suppose it will take Congress to come up with a solution, if they can.

Our gang of five and Hollie are somewhat paranoid regarding our own safety now in light of this involvement of ours in uncovering the degree of activity by this widespread band of drug cartels—including how these potentially extend inside the government itself. At this point, we have done as instructed and have placed all the original documents in our possession in safety deposit boxes in various locales, carefully using relatives with different surnames to place another layer of separation between ourselves and this critical data we seized.

Percy, Hollie, Bill, and I are having lunch by the pool a few days later.

Suddenly, I exclaim, "Egads, I have some new info I forgot I even had till just now. I talked with Glenn in private before he was taken to Fort Leavenworth. He gave me—no, he told me—of a flash drive he'd made. It was stashed in an urn of his father's ashes on the mantle of his living room. I retrieved it and put it in my bra. When I got to Leavenworth, I put the flash-drive in my toothbrush case, as it just slipped in. I guess it's still there!"

Percy replies, "Go get it right away, Gee, and we'll boot it up on my laptop."

I retrieve the flash drive and once the device loads, we retrieve Glenn's long confession of his activities. "This along with Cassie's confession now provides us with a complete picture of his activities in conjunction with the cartels. See all the references to various politicians? Their names seem to be garbled though. Do you think he used some sort of code for those? How can we unravel it?"

Hollie says, "Nobody has a name Senator Dqoyj. What do you suppose it stands for?" I think for a minute and then answer, "Remember, Cassie said Glenn could not remember more than one combination and that is why we were able to get into all his safes so easily? There has to be a simple answer to this question of an I.D. code for the politicians or Glenn would have had trouble even writing it. Let's take down three or four of the names and all work on deciphering it."

At breakfast, the next morning Bill reports with excitement, "Hey, I've done it, gang, I've cracked the code. In fact, I beat your hotshot Karen in figuring it out. Turns out it's pretty simple. Take Dqoyj and back up on your keyboard one letter. The only problem is the 'q' which is at the left end of the keyboard. Just roll it back to the end of the bottom row and it becomes an 'm.' That senator is named Smith." We try it out on several other names, and several are revealed, but many are not.

Percy then says, "Hmmm…Glenn must have changed the code for some reason at one point. What could that reason be? So, what's the similarity of the five names we uncovered?"

Hollie responds, "And where are these five politicians located? Are they not all from the east coast? What happens if we move the letters in the opposite direction?"

We try it and discover several more names, but there are still many unrecognizable names. The ones we have just discovered are from the West Coast.

Bill then says "Ok, let's try moving the letters up or down and we may find politicians from the north and south." We work on it and soon all the names become readable.

"Maybe Glenn was cleverer than we thought. He certainly knew how to give money to politicians and get something on them. I wonder how long it will take the FBI to break his code? They have whole floors of codebreakers with sophisticated computer programs. When we give them this flash drive, let's tell them we think we have the code, but we don't want to give them bad information. It took us a day to figure it out. What's your bet for the FBI?"

A few days later, Senator Throckmorton calls and updates us with progress on the operation. He reports Glenn has already been tried in a Wyoming court for attempted bribery and given 10 years in a Wyoming prison. He tells us VP Cheney was previously apprised of the magnitude of Glenn's crimes and his influence in Congress, which began during the Bush-Cheney years in office. Cheney kept the press in the dark on the matter and had only a minor note added in the Law Record which indicated the trial and sentence. Which prison Glenn was put in was kept a secret along with his real name. The lightning quick and virtually secret trial had been purposely arranged to keep Glenn safe as he might need to be a witness in future trials of drug cartel leaders.

As Operation Clean Sweep got underway, one of its corruption-tinged senators retired, citing poor health. Two other senators have indicated they too are retiring and will not run for re-election. And another has been replaced in his role on the Homeland Security Oversight Committee. New money laundering laws are now in process to make usage of drug money more difficult.

Glenn's five homes have been confiscated and their co-owner cartel members arrested. The FBI is actively investigating their previous activities in the U.S.

As this update is being provided, I can't help but smile and say, "That's such good news, Senator. We also have some additional information we can turn over to the FBI, and this should clinch their cases. We have flash drives of both Glenn's and Cassie's confessions which outline in detail all their activities over the past nearly-13 years. We were holding this information to see how you and your governmental colleagues would perform. Sorry to have distrusted you, but given the nature of this highly sensitive and damning information, we felt we needed to protect ourselves in case you or others are in the pockets of the cartels."

"Well, I understand your concern and cautionary maneuvers, and I also thank you for your honesty, Gee. I suspected you had more information than that contained in the four safes. Can you go ahead and deliver this information to the FBI chief now? I will tell him you will meet him Friday at his office, what's good for you?"

I nod in agreement, "Noon on Friday will be fine, Senator."

Bill and I subsequently prepare for the trip to Washington. We include flash drives of the two confessions as well as the flash drives of Cassie's ledger. We call Ma Mah and tell her of our upcoming meeting with the top brass in Washington. It turns out she's also going to be in D.C. for a fundraiser for the hurricane victims on Friday evening and decides on the spot she wants me to address the gathering and report on our Taft Plantation Tent City. We agree to speak of our disaster relief camp, and our plans for the construction of model tent cities to be replicated in other regions following natural or man-made disasters. Maybe via this exposure we can attract other donors to help push our project forward.

On Friday morning, we leave very early in order to arrive in Washington in time for the noon meeting. Having disposed of the bugs, our plane is under 24-hour camera surveillance, so we're assured no one has been near it. Bill nevertheless checks it out thoroughly just in case. We land in Virginia at a small airport not far outside of D.C. A cab delivers us to the FBI headquarters just in time for our meeting.

With little waiting in the reception area upon our arrival, we are ushered into the Director's office and seated at a small conference table. Somewhat to our surprise, lunch is delivered for the three of us shortly after we've been greeted and seated.

I begin by saying, "Chief, you will find everything you need in these six flash drives. The conspiracy is even bigger than we first indicated. There are numerous politicians involved to varying degrees. The names of these individuals referenced in Glenn's confession are in code. We think we have broken the code, but we're certain the FBI will quickly penetrate it. Put flash drive five in your computer and project it onto the screen as it will display the beginning of Cassie's ledger, which actually fills three flash drives."

Once the ledger loads, he glances through it and says, "This appears to be very complete information indeed. How'd you get it?"

"We received it from Cassie's sister in Joplin. We believe she's being watched by the cartel—but maybe it's the government? We've hired two private detectives to guard her for the time being, however, we'd appreciate turning that task over to your agency. She has given us all the data she received from Cassie, so she's of no further threat to the cartels, but I'm also quite sure they don't know that."

"We can take care of that and even provide her with a new identity if she desires it. I don't know how to thank you two for all this information, not to mention all the risks you've taken. Do you two require further security?"

Bill shakes his head and responds, "We don't think so, but they have tried to kidnap or kill us three different times to date. We have a security system plus on-site security force at Taft Tent City, and they're watching the camp. Perhaps you could place a couple of agents in our security force? We have two retired FBI agents on our security force. They've been terrific but they need to return to their retirement activities. And I'm sure several criminals have come through the area already. Your agents might even recognize them. Our team is only focused on preventing incidents inside the camp itself, by and large."

"Yes, I definitely think we need to place some agents on your force. I had heard you already have a retired FBI agent there as he was one of the displaced refugees. I'll make the arrangements and will select ones with the proper Southern background and accents, so they'll blend in and not be noticed."

Two days later, a pair of FBI agents show up at our tent city, but convincingly put forward the story they were refugees from the storms who had been holed up in a flooded supermarket for several weeks before making their way to the camp. They volunteer for the Security Force and each indicate they have previous experience in law enforcement. They do not disclose their actual identities to others but do make themselves known to Percy and me. We have them review security procedures around the Taft Plantation; after their review, they report they think it's quite adequate. However, they do recommend we place an alarm in the Plantation's gatehouse for emergency situations to augment our normal contact via intercom. Additional cameras are also put in place three miles down the road at the turnoff to Highway 42.

A week later, the security cameras captured footage of two black vans turning off the highway and heading toward Taft Plantation. Security watch sent a signal to Security headquarters as well as to us on each of our cell phones. Percy wondered aloud upon receiving the notice, "So who do we think these guys are? They don't look like refugees to me. Probably some kind of government officials or committee members sent to check us out. But they should have given us a heads up. We better get ourselves together quickly and try to appear prepared."

Our volunteer gatekeeper stops the car at a checkpoint and asks the vehicle's occupants for identification and whom they wish to see. They claim to be CIA and have a warrant to search the mansion and grounds. The gatekeeper says, "I will have to call the house and inform them." Two agents in the lead vehicle quickly pull guns on her, apprising her she's under arrest. She hits the concealed alarm button below the desk and sirens begin to squeal. The two vans rev their engines and the first accelerates, bursting through the gate as they both speed toward the mansion, the second vehicle just a few feet behind the first and both are clearly flooring it.

Screeching to a halt with the second van skidding slightly, eight guys attired in black head-to-toe jump out of the vehicles and charge up the stately stairs toward the front door. Alarmed by the suddenness of the siren wailing, I meet them mid-porch and demand to know who they are. "We're CIA agents and we have a warrant to search the property." All of them have drawn weapons and these are pointed straight at me.

"I don't think the CIA has any jurisdiction here at Taft Plantation. On what grounds are you here?"

"The FBI has informed us you raided houses in three foreign nations. That gives us all the legal justification we need."

"No, it doesn't. This is American soil and we are U.S. citizens."

"No matter, we are coming inside and conducting the search as instructed."

At that moment, our two on-loan FBI agents accompanied by 20 members of the Security Force quickly descend upon the scene, surrounding the eight men. All their guns are drawn and pointed at the group. One of our agents then shouts, "I'm an FBI agent. We have control of this area, and here's my authorization. Drop your weapons or you will be shot immediately." He cocks his gun and rushes over to the CIA agent. "Drop them now or die."

The CIA agents drop their weapons as they're far outnumbered, outgunned, and now realize another federal agency is already involved in the operation. Their hands are placed behind their backs and each are handcuffed with zip ties, all their identifications are confiscated. As soon as he can see the intruders have been secured, Jeff, our FBI agent, calls his boss and relates the story. He's informed in response that the CIA will be immediately contacted by the head of the Bureau, and this operation, if it is real, will be explained.

A short while later, we get a call back from the FBI bureau chief. It seems the CIA had not yet been drawn into the investigation, although much of the information and activities of our operation involved foreign nationals. We then learned the FBI thought, rightly or wrongly, that there are cartel operators at work inside the CIA. So it had been determined by Senator Throckmorton and the FBI they wanted to take care of certain situations before the CIA and numerous foreign governments became involved.

The CIA was at Guantanamo and observed our special ops helicopters and the involvement of the four of us. Shortly thereafter we learned we were identified from photographs, especially Percy and Jackie, who each have a certain degree of profile with the news media. After fixing on Percy, they followed the trail to the Taft Plantation.

I meet with the eight prisoners saying, "Look guys, this is a big mistake on your part. We have already provided everything we know to the FBI, which is mostly speculation and a little data. You need to deal with the FBI directly on this matter. We only have these two agents here for our personal protection and to help potentially ferret out any criminals who may be posing as refugees in our Tent City. Please deal directly with that agency and leave us alone. We are strictly in the refugee rescue business here."

Just then, one of the prisoner's phones rings, I cut him loose so he can answer it. They are told to abandon the mission and return to base. "How can we? They've got us rounded up and in handcuffs, plus they don't have authorization to release us."

I take the phone from him, "Who's this? How do we know you're CIA and not with a drug cartel? I won't release anyone until the FBI bureau chief tells me to. We can take them all to the county jail in Bixby, and I think it'll be bad PR for you guys if a local newsperson gets a whiff of this."

A half an hour later, my cell rings and the FBI chief himself gives us the authority to release our prisoners. However, in doing so, we're told to keep their guns and I.D.s. The chief informs me their computers broke the code in 32 minutes of computer time. One name does appear on two different runs of the four codes. Do you know which name is correct?"

I laugh, "Four of us figured it out over a bottle of wine. After we broke the first code, we discovered the political names were all in the same area of the country. There are four codes: east, west, north, and south. The correct name and code are therefore governed by the section of the country that politician represents. I guess your computers did not make that leap. Glenn had a simple mind, so we knew going in that the code had to be simple as well."

We released the eight, gave them each a cup of coffee, and then sent them on their way after they'd sat and collected themselves for a bit. I then called the entire Security force as well as the gatekeeper, asking them to gather poolside where we open several bottles of wine and serve them some snacks. I thank them for their service and introduce the two FBI agents who are now part of our small force, and also apologize for keeping their identities secret from the group. Looking around as everyone helps themselves to the refreshments and are beginning to visibly relax, our people seem relieved and in a good mood as they chat animatedly with one another, especially as some lively music begins to play over the sound system. *(Doesn't the music always play at the end of a movie scene and slowly fade away? Why couldn't this tale be made into a movie? I'll bet Karen and Gee think it could. Life in a novel certainly can be exciting. So...what's next?)*

CHAPTER 21 Building tent cities

It's the morning after. I awake with a start…but today it's also a nice awakening. Bill is kissing my neck and clearly feeling amorous. "Gee-Karen, or whoever you are, you certainly were brave facing those eight gunmen last night. How'd you know they were CIA?"

"They didn't look like drug dealers, and none of them were Latino. They were playing macho, but I thought they'd have a hard time explaining one of us being killed."

Changing the subject, Bill whispered in my ear, "Listen, we don't have much on for today…do we have to get up this early?"

At noon, the phone rang and it was Ma Mah calling, "Gee, your speech in Washington was great and it's inspired some investors for your Tent City project. Can you meet us in Nashville with some sketches to review tomorrow at noon? I have a group of 10 investors who want to look at the project. They will want to visit both Mayflower and The Taft Plantation to see your two projects. Are you free?"

"Yes, we're free for such a meeting. Ok, Bill and I will be there, Percy will prepare for the visits here and at Mayflower. I must say, Ma Mah, you don't mess around, do you?"

"Not where my wonderful daughter's concerned. By the way, I also wanted you to know I spoke again with the Boston D.A., and I believe he's going to let the whole matter slide. What did you do to those bounty hunters?"

"I believe they have left the area and gone into another line of work."

"Did you really hog-tie them and leave a dead fish in their van?"

"Well, we might have had a little part in that—it was a single shrimp actually—but my Maine Sons of Liberty were the responsible actors. We must all go up to the cabin sometime soon, Ma Mah. Hey, do you remember Van?"

"Wasn't he the one you lost your virginity with?"

"Ma Mah, *how can you know that?* You weren't there!"

"I saw that look on your face the next morning and it took me back to my girlhood—I should say, womanhood."

"Mothers don't talk with their daughters like this. Some things are private."

"Hey squirt, you are 38-years-old. That's a liberated age, is it not?"

"I guess you were more aware of my goings-on than I thought at the time. Alrighty, I'll get busy on those renderings and will see you tomorrow with your investors. Love you!"

Early the next morning, Percy, Bill, and I fly to Nashville for the meeting with Ma Mah's monied individuals. The presentation itself goes well. Our plan calls for multiple add-ons to what is being done at many refugee camps. One significant difference in our camp plans are that the refugees themselves run their tent cities in a democratic way, electing their own leaders. Camps are scattered over the world in many different environments. Insulation is important for both heat and cold. Some areas require mosquito netting. We have plans for group and smaller kitchen units, and also for meeting and dining tents. Key features include water reclamation units to handle sewage and wastewater, portable well drilling rigs, desalinization plants, medical clinics, hospital bed units, and for isolation wards for dealing with infectious diseases as well as playgrounds, libraries, and school units.

Our plan is to standardize these features as units and construct them at Taft Plantation. We're now phasing out tobacco production and have closed the operation. The empty warehouses will be used for construction and assembling of the tent city units. The CDC plans to keep the small isolation unit in place here for the time being just to be on the safe side, but is deactivating the larger facility as the patients recover.

The investors like our plans and agree to fund the final designs and initial production of 20 tent cities. Between natural disasters and civil wars, relief organizations can easily fill up 20 tent cities. One of the investors is Japanese and asks if we can come to Japan and meet with Harry Honda who he indicates would like to support the project with money as well as various materials his factories there already produce.

Bill and I agree to make the trip the following week.

After the successful meeting, Percy and I have dinner with our mom. He remarks to her, "Ma Mah, you certainly move rapidly for an old gal. How did you get the 10 of them together? And so quickly too? Luckily one of them had a large airplane to bring you down here, so that obviously helped."

"Speaking of planes, I would like my nice plane with the red heart back please. You two have been using it a lot and Gee has also stolen my pilot, although I guess I won't be getting him back. I know you two need an airplane, so I've been looking at a new one for you and I've chosen an XB-248, if that meets with Bill's liking, that is."

"Wow! Ma Mah, that's one hot ride—plus it also has more range than we have now so we would be very happy with it. One thing though, let's ensure it has no logos or markings that easily identify us as there are too many people who may be after us."

"Well, I don't care for the sound of that disclosure, but otherwise that's good, I'm glad you approve of my choice., Bill Actually, the plane's already been ordered and will be available in three weeks, so it'll be here when you get back from Japan. And, listen, you two plan on having some fun while you're over there. Now we need to take two investors down to Taft to see your Tent City. I've hired a new pilot and he'll meet us at Taft and fly me and my plane back to Boston after we've seen what you're doing at the plantation. I want to meet Hollie and see her animal rescue facilities also. I've been hearing lots about her from Percy. In fact, he's sounding quite smitten – so I assume we have a little romance going on there too....yes?"

I mumble half under my breath, "Is there anything we can do without her immediately perceiving what's going on?"

The trip to Taft went well. Everyone liked our facilities. Ma Mah loved Hollie as well as her menagerie of animals. The new pilot arrived at the mansion a short while thereafter. Turns out he's a pilot who retired early from American Airlines, is highly personable, and Ma Mah clearly likes him. After some introductions and shaking of hands, Bill takes him to the plane and acquaints him with what he refers to as its "personality." He then cleans out all of our personal items, but makes sure Ma Mah's liquor cabinet contains her favorite drinks. He also restocks the refrigerator for the return trip. Bill supplies all the maintenance records to his replacement telling him, "If you have any questions or problems, just speak with George, he's the mechanic at the hangar where we keep the plane."

We are now busying ourselves making arrangements for the trip to Japan. I wish I had brought more of my clothes from Boston as what I have on-hand at Taft is pretty slim pickings. I call Pierre, my dressmaker, and have him rush three outfits to Atlanta as that's where we'll depart for our Japan trip. I ask Bill, "So how're we going to get to Atlanta from here? Ma Mah's taken the plane." Bill then makes a quick call and asks a pilot pal of his at the Bixby airport if he can fly us to our destination in Georgia. It's helpful indeed to have friends who own planes.

As Bill and I finish making preparations for the upcoming trip overseas, we decide to do as Ma Mah suggested and work in a little vacation thereafter. My clothes arrive in Atlanta and we also now have pictures as well as plans of our tent city project to take with us to Tokyo.

Our flight to the other side of the planet takes over fourteen hours and we try to get in as much sleep as we can en route to help with the time difference. Upon landing and retrieving our luggage, a black limousine picks us up at the airport *(aren't they always black? No, those used for weddings are white)* and we're then whisked off to Harry Honda's well-appointed estate. Upon being greeted by a butler at the door, we're escorted to our room and told to settle in, and that Mr. Honda will meet us at six p.m. for cocktails in his home conference room.

After enjoying a bit of time to relax in our sumptuous room, we retrace our steps inside the spacious abode, heading down the broad staircase and finding our way to the conference room, thankfully arriving on-time. After a greeting, we bow when meeting Mr. Honda who quickly puts us at ease by saying he has already warmed to our project and says he would like to supply much of the canvas from his canvas factory. He indicates he'll also give us a good price plus will donate generously to the project.

As Bill and I turn and smile at one another in response to this news, Mr. Honda then extends his hand saying, "Pardon me, but aren't you the woman who shot the Boston Symphony killer?" Surprised, I admit that I am.

"We had not thought that the news would have made it's way here to Japan."

"Well, it has as we follow American news regularly. If the press finds out you're here, they'll be all over you with questions, so I'll try to shield you from their onslaught. Instead of you being so visible, it'll probably be best if Bill and I give the presentation and answer their questions. You might just slip out and get in the limo and avoid them altogether. I'll arrange for one of my security guards to prevent them from talking to you. Is this alright with you?"

That sounds like a good plan to me. I definitely am not interested in doing any more talking about guns just now, especially as I'm aware the Japanese are not fans of everyday folks owning guns.

The press and TV are at the conference in sizable numbers. We three pose for pictures and Harry Honda leads the discussion in Japanese, and then in English. Bill adds to the presentation. I point to my throat and cough and head out the back. One reporter follows but a guard steps in front of him to halt him following as I make an exit into the limo.

TV and newspapers are full of the project that night and the next morning. Of course, even though I thought I had made only the most cursory of appearances, one diligent news outlet discovers my ties to the Boston Symphony massacre and soon a bevy of them are commenting extensively on the incident in what was supposed to be their tent city coverage. Upon seeing this aspect played up in both print and TV coverage, Bill shakes his head, , "Well, so much for sightseeing in Tokyo."

I reply, "No, I'll just be Karen on this trip. Too bad I bought those three new outfits though. It also just occurs to me, this news coverage might well be seen by members of the cartels too. Maybe we could dye my blond hair black and I'll make an effort to be a really slovenly-looking Karen. By the way, I need to go see my friend Joe Kuchimura at Special Operations soon."

I call Special Ops, ask for him, and am patched through to his cell phone. "Joe, this is Karen Hunt and I'm here in town and need to meet with you."

He replies, "I didn't know you were in Tokyo or I would have looked you up. Where are you?"

"We're staying at Harry Honda's mansion, but have just concluded our business with him."

"Are you with Gee Lowell? I saw the press coverage."

"Well, yes. I will confess to you, Joe, I'm actually Gee Lowell and Karen Hunt is another life I lead. I'll explain everything to you when we meet, ok?"

"Wow, that's a shocker, I'll be waiting to hear all about it! And, yes, I definitely want to see you. Don't come to the office though. Meet me at a quiet little invitation-only tea house that's just five blocks from our office. Can you be there at one p.m.? When you arrive, tell them you're there to see me."

As the time approaches, we proceed to the tea house with me dressed as Karen (having rushed quickly to a local store for some bland duds) and Bill is similarly outfitted in tourist drab. After supplying our I.D.s, we're admitted and ushered into a private room. Shortly after we're seated, tea is served and then Joe appears. (I'm struck by the oddity of so many Japanese here having American names and wonder why that is.)

I introduce the two men. He bows, and turns to Bill, saying, "I met Karen three years ago, when she was on the trail of a jewel thief. I think she called the case the "The Merry Christmas Jewel Heist.' She was successful in retrieving the highly prized gem, and in the following year, we rounded up fourteen jewel thieves all told—it was a very big deal here in Japan.

Turning to me, he continues, "We thank you so much for helping us break that case."

"You are far too generous. You did most of the work and I just tagged along."

"Tell me, what you have been up to? Or how I can help you? I'm not certain why you've asked to meet."

"Well, Joe, one of my college friends was killed at a reunion of ours not too long ago and poking into it has provided a trail to the drug cartels. As a result, we have been watched, threatened, and had three attempts on our lives thus far. I fear this publicity I just received will lead them to us while we're here visiting in Japan. Bill and I are going to vacation in the country north of Tokyo for a couple of weeks. It will be a low-key trip and we'll be dressed very casually, as we are here today. However, especially under the circumstances, I feel naked without a pistol in my purse. Can you get me one?"

"Well, you know how we are about guns in our society which is much different than yours. However, the criminals carry guns, so I must carry one also. I will loan you the gun I carry, and don't worry, I have other ones back at the office. It's a .38 with five bullets. Please try not to kill anyone while you're in country though. It would be a real mess here in Japan for both you and me. If by chance the people you're concerned about find you, *call me,* and I will get them picked up, ok? If they confront you, try to capture them and we'll take it from there. So, in this case, it is my hope I will not hear from you during your stay! One note on this gun, it has a hard trigger pull and thus tends to make you shoot to the right. Let me also round up some plastic ties and a canister of pepper spray for you, you can keep those in your purse too."

"Oh, good thinking, thank you, Joe. And, believe me, we will try to stay out of trouble."

After we finish our tea, Joe has us accompany him back to his office where he ushers us inside, closes the door, and discreetly supplies me with the promised protection. Bill shakes hands with him as we offer our thanks, and I give Joe a quick hug. We depart and leave newly-armed and

I'm feeling immediately safer. Bill cocks one eyebrow, saying, "He really seems like a nice guy."

I nod and reply, "I believe Joe and Karen together could clean up the world of crime. In fact, if you don't work out, I could really go for Joe," I say with a wink.

Turning his head and smirking at me, Bill says, "Naw, you two would burn each other out in less than a year. I'll tell you what, let's take off and go on our vacation. I have a bit of a surprise arranged and have reserved a place north of here. We'll grab the I-train out of here tonight."

Back at his sumptuous estate, we thank Harry Honda for joining our project, not to mention his efforts regarding the press, even though our attempt to conceal my identity backfired. Giving me a quick once over, he then wonders aloud at my attire. I tell him of our vacation plans and desire for privacy while traveling. Harry then says, "When you're ready to depart, we'll have you slip out the back servants' entrance in one of my employee's old brown Hondas (of course), and he'll deliver you to the train station."

The I-train whisks us rapidly north to our destination. Upon arrival, Bill heads off and picks up a rental car he's arranged and, once on the road, we proceed fifteen miles to a secluded guesthouse. A bottle of champagne and two trays of sushi greet us upon our arrival in the room. It's been a busy day and the chilled bubbly and fresh seafood are the precursor for a gentle but deep sleep. The next day we're planning to explore the area.

Again, I'm awakened with a loving start to my day—that guy is kissing my neck again. Do I or don't I need a bit more sleep?

We have a late breakfast of fruit and tea. I am beginning to really like tea, it's a nice change from coffee. The guesthouse is currently accommodating three other couples but, for the most part, we rarely see them. The place itself is situated on top of a large hill overlooking an agricultural valley, with multi-hued fields apparently nearing their harvest. A volcano is located in the distance to the northeast. We take long walks on the paths alongside the fields and head on into a small village located about two miles from the guesthouse which proves to be a long and satisfying stroll in visiting this much-different culture…

As we return to our room, the sun's going down, and Bill opens the sliding doors to fully take in the view. Two chairs are situated next to each other and positioned toward the setting sun. On a small table in between the two chairs I spy a flask of what turns out to be warm Japanese wine accompanied by two small cups. Bill motions to one of the chairs, "Sit down and let me pour you a small bit of this saké. This time I am going to do it right with no interruptions."

Pausing to clear his throat, he lowers his head and smiles at me mischievously saying, 'Ok, now I would like to raise this cup and offer a heartfelt toast to all that you are…and ask for your hand in marriage- will you marry me, my love?"

"Oh, yes, this is just perfect, Bill. What a wonderful spot to pop the question. Yes, I will marry you!"

The ground suddenly shakes—not violently, but with a bang and a bump.

I jump up from my seat, "No, that damned geologist has not yet had enough earth-related problems—hurricanes and earthquakes. What is this now, a volcanic eruption? Will we end up like the people in Pompeii, buried alive and preserved in ash? Does he just lay around thinking up this stuff?"

Bill pulls at my arm, tugging me back down, onto his lap this time, "No, Gee, the hurricanes and earthquakes were real events. This is just a bump—no big deal. God sent it as a period to my proposal. Here, give me your hand…this is a token of my affection, and is also my pledge to you." He slips a gorgeous ring on the third finger of my left hand.

"Oh, it's beautiful Bill. I love it. *I love you.* And I will remember this idyllic day always."

The two weeks we spend in the guesthouse pass rapidly. We don't bother our brains thinking about any of our current or previous problems. Instead we discuss everything else—life, possible children, where we might like a home, each of our favorite books, foods, drinks, our childhood, our parents—and our favorite music. We listen together to all the special songs we once loved—Alexa has taken over the world—so "she" retrieves and plays special tunes from the past for us within seconds of each request.

"This is just such a delicious escape—can't we just stay here, Bill? I don't want to go back to the ole' rat race."

"But what about our tent city project? By now, Harry Honda has probably turned out 100,000 tents. And Ma Mah has probably raised a couple more million dollars. Percy's likely building the factory and hiring our local refugees. But…you're right. This has been a wonderful getaway. Hey, I know…let's promise each other we will do these sorts of retreats from reality four times a year. But I just realized…in all our discussions, we haven't gotten around to deciding where we should have our wedding, or how many people we should invite—do you want to wear a white wedding gown, or would you rather be wed in a bikini?"

"Oh, I don't know at this point in time. Something will happen that will show us where and when we should tie the knot. Maybe Percy and Hollie will get to this point and we can do something together. What do you think?"

"I would share our day with them. We have all definitely become very close in the past few months."

As our too-brief time out from regular life ends, we pack our suitcases, check out of our own private Shangri-La, and take the I-train back to Tokyo, calling Joe before departing who then picks us up at the station. Once in his car, I stealthily return his gun, pepper spray, and zip ties to him straightaway. "Well, you'll be glad to hear we didn't kill anybody this trip—maybe next time. Hey, look at my shiny new ring, Joe. It was an eventful vacation!"

Upon hearing our news, he smiles and says all the right things to the newly-engaged couple he's chauffeuring and graciously drives us to the airport, sharing some more about information about this lovely country of his with us en route. We say our goodbyes upon reaching the terminal where he drops us off out front, departing with a hearty wave. Once inside the airport's first-class lounge, I head to the ladies and change back into my Gee clothes, retrieving my Gee identification just before we proceed to the airline counter.

CHAPTER 22   Journeying east to China

After what feels like an endless amount of time in the air, we finally arrive back on U.S. soil and are soon returned to the Taft Plantation where everything has clearly been moving at a furious pace in our absence. The warehouses have been cleaned out and repaired to begin fabrication of the tent units. The city council has interviewed everyone in the camp who's expressed interest in being part of the project. Volunteers are already working alongside Percy and Hollie. Five full-time staff are taking over many of the day-to-day demands of making the factory function well.

Harry Honda calls me on my cell. He informs me he's discovered a warehouse full of generators, approximately 900 of them. Turns out they're a discontinued line with pull starters while all of his new generators have battery-powered starters. He tells me he's donating the 900 to us, plus offering the new line to us at just slightly above their cost to manufacture. As I express my astonished appreciation, he then tells me that 600 generators are already being loaded onto planes for the flight to Atlanta, and says we're free to send those wherever we need them. He also reports a ship is being loaded with the rest of the old generators plus 1000 of the newest ones. Additional relief supplies of food and water are also onboard. I tell him to please direct the ship to head directly to Puerto Rico.

Percy then leans over and tells me while I'm still on the phone with Henry that the 600 generators should be distributed around the Caribbean to support existing relief efforts there.

It's 3:45 a.m. and I once again awake with a start. I'm feeling rattled and quickly realize I've been dreaming about Cassie's murder. I nudge Bill and, as his eyes open sleepily, I tell him of my dream. Something is stirring in my mind. He says, "It just has to be one of the girls from the reunion, don't you think? You girls or the sheriff would have seen any man who might have been there."

"I'm just thinking…someone said something to me about who could have done it. I remember now! It was Glenn. When I had that private interview with him, I told him we would pin the murder on him. Glenn maintained he was not the one, kept saying how much he loved Cassie, and that his affairs meant nothing to him. The last thing he whispered to me was, 'I think Kathleen killed her.' Yikes, I can't believe I'd forgotten he said that!"

Kathleen is one of your alumni, isn't she?"

"Yes, she is. We never called her Kathleen though, she was always Katy to all of us. I suppose it's didn't actually register in my mind that Kathleen is Katy. Oh m'gosh, Bill, I must call Jackie and Charlie right away and have them check her out. Thinking back, she sure didn't tell us much about herself at the reunion. I'm not even sure where she resides, or what she's doing for work these days."

After getting a couple more hours sleep, it's finally time to get up. Not long after downing some coffee, I call Jackie and tell her of Glenn's statement. She responds, "Well, Cassie certainly did not know about Katy—if she was having an affair with Glenn. Remember, we found out that Glenn made lots of trips to Pittsburgh, but never rented a car? Katy didn't say she lives in Pittsburgh. In fact, doesn't she live in Ohio?"

"I don't know. I never discussed where she lived or what she's been doing."

"Don't you remember when we were in college…Katy was always very possessive and easily became jealous if anyone even talked with her dates? I will get Charlie to check her out and get back to you. Maybe this is the lead we've been waiting for."

The next week goes by quickly and progress continues on the construction of our Tent City factory. Many experts are now returning to the area from Florida and Texas who have expertise in water reclamation, power generation, solar and wind power, bio-mass power generation, etc., and many of these highly knowledgeable professionals stop at Taft Plantation with suggestions and/or supply contacts for our new venture now that the word's gotten out about our project through various channels.

The first tent cities will be sent to central Africa to Doctors without Borders camps which are taking care of refugees from civil wars in the surrounding countries, and others are dispatched to several islands in the Caribbean recently devastated by hurricanes.

Having learned the storms and earthquakes have also disrupted many zoos in Mexico and along the Gulf Coast of the U.S., Hollie is receiving animals from several of these facilities in their aftermath. One such critter is an 18-month-old panda bear whose mother died in a recent flood. Pandas have made an amazing recovery in the wild, and now number over 2000, most of whom are still located in the wild mountainous regions of South Central China. Ninety-nine percent of a panda's diet is comprised of two special types of bamboo. The cub is still able to eat some other types of food, but she soon discovers obtaining the right kind of bamboo is a problem for Hollie—especially as they need 20 – 30 lbs. of it per day.

The panda cub's mother was on a 10-year loan program with China, so of course they now want the cub returned to China.

Bill suggests, "We can fly the new plane to China, with a couple of stops. I can adapt a cage for the baggage compartment, as well as heat it for the cub's comfort. Percy, can you contact the proper Chinese authorities and arrange for the transfer?"

It takes over three weeks for the U.S. State Department and the Chinese Foreign Service to confer and arrange the trip. By this time, we are all in love with the furry little panda cub—she's adorably precocious and no one wants to give her up. However, the Chinese are insistent, so we continue making our plans to return her.

Having made pretty good progress with her inquiries, Jackie calls with new information on Katy. "Ok, Gee, it turns out she lives just over the border from Pittsburgh in Ohio. She has a flashy new, red Jaguar convertible, and a black Ford SUV with dark tinted windows. Until recently, Katy worked in a bank in Pittsburgh, which is apparently where she met Glenn. She now operates an investment business which has several foreign clients. It appears she's doing the same kind of business that Cassie did."

"Well, that confirms why Glenn never rented a car when he was in Pittsburgh. Katy just picked him up at the airport. What kind of a house does she live in?"

"Previously, she lived in an apartment. Now she owns a large home in a gated community. It has six bedrooms, a pool, sauna, and media room that seats up to 15 people. She runs much of her business out of her home, but she also has an office with three employees in Pittsburgh. The gated community has a staffed gatehouse where one must check in, and the attendant calls to arrange for visitors to gain entrance."

"So, where'd she get the money for this operation? You think all of it came from Glenn?"

"Charlie has been tracing the foreign investors. Several of them are from China, especially from Hong Kong."

"Jackie, don't I recall Katy had some Chinese relatives? Wasn't her middle name Heng or Chinn or Chiang or something?"

"My, you do have a good memory, Gee. And, yes, her middle name is Chiang. Her grandfather was British, and he married a Chinese woman from the Chiang family, her mother was therefore half Chinese. She married an American businessman, and on a trip back to the U.S. Katy was born, and is therefore an American citizen."

"What did you find out about the Chiang family so far?"

"They were, of course, in the import/export business. And they also were apparently in the drug trafficking trade to both the U.S. and Great Britain. In fact, we think Katy is dealing with some of her relatives in the drug business."

"I wonder if there's a problem or competition between the Asian drug cartels and the South American cartels? Glenn may have gotten himself into more than he bargained for."

Bill then joins in saying, "I think Jackie and Charlie should go with us to China. We'll stop for a little vacation in Hong Kong and maybe find out some more about Katy." Jackie had already been excited when hearing of the panda, so she quickly announces she wants to come to see it and says she's also open to possibly accompanying us to China.

I reply, "Do you think we should inform the CIA and the FBI of our suspicions about Katy…her investments and Chinese connections?"

Jackie nods, "Yes, I think so, so let's do it. The FBI may spook Katy out of hiding and we can maybe pin Cassie's murder on her. I can't leave here for at least a week though as I have some social commitments. I do want to see your cute panda bear though. Is there a rush to get the cub back to China?"

"No, we can wait for two weeks to leave. By then all the paperwork will be here and preparations for the cub fully completed. Maybe we'll know more about Katy by then."

Not long thereafter, I phone our contacts at both the FBI and the CIA, reporting our findings and suspicions of Katy and her newfound wealth. Even though Glenn is now in prison, their investigations and related arrests are continuing. The drug trade is slowly feeling the pressure of their attention. The FBI and CIA are also very interested in the Chinese connection as drugs infiltrating the U.S. from Asia are as big a threat as those from South America.

The Earth keeps dutifully spinning and two weeks quickly pass. The Japanese ship has now reached Puerto Rico and the generators and supplies are being put to good use. Tents and building supplies are pouring in from the continental U.S. courtesy of Mr. Honda and his goodwill arrangements.

Jackie and Charlie arrive at the plantation and are eager to meet the panda cub plus inspect the animal rescue farm. While Hollie's farm is supposed to be for wild animals, the hurricanes have displaced many household pets. Therefore, a large kennel has been constructed to house them, and horses are confined to a special field, away from the wild, grazing animals. Hollie tells us, "As people reconstruct their homes, they will come retrieve their animals from us…we hope." She says she wants to concentrate on the wild animals overall, rather than domesticated ones, but is glad she can help out following the hurricane and all the households its upended.

We receive a call from the FBI with an update on Katy and her ties to the Asian drug market. It turns out the damning evidence against her was piling up and the FBI was already poised to arrest her. Just before this could happen though Katy flew off to Hong Kong. We fear she will disappear and not return to the U.S. I ask, "Are you working with the CIA? Are they poking around in Hong Kong?" Of course, it turns out they have not coordinated their efforts with the CIA.

After that call concludes, I phone our contact at the CIA and bring them up to date telling him, "We will be in Hong Kong at the end of next week or soon after. Years ago, Katy introduced me to one of her Chinese cousins. I will try to contact him and possibly see Katy while there. Can you have an agent accompany us to that meeting? Is it possible to arrest Katy in China and get her extradited back here to the States?"

He replies, "We have been working with the Chinese government in an effort to try and halt the drug trade to the U.S. If you find her, possibly we can deliver her to a Chinese jail, and then our diplomats can petition the Chinese government to send her back here for trial."

I then provided them with the information on our hotel arrangements, and he gives me a number to call so we can arrange to have an agent meet us when we arrive.

Well, it's on to another new adventure. Will this one be dangerous? I suddenly realize we don't have any weapons to protect ourselves. Maybe I should hide Karen's pistol in the plane. At least we would have a back-up…but then it occurs to me it might be difficult to get it off the plane and through Customs. Hopefully, our CIA agent will be armed.

We had planned for the six of us to go to China, but Hollie announces she just can't bear to be on-hand when the little cub is turned over. Therefore, she excused herself and Percy from the trip, saying they both needed to take care of all the animals currently at Taft Plantation as the number of critters has continued to grow so dramatically. "So, you're going to leave it to the four of us, or five if you count Karen, to take on the Chinese government and the Chinese drug mafia?!" Hollie nods her head, "Sorry, but I just don't want to be a witness to giving up that sweet little cub…Candy, as I call her. She's just so cute and cuddly."

The flight goes without incident, although it's once again an interminably long jaunt to reach Asia, but we finally land in Beijing. An animal customs agent is waiting for us upon arrival. The cub is quickly but thoroughly examined for disease and we are subsequently informed by the agent we're now released to fly to central China and the cub's new home. We're told the agent will accompany us to the animal preserve. The Chinese are so happy to see the wee panda cub. We are assured effusively she will be given the best of care, but also told she must be kept in isolation for two weeks as a disease control precaution. We spend a couple of days at the preserve and get to see a number of adult pandas as well as other animals in the preserve. We fly our customs agent back to Beijing and, after refueling, our plane takes off for Hong Kong.

Upon arriving, we check into our hotel, freshen up *(what does this mean? How does one freshen up?)*, and decide to try our luck at the gambling tables. In three minutes, I manage to lose $100. "Well, that's my limit, so

I'm quitting. I never have any luck at these places. What makes people want to gamble? The odds are always with the house!"

Jackie replies, "I think there's a part of all of us that likes the idea of being rich—or just getting money for free. Whenever there's a mega-million jackpot, scads of people buy tickets—in spite of the fact the more tickets sold the greater the odds of you not getting the winning ticket."

Downstairs in a shop off the lobby I buy a disposable cell phone. Moving to a semi-secluded chair by a tall indoor tree I flip it on and call our CIA agent contact. "Hello, this is Gee Lowell. I understand you are our local contact. I'm in Hong Kong now, so when and where can we meet?"

"This is Jerry Chinn and, yes, I am your contact for your stay here. I will meet you in the morning at eight a.m. in the local fish market just five blocks east of your hotel on the waterfront. Pull out your compact and fuss with fixing your hair or putting on lipstick. I'll find you."

That evening, we play regular tourists, checking out all the sites around the hotel. After several hours, we have a late dinner and retire to the hotel around eleven p.m. We have a nice suite on an upper floor with two bedrooms, a living room, and a well-stocked bar. The décor is a strange mixture of modern western style furniture combined with Chinese cabinetry. The oriental rugs topping the wood floors are slightly worn but look to be old collectors' items. The bathrooms are sleek, modern, and covered floor to ceiling with limestone tiles. *(My geologist tells me it's Indiana Salem Limestone. He just can't stop poking his nose into my novel.)*

I awake with a start—ok, where am I now? I hear the tinkle of the adjoining casino's one-armed bandits. Don't people ever quit playing them? Cracking the window open a bit and blinking into the still semi-dark dawn, I hear the bustle of the city, with shopkeepers and vendors already beginning their day on the street below. I also smell food cooking somewhere close by. It's just after six a.m. and we must grab some breakfast soon and get ready to meet Jerry Chinn. I wonder what today will bring. I'm feeling pretty confident we will we find the Chiang family, but might that prove dangerous? I remember Katy's supposed to be here in the city. Will she suspect we know about her illegal activities? I sure wish I had Karen's gun. I suddenly realize we could be made to disappear so easily in this densely populated mass of humanity (with over 7 million residents, Hong Kong's population nets out at approximately 6,300 people per square kilometer).

Once downstairs, we all collect around the bar's island for coffee and western style biscuits and sweet rolls. Bill asks, "Should all four of us go together, or should we split up? Gee and I could meet Jerry Chinn and pick you two up later. We want to be inconspicuous, if possible."

Jackie answers, "Four Americans out at eight a.m. sounds real conspicuous to me. I wonder why he had us meet him so dang early? I'm never up and out at this hour of the morning!"

Fed and caffeinated, we stroll down to the fish market, carefully timing our arrival. Jackie and Charlie check out one area while Bill and I take the other side of the market. At eight o'clock precisely, I take out my compact and start to apply more lipstick.

A man with a newly-purchased fish exclaims to me, "Good morning, you like our fishy market?" He then lowers his voice and says just above a whisper, "Would the four of you please follow me to the street? I have a limo waiting. My name is Jerry Chinn." He proceeds slowly toward the street in front of me and I nod to Jackie and Charlie who quickly follow. We climb into the black limo with its dark windows and it soon heads off.

"I know it's early, but I wanted to spend some time with you at our drug enforcement headquarters. Langley has informed me about the four of you and your role in uncovering the means to put many of these people away for a long time."

The limo winds its way along narrow streets, including turning down several alleys. We finally descend into the underground garage of what looks like a warehouse. Once the vehicle parks and we step outside,

Chinn steers us to a wall with a large mural of Hong Kong Bay. He places his right hand at a strategic spot and the wall suddenly opens to reveal a concealed elevator. Chinn ushers us inside it, pushes a button, and we quickly descend down another three floors, my stomach dropping in the process. The door opens to a lobby with two armed guards seated on either side of the elevator's door. We walk through a metal detector single file. Afterward, badges with our pictures are given to each us to wear around our necks. I wonder where they got our pictures? Especially as they're different from our passport photos.

Next, four new iPhones are distributed among us. They appear to be standard issue with many of the usual apps and games installed. However, to reach special data we may want to save or refer to, each of us has to put in a four-digit code plus our own fingerprint. That data will otherwise be inaccessible to anyone other than the one who owns that particular phone. I think Karen certainly needs this kind of a phone. I'm also hoping this one's now mine vs. one I can only use while here in Hong Kong.

We follow Jerry and proceed to a small conference room. Once inside and seated, he begins projecting images on a large screen. "These are the leaders of the Chinese drug cartels, with a description of their past criminal activity. However, we can actually only prove a small portion of this activity at present. To find your friend, Kathleen Chiang, you will initially meet with her cousin, Chad Chiang, whom you indicated you had previously met in the U.S. I have run down his international phone number, which you might also have found online. I suggest you call him and set up a luncheon meeting at Hwang Ho Restaurant, which incidentally is owned by another cousin of his. Tell him you have hired a tour guide—me—and there will be five of you for lunch. You can tell him the three guys, Bill, Charley, and the guide (me) want sushi, so we'll plan on sitting at the Sushi bar. You and Jackie are Kathleen's college friends and don't like sushi, so you two will dine with him alone and talk about where to find Katy."

"That sounds like a good plan," I reply. "And what shall we tell Chad concerning Katy?"

"Maybe that you called her investment office looking for her, and they told you she was out of town visiting relatives. You asked if she was in Hong Kong as you knew she had relatives there. They replied they didn't really know her itinerary but indicated that might be the case."

"How can we record this conversation without him knowing it?"

"Show him your new phones you just purchased. Lay them on the table and tell him you don't want to be disturbed while on vacation and ask him, how do we turn them off? Hand him one of them and he will no doubt show you the button to deactivate it and push it. The phone will go blank, but will still be on. On these special units, you must push the button twice to actually turn it off. To turn on the screen, tap it three times. If you want to take a photo, point the thin edge side of the phone in the direction of the suspect and say rapidly—"yes-yes." The photo is set to a wide-angle format and optimized for low light situations as the flash is deactivated – once taken, the images of individuals will be compared and identify any subjects from the police data already downloaded into your phones."

"Take a picture of all the people you encounter in these meetings. An app in the phone will automatically process a dossier on each of them we have a file on. You can look at that information later. Of course, don't let them know you are taking their picture. These drug people try to keep a low profile and try to make certain their photos aren't captured…ever.

"Additionally, our own intervention in monitoring your access to these targets will include our ability to remotely activate your device's audio recording app, thus ensuring your entire interaction is taped, so you don't have to worry about that key aspect yourselves."

After being given this initial prep, I call Chad and tell him I heard Katy was here in Hong Kong. He remembers meeting me in America, and I quickly suggest we have lunch at the Hwang Ho restaurant as instructed, and he agrees to meet today. He indicates he's not sure he can get Katy here today as she's out in the country at another relative's house, but says he will try to contact her anyway.

We continue to talk with Jerry Chinn about the drug trade. "Do you think we can arrest Katy for drug smuggling and have her brought back to the U.S.?"

"We've checked into her operations—namely her investment business in the U.S.—and, at this point, we have no evidence of any impropriety in her investments. Some of her clients are Chinese and possibly involved in illegal drug trafficking, but all the investments themselves have been handled properly. We also have thus far found no evidence she is laundering cash for them, or for Glenn. Therefore, we can't just arrest her. However maybe you can get something out of her. A confession would be ideal. Other than that, it will be difficult to make a case against her with what little we have now. Make sure you record all your conversations with her, no matter how trivial they may appear."

We proceed to the Hwang Ho restaurant and our lunch meeting. The boys head for the sushi bar as planned, and Jackie and I meet with Chad at a quiet table in the back of the restaurant. Three Chinese men are seated two tables away from us. We mentally finger them as Chad's bodyguards.

"It is good to meet you once again, Ms. Lowell. I am sorry that Katy cannot be back until tomorrow evening. I told her where you are staying though. She will contact you at your hotel later today, at six p.m."

"Oh, thank you Mr. Chiang. And please call me Gee. By the way, we just bought some new cell phones when we were shopping. Can you please show us how to turn them off? I already gave the new number to my office but don't want to be bothered by business from home. That's actually why I didn't bring my own cell on this trip."

Chad takes the phone and pushes the button and the phone goes blank.

Jackie then asks him, "Is this the button?" She pushes it and her phone goes blank. We lay them on the table, one pointing toward Chad and one pointing toward the three body guards. "Yes, yes, thank you Mr. Chiang."

"Please call me Chad, and may I call you Jackie?"

"Yes, yes, of course you may."

We then proceed to enjoy a lovely lunch and chatter back and forth with him about sights to see in Hong Kong.

After our touristy discourse, I ask, "So, what business are you in, Chad?"

He replies, "I am in the drug business. Because you are a long time acquaintance of a family member I can share with you discreetly that we have two drug businesses here in Hong Kong: one in supplying drugs to pharmaceutical companies for medicines, but also one in illegal recreational drugs. Rest easy though as although I have taken you into my confidence in this way, I am in the legitimate drug business, thank goodness. Your friend, my cousin Katy, is in charge of our family's investments in America. In recent years, we have invested many millions in the U.S. and have also been involved in joint American-Chinese ventures. China, as you know has become very aggressive in foreign markets. We here in Hong Kong have historically been in business worldwide. We are using our expertise in helping new Chinese startups gain access to international markets."

I reply, "That's very interesting, and it sounds like you've been very successful indeed. So, I have a question for you if I may. Jackie and I both raise money for good causes. My family has the Lowell Foundation and Jackie has the Need Help Foundation. In view of recent natural disasters and migrations of people from civil wars, the Lowell Foundation is now producing tent cities for refugees. We have many investors from several nations, but the needs of people seem endless. We are currently sending tent cities to South East Asia tsunami and earthquake victims. We would love to add you to our investor list, do you think you might be willing to provide some underwriting of our efforts?"

Chad replies, "I am sure the family can support some of your causes. The tent cities project sounds like an interesting venture with lots of ramifications and potential problems. We can supply you with chemicals for sanitation, sprays for insects, and various medical supplies. Discuss your needs with Katy when you see her, and I'll arrange for her to help you."

Jackie replies, "Thank you for your offer. Yes, we are aware to some extent of Chinese trade and the past role of Hong Kong in world trade. I'm sure Katy can give us some more insight when we connect with her. Thank you for a wonderful lunch. I am sure our men have had their fill of sushi and saké by now. We will take our leave from your gracious company."

Back on the street, we stroll back toward our hotel. Jerry Chinn exclaims, "That worked perfectly, I heard your entire conversation. I thought that Chiang's explanation of his business was interesting. It appears he was accurate, and he is legitimate. Maybe one of his bodyguards is also attached to one of the other members of the family in the illicit drug trade."

I reply, "Unless you can find something illegal going on, it looks like Chad and Katy are maybe alright. You know what's odd though? I don't remember telling Chad which hotel we were staying at! I wonder…is he watching us?"

Jerry answers, "If Katy's office contacted her after you talked with them, then maybe they were looking for you. Chad Chiang made no reference to your drug chase of Glenn and Cassie. If he is part of that network, then he may already know about some of your activities."

"Do you think we're in danger here, Jerry? Are you carrying? Do we need your people to protect us while we're here?"

"It is possible you may be in danger, although I doubt if they would kill you as that could potentially bring too much attention their way. You may be safe but do be careful. We already have someone watching out for you 24 hours per day. I am going to leave you now but I will be back here at 9:30 tomorrow morning and will play the travel guide for you two, in case others are monitoring your activities. Wear some good walking shoes."

The next morning my lover man wakes me by kissing my neck again and then nibbling on my ears. "Bill, what do you think today will bring? Do you think Katy's going to turn out to be guilty of Cassie's murder?"

"Hey, we're on vacation, missy, at least for a bit of our time here. Pay attention to my kisses please…at least for a little while. Today will pan out as it's supposed to. Do you want some coffee? I just brewed some before you woke up."

A marvelous day greets us once outside and on our way, and we're treated to many new sights accompanied by a running dialogue from our Chinese CIA agent-cum-travel-guide. He really knows the city and countryside hereabouts. Once back at the hotel later in the day, we await Katy's arrival having chatted with her briefly yesterday. Jerry will not be there, but will be listening to our conversation remotely.

Later on, we hear a gentle tapping on the door and let Katy in, welcoming her inside with big hugs from Jackie and me. We're glad to see her, in spite of our suspicions she may be a murderess. "There is so much to tell you. I have been so busy since our reunion, and Cassie's awful murder. Were you two aware I knew Cassie well and that I even knew Glenn? By the way, I also know of Cassie's and Glenn's illegal business with the drug cartels. In fact, early on, Glenn contacted me to arrange a safety deposit box at the bank I worked at in Pittsburgh."

I ask, "Did Glenn put the move on you? Were you in love with him, Katy?"

"No, absolutely not, I sized him up from my first encounter. Yes, he put the move on me alrighty. But I knew he was married to Cassie, and so I rejected him. He was pretty charming though and eventually, after some subsequent meetings, I did have a pretty casual fling with him. Cassie had already told me she knew he had sex with many of the women he met, both personally and professionally. She also warned me not to fall in love with him as she had, she was actually concerned it would only lead to massive hurt on my part."

"So, how'd you get together with Cassie? Did she ever come to Pittsburgh?"

"The first time I met her, after Vassar, was the one time she did come to Pittsburgh. She convinced me to quit being just a teller at the bank and become a financial planner and stockbroker. She also warned me about Glenn's nefarious activities. Cassie wanted to have some legitimate investments that were not entangled with his businesses. So, I eventually setup an investment company for the two of us with Cassie as 90% unlisted owner and me as 10% owner. I was however 100% of the recorded owner. My Board of Directors included myself, Cassie, and Cassie's sister, Lisa. All distributions of assets were to be determined by the three of us. Lisa and Cassie held their interest in joint tenancy. Lisa is now the heir of 90% of a company worth $40M."

"What about Glenn? What'd you do for him?"

"He was trying to launder drug cartel monies. However, I refused to take any cash from Glenn, and insisted on accepting only corporate checks from him for companies with legitimate owners. I ran whatever background checks I could on some of these people and refused to take any checks from people under indictment, or who appeared in the news with possible drug connections referenced. I am as clean as I can be."

"I remember you mentioning at the reunion you have a Jaguar and an SUV, where'd you get those, Katy?"

"I lease them from one of Glenn's corporations. Cassie prepared the documents for the leases."

Jackie then asked, "And who owns the big manor house estate?"

"Hey, wait just a minute here, you two," Katy suddenly straightened up in her chair and scowled at each of us, turning from side to side and glaring. "Hey, what gives? I never told either of you anything about where I live. Has somebody actually been *investigating* me? How do YOU know what sort of house I own?"

At this Jackie glances at me with a quick nod and takes the lead, "I'm sorry, Katy, we should have told you when we first started in on this topic; I actually hired a private detective and everyone at the reunion has been investigated as a result, even Gee and I.

"So at this point, we do have some questions for you as a result, but they're the same ones being posed to everyone in our group in terms of anyone's connections to Cassie and Glenn…so, if you don't mind?" She cocked her head at her and then smiled encouragingly at her quarry.

It took close to a minute while Katy then seemed to process this response. Once she seemed to visually relax a bit, she then continued,

"I own it, under my own name, and have a sizable mortgage payment each month. Glenn wanted a big place with many bedrooms so he could have clients stay while they were here in the U.S. Two of his corporations pay me for that option plus to cover staff to serve their needs during these visits."

"Is that legal?"

"Yes, I assure you it IS. I dutifully file as a bed & breakfast and pay TOT (Transient Occupancy Tax) for their stays. As an inn owner—how am I supposed to know anything about my guests? I just turn a 'blind eye.' *(What is a blind eye? Where did this saying come from?)*

I then ask, "Did you know Glenn's been arrested and tried, and is now in prison?"

"No-o—I was aware he had been indicted but didn't know about a trial or imprisonment. Good grief, it's not been that long since I last saw him. How bizarre!"

"Did you know the FBI has been to your office and they've been looking into your connection with Glenn?"

"Yes, and I've been *freaking out!* My office called me with that news and also told me you'd called and were coming to Hong Kong. Listen, my records are clean, Gee. They won't find anything illegal in my activities whatsoever. Please believe me."

"Well, they have found a lot in Cassie's records though. She appears, at least in the legal records of docs on file, to be more guilty than Glenn. If she were alive, she would be facing more prison time than Glenn."

Squaring back her shoulders, Jackie then asks sternly, "So do you think Glenn killed Cassie, Katy? Or…did you kill her?"

Katy responded immediately, "Hey, c'mon you two, I had no reason to kill Cassie. I knew she was into Glenn's illegal businesses as the CEO, the President, or Secretary, etc. of many of his corporations. But how could she testify against her husband?"

Jackie then said, "Charlie found out Cassie was previously married before Glenn and was never legally divorced. If Glenn knew that, then he had a motive as the wife thing was no longer applicable in protecting him from her testimony."

"Yeah, well, that may be true—if you say so—but I don't think Glenn knew any of that. He always laughed when he said Cassie would take the heat and couldn't testify against him because they were married."

At this point, I jumped back in, "Well, I guess perhaps we'll never find out who killed Cassie, unless someone confesses to it. Ok, let's change the subject. Katy, tell us about your relationship with your Chinese investors. The FBI will be checking your records very thoroughly. And everyone knows there are a lot of drugs run through Hong Kong. Your cousin Chad seems like an honest businessman, but he's aware of the Asian drug cartels. Are any of your relatives or Chinese investors tied into the illicit drug trade?"

Katy shakes her head, "Chad's warned me about some specific investors, and I have quit doing business with them as a result. I just got back from the hill country where I was seeing some other relatives of ours. It seems several of them are raising poppies, and don't want to talk about their market. In that district, raising poppies is a major source of income. Until the Chinese government ceases to tolerate it, I fear it will continue."

Bill then announces from the couch where he's been appearing to nap while eavesdropping, "Ok, ladies, let's all go to dinner. This whole thing is too depressing. We stopped here in Hong Kong to have some fun. When we get back to the States, we'll be right back in the emergency relief business again. Did you show Katy pictures of the panda bear we returned to China on the first leg of our journey here?"

Katy responds, "Frankly, I'm tired of talking about all of this too. I think I'll just stay here in China until the lawyers prove my innocence so I can return to my investment business. Tomorrow, I will take you all on a boat trip around the bay here. There are a lot of neat stops and interesting things to see."

Three days later, we leave for the U.S. after having had a nice time playing tourists with Katy as our guide. It certainly appears she isn't Cassie's murderer. Another dead end?

CHAPTER 23   Facing the Boston D.A.

The return flight is uneventful. We fly to Chicago and drop off Jackie and Charlie. The four of us are sad to part as we've spent so much time together recently. Jackie says, "Hey, when are you two going to get married anyway? Don't you think it's time? By the way, I forgot to tell you, Charlie's proposed to me and I accepted. Maybe we should think about tying the knot together somewhere. What do you two think about that idea—maybe in some exotic place like Tahiti?"

Smiling at my longtime pal who's now beaming, I tell her, "Well, we hadn't thought about a place or time just yet. The engagement actually took weeks before Bill finally presented me with the ring just recently in Japan. I hope we can have an uninterrupted wedding when it finally does happen."

Bill adds, "Hey, Percy and Hollie are now engaged, maybe we should make it a three-couple wedding. Gee and I are up for it and actually already discussed it. So you two think about it, and we'll talk with Percy and Hollie!"

After a bit of post-travel decompression in Chicago, I call my lawyer to see what progress he's managed to make with the Boston D.A. Turns out the D.A. still wants to question me further. Upon hearing this news, I think it's time to confront him and decide to fly on back to Boston. After that call concludes, I ring up my contact with the FBI and bring him up to date on our China trip. After underscoring this most recent display of my civic duty, I then ask him if the FBI would please call the Boston D. A. and get him to give up on the idea of arresting me. He said he would talk to his boss and see about getting a call in to the D.A. as requested.

A bit later on, I phone Ma Mah and tell her we are heading home. She says she'll have James pick us up at the airport. As we prepare to land, I put my chip back in my Gee cell phone. I am now once again visible to tracking being done by the Boston D.A.'s office.

After we disembark from our two-hour flight, James is dutifully waiting for us as we deplane. He loads our bags into the vehicle and exclaims, "Ms. Gee, it's good to have you back. I have your drink ready for you at the house—Glenlivet with two drops of water, and a cold Coors Lite for you, Bill. But would you rather have something different today?"

"No, I like Coors, but for your information, I do drink other things besides beer."

Once we're settled inside and back on the freeway, I ask our driver, "So…what's new, James? How is Ma Mah doing these days? I do worry about her."

"Your mother has slowed down a little with her fundraising events. I think age is beginning to tell, although don't say anything to her about it or she will bite your head off."

"You can't make her slow down a bit more, can you?"

"No, I can't, but she has mentioned that she wants to turn over the Lowell Foundation to you and Percy to run. She hates all the paperwork and dealing with accountants and tax people. I hope you and Percy can dedicate more time to the foundation in the future. It would surely please her if so."

Striding into our spacious living room, I cross over to where she's seated and plant a quick kiss on her cheek, "Ma Mah, I am *so* happy to be home. I'll bet you've been lonely without Percy or me hanging around and making our messes. Speaking of messes, have you had any more conversations with the D.A.?"

"Yes, and I'm glad you're now here. I have missed you too, daughter. I have also planned dinner for just the three of us tonight. I want you to give me a rundown on all your activities since you've been away and traveling hither and yon. By the way, I received a copy of the Liberty, Maine newspaper with your complete speech to the town gathering. I wish I could have seen the contest there—looks like I've made quite a feminist out of you…at last!"

Dinner was served and happily included some of my favorite dishes: boiled lobster, corn on the cob, and Crème Brulee for dessert. There was also a pale ale served with the lobster and a nicely aged port with our dessert.

"Ma Mah, I haven't told you much about Cassie's murder while we were at the Vassar reunion. Jackie, Bill, Charles, and I have been busy trying to track down her killer. In the process, we uncovered connections between the South American drug cartels and Cassie and her husband, Glenn. In fact, we've uncovered information that has actually already led to several arrests as we supplied our information to the FBI as well as the CIA. We have also been involved with Senator Throckmorton, who sits on the Homeland Security Oversight Committee. We have discovered the drug cartels have developed reach inside our government. That matter is an ongoing investigation. A couple of senators have decided not to run for re-election as a result of these matters coming to light and each are now making some very substantial contributions to fight drugs and opiate addictions to provide some "cover" for their potential or alleged roles. Bill and I have been followed and threatened by these drug cartels. And we're currently being protected by the FBI in the U.S. and by the CIA when outside the country."

Upon hearing this news, Ma Mah shakes her head, nearly dropping her fork which has been paused in mid-air during this revelation, then saying, "I had no knowledge of this, but I had an inkling you were into something big. And I'm pretty sure there have been people watching the house here. I certainly hope they're the FBI and not the drug thugs. Will you check on that please? Straightaway?"

The next morning, I bound out of bed, quickly throwing on a swimsuit and doing laps for a half an hour and then took off for a morning run. Returning back, I realize how glad I am to be back in my closet, I've had so few changes of clothes over the past few weeks. I busy myself throwing a bunch out as I'm just tired of them. And as I look over "her" section, Karen really needs to dress better. I must have a chat with her about it.

The phone rings—my Gee phone. It's the Boston D.A. and he cuts right to the chase, indicating he'd like to have a meeting. "I got three calls first thing this morning: from the head of the FBI, from the head of the CIA, and from Senator Throckmorton on the Homeland Security Oversight Committee. They all told me that you were working for them and to lay off you. Could we have a meeting so you can provide me with a briefing of whatever it is you're currently working on? I would also like you to clear up the problem with your fingerprints."

I then replied, "I know that by now you must be aware of my detective business operating as Karen Hunt. My office and my records are in western Massachusetts at my fiancé's cabin. Could you meet me there and I will reveal to you what I can of my role in fighting the drug traffickers?"

"Ok, I could meet you on Thursday, say by 10:00 a.m., I think I can get there in about two hours. Give me the address."

I provide that for him but couldn't help but poke him with a little jab. "So, what did you think of my speech to the community in Liberty, Maine when I was hiding out from you?"

"Well, to tell you the truth, I thought that maybe you really were a vigilante taking on a paramilitary group. How'd you beat them at their own game?"

I laughed, "I'll gladly tell you all about that episode over a glass of wine one of these days."

Bill and I decide to go out to the cabin on Wednesday evening. "We might need to clean up the place before the D.A. arrives tomorrow. I think I would like to drive the Lamborghini, as I haven't felt that kind of horsepower in a while. You've never driven it, have you Bill? Maybe I'll let you take the wheel on the drive back. My insurance won't be able to bear tickets in both directions."

"Now what exactly are you going to tell this clown? It sounds like he has Karen's fingerprints on file but of course it was Gee who used the gun to kill the perp."

"I guess I like the dead twin story the best, as it explains both of us having the same fingerprints. Hey, don't you have an urn of your dead uncle's ashes on the mantle of the fireplace in the cabin? I could show those to the D.A. and, with a few tears, convince him the story's true. What do you think?"

"You know, Gee, if I had your imagination, I would become a novelist." *(Doesn't everyone want to write a novel? So, what is holding you back, dear reader?)*

Wednesday evening, we zoom out to western Massachusetts to Bill's cabin. "Bill, is this your only home? Where do you stay in Boston?"

"If flights are not scheduled for you or Ma Mah, then I just stay out here. If I get caught in Boston, my sister lives just a mile away from the Lowell mansion, so I stay with her. I have my own bedroom and closet there, so I have what I need—in fact, it'll be time for you two to meet each other soon."

"Definitely! Hey, this is a nice, roomy cabin. The third bedroom works well for Karen's office, especially her files. But where do you see us living once we get married? I'm used to lots of space and we'll need four bays for our cars. It doesn't look like we could add a four-car garage here."

"I guess I hadn't thought that far ahead."

"Bill, do you have a problem with me having the money in our future family? I'm sure you're aware I can easily provide whatever we need. The only problem is, can you deal with that emotionally?"

"I have to admit I've wrestled with that a bit, and I'm not sure whether it will be a problem. However, I do realize I need a job that brings in more money than a private pilot's salary."

"Well, it's interesting you say that as I may have a possible solution. Remember James mentioning that Ma Mah wants Percy and I to take on more responsibilities in the Lowell Foundation? However, these days Percy seems to be buried in the Taft Plantation, Hollie's animal rescue, and the creation of the new Tent City factory project. The Lowell Foundation will no doubt put lots of money into those ventures at Taft Plantation. That will leave the rest of the Lowell Foundation charities for me to run. And I will need lots of help. Are you willing to learn a whole new arena?"

"You bet, I'm willing to take that on. Although I would like to remain as your pilot as well as I do love to fly. What will the Foundation pay me?"

"That was a straight arrow response. I like it, you don't mess around, buddy! I think as a foundation, we can only pay you a minimal salary of, say, $100,000 per year. Combined with my trust fund monies, we can live on that, unless we have too many children that is—you know how expensive private schools are!"

"Y'know, during our time in Japan, we talked about this topic a bit, but I'm not sure we ever got down to brass tacks—so how many do you want? Or are we sure we want to have any? After all, we would be able to have more fun without them, but I'm open to whatever you want. But, now that we're addressing the issue, aren't you getting a bit old to have your first child? Maybe instead we could adopt some teenagers and not have to go through the mess of diapers, terrible two's, and all that business, what do you think?"

"Well it's a surprise to hear you say that, Bill, I thought all men wanted to have a male heir. Maybe you don't? If we decide to have children, I would be happy to adopt. There are certainly too many unwanted children in this world already. You should be warned though, I don't know what kind of a parent I'd actually be—having been raised by nannies and parents who were rarely home and always busy when they were. Probably, by most standards, I am a little weird—with Karen and all."

"Gee/Karen, I like your weirdness. I think you are a very caring person and will make a lovely mother. I think this is enough discussion for now on this matter though, let's call it a night and hit the hay please."

I awake with a start—oh, now I remember, the Boston D.A., George Homely, is coming here this morning. I hope he's not bringing police along with him and actually just accepted my invitation in order to arrest me!

Bill and I have breakfast and I then dress as Gee, with a nice casual outfit of tan slacks and a pale green top. I have my hair down, and it's now back to its normal black color. I put on some very red lipstick. Ok, I'm ready for Mr. D.A.

He arrives driving a Boston City vehicle. He gets out of the car and stares at my Lamborghini—no doubt with a bit of jealousy.

"Welcome, Mr. Homely, or do I say Mr. District Attorney?"

"Just call me George. This is just supposed to be a friendly visit. You certainly have your cheering committee working diligently on your behalf, I must say, Ms. Lowell. Last night I also ran into Bernie Sanders, and he told me you were a hero and asked me to please get off your case. How ever did he know about your matter?"

"Well, Bernie called me for a visit not long after the shooting and encouraged me to run for political office. I told him about my problem with my fingerprints and my dual life as a detective. But I just want to continue to promote certain social causes, raise money for them, and convince others to run for political office."

"I guess your motives appear just. I would however like you to clear up this fingerprint problem of yours. How do two people have the same fingerprints?"

"It's actually a long story but I'll try to simplify it for you. Come on inside, George, I've just made some coffee, I'll get you a cup.

Once we're seated at a small dining table near the window and I've placed some spoons, sugar, and a small pitcher of cream on the table, I collect my thoughts and launch in.

"You see, I was born an identical twin, with identical fingerprints. Karen was born first, three days before me. She had serious physical problems and was put into isolation for more than two months, and she also required several operations. Another child was born the same day, also with serious problems. Her parents spent virtually night and day at the hospital. My mother had me to take care of along with the numerous social engagements necessary to run the Lowell Foundation. She visited the hospital each day to see Karen and became friends with the Hunts. As they got to know each other a bit, she learned they couldn't afford the hospital expenses for their sick daughter. My mother subsequently arranged to pay for that care on their behalf. But then their baby girl died. Astonishingly, albeit after a brief absence, the Hunts returned to the hospital again and again to spend time with Karen. When she was about to be released from the hospital, she required constant attention 'round the clock. Ma Mah felt she already had her hands full with me, but mostly out of compassion she made an offer to the Hunts: they would take Karen and care for her until she was healthy enough to join the Lowell family. Of course, after they took her home, the Hunts fell in love with her in a very short while and wanted to raise her as their own child. Reluctantly Ma Mah finally agreed to it. She also paid off the mortgage on their farm plus sent them a monthly stipend.

Karen was homeschooled by Mrs. Hunt. Ma Mah also arranged to send educational experts to teach her certain skills. In the meantime, I grew up not knowing anything about Karen's existence, or that I was a twin. About eight years ago, the Hunts were killed by a drunk driver. Spurred by a combination of grief and vengeance, Karen decided to become a detective in order to track down who killed her parents. She never succeeded. In going through the Hunt's estate matters though, she discovered all kinds of paperwork which led her to the Lowell's...and finally to me.

She called me out of the blue one day and just told me bluntly she was my sister. We arranged to meet straightaway, and she told me the story, and she also brought various documents along with her—and of course I felt like I was looking in a slightly disheveled mirror once we were in the same room together. Ma Mah then verified everything when asked. Karen, because of her disabilities, needed help in her detective business, so I ended up assisting her a bit on occasion. However, she died from health complications five years ago now. However, her business phone kept ringing and, without really thinking it through, I ended up just taking over her detective business. I'll show you the files of our cases."

During the latter part of this conversation, I wipe off my red lipstick, pull my hair back into a ponytail. And then put on an old shirt covering my blouse. I stand up with a slouch and I am Karen.

"Do you see how easily I morph into her?"

I take off the shirt, drop my hair, get out my compact and quickly reapply my lipstick. I then cross the room to the mantle and pick up the urn. "These are Karen's ashes. I so wish I'd spent more time with her, she was an amazing person!" The tears begin to trickle down my cheeks as I think of poor Karen and quickly grab a tissue.

The D.A. lowers his head, his eyes gazing into his mug of coffee, silent for nearly a full minute, and then replies, "That's a truly astonishing story…and I can now see how you became Karen. I am not sure about the legality of any of this however."

"Well, I have recently discussed the situation with my lawyer. I have also registered with the State of Massachusetts and have filed and received a d.b.a. for G.W. Lowell to operate as Karen Hunt, Detective. Does that satisfy you?"

"Well, hmmm, I think it does…ok, I guess I can close that case now. But why and how did you get the dead policeman's gun?"

"It was less than 10' away from me, with the sheath unbuttoned. The killer was emptying his clip and had several more with him. There were no other police or security at the event. Someone had to act, and I know how to use firearms. I could have just run and protected my own safety, but Doris and Clarence had unwittingly taken bullets meant for me—I was alive, on "borrowed time,' so I had to act to try and save others, in addition to myself."

"Yes, well I guess you did accomplish that. In retrospect, I apologize for having been so hard on you. I must have received some questionable intel right after the event which planted a suspicious seed in my brain where you were concerned. I think this wraps up my questions though. We'll now consider the file closed, so you're free and clear, Ms. Lowell. Someday soon, I would like to have lunch and have you tell me about the Maine Wolverines though. Your speech which was printed in the Liberty newspaper was quite a tale."

"Ok, George, I promise to do just that. Actually, will you stay and join us for lunch today?"

"No, I'm afraid not, I must get back to Boston as I have a meeting at five this afternoon and have some more work to get done beforehand. Thank you for the invitation though."

"Before you leave, Mr. District Attorney, I would also like to provide you with a confidential list of people we—meaning the FBI, CIA, and Homeland Security—are pursuing as drug traffickers in the Boston area. Bill and I uncovered some evidence indicating these people are drug dealers who are connected internationally. I'm sure you're already aware of at least some of the ones operating regionally. Before you arrest anyone on this list, please call my contact at the FBI. This is his 24-hour number. For your information, the FBI is currently working on verifying our information. My understanding is they have undercover agents who may appear to be associated with some of these people. We don't want them unwittingly arrested by the Boston Police, that will only slow down their efforts. When the evidence is in hand, the FBI and the other agencies want to remain in the background, as they have in many of these operations going on around the world. No doubt, your office can receive most of the accolades for breaking this local drug ring in due course. Bill and I absolutely want to remain anonymous in this matter, by the way. Can you commit to this?"

"Yes, I can commit to calling the FBI before taking any action in our jurisdiction on individuals on this list of yours. Of course, we already coordinate with them on a regular basis. Remember the Boston Marathon massacre? Let me have a look at your list."

I hand it to him after which he scans it briefly, then replies, "Yes, I recognize some of these names. Possibly we already have evidence we can add to your investigation. I'll make contact with the attorney overseeing that case to get the files reviewed and will make a point of talking to your agent tomorrow. Thank you for supplying this information, much appreciated"

At this, he gives a little wave as he exits the front door, strides across the porch and down the steps, getting back into his city vehicle. Turning on the engine, he pulls forward to make a U-turn in the wide driveway and then heads off, noticeably slowing down as he makes his way past the Lamborghini. Bill and I breathe a sigh of relief. He turns to me and exclaims, "Hey, I didn't think you'd actually use the urn. How in the world did you cry so easily?"

"Well, I was just thinking about Karen and how I miss her so much."

"So are you actually going to give her up? Who will you talk to in her place? I am of course offering myself up for this role."

"I don't know if I can ever give up Karen completely, although lately I can't seem to keep the two roles separated. What do you think that means?"

"Maybe it means you're finally feeling "whole" now, darlin'—and no longer have the need of an imaginary friend."

"Hmmm. Well, I never thought of Karen as imaginary. In fact, she is far more real than almost all of my school friends."

Just then Karen's phone rings. "Don't we ever get time to just enjoy each other? If this is a new case, I'll try to turn it down."

I answer simply, "Hello."

"Is that you, Gee? Jackie gave me this number. It's Rosalie (Vassar roommate)… and I…I need your help please. The FBI has impounded my recent shipment of furniture from my hometown in Argentina. I fear my whole import/export business is in jeopardy. *I may even be arrested!*

They're t-t-tearing everything apart, claiming the merchandise is filled with drugs. I have no knowledge of any of this. Can you help me, please, Gee? Can you go with me to Argentina right away?"

"Why do you think I can help you, Rosalie?"

"One of the FBI agents let slip to his partner the comment, 'I wonder if this relates to G.W.'s investigation of the South American drug cartels?' I knew that had to be you, as there is only one G.W. after all, so I tried calling you, but the phone company said the number was out of service. So, I called Jackie and she gave me this number."

"I'm *so* sorry to hear this news of yours, Rosalie, but we literally just got back to the States after being away for weeks. Can you possibly come to Boston and maybe we can figure something out."

"Ok, yes, I can be there sometime late in the day tomorrow."

"Alright, let me know when your flight gets in and I'll arrange to have our chauffeur, James, pick you up. We'll have cocktails waiting by the pool when you arrive. See you manana, Rosalie."

CHAPTER 24   Argentina awaits

James picks up Rosalie as planned and deposits her at the Lowell Mansion just before 5 p.m. the next day. I was surprised to discover she drinks gin martinis, for some reason I always associated her with more fruity South American type drinks and made a comment along these lines. Once she'd settled into her chair and had a quick sip, she said, "Gee, you know I've been in the U.S. since I was three years old and I am an American citizen."

"Hmmm, how about that? I always thought you spoke with a slight accent. And it was certainly not a New York twang."

She giggled and shook her head, rolling her eyes a bit she said, "Oh, I started using the accent in college during my Vassar days. The boys liked it and so did some of my professors. I think I got higher grades by using the accent."

"Sheesh, I didn't realize you were that devious! It just goes to show that one doesn't really know people, sometimes we're actually quite different inside."

"Jackie mentioned the name Karen. Who's this Karen?"

"Well, Rosalie…touché! You see, Karen is *my* secret inside life. When I'm Karen, I'm a private detective. Gee is the socialite. It's a long story and will require many drinks to explain. So, for now, let's get into your problem. So what's this about drugs and some alleged tie to your furniture company?"

"Ok," she then took more of a gulp of the martini this time and seemed to settle herself for a minute, briefly closing her eyes. She looked up with an earnest look on her face and continued, "I operate my business, American Fine Imports/Exports, from New York City, and I have a showroom located just off Times Square. One of my lines of imports is handmade furniture from my parents' hometown in northern Argentina. It's a poor area and my furniture sales have helped the local economy there. However, in the last year, there have been production issues that seemed to have no explanation vs. in previous years, I guess the drug cartels must have gotten to them somehow, that's my worry anyway. But I just find it so hard to believe that my cousins knew anything about the drugs being smuggled into the U.S. inside the furniture. I need a detective to go with me and help discover how this happened."

Bill then says, "Well, other than the disturbing reason for traveling, this sounds like a good trip. I've never been to Argentina or the Pampas region."

Rosalie turns to him, explaining, "My town's north of the Pampas in a wooded forest area. However, we could also take a quick run to the Pampas and get you on a horse to ride if that interests you."

I'm feeling a little impatient at this point for some reason—probably because I cannot *believe* this Boston socialite is yet again being dragged into contact with international drug thugs—and I purposely switch the focus of the conversation. "So, Rosalie, what did Jackie say about our recent adventures?"

"She told me about you returning the panda bear to China and you seeing Katy in Hong Kong. I had totally forgotten she was part Chinese. What's she doing there anyway?"

"We had a good time with her. She has something to do with some family investments in the U.S. I guess she was meeting with them about it, she didn't really say." (I did not want to disclose too much to Rosalie as she might be more ensnared in the drug cartel's clutches than she's letting on.) "Let me change the subject yet again though. It seems that Cassie's murder keeps coming up whenever any of us alums get together. Jackie, Katy, and I beat our heads together in Hong Kong discussing it, but to no avail. The police already consider it a cold case now, so nothing more will likely happen on their end to speak of. Do you have any thoughts about it, Rosalie? What do you think may have happened? Or why?"

"Well, I have mulled it around in my head also—after all, that was a horrific experience, being with an old friend from college catching up one minute and the next day she's suddenly dead. Killed! I just can't believe any of our Vassar girls murdered Cassie though. Could somebody else have sneaked in there without us seeing him?"

"I thought Cassie's husband, Glenn, was the best suspect, but he appears to have an alibi. Did you ever meet Glenn, Rosalie? He was kind of charming to women."

"No, I never met him myself. Cassie had called me a couple of times fairly recently. She was looking for a particular piece of furniture for her patio in Kansas City. I ended up shipping her a complete outdoor set of pool furniture constructed by the artisans in my parents' village."

I think maybe this is the connection with the drugs and the furniture. Cassie may have shown one of her drug clients the massive legs on the pool furniture. "Rosalie, did Cassie ever tell you about her investment business?"

"She just mentioned she was into handling investments for some South American clients. I remember her telling me she had a couple of low-risk, high-return investments and asking if I had any money. Sounded to me like a sales pitch I wasn't in the mood for at the time so I told her I had no extra cash currently but would keep her in mind for the future. We never discussed anything further as that was actually the last conversation I had with her. Oh, poor Cassie!"

I lean over and pat her as she's suddenly become so emotional. "Well it's a good thing you didn't get back to her. Glenn was recently tried for illegal money laundering and I believe he's now in prison."

"Oh m'gosh! Did this happen before Cassie was murdered?"

"No, it's a recent development. Cassie was involved as an officer in several of Glenn's corporations, so she would have been indicted too- IF she hadn't been killed that is."

Rosalie then replied, "Remember how depressed Cassie was at the Vassar Alum reunion? In fact…thinking back…didn't she jump off your boat and nearly drown at one point?"

"Yes, she did; in fact, I thought it may have been a suicide attempt at the time—or that Jackie pushed her. You know, Jackie did know Glenn and apparently he was setting her up in hopes of them having an affair."

"Oh, I can't believe Jackie pushed her, or for that matter, that you pushed her."

"Cassie did maintain she was not suicidal when we talked to her about it afterwards. I know that Jackie and I did not push her. The point is…somebody killed her, and it appears to be one of our group!"

Bill then broke in, "Ok, ladies…I'm sorry but I've had enough of this talk just now. Let's give our brains a rest from these sordid matters for just a bit please. The pool is warm. Let's all go for a swim, ok? You just got here, Rosalie, as did we. We need to spend a day or two and plan the Argentina trip and we can discuss along the way more of the background information needed. The plane is being serviced and checked out, so it may be a couple of days before it's ready to travel and I can file a flight plan."

The next morning, I'm up and out early for my morning run, having so badly missed this energizing way of starting the day recently. I stop on a bench for a quick rest, guess I'm getting soft and out of shape. Even as my body temporarily slows down, all these details keep running through my brain. So now we have a new international drug smuggling problem. Rosalie appears innocent, but who knows at this point in time? This jaunt to Argentina will hopefully give me a better perspective. I decide to call Senator Throckmorton and bring him up to date on my meeting with the Boston D.A., along with an update on this alarming new matter that's suddenly arisen.

Ringing his number, Laura Lee answers the line. She is enthusiastic about our tent city factory project, saying "The Senator is telling everyone about it. I think there's some government funding he's in the process of sourcing. If not, the government may be a large purchaser of the tent units themselves. Supplying these tent cities for refugees gives us a lot better PR than selling them guns and training them to kill each other. The Senator is in a meeting. Isn't he always? Can you take a call this evening, Gee?"

"Anytime, at his convenience, but please tell him we are leaving in two days for Argentina. Our college chum, Rosalie, has a problem with U.S. Customs. It seems that some drug cartel there got a hold of some furniture she was importing, and filled the hollow legs with drugs, which was discovered by Customs when the freight arrived. Bill and I are flying with her to Argentina to see what we can find out as she's utterly bewildered by this news."

Ma Mah hosts us for dinner that evening. She has also invited four of her friends who 'just want to meet the heroine who killed the Boston Symphony maniac.' Will this notoriety never end? I wish Karen had killed the perp. Too bad she doesn't like classical music, or she might have been the one at the symphony that night! While I can pretty much manage to keep her hidden—other than those well-honed marksmanship skills of hers—socialite G.W. Lowell is out there front and center for all to see. I now fear another one of those evenings awaits!

The meal goes well, although I do my best to dodge direct discussion of the massacre (which will only serve to lose my appetite). "Please just read the papers. They have given accurate accounts of the whole horrible ordeal. What I would like to talk about instead is getting rid of fully automatic weapons and semi-automatics which are easy to convert into fully-automatic weapons. Did you happen to read the account of what I started in Liberty, Maine?"

One of the well-coiffed ladies nods, replying, "Yes, we did read about that, your mother sent the first article our way. It is amazing that you transformed that paramilitary group into real American citizens. Were you aware that 60 Minutes did a follow-up story on the Sons of Liberty? They now have all their children in public schools and three members of the group, or their wives, have already been elected to the school board. One of them—Van you called him— is now the Mayor of the town following his predecessor's resignation. That one man, Buck, is finishing his law degree and working part-time as a paralegal for his father. The multi-shot piles of welded clips are also showing up in many of the surrounding towns and villages."

"No, we were out of the country at the time and missed that program. Do you think we—or you personally—could start a program here in Massachusetts to get these clips off the streets?"

"Now that you bring it up, yes, we really should. Ok, we'll start talking and writing about it. We can even setup some town hall meetings. Would you agree to speak at some of them please, Gee?"

"Yes, ok, I can do that. And I'll also contact Buck and Van—now that they're bona fide TV stars—and see about having them talk at the meetings about Liberty's and their own personal transformations."

As I'm expecting a call from Senator Throckmorton, I excuse myself after dessert as my phone is buzzing. "Hello, Gee. I understand you called. Hey, I can tell you interest is running high on your tent city project. However, it needs one new item we haven't discussed before. The tents need furniture, particularly furniture that can be folded up or stored easily. Please see what you can do about that."

"Ok, I will, Senator. But I wanted to let you know we're leaving tomorrow for Argentina with a friend in the import/export business, and I wanted to touch base with you before we take off on that trip. In brief, as I told Laura Lee, she's been importing furniture from her family's hometown west of Cordoba in Argentina, and the last shipment had drugs inserted in the hollowed-out legs. She claims no knowledge of this. She has been importing artisan furniture from her cousins for years with no problems. Somehow the drug dealers have either influenced the family or modified the furniture directly without their knowledge. We are flying down to check it out for her."

"Well, I can go ahead and call President Macri—he's a friend I've worked with before. I will have him put a federal drug enforcement person of theirs at your disposal during your trip. Maybe you can catch this at the embryonic stage, hopefully anyway."

"Great! This will give us another line of attack. Surely the Argentine government knows about these drug traffickers, at least to some degree. Oh, by the way, Senator, I met with the Boston D.A. recently and was finally able to straighten out my problems with him—and I especially wanted to thank you for contacting him on my behalf. I also gave him a list of the suspected drug operators in Boston and put him in touch with my FBI connection. He's also going to coordinate their activities with the FBI and share information. I hope the info we passed along helps lead to many arrests."

"Sounds good, and you're welcome, I'm relieved to hear that matter's behind you now. Listen, you will want to refuel in Buenos Aires. I'll arrange for the drug enforcement person to seek you out when you land there. Good luck. I hope to see you soon, Gee."

A bit later, I meet Bill and Rosalie at the pool for an evening swim. I tell them about my conversation with Senator Throckmorton, and the drug enforcement person he says he'll have us meet up with in Buenos Aires.

"Gee, I wish I had your contacts. You go right to the top, don't you?"

"You know, I had an old friend who told me, 'Always go to the top. Never talk with anyone who doesn't have the authority to say yes.' And I try to do that whenever I can. Hey…it works!"

Bill then tells us, "Ladies, the plane will be ready in the a.m. We will need to make a couple of stops for fuel en route. I've hired a relief pilot to accompany us on the trip, and I've had the plane stocked with food and beverages. You might want to see if there's anything else you want to take along."

Ah-h, yet another new adventure. So who am I? Am I Gee, or am I Karen, or do I need to "be" both? The Argentine cousins are probably middle-class workers. The drug agent is a government worker. I guess Karen is best for this gig. If we have to attend a big deal social affair in Cordoba, then I can morph back into Gee as needed.

At eight a.m., James drops us at the airport. The relief pilot is already inside the plane and checking the controls. His name is Lloyd, and Rosalie tells me under her breath she thinks he's kind of cute. I never think of guys as "cute"! Perhaps Lloyd is handsome, but definitely not my type.

Hey…a mental rubber band snaps inside my brain—I'm engaged to Bill! I wonder how he compares my looks when I appear as Karen vs. my appearance when I'm Gee? He did dodge the question when I asked him about which one of us was better in bed. And, frankly, I think I have better sex as Karen than as Gee. After all, Karen is imaginary, so she can freely do anything at all and is completely uninhibited. And I was worried for a time about losing Karen's identity, or that it was merging into

Gee's identity. Nope…I'm now pretty sure I will keep the Karen identity around for life. Gee's an uptight socialite. Karen is free of that! *(Isn't it interesting that I had this entire conversation with myself only as Gee. Karen never jumped into the conversation with her thoughts or desires regarding our "separateness.")*

We fly to Miami and spent the night there. After refueling in the morning, we departed at six a.m. and fly the lengthy distance down to the capital of Brazil, Brasilia, for our next stop. We landed early afternoon the following day in Buenos Aires. Our assigned drug enforcement agent meets us as planned upon our arrival. He introduces himself as Ricard Santos.

"Welcome to Argentina. I know little of your background but have heard you have been important in producing evidence to fight the drug trade. We do have a challenging drug problem here in Argentina, but not to the extent that you have in the U.S. Please tell me why you are here."

Rosalie then introduces herself and launches into her story of her family business's sudden involvement in drug smuggling. She tells him she simply cannot believe her cousins would be involved though and lets him know this is what we are now here to find out. Her cousins live just west of Cordoba in a small town, Villa San Nicolas, which is located in the foothills of the Andes. She says to him, "We plan to fly to Cordoba, spend the night, and rent a car. Then we're on to Villa San Nicolas in the morning. Can you tell us anything about the drug dealers in that area?"

Ricard replies, "Cordoba is a big city of 1.4 million people. It is surrounded by rich agricultural lands where all kinds of crops are grown, including drugs. Villa San Nicolas is at the edge of the forest in the low foothills of the Andes Mountains. The wood that your cousins use surely comes from these forests. There probably are secluded glens in the forest that also are used to grow drug-producing plants. Your cousins may have stumbled upon one of these clandestine crops."

We stay in Buenos Aires as planned and decide to catch a little of the local night life. The next morning, it's a short flight to Cordoba and Ricard suggests we spend the night there. He tells us he wants to confer with the local drug enforcement people. We are lucky in getting tickets to a local rodeo scheduled for later that day where we can see the Argentine gauchos perform. Ricard meets us for dinner and another evening's round of visiting nightclubs—so far, this South American gig has just been one delightful party.

At one point in the evening though, Ricard leans in close and tells us, "Listen, I have now met with our people regionally. I'm informed there is newly detected drug activity in the Villa San Nicolas area. The early reports are these guys are well-armed with automatic weapons and have forced several people into the area's drug trade."

I ask him, "Are you carrying a gun, Ricard? Can you get me a small hand gun and also a long-range riffle?"

"Yes, I always carry a pistol myself. However, I am not sure that it is legal for you to have these guns in Argentina as you request. I do know a local gun dealer here in Cordoba. I will introduce you and turn my head. Whatever deal you make, is your deal. I know nothing about it. I understand your need to be protected, but that's the best I can do."

On the way out of town we stop at a large gun shop. Ricard goes with me into the store and finds his contact who is one of the clerks in the store. He tells the clerk to rent me whatever I desire in guns and that I will return them in one week, he then turns and heads back outside to the car, saying over his shoulder, "But I wasn't in here today." I pick up a .45 caliber as well as a .38 caliber pistol, plus a long-range rifle with two ten shot clips. I also ask the clerk for a box of ammunition for each gun. He produces a rental agreement and I scrawl an illegible signature on the agreement. I pay him $300 in cash, pack up my new merchandise, and leave.

Back outside, Ricard says, "You see, we have our own gun problem here in Argentina. If you get into a gun battle with any of these drug people, try to just wound them. If you kill them, it will involve much paperwork and no doubt you will not be able to leave the country for several weeks at a minimum until the situation is resolved."

Bill chimes in at this point, "Well, I certainly hope we don't have to use these. As for me, I'm really just learning to shoot pistols. But Karen here is an excellent marksman…er, markswoman."

Ricard replies, "I thought your name is Gee!"

I reply, "Actually my detective alias is Karen. And, yes, I am a good shot. But Bill here is being modest. He has also become a first rate marksman in recent months."

We stash the guns under the lid over the spare tire of the rented Land Rover and head off to Villa San Nicolas. Rosalie wonders aloud what she has gotten us into. With this remark, Bill and I quickly glance at each other, saying nothing. Thankfully Lloyd seems to have dozed off.

A four-lane highway connects us rapidly to the small village. Rosalie tells us her cousins live on the corner of El Pais and 25 de Mayo streets. The town itself is a small dusty village with the mountains rising on its western edge. We easily find our way there with our GPS app on our cell phones. Incidentally, I still have my Chinese cell phone with its special features. However, the drug cartel data from the Hong Kong police has now disappeared from my phone. The camera and the recorder work just fine though and I've now set that app up so I can use its voice-activated feature, even when the phone appears to be off.

Now that we've arrived, Rosalie calls her cousin, Luis, and tells him four of us are on our way to his house. We leave Lloyd, the relief pilot, in Cordoba in case anything happens to us. We inform him to just go around town and see the sights and I tell him I'm sure he'll enjoy his stay while we are out prowling around the countryside.

Luis has two houses on the property and is able to put the four of us up in one of them. The furniture factory is next to the houses on the corner of the two streets. Luis's wife, Lucita, prepares dinner for us that night. To contribute, we produce some bottles of wine we had purchased at a vineyard outside of Cordoba where we stopped briefly en route.

At one point, Rosalie turns to Luis and asks bluntly, "Did you know there were drugs in the legs of the furniture you sent me?"

Luis seems surprised at this but then quickly replies, "I was afraid there was. Three men with guns instructed me to place legs on the furniture which they had brought with them. I had no choice but to do what they wanted. The furniture was to be shipped to you for a client named Jerry Smith."

I ask, "Did they make the legs, or did you make them?"

"No, they were already made when they brought them here. I simply attached them to certain small tables, similar to our regular line. I was afraid that there were drugs in the legs, I'm so-o sorry."

Ricard then asks, "Where do you get the wood for your furniture?"

"I have a supplier about five miles up in the hills. Often, he brings me the wood, but sometimes I go out there to get it myself."

"And are they growing drug crops around there?"

"I have not seen any, but there are several locked gates, each with a couple of armed guards. I don't think that they are guarding just the forest."

"Luis, have you seen any of the three gauchos here in town? Have they brought you any new legs for shipment?"

" I have seen their truck at a local bar, but I never go to that one… there are always a lot of fights in there. No, they have not brought me any new legs to install."

Rosalie then says, "It has been less than two weeks since the FBI and Customs seized the furniture with the drugs in it. Do you think the word has made it back here by now?"

I join in, "I think it's at least possible they don't know as yet. So, was this Jerry Smith supposed to pick up the furniture from Customs, or from your shop?"

"No, he was supposed to pick up his order from my shop. I had not heard anything from him when I left the store, but of course I was the one who should be contacting him re: the furniture's arrival. Shall I call and find out if he has called the shop?"

At this, my brain kicks into Karen mode, "Yes, Rosalie, call your shop and see if he has checked in. Ricard, what do you think of this plan I have working in my head? Suppose we—Luis?, Rosalie?, myself? contact these people at the bar and suggest a meeting. Maybe we tell them the drugs were discovered, but we now have a plan for future shipments. We tell them we would like a meeting with the principal owners. But then say that even though we have this plan, it will cost them for us to implement it."

Ricard thinks about it for a minute, then responds, "Yes, we could have Luis contact them at the bar. They will want to check us out before they call any of their superiors though. We have Luis tell them to come to the shop in the evening when the workers are not there. We know they carry guns. There are three of them, but five of us. We make sure they see our guns, but two of us are women, so they will no doubt consider us to all be on equal ground. They will come," he announces with some certainty in his voice as he nods.

The next day, we tour the furniture factory. I tell Luis about our tent city project and that we need serviceable but foldable furniture for the project, just very basic and functional designs. We will initially need hundreds of pieces of furniture for two committed projects slated for Africa. We provide him the sizes of the tents and ask him to have his staff come up with furnishings which will fit the tents.

Luis then drives Ricard and me in his truck out to meet with his wood supplier so we can get a feel for the countryside regionally. I note the roads which look like they're receiving the heaviest use from vehicle traffic. There are indeed guards posted at several gates, but no sign of any dogs—my guess is that nobody sneaks around areas where there are armed guards. Their only fear is a police raid, and I would guess that they have informants to tell them when one might be imminent.

Back in town, we cruise by the local bars and Luis spots the drug guys who look like ordinary gauchos, except for their shiny, new, expensive boots. They are just arriving at the rough-sounding bar we'd been discussing. We park around the corner and Luis goes inside the dark, smelly, smoke-filled building, Latin music is blaring from a vintage-looking jukebox. He informs them that his cousin, Rosalie, from the U.S is here in town with a potential buyer of their products. "There was some mix-up with their last shipment," he says, but then tells them Rosalie will discuss that situation with them. "Can we have a meeting at the furniture factory in one hour?" They agree to come as soon as they have a couple of beers.

An hour and a half later, the three show up at the factory. We see the bulges of their guns under their shirts, just above their waists. By contrast, Bill and Ricard's guns are clearly visible. I take charge of the meeting and usher the three to a large markout table where furniture patterns are traced out and cut and tell them to sit down. I lay my pistol on the table with a sharp thud. "Gentlemen, we will lay down our guns here today, and also ask you put yours down as well, por favor. I also want everyone's cell phones out and placed here on the table. Yes-yes, I am turning mine off. Please turn yours off now too." At this they turn and glance at one another, grumbling, but then slowly comply. One says, "And who are YOU, gringa, to tell us what to do?"

"I just may be the one who makes you rich, OR I may be the one who kills you, if you don't comply with my orders." I snatch up my pistol from the table and point it at the questioner's head, who is taller than the other two and possibly a bit brighter. The other pair appear quite drunk. "You with the mouth, what's your name?"

"Ok, ok, lady. I was just asking. My name is Garcia Moranes. These are mi amigos. What are we here to talk about?"

"I want to meet with your bosses. And next time we have a meeting, I want it to be prompt. Comprende? Your last shipment in Luis's furniture was so poorly packaged that the Customs' dogs immediately found the drugs. That should be easy to fix, and I can show you how to do it. That was small potatoes and the loss is hardly worth talking about. By the way, you should tell your bosses. Remember this next part carefully! Cassie's dead, and Glenn is now in prison for it. I am taking over their business and will be the one dealing with your bosses. I don't want to spend a lot of time down here in this poor excuse of a town though. Therefore, I want a meeting tomorrow night or the next morning here at the factory. Let Luis know when we can meet. We can close the factory for the afternoon and thus have privacy. As it'll be daytime, they'll be able to readily see we won't have any policeman on-hand ready to arrest you. I don't like cops any better than you do. That's all I have to say. Ok, on your way. Good night—buenas noches, hombres."

"Yes-yes, that is my cell phone." I pick up the phone and my gun and stride out of the factory. The three stooges pick up their phones and guns and stumble out, clearly they each had more to drink than just a couple beers.

We return immediately to Luis's house. Bill heads to the small bar cart and pours us each a stiff drink. Ricard exclaims as he sinks into the sofa, "My God! That was beautiful. When you snatched your gun, and put it to his head, I thought he'd wet his pants! What do you think they are calling you? You were the most perfect 'impatient bitch' that I have ever seen, pardon my French!"

Bill then laughed, "And just think, yours truly is actually engaged to this woman!"

Rosalie then replies, "Well, even though they probably don't know who Cassie and Glenn are, I bet some of their bosses at least know Glenn. That bit of bait may be sufficient to get their attention."

Ricard then asks, "So, did you record the conversation?"

"Yes, I did, and I also got pictures of the three of them. Let me show them to you, and thanks for reminding me as I'll shut off the recording app now too.

"Once I get pictures of the bosses, you can send them back to your department. Hopefully we can get enough conversation on tape to implicate them in their drug business. What we need now is to arrange a shipment of the goods. Maybe we can get an invitation to their place of business."

The next day Luis gets a phone call setting up the meeting for the following afternoon at two o'clock in the factory. They demand that the power to the factory will be turned off for the meeting.

The factory is being watched until after the meeting. Sleepy bums with dirty woolen ponchos appear to be asleep in positions that view all the surrounding streets.

At five minutes to two, a pair of black limos pull up just outside the factory. Luis flips off the power to the factory at the main breaker box on the side of the building. Five guys with automatic guns then exit the limos and quickly station themselves at various doors to the factory. Luis and Bill station themselves outside of two doors adjacent to the parking lot. Luis has an old shotgun, and Bill's in possession of the semi-automatic rifle.

Ricard, Rosalie, and I will conduct the meeting. Three well-dressed drug lords represent the other side. They're accompanied by three more bodyguards. No wonder it took two sizable vehicles to transport them and their entourage.

I begin the conversation, "Welcome, gentlemen. I see you are more punctual than those other three clowns were. Could you have all your bodyguards stand over near the door por favor? That way, it's three of us and three of you. The power is off as you requested, and the cameras don't operate without power. Here is my gun. Here too is my cell phone. Would you like to turn it off? One of them switches it off and lays it on the table. Yes-yes, would you also switch yours off? Thank you. We don't know each other, so it pays to be careful."

One of them speaks, "Moranes said you mentioned something about Cassie and Glenn. I know them very well. I did hear that Cassie had been murdered. What exactly happened to her and where is Glenn now?"

"Glenn was arrested for Cassie's murder and tried in a little-publicized court in Montana, or Idaho—I don't know which. I heard he's now in prison, but I don't know which one. I knew Cassie quite well and have now taken over some of her business dealings. The FBI is looking into a couple of Glenn's corporations. I haven't heard anything more than that. With my personal holdings, I have acquired and/or made proposals to merge over three billion dollars' worth of assets. Although you haven't given me your individual names, I would guess you own a large portion of some of these assets. I have spoken with a couple of senators on the

Homeland Securities Oversight Committee about their ties to Glenn. Since Glenn is now gone, I will now be your contact with those gentlemen."

"My name is Aldo Casio and, yes-yes, I knew and dealt with Glenn many times. He and Cassie put me into many fine investments. I will now need someone whom I can trust to deal with those assets. There is much more than three billion dollars at stake here. Is that not correct, gentlemen?"

I then responded, "Since I have already purchased some of the assets, I guess I am already into your business."

"Yes, you are. My name is Rolando Longstreet and I have 35% of several of Glenn's corporations. I have made so much money from drugs that I am now retiring from that business. I need to have my assets managed in a legal and proper way with a good, honest money manager. I don't want them seized because of laundered money transactions from other clients like Aldo and Jon here."

Jon's head turns quickly upon hearing this and he says angrily, "Wait a minute. You made your money on drugs. You laundered lots of money in the past. Don't you suddenly get all high and mighty on us!"

"Gentlemen, gentlemen, I can handle both sides of this equation. I have a friend, Kathleen, who operates an investment business. She does not deal in cash but only with checks from clean businesses. I can place Rolando in contact with her."

Jon has seemingly regained his composure and replies, "Alright, that settles that problem I suppose. The drugs were mine that your Customs agents found. I don't know how they found them though. They were double wrapped plus sealed with wax."

"Where did you turn the legs for the tables? Were they in proximity to the drugs? It is possible that the wood itself had picked up a residual drug scent."

"Si, si, you are probably right. The legs were turned next to the packing table." As he says this, he thumps his hand against his forehead in realizing their stupidity.

I nod and say to him, "My solution is to have Luis turn the legs containing the hollowed-out drug compartment. Take the cardboard out of the center of a roll of paper towels. Double wrap the drugs and place them inside the cardboard sleeve. Seal the ends with wax. Deliver them to Luis. He can spray paint the outside of the sleeves to cover up any remaining smell. Once the tables are put together, Luis can give the whole table another spray of paint or varnish. That should take care of the dog-sniffing problem."

"Well, little lady, you have a good mind for these things. Would you like to help us design a compartment for cars and trucks? How about designing us some fake bananas? In the meantime, I will prepare a new shipment with your suggestions."

Aldo then says, "It looks like we may be in business together alright but we do still need to check you out though, I'm sure you understand. Give us the names of the entities you are operating under. I will also talk with Senator Closs and see what he knows about you. I will give you my number in Bogota—we will meet there in three weeks to close the deal. I think this meeting is now over."

The three stand up and head toward the exit. I have pictures of them and the names they gave us. Soon we will know if these are their real names. Again, it seems anti-climactic. There was no shoot-out, sudden raid, or arrests as they calmly stride away outside the factory. Ricard promises us things will happen in the future. Luis says he'll inform Rosalie, Ricard, and me when the next drug shipment will leave Argentina. I will then alert the FBI and we will see if the shipment clears Customs.

We return to Cordoba to pick up our plane and then begin trying to find our relief pilot, Lloyd. He does not seem to be at his hotel, and we're told by their front desk staff he has not been seen for two days. At this report, I immediately worry that the drug people have taken him as an example to us of what can happen if we are not being straight with them.

We then tour the nearby bars and cafes asking for news of our missing pilot. At the Americana Bar, we hear tell Lloyd has spent many hours there with a particularly hot number named Carmen. We then chat up some local teenagers hanging around the corner. Ricard asks them if they know where Carmen lives? "Quién sabe?" I slap a $20 bill in the eldest of the group's outstretched hand. He then nods and gestures down the street toward a small two-story hotel. I question, "Hotel?" He shrugs. I slap another $20 in his hand. "Si, hotel, yes, ahí."

We proceed to the small Amiga Hotel, and enter the cramped lobby painted in shades of orange and vivid red. Large paintings of matadors battling ferocious bulls are featured on a wall-to-wall mural behind the desk. We question the clerk about the "lady" in question and he then points us to room six—although another $20 is required to obtain this information. We hear music coming from inside as Bill knocks on the door, but no activity. After 30 seconds or so, he pounds on the door and yells for Lloyd. Carmen opens the door, seemingly nonchalant about the intrusion, and points to the bed. "Él está aquí, señor."

I walk inside a cheerfully decorated room which Carmen obviously uses for both her home and "business"…whatever that may be. Heading to the bathroom, I quickly return with a glass of water which I proceed to pour onto the head of the drunken lug sprawled across the garish floral-patterned sheets. "Hey, what happened to that cute guy you were describing to us, Rosalie?" She laughs in reply, "Well, obviously Carmen roped him but good!"

We pull Lloyd to his feet, wait while he tucks in his shirt and runs a comb through his tousled hair as he tries to shake his head sober, and then we proceed to steer him to the waiting taxi, one of us on each arm and the other two guiding him gently from behind. He then begins to sob, "Just leave me here. Don't you realize I'm in lo-o-ove? After a short drive, we get him back inside the hotel and up to his room where Bill and Ricard pull off his clothes and dump him in a cold shower while Rosalie and I plop down on the edge of the bed.

Bill exclaims, "Well, ladies and gentlemen, sorry to report, but he clearly can't fly for at least 36 hours—maybe longer."

Ricard offers, "I could have him put in a local jail cell for a day or two to sober up. You all could play and see our sights until he's ready to resume his duties."

"Yes," I nod in agreement, "Go ahead and have him locked up. Thanks, Ricard, that oughta make a lasting impression on him."

Rosalie then says, "Well, in the meantime, I will have my cousin, Luis, come to town and we can finalize the deal for the furniture for your tent cities."

"And I will take your photos of the group and the recordings to our drug enforcement bureau," Ricard says. "Possibly we have enough to arrest them. Is there any way you could get Glenn to testify against them? I know he's in prison, but maybe that will help—that would put them away forever."

Shortly thereafter I forward the photos and recordings on to the CIA in Washington via a special FTP account they've setup for my use. Turns out the three had actually used their real names when introducing themselves. The pictures of them then verified their identities. Their arrests are now to be determined at a higher level in coordinating between our two countries.

Forty hours later we are in the air—piloted by a sober and seemingly sheepish Lloyd and a happy-looking Rosalie who, for some unfathomable reason, still appears smitten.

CHAPTER 25   United...at last

Arriving back from Argentina, although pretty tired from our jaunt south, we decide to stop first in D.C. and arrange an impromptu meeting with our contacts at the FBI and CIA. We convince them that Rosalie was an unwitting victim of the drugs smuggled into the country via her furniture imports, also alerting them to the next scheduled delivery being setup, and informing them of precisely how the drugs will be concealed. Having already digitally supplied the materials we obtained of these recent interactions to them, we're told this evidence, in combination with the next shipment of drugs, will be enough to arrest them on American soil, or in other cooperating countries.

After leaving Washington, we drop Rosalie in New York City, and Bill and I then fly home to Boston. Ma Mah herself opens the door as we arrive and is clearly glad to see us, hugging us each warmly. Soon after we've taken a short while to freshen up, we head down the staircase from the second floor to meet up with her in the library for an afternoon cocktail. Ma Mah exclaims, "I am so relieved you two are back in the States." Reaching over and patting each of us on the hand, "I wonder if you can now slow-w down enough and spend a little time here for awhile please?"

"Oh I hope so, Ma Mah. We've missed you too," I tell her as I reach around her slender shoulder, giving her a quick one-armed squeeze.

"Since you two are now engaged, we should also talk about wedding plans—don't you think? After all, I am getting old and would like to see my only daughter married, thank you very much."

"Well, that's certainly a reasonable request—but so much has been going on with all this international back and forth we haven't made much headway on any decisions to speak of. Do you know what Percy and Hollie want to do in the meantime? You know Percy gave her a ring, right, Ma Mah? Well, we all have talked briefly about having a double wedding. What do you think about that?"

"Oh, I *like* that idea! Two weddings, but only one mess, all the same relatives on our side, but then Bill's relatives and Hollie's relatives. Hmmm, sounds too sizable a guest list to have here at the house though. Where else would the four of you like to hold the ceremony?"

"I like Boston, but a rented hall certainly doesn't sound very romantic. Maybe we should consider some scenic spot somewhere else in the world?"

As it happens, Percy phoned later in the evening. "I'm sending out written invitations for you all plus some of my friends to come down to Taft Plantation for our Grand Opening. Everything is finally complete, and the decorators are just putting the finishing touches on all the rooms. My new chef is preparing a full menu and is busily breaking in the kitchen help. We will be ready in two weeks, but you three can come early if you wish."

Ma Mah says, "Sounds delightful. You two go down to the plantation a couple of days early as your brother suggests. I will then take my plane down the day before the celebration. I shall also bring two of your cousins with me, plus a gentleman friend."

"Really, Ma Mah? So, pray tell, who are you seeing?"

"Well, you probably know him. He's James, our chauffeur."

"What? How did that happen? I guess we shouldn't leave you unsupervised, madame!"

Laughing, and with her cheeks suddenly displaying a hint of a pink, she replies, "You're probably right about that. You know I hate to drink alone, but I do love my five o'clock martini. So, one day, I invited James to join me, and it became a habit every day since. He has been here so long that he knows all the family secrets. We talk a lot about you, Gee, and the horrible murders you've been entangled with—he also helped me wrestle with your dealings regarding the D.A., before that mess finally got sorted."

"Well, I think this is just lovely news, Ma Mah! You need male companionship. I hate to tell you, but some of your female socialite friends are horrible! What's her name? Tallulu Crackenback—she drives me nuts—although I must admit this romance of yours will surely spur a bit of gossip among that crowd!"

The next ten days pass with no further incidents, no phone calls for Karen's services, no reporters, and no lurking hulks invading my dreams. Each day I awake normally, maybe a few times with Bill nuzzling my neck, but none of those sudden being-jolted awakenings have occurred of late. I guess life is getting boring. Will married life be boring? Am I ready for that? I wonder...........zzzz.

Soon we're off again to the Taft Plantation. Percy has a new stretch white limo and the driver pick us up at the airport. Bill comments to him as we climb inside, "I guess Percy and the senator finally arranged to get the airstrip runway re-paved. It's also now 500' longer," to which the chauffeur nods obligingly.

Arriving just outside the entrance to the mansion, the limo pulls up and stops. We're instructed to exit the vehicle. As the driver holds the door open for us I say, "Hey, wait a minute, is that you, Jackson? I didn't recognize you all cleaned up and in a uniform. How'd that happen?"

"Mr. Percy said I was getting too old for all that heavy construction stuff and asked would I like to be a limo driver? How could I refuse? My wife loves this outfit. Mr. Percy also hired her to manage the cleaning help. Believe me, she is one tough boss. She also wears an outfit of her own design, and she's also designed uniforms for all the cleaning staff, as well as the yard staff. I think we all look pretty spiffy!"

Bill exclaims, "Hey, that's splendid, Jackson. I recall wanting to get you away from Barney's construction staff. This is a perfect role for you, and the ride back here was very smooth indeed, thank you."

I then ask, "What about Pegleg Joe, or Robin Hood, is he still wearing that kooky green Merry Men outfit?"

"My wife, Oprah, couldn't do anything about Robin Hood. He will never give up being that character now, I fear. Anyway, everybody loves his antics and that getup of his He's gotten real good with his bow and arrows recently too. Now he challenges everyone who visits to a shooting contest, which he usually wins."

A horse-drawn carriage pulls up while we're having this brief exchange and Bill and I are escorted to the fold-down steps of the open carriage compartment. Jackson then introduces us to his cousin, Andrew, the driver. The carriage has been recently restored, the vintage golden oak wood now varnished and gleaming. Plush seats upholstered in purple velvet face each other, and Andrew assists us as we step up inside.

With the pair of horses sporting gleaming coats as well, we then proceed clippity-clop down the long entrance road, which has also been newly repaved. The two palomino horses are immaculately groomed and trained in lively high steps, but they trot at a slow and measured pace, nevertheless looking theatrical indeed

Looking up as we traverse the long drive I say, "I remember these two rows of trees with the Spanish moss. They look just lovely with everything tidied up now. Oh, and I see Percy has had a row of red roses planted on each side of the road. And there's another row of small plantings just inside of the roses."

Andrew replies, "There are pansies this time of year and yellow tulips in the springtime. Isn't it beautiful?"

After a few minutes, the carriage stops at the front portico. As we descend Percy comes out to meet us. "So, how did you two like the carriage ride? I'll bet Ma Mah will love it. Where is she, by the way? I thought she was flying down with you?"

"She decided to arrive one day before the event. She's also bringing James and two cousins. I hope you have room for everybody…do you?"

Percy replies, "We now have a total of 36 rooms. I ended up tearing down the two one-story wings and replacing them with two-story wings, nine down and nine up in each wing. The area between the two wings is now a vaulted roof covering the dining area. I've also had enough solar panels put on the house and carriage house to completely handle our energy needs. Ok, you two, go on inside and stash your things in Room 9 which opens onto the pool. Hollie and I will meet you out there in forty-five minutes at the pool bar."

As we survey the fully renovated property, Bill and I agree the rooms are wonderful, very tastefully done in the old Southern style décor. We meet Hollie and Percy as arranged, and I ask her, "Where did you get all the old reproduction photos and artwork from this area and what looks like other parts of the old South?"

She replies, "I talked with your friend, Laura Lee, the senator's point person, and she actually came up with a good part of this collection. In fact, a few of these photos are from the senator's own personal collection. Aren't they splendid?"

Percy moves over and sits down next to Hollie. He takes her hand saying, "You two know we're engaged to be married. We considered tying the knot at this opening event, but then the wedding celebration would overshadow what we've worked so hard to accomplish here at Taft Plantation. Actually, Hollie has now decided she'd like us to be married at the refuge with the animals surrounding us. We could then have the reception here at the mansion."

I reply, "That sounds like a good advertisement for the animal rescue farm. What would you wear for a wedding dress?"

Hollie tilts her head to one side and glances off into the distance momentarily, "I don't know yet. I vacillate between a formal, traditional white dress vs. a less formal look I know I'd feel more comfortable in."

"Well, you can bet Ma Mah would prefer to see Percy attired in more suitably fancy traditional togs."

At which Percy then replies, "We all have batted around the idea of a joint wedding for the four of us, and I'm sure Ma Mah would like that held in Boston."

Bill joins in, "Say, maybe we should make it a triple wedding with Jackie and Charlie? We did brainstorm a bit about that idea when we were with them overseas."

Percy replies, "When they arrive, maybe we can have a group discussion about this topic together. Once Ma Mah's here perhaps we should invite her to be part of the conversation too."

On the appointed day, Ma Mah, James, and company arrive, and the two restored carriages will clearly get lots of use over the next few days. Ma Mah exclaims that she adored the carriage ride up the glorious entrance road to the mansion. "Oh, Percy and Hollie, I just love this elegant arrival that's been created for your lucky guests. You need to give the mansion its own name though. The Taft Plantation is fine, but the manor house needs its own name. Have you thought of one?"

Hollie replies, "That's a terrific suggestion, but I don't have any ideas just now. Maybe, we should have a suggestion box for our guests tomorrow to suggest names?"

The day of the opening celebration arrives. The caterers show up at seven a.m. and begin their bustling preparations. The dining area is set up as a buffet. Tables are moved around the pool with additional tables scattered over the lawn and around the gazebo, where a local band will be performing.

Senator Throckmorton and Laura Lee arrive early and are treated to the carriage ride to the mansion. "What a marvelous and memorable approach, and I always enjoy seeing some first-class horse flesh at work. Your landscaping is also beautiful. Ah don't think that Ah have been here since we first set up the tent cities. But that was only a year ago, as Ah recall. However, did you get my relatives to perform and restore this place in such a short span o' time?"

I answer, "Well, actually, Percy gave them some real incentives, Senator—more than just money. By the way, all the workers and virtually everyone from Bixby will be here today."

Percy adds, "At two o'clock all the workers will break and join in the celebration. These people have all become friends, as well as coworkers. If you need anything after two, I'm afraid you'll have to get it for yourself."

Percy's toast

Clinking his pen against the side of a champagne flute to gather everyone's attention, he begins, "Welcome, family, friends, guests, Senator Throckmorton, plantation workers, and residents of Bixby. Welcome to the newly-resurrected Taft Plantation. In a year and a half, we have collectively transferred this old termite-infested mansion into something that transcends its earlier bygone splendor. And yet we've kept the historic fabric intact, as you can see.

"The rough n' tumble tobacco buildings have been rebuilt and transformed into new businesses. We still have one warehouse dedicated to the tobacco industry, it's mostly involved in processing tobacco our neighbors are still growing. It is our hope however that you will convert to different crops in the next year or two.

"Horses are also back on the plantation now. Some of these horses will be ridden hereabouts—some are being raised as race horses, and some are being trained to high-step and will pull our restored vintage carriages to be used by our guests. The depleted soil is being rejuvenated by cover crops of clover, alfalfa, and blue grass. A couple of the fields are now growing corn and barley, which are being used to start a new bourbon whiskey distillery housed on-site. As you know, Hollie has brought her animal rescue operation here, which now utilizes nearly 50% of our fields. At present, we have two lions housed there, and their roars in the night are marvelous to hear. When you first hear them though it'll likely raise the hair on the back of your neck!

"The tent city factory now employees over four dozen people and we have orders to be sent to refugee camps located in ten countries. Your town of Bixby is undergoing a face lift as a result of all this new economic activity, and the early benefits on display are newly-paved streets and the addition or improvement of other infrastructure. The six bars in Bixby have each been refurbished and are becoming boutique eateries for the tourists who are beginning to visit our animal rescue zoo. My favorite bar is the My-Oh-My Club, which now has sawdust floors, cracked mirrors with fake cobwebs, and fake electric candles for lighting. And Pullium's Bar has the best barbecue in the area.

"As you may have observed, solar panels are covering the roofs of many buildings. We are also supplying nearly 75% of our electric needs from the solar panels on our warehouses.

"New condominiums are being constructed in place of the old slave quarters. However, one of the slave quarter buildings has saved, refurbished, and has been set up as a small museum of sorts as it houses items and photos from the pre-Civil War era locally as we should never forget that part of our history—and those of us who were born here trace our heritage back to those days.

"The temporary tent city we setup after Hurricane Harvey has now decreased in size from 1500 people to around 100 currently. These folks will either move on, move back to their previous homes if they were able to be restored or rebuilt, and some may decide to stay and acquire one of the condominiums currently under construction. But I'm rambling on too long.

"I am glad I inherited the Taft Plantation, it's been a privilege to resurrect it, and now Hollie and I consider ourselves part of this community. Ok, it is now two o'clock and the plantation staff is dismissed from their duties of serving you. This is a time of celebration, so we've invited them to join us in today's fun. If you need anything besides what's on offer at the bars or buffet tables, please check with the catering staff in the kitchen or ask one of us. And now, folks, it's officially party time. Incidentally, Robin Hood and his Merry Band have an archery contest scheduled at three o'clock. You are invited to match your skill with a bow and arrow to that of our own Robin Hood. I think Gee and I will each take a shot. Although I know my sister, Gee, will be hard to beat."

After an encouraging round of applause, the festivities then proceed, and it's easy to see everyone in attendance is nodding, smiling, and looking enthusiastic as they survey the newly-renovated surroundings that have been the focus of such a protracted restoration process. A short while later, sure enough, Robin Hood beats Gee in the archery contest.

(I wonder if she let him win?) A new cleanup crew from Hornby shows up at eight p.m. and swiftly handles tidying up the bulk of the post-soiree mess. It was very generous of Percy to not want our crew to have to do the work today. However, they'll be back at their posts tomorrow and will finish up the balance of the cleanup duties then.

Ma Mah calls a meeting for the next day at eleven a.m. to in hopes of drilling down in earnest into the discussion of wedding plans for the six of us. At precisely the stroke of eleven, we three couples gather to meet her, and she quickly hands us each a yellow legal pad and a pen saying, "I want each of you to answer the following questions.

"Where (what city or place) do you want to have your ceremony? Or…do you instead want to have separate ceremonies in different places?

"What do you want to wear? Formal clothes and traditional wedding gowns? Or maybe bikinis on the beach?

"Who do you want at the wedding? Just family? Friends?

"What type of a service do you want? A minister? Bishop Mahaffey? A licensed friend? Do you want a mass or other religious ceremony? Or a handfasting?

"What kind of reception?

"Honeymoons. Separate or group? Where?"

Percy scans the list, saying, "I guess what we have here are seven people making the decisions. Is it even possible we can all agree on these six main topics?"

Ma Mah jumps right in, "Well, it is "your big day," so I will be happy to go along with whatever you all decide, I'm just here to help, not "decide," that's your job. However, I'll nevertheless share my preference which is that I would like my daughter and son to be married in Boston by our bishop. And I now promise to stay out of the rest of your discussions. So, if you'll excuse me now, James and I will be having our lunch in the gazebo. Maybe by dinner tonight you six will have made some decisions. Please try to make some progress—I'm getting old and would like to see this blessed occasion happen before I die please."

Smirking at my delightful mother as she turns on her stylish heels, she takes James' arm, and departs, and I swivel back to the others, "Ok, let's all separate and answer these questions as individuals vs. couples for an hour and, come back together, and then we can jointly review our thoughts and wishes. Surely, we have each been thinking about our wedding—what's your ideal fantasy, folks? Let's brainstorm."

I retreat to Robin's shooting range behind the gazebo and try to collect my thoughts. Ma Mah prepared a good list of questions, but she forgot one element. Years later, when I look back on the event, I want to reflect on the day with happy thoughts. And, after all, who knows what the future will bring? Bill and I may grow apart, one of us may become sick or even die, or we could even end up divorced. But this wedding is our day and should produce idyllic memories. Should we even share it with Percy & Hollie, Jackie & Charlie?

Let me deal with the first question—where to have the wedding(s)? Should we let fantasy drive our selection? Most of us have our areas of comfort—temperature, climate, things around us that make it feel like home. So, should we just go ahead and be married in our family home?

How much are we governed by tradition? How much by genetics? What is the role of romantic dreams in this decision-making? When I was growing up, Ma Mah and Pa Pah were always traveling to exotic and faraway places. Karen and I fantasized about going with them. We often researched their destinations and nurtured our own daydream experiences in those places in their absence.

Well, I didn't do very well with question one, how about question two? What do I want to wear? This one should be easier. My designer will have endless suggestions and will take all my nebulous ideas and create something that culminates them all into a just-right look, knowing me as he does. Do I want a traditional white-but-shockingly-topless wedding dress? Should we change the color to say red or purple? What does color do to dress? We don't want black of course, that I know. Black is associated with funerals, and in most societies, it's associated with death. Maybe, when I die I will want to be draped in white, placed on a long wooden Viking boat with black ringed sails and sent burning out to sea (naw, that sounds like a male thing!).

Ok, setting aside the planning of my funeral for the time being, so what about question three—who do I want attending my wedding, our wedding, that is? This may be the easiest one. I want close friends and family to be present. This would include Percy and Hollie, Jackie and Charlie, plus Ma Mah and all the cousins, my Vassar friends, and the list goes on. Now if Percy and Hollie come up with their friends and Hollie's family, the numbers increase of course. Then there's Jackie and Charlie, plus their families and friends. Since everything we do in the family's charity work seems to have political implications, I realize then we must also include our political friends and key nonprofit contacts on the guest list too.

Hmmm…at this point, I don't see how we can reduce this number to less than a thousand all told!

Question four, what type of a service do I want? Since I was raised Catholic, it seems that a Catholic wedding service and mass, possibly conducted by the bishop, is the obvious choice. No doubt the bishop can obtain a Papal Blessing for us since neither Bill nor I have been married before. I would like a High Mass sung in Latin with a large choir also singing the Latin Mass. However, I doubt that the rest of the group will go for this. Percy could opt for it, even with Hollie, as her first husband died. However, Jackie's a recent divorcee, and I don't know about Charlie's prior life before he met her. Well, this one could definitely pose a problem, but then it occurs to me—we could be married in different churches on the same day and have one giant reception.

Question five is about the reception itself, what do I want? For a thousand people, a sit-down dinner would be difficult—both to produce quality and get it served in a short time. I guess a buffet is possible if we have enough serving areas to reduce the length of the buffet lines. Maybe just circulating trays of hors d' oeuvres if plentiful enough could fit the bill. Of course, we need lots of liquor, especially champagne, and a huge cake with figurines of the six of us perched atop it—or should we have three individual cakes instead?

At this point, I'm not at all sure I'm actually making much progress with this mental exercise but am now up to Ma Mah's final question, about the honeymoons. Probably we will each have ideas on where to have this most memorable of trips. Maybe we could have a week together someplace and branch out from there for another week or two for each couple on their own. Where in all the world would I like to honeymoon? Hmmm. Certainly, it will need to be in a romantic and very beautiful place, but with Bill at my side, I know it will be a gloriously delightful time wherever we go. Remember that delightful getaway he arranged for us after the Boston Massacre? *(I'll bet author Tom will want us to climb a mountain, maybe Mt. Kilimanjaro, or Mount Fuji, or even have us head to a base camp in the Himalayas! He might pick an ice palace in Scandinavia, or a visit to the South Pole. But why would I want to make love in those frozen settings?)* Honeymoons on the beach of a small island surely sounds much more appealing.

I can only hope the group comes up with better suggestions. Otherwise, we may have to end this book without any marriages. Well, another option is to just "live in sin!"

The afternoon whizzes by and we reconvene to discuss our potential plans. As we begin to compare notes, it appears everyone else had as hard a time in wrestling with these questions as I did.

Tradition and family/friends were the group choices. As to location, Percy and I were close in wanting our weddings in Boston, performed by the bishop, with a high Latin mass. This actually surprised me as I couldn't believe Percy was so willing to go this more predictable route, although having attended a boy's school, one has tradition stamped into one's soul at an early age. Jackie and Charlie indicated they wanted to be married in an Episcopal church in Chicago. We discussed having videos shown in each other's churches of our weddings, but quickly decide against that idea. I wanted Jackie as my maid of honor, and she wanted me as her maid of honor. The compromise was that the four of us would be married on Friday in Boston and then Bill and I would go to Chicago for Jackie's wedding on Sunday.

The receptions would follow the weddings. Jackie wants a dinner reception and Bill and I decided on a buffet. Our Vassar roommates were all invited and will pick either my wedding or Jackie's wedding, depending on their other commitments and locales. A couple of them may make both weddings.

We all agree on traditional wedding dresses and suits. How boring! My designer Pierre is selected to outfit the four of us. The men will be dressed similarly, but Hollie and I will each have different wedding dresses to best suit our own figures and style.

The siblings get hitched in style

Having opted for traditional services, shortly after these decisions are finally reached I contact the bishop and the church to make the arrangements. The Bishop says he is ecstatic to perform the double marriage ceremony and the High Latin Mass for us. I arrange for the 30-member choir to also sing the Latin Mass. Luckily, they still practice it regularly and perform it once a year.

We agree on the traditional Catholic wedding ceremony, although I do not like a couple of the phrases typically used in the vows. Much to my delight, our bishop agrees to my requested modifications (who says the Catholic Church is unbending?!).

Once the guest lists are compiled, reviewed, and re-reviewed, over 700 are people invited to our double wedding. Most of them are there for the day's festivities with perhaps just 50 or so only attending to witness the wedding vows. Ma Mah has related all of my adventures to the bishop, including my killing of two bad men. I have a long discussion with him on this and other topics in the confessional booth. He than grants me absolution for my sins. After all, taking a life is a sin, in spite of the circumstances.

The Mass and services are simply beautiful. Both Hollie and I pick wedding dresses with long sleeves. Hollie's gown is a lovely creamy hue, whereas mine is sparkling white. Flowers adorn the alter and at the edge of each pew. A white runner is rolled out along the center aisle. Two flower boys scatter red rose petals along the path. Hollie's father, who we had not met previously, proudly escorts her down the aisle on his arm while James graciously escorts yours truly to the alter (too bad that Pa Pah had died so many years ago, I found myself missing him more than usual on my big day, sigh).

As the wedding ceremony began, the bishop asked me, "Gertrude Winifred Lowell, also known as G.W. Lowell, also known as Gee Lowell, also known as Karen Hunt, do you take this man, William West Scott, also known as Bill Scott to be your lawfully wedded husband?" The audience gasps as most of them do not know of Karen Hunt. There is much whispering back and forth in trying to figure out how I can also be a person named Karen Hunt.

Thankfully, the attendees are quickly diverted by the solemn yet joyful ambience inside the historic stone church, illuminated today by glowing candles, and bedecked by a masterfully massive display of white roses, both full-sized and petite tea varieties, which are spilling onto both sides of the altar's main platform and are intertwined with dark green ivy—the flowers' scent perfuming the stillness of the air which is soon pierced by the angelic voices of the choir performing their ancient hymns.

Eyes mist among those in the rows on both sides of the massive cathedral as vows and rings are then exchanged, a soloist performs Ave Maria, and the ceremony concludes with each couple beaming, and kissing as the bishop pronounces they're now married. All four then turn joyfully to face their cloud of happy witnesses who break into applause as they proceed back down the aisle, marking the official start of each couple's new life as husband and wife.

The reception follows at Kennedy Park. It is a beautiful autumn day with the maple leaves just beginning to turn. As we arrive, a Scottish bagpiper awaits and leads us from our limos to the voluminous white tent, again bedecked with garlands of ivy and white roses. Just inside, we head onto the dance floor where the musical duties are then turned over to a small band. Bill and I have a traditional dance or two together before being seated in the place of honor at the head table. As champagne is poured to the large assembly of guests, glasses are raised and everyone toasts the two couples with smiles and clinking of crystal flutes.

After kissing Bill yet again, I stand and address the crowd, "Thank you all for coming and sharing our joy with us on this most special of days for the two of us. However, I'm sure most of you are wondering about Karen Hunt whom the bishop mentioned in our service. I must confess I have been leading a double life for quite some time—as a socialite and also a private detective. I don't know whether this dual identity will continue or has now merged into one life with my new husband, Bill. I suppose time will tell if Karen is needed to handle some future mystery—in fact, it now occurs to me that I've been trying *so* hard to keep this secret over the years and yet everyone seems to be very accepting of this unusual quirk of mine once I disclose it...and I trust that's been the case here today in my sharing of this revelation with all of you. My second announcement is that I'm now going to change out of this beautiful wedding gown into clothes more suitable for enjoying our buffet meal. Frankly, I don't know how anyone could eat lobster with drawn butter in a wedding dress!"

The feast includes all of Percy and my favorite foods: along with the fresh lobster there are steamed clams, raw and barbecued oysters, corn on the cob, real baked potatoes (from an oven not a microwave), Boston baked beans, julienned green beans, and cranberry and pumpkin pie for dessert. Of course, we have to have the traditional wedding cake too—with two sets of figurines topping it—but I'm only going to eat a small slice of that. The champagne flows along with the local Sam Adams beer. There's rum also, as it was one of the causes of the American Revolution.

There is however no wine and there's also no beef or other meat. We had thought about deer meat, but I could not bring myself to think about the killing of deer. Turkey was a possibility, but it's often too dry. The menu we decided on is what Percy and I remember from the Lowell reunions of our childhood. The memories of those long-ago gatherings have kind of faded away in recent years. Maybe we should revive the old family reunions?

It was a gorgeous and utterly perfect day, and truly one to re-member. But the next evening we take off to fly to Chicago for Jackie and Charlie's wedding. Sunday late afternoon just as the sky is darkening, we gather with the other guests at the Episcopal Church for a lovely and moving service, mostly written by Jackie and Charlie themselves. Jackie has chosen a striking red wedding gown to accentuate her complexion and red hair. There were nearly 400 people in attendance. The recep-tion included a sit-down dinner with a choice of prime rib, salmon, and chicken, accompanied by a seemingly endless flow of both champagne and wine. Another successful tying of the knot.

CHAPTER 26 Whodunit?

After our lengthy group discussions of all the gorgeous spots in the world, we all decided to spend one week together on Qalito at the Castaway Island Resort in the Fiji Islands. On Monday morning, after we have sobered up from our collective nuptials, we six newlyweds pile into our plane with Lloyd, the relief pilot (and thankfully sober), who's at the controls for our lengthy flight to Fiji. Bill will spell him on the trip.

Ahhh, an entire week luxuriating in the sand and surf. What deliciously decadent relaxation! Each day we all meet up for drinks at sunset. As our collective honeymoon winds to a close, Jackie and Charlie will next be dropped in Oregon to spend some time secluded in a cabin in the coastal woods there. Percy and Hollie are heading to Vancouver where they will take an Inside Passage cruise and gaze at glaciers. *(That geologist keeps sneaking into my story!)*

After finishing up his flight duties, Lloyd will visit relatives in Seattle for two weeks and then pick the four of them up for their return flights to Chicago and the Taft Plantation.

Bill and I are taking a sailing ship, a schooner, from Fiji to Australia. We'll just have a skeleton crew aboard and we will each help to sail the ship. We both love to sail, but somehow our busy lives have given us precious little time to pursue that pleasure in recent years. A long sail on a warm and tranquil ocean, what could be better?

Before we all head out in these various directions though, we decide to review Cassie's murder together one more time, and pool our brain power. Surely there are clues that point to the murderer. *(This book is about to end, and our six main characters must solve this crime! They have screwed around with trying to solve it for 25 chapters thus far. Why are they so slow or blind? Isn't the murderer easily pointed out in the book? Even I (or maybe only I) know who the murderer is. Do you still not know?)*

I call our group of sleuths, Jackie and Charlie, Bill and I, along with Percy and Hollie to re-examine the facts and see if we can identify who slayed Cassie. We interrupt our honeymoon festivities and meet up at a quiet corner of the Tiki Bar. We each order a Mai Tai and try to focus our collective minds on the murder. I have appointed Percy to be the leader of our discussion—maybe we need him to more objectively examine what leads we've been able to compile on our own thus far.

Percy begins, "Ok, what do we actually know about the event itself as well as the pool of possible suspects? I know you just can't bring yourselves to believe one of your Vassar friends actually killed Cassie. So who might have wanted her dead...and *why?*"

I responded, "Jackie and I were at the Vassar reunion, so we were probably less than a couple hundred feet from the murder, while it was happening. But we each saw nothing and also saw no one running away or leaving the scene.

"Debbie discovered the murder scene and Cassie's body. She must have been in the closest physical proximity. So, what did she say? Did she see anyone leaving the area right afterwards?

I reply, "She said at the time she saw nothing, and just stumbled onto Cassie's body. Cassie's husband, Glenn, has emerged as the chief suspect behind the murder thus far."

Percy asks, "Alright, but since Glenn was apparently not in the area at the time, who did he know in your group who might have done the deed at his behest?"

I answered, "We discovered Katy knew Glenn and was performing investment purchases for him as well as the cartels. They also, according to Katy, did have an affair. However, Katy maintained it was just sexual and that they weren't in love, so she said quite adamantly she wasn't jealous of Cassie. Incidentally, Katy and Cassie were staying in the same two-unit cabin, so they may have walked back together to the cabin."

"And what did Glenn tell you about Cassie and Katy?"

"Glenn maintained he loved Cassie and she loved him, but he claimed she understood his sexual needs and the affairs that resulted. He told me we should look at Kathleen (Katy) as the possible murderer."

"Do we know if anyone else in the group actually knew Glenn?"

"No, we don't know of anyone for sure. However, we also know Rosalie was in the import/export business and was apparently forced by the cartels to bring in drugs concealed inside her furniture for them—but how this might relate to Cassie's business is uncertain.

"We also know Debbie was a stockbroker, so she might have been contacted by Glenn or Cassie in her professional capacity. We have no evidence of that though, mind you. Jackie, what did Charlie find out about Debbie when he looked into her background?"

"This is an interesting story that Charlie's actually still working on," Jackie says "It seems Debbie and her husband were divorced three years ago, but are still working together in their St. Louis investment business. Debbie has her own condo, but it turns out she spends many nights staying with her ex-husband. Three months before their divorce, they moved into a newly-built house in the Virgin Islands. They spent one month there together, I guess on vacation, and then filed for divorce. They then returned to St. Louis and bought Debbie the condo. After a couple of months, Debbie went back to the Virgin Islands to stay in the new house. Six months after the divorce, Debbie married her South American neighbor in the Virgin Islands. His name is Rolando Longstreet."

I reply, "My god! We just met him in Argentina! He's one of the drug lords."

Jackie then says, "Can this somehow be connected to Cassie and Glenn?"

"Yes, it definitely can be connected. We got the drug lords to meet with us as I told them I was taking over Glenn and Cassie's businesses."

Percy then adds, "Ok, this reveals the connection to Glenn and Cassie—but what would Debbie's motive be for killing Cassie?"

I said, "I don't know, but what if Rolando was trying to cover his ties with Glenn and Cassie? Debbie and her ex-husband have a legitimate investment business. Rolando is trying to detach from the drug cartels, if we believe him, that is. His marriage to Debbie might give him an edge in becoming an American citizen. Also, with the marriage and ownership of property in the Virgin Islands, it provides him with a stronger American association in terms of gaining citizenship."

"Yes, Gee," Percy replies, "that sounds like a possible motive, but how do we prove it? We need to make the strongest connection to Glenn and Cassie. But, realistically, the other two drug lords you met with may have been the ones, not Rolando.

Bill then adds, "Up until now, I knew little of Debbie, as she has been a minor player in Gee's story. Shouldn't we have known more about her before this stage?" *(What kind of a novel introduces the potential killer in the last few pages? Is that not against the rules?)*

Percy responds, "Is there anyone else we haven't considered as the possible murderer? Have you all revealed everything you know about Glenn and Cassie?"

Jackie lowers her voice a bit and then says, "I haven't told you, but I met Glenn once at a fundraiser for hurricane victims I was funneling through my foundation He gave me a check for $50,000 for the cause. I had a couple of glasses of wine with him and found him charming. I do believe both then and now he was lining me up for his next affair, or at least a roll in the hay."

"Why didn't you tell us this earlier, Jackie?" Bill asks, astonishment in his voice. "This lack of disclosure until now also puts you on the suspect list."

"Well, I was just embarrassed about the whole evening."

I then chide her, "Tell us more about it please, missy. I glean a hint that something happened between you two at the time. Maybe a juicy story you're hiding?"

Jackie reluctantly replies, "Ok, I'll confess. I sized Glenn up immediately as a cocksman wanting to add me to his list of conquests. He suggested we have a glass or two of wine together. I told him I knew a quiet little Italian restaurant where we could duck into a dark booth toward the back and be out of sight of most of the rest of the patrons.

"I had already received the check from him, so I knew I could do anything I wanted to at that point and made sure it was safely deposited. So, I told my chauffeur, Edward, that I would be ready in an hour for him to pick me up at the restaurant. Glenn picked me up and drove me there in his rental car. We waltzed on into the restaurant and the head waiter greeted me. "Good evening, Ms. Horton. How can I be of assistance to you?"

"Oh, Salvadore, it's so nice to see you again. Will you please seat us in a quiet place, maybe toward the very back. Set us both up on the bench side of the table and please bring us a bottle of your best champagne, a cheese fondue, and a chocolate fondue too."

He replied, "Very good, there is also no one seated back there at present. But I thought you did not care for cheese fondue?"

"Oh, I just love chocolate with champagne, but my date will no doubt enjoy the cheese fondue." Shown to our table, we snuggle up together on the bench side of the table. Glenn then proceeds to tell me how pretty I am and how attracted he is to me.

"I asked, quite innocent-sounding, "But I thought you were married?" He then admitted that was the case, but he also quickly added that he needed more sex than he got from Cassie, but did try to then explain they were actually happily married."

I interrupted Jackie's story, "Didn't we hear this very same story from Katy? Weren't these lines almost identical?"

"Yes, they were. I had already decided I was not going to have sex with him, but that I would just string him along. Since we were next to one another on the bench seat, Glenn moved closer, put his hand on my leg, and then started telling me how hot he was for me.

"So, I said, 'Oh, right, I'll bet you say this to all the girls.'

"He said, 'No,' and just kept telling me I was very sexy."

"Then he said, 'Let me see if you are hot?" But before he could reach for me, I placed my hand on his pants and could feel him getting hard. I unzipped his pants and pulled out his penis. "Oh, that feels like a good one. I wonder what we should do with it?" I pegged him as a quick come, so I started stroking it. He kept getting harder. I kept stroking it and whispered. "I am getting so-o juicy. My clit is beginning to get hard." Soon he came in my hand and I then rubbed it all over his pants. I said, "Gad! Glenn, I'll bet you have left a lot of dissatisfied women out there.

How soon can you get it hard again? Can we then do something with it to satisfy me?"

"I then told him he should go to the bathroom and clean up. He nodded, looking down at his trousers as he stood and headed off to the restroom, turning sideways as he walked, and holding the cloth napkin in front of him. As soon as he was gone, I called Edward for my waiting limo. I picked up Glenn's car keys he'd left on the table and dropped them into the chocolate fondue. I took a last long gulp of the pricey bubbly and turned the half empty bottle over into the wine bucket. I just hate wasting good champagne.

"I then got out my compact, applied some bright red lipstick, and left a kiss on the other white cloth napkin, placing it on the table. After all, he needed a kiss goodbye. I pulled out the chair next to the bench and poured some of the cheese fondue on the chair. I carefully left the chair so that Glenn would sit down in it when he returned.

"Salvadore asked me on my way out, 'How was everything this evening Ms. Horton?'

"Oh, it was just perfect, thank you. My date is having a little trouble this evening though. Please do me a favor and give him a hard time, will you?" I then grasped and shook his hand, thanked him, and thrust a hundred dollar bill into his palm, waving goodbye as I turned and headed out the door.

"You know what? I never heard from Glenn again…!"

We all break down laughing. Hollie says, "That is the *best* story. I have always wanted to do something outrageous like that to those dates with their busy little hands pawing at my leg under the table. You planned it, Jackie, when he suggested the glass of wine. My, you are a devious little tease, m'dear!"

Percy shakes his head, "Well, is there anyone else who should be on the list? Don't we have a butler handy? Isn't that low-profile servant always the murderer in old whodunits? I guess we don't have one in this one. So, ladies and gentlemen, WHO is our killer?""

No other names of suspects were supplied, the group was silent for a bit.

Percy then says, "Ok, ok…let me make a couple of observations. Who was on the boat when Cassie fell overboard? Wasn't it Jackie and Gee? Didn't Katy run over Cassie with the canoe when you were leaving the picnic on the island?"

Bill then answers, "That makes three suspects then: Katy, Jackie, and Gee, who seemed to be having the most interaction with Cassie during the reunion."

At this, Percy says, "Dear sister, I hate to say this, but you are the only suspect on the list who we know has actually killed someone. In fact, you have actually killed two people, counting the drug cartel thug who was going to either kidnap or kill you. I'm sure the Boston D.A. would put you high on his list."

I then cry, "How can you say this? That really hurts my feelings, Perc. I have always objected to killing—animals, people. After all, I'm even opposed to the death penalty. I had absolutely no choice at the Boston Pops as the perp would have kept on killing until he was put down. That drug guy was at point blank range and had just fired a shot between Bill's legs—his next shot would have killed him! I simply reacted to save the one I love. In fact, I think this proves a point; if someone threatens your nearest and dearest, your children, you'll do anything—including killing them—to protect your loved ones.

"Cassie's murder is a completely different situation though. At the moment of her murder, she was threatening no one, especially none of her friends. She obviously knew something about someone connected to the drug business, and so it seems concealing that information was the motive for her death. Obviously, I have no connection to the drug cartels, and absolutely no motive to kill Cassie."

Jackie then says, "Oh, c'mon, don't get wound up, none of us actually suspects you, Gee. And I'm afraid you're totally off base with your observation, Percy. Say, there is one thing I remember now that we haven't talked about already though. The murder weapon was found by Gee. Were there any fingerprints on it? Were you able to run down a registration on the gun? I just realized I never heard any updates about that."

"Nope, there were no fingerprints on the gun nor on the ammunition in the gun. The gun itself was unregistered and thought to have been bought on the street. Ballistics showed it had been used in Miami for a drug-related murder, that's all we know."

Charlie then says, "That's interesting, and possibly pulls it back to Glenn. He made lots of trips to Miami. The drug cartel could have given him the gun and he gave it to the murderer—Katy?"

Bill cocks his head for a moment, thinking, and then responds, "Good thought, but how would Glenn have got the gun from Miami to Pittsburgh?"

I then reply, "You can check guns through in your suitcase or with special handling."

"But would Glenn have wanted to take that risk?" Percy then asked. "Suppose it was confiscated and ballistics or registration checked? That was probably a serious risk most of us wouldn't take."

Bill says, "There are ways to get it through without discovery. Karen here has a metallic oriental box she's used to transport her weapon in while traveling."

"So…where do we go from here, gang?," Percy asks. "Nothing seems to be iron clad and there is certainly no compelling evidence which will actually convict anyone, everything just seems so vague and circumstantial. Glenn's also in jail for who knows how long. Katy's staying in Hong Kong until her lawyers can clear her relationship with the Asian drug cartels. That may not even be possible. Rosalie and Debbie are possible suspects—but you've uncovered little thus far to connect them directly to Glenn and Cassie."

Think of how many unsolved murders there are in this country every year. Is this to be another one? Maybe you can get one of them to confess, or maybe you can turn up some additional condemning evidence? Until then, it appears this may just remain on the unsolved murder list.

CHAPTER 27   Playing the End Game

Since Gee cannot complete the novel, I, Tom Cochrane, must step in and take command now. Gee and Bill are lost, marooned, or dead. At this point we cannot be sure of their fate. Several scenarios are possible based on their last adventure. Maybe they will resurface unharmed, or maybe we will receive news of their whereabouts…or their demise. All efforts are being made to locate them.

Here's what we know now.

At last report, newlyweds Bill and Gee were sailing in the South Pacific on a small schooner with a crew of five. The ship normally sailed with a crew of fifteen, hosting up to twenty passengers. They left from Fiji to sail to Australia where it was then due for an overhaul and reconditioning in dry dock.

The ship's skeletal crew for this voyage included the captain, first mate, engineer, cook, and a sailor. Gee and Bill agreed to help man the sails during the voyage. Beyond these basic facts, we know little else.

Three days outside of Fiji, communication with the vessel ceased. There was no distress call. So, what, pray tell, has happened to our heroes?

Scenario 1:

Perhaps one of the members of the crew goes berserk. Possibly he locks up his captives in the galley-dining area after making who-knows-what demands. What could his intensions be, or where might he be heading after seizing control of the ship? Might he have actually killed some or all of those onboard?

Since Karen always responds proactively in suddenly dicey situations, can she slip out of makeshift restraints, wriggle out a porthole, and sneak up behind this madman and disable him? Surely, she cannot be one of those already killed! The heroine never gets killed in a novel, right? That only happens in Shakespearean tragedies.

Scenario 2:

A disease or plague may have infected some of the crew. The radio must be out of service or we would have heard, and medical help would have been dispatched. Maybe one of them fell out of the rigging and needs critical medical attention.

Maybe the generator has failed, and all electronic equipment onboard is out of service? Without GPS, can they sail the ship by dead reckoning to the nearest port?

Scenario 3:

A sudden but severe squall has taken its toll on the ship. The boat is taking on water, even though the pumps are working at capacity. As the water rises in the hull, the engines are flooded, and the pumps stall. The ship is beginning to sink.

Will they have to abandon ship? Can they launch a lifeboat in such a large storm? Maybe they are out there somewhere on the ocean, just bobbing in a small craft, with supplies of water and food dangerously dwindling.

Scenario 4:

Since the ship is undermanned, some of the time it's running on autopilot. Maybe the crew member on watch fell asleep. Everyone else is asleep and the sound of a large crunch or crack awakens them.

They may have run aground on a reef far from any island. The underground formation might be situated off a deserted island or a small atoll. They may have somehow scrambled safely to land, but have no way of contacting the outside world. They will have to wait for us to somehow find them.

My questions for you:

Which ending would you prefer?

Are the four possible endings the beginnings of a new book?

Will the two girls wake me in the middle of the night imploring me to save them?

Will two or four of the other main characters come to the rescue of Gee & Bill?

Was this novel so bad that I should just let all of them die?

The choice is yours, gentle reader.

This novel has been fun and exciting for me. *(Although, admittedly, what good novel leaves this key whodunit question dangling? I thought "the rule" is to solve the crime in the last five pages of the book. What kind of novel is this to leave the crime unsolved?)*

Give me your thoughts. In fact, why don't YOU write the ending? I will then put the best endings on my website and possibly weave them into a second novel. Send your recommended conclusions and comments to: **hello@RiverBeachPress.com** (the website where you can read about my two earlier books – both of which are nonfiction, mind you!)

Is *this* how it Ends?

This amazing Tale dost end,
But the story is not over.
Certainly, Cassie's murder
Is not resolved.
Karen and Gee,
like Don Quixote,
are still tilting at windmills.
The drug problem is
still with us.
New murders
occur around us every day.
More of us are
packing guns.
The 'Wolverine' groups
are in every state.
But, did we not have fun on the journey?
How can one forget
Pegleg Joe
in his Sherwood Forest
prancing around as Robin Hood?
Should we have another book
Or just end this tale here?
The choice is yours.
Me thinks that
Gee's pen is ready!

Questions? Comments? Or otherwise want to get in touch? Please visit:

www.RiverBeachPress.com

Or drop a note:

River Beach Press
PO Box 358
The Sea Ranch, CA 95497

If you enjoyed *Entwined -- In Mystery & Murder. . .x 2* please leave a review on 

...and THANKS for any other sharing you might do on this book's behalf!